RECURVE RIDGE

When Mari crashes into a mountain man,

she isn't sure if he's her salvation...

or her new tormentor.

SAVAGE MOUNTAIN

DOVE PRIEST

RECURVE RIDGE

HOT TREE PUBLISHING

DOVE PRIEST

For information, contact the publisher, Tangled Tree Publishing.

WWW.HOTTREEPUBLISHING.COM

EDITING: HOT TREE EDITING

COVER DESIGNER: BOOKSMITH DESIGN

E-BOOK ISBN: 978-1-923252-23-3

PAPERBACK ISBN: 978-1-923252-24-0

DISCREET PAPERBACK ISBN: 978-1-923252-29-5

AUTHOR'S NOTE

Robin Hood has been my favorite fairy tale/legend since I was a child watching Errol Flynn, Kevin Costner, and of course, Mel Brooks's nineties spoof *Men in Tights* featuring Cary Elwes—another childhood hero also appearing in *The Princess Bride*. I desperately wanted to rewrite Robin's story in my own way, but my vision seemed a little askew compared to the mainstream one floating about. More recently I've harbored a slight obsession with the BBC version featuring Jonas Armstrong as Robin and Richard Armitage as Guy of Gisborne.

But my fangirling of the outlaw who gave to the poor delves deeper than that. I spent time in Bristol during my hub's secondment in the UK, and I dragged the family to Sherwood Forest in the middle of winter.

It's stunning (and well worth the walk if you get the chance).

I took so many photos of the multicolored leaf mulch that covered the ground. And if the leaves were down there, that meant that those trees were... bare.

My creative mind kicked into gear. There was simply *no*

way a ragtag outlaw army could possibly hide in the forest during winter (yes, it was meant to be summer while they were in hiding, but many of the stories push over more than one season). The Robin Hood Tree, an absolute behemoth of a Major (English) Oak purported to be the home of the Merry Men, has an enormous base. Tall branches extend straight up to the graying sky, and in the weeks after Christmas, the entire tree stood naked. People barbequed around it. Kids sang songs and danced around the trunk—all in crystal-clear view—and I could hear them for *miles*. Quite literally.

It occurred to me that my desire to write a Robin Hood retelling might need a new location, and that bugged me. Badly. The history and archaeology major in me balked. I set the project aside, letting the idea stew until I returned home. Then I decided to research the "real" Robin Hood story in greater depth, plowing through sites and libraries back home in Australia.

Robert Fitzooth, Earl of Huntingdon from Locksley, appeared to be the original inspiration for the tale, and over many years of retellings, the legend evolved to become the one we recognize today.

For me, that story still wasn't the right version. Robin and Marian's romance I absolutely understood. That level of *knowing* they were perfect for each other, plus the flirty banter... that topped up my romance tanks just fine. But for me, the Merry Men, who shared everything with Robin, who had his back, shared his pain, and were just as passionate in their own ways...

It stood to reason in my head that if Robin loved Marian, then his men would too.

Finally, I had the core premise for a series... and then a friend gave me the setting I searched for. Thick evergreen forests and remote locations for my outlaws to hide within and retreat from a society who proclaimed to hate them yet needed what they offered.

Recurve Ridge was born featuring characters inspired by Robin's original Merry Men—Little John, Alan-a-dale, Much the Miller's son, and of course, Will Scarlett. And with Team Good Guys came the baddies contingent: a reborn Sheriff of Nottingham as a foil for Robin and a twisted-as-always version of Guy of Gisbourne lurking in the shadowy realm ready to ruin the innocence the story revolved around: their combined obsession for Marian.

I hope you enjoy my version of my favorite legend in a contemporary setting and who I envision Robin might be today.

Dove xx

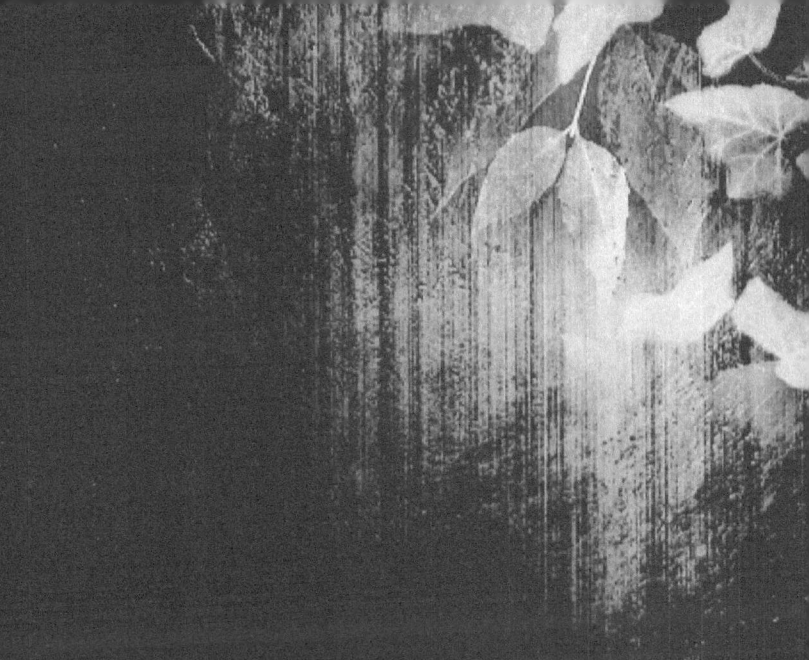

Fairy tales are true,
if you believe hard enough

To Tony, Emily, Harry, and Charlotte,
who traipsed miles across Sherwood
Forest looking for a legend who
resided in my head all along.

PROLOGUE

MULCH SCATTERED BENEATH MY FEET AS I TORE through the forest, its soft crackle overriding a brittle roar that consumed all thought inside my head.

Get away. Can't stop. Don't let them catch me.

If I went back, I might never get out.

No "might" about it. I couldn't go back to that table. The shadows. The hands—

—can't, can't, can't—

I couldn't stop, not even if my brain kicked into gear. Something primal had been activated, and my body entered flight mode without my mind's permission. Not that I needed to give it. Every nerve ending numbed in a desperate bid to survive, leaving me a willing host carried away from horror and death and seeking the facade of freedom and safety.

There was nothing worse in the woods than him. The darkest monsters resided in their plush upper-class digs, not out in the roughened forest like wild mountain men... right?

Wrong.

I would discover just how dark the monsters in the forest could be.

Myself most of all.

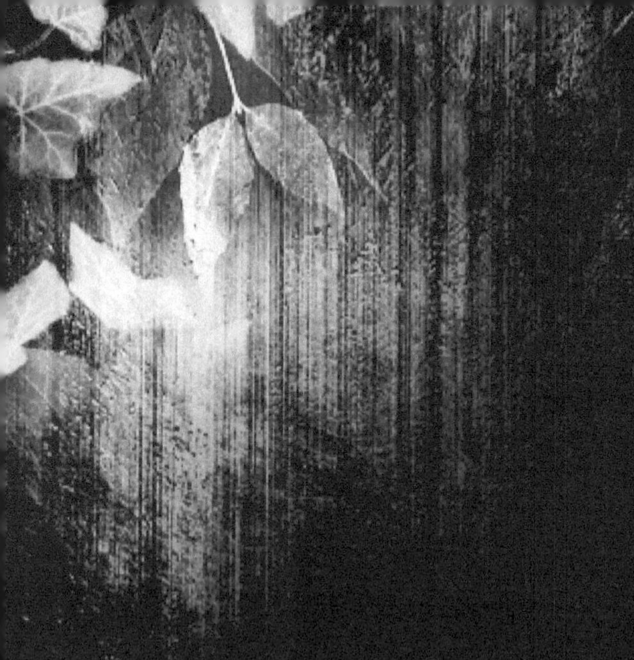

Robe

1

ROBE

BODIES LITTERED MY CABIN FLOOR IN VARIOUS STATES of déshabillé. Stale piss and body odor overpowered the ever-present scent of spruce and brisk mountain air my remote ridgeline in the Adirondacks failed to combat.

One man groaned, and I knew they weren't out for good. Still, it annoyed the shit out of me that I couldn't use my own living space.

"I came out here to be alone," I grumbled, gesturing to the mountains that surrounded my forest cabin. "Not host an overage frat party every damn night."

My college years were well behind me. Easy days with no sense of responsibility and even less care factor. Those days were gone, trapped behind an unopenable door of my own making.

"Yet you take in strays with the heart of a philanthropist and the ease of a five-dollar hooker." Jonothan Littleman pressed a mug of black coffee into my hand. Thick blond hair that matched his wild beard shot through with the occasional strand of silver cascaded down his back. He looked less like an Upstate New York taxpayer and more like a Viking who had stormed my house and taken up residence. The latter was true, in retrospect. "Be honest with yourself. You came out here to hide behind a mountain and lick your wounds."

"And hide the devil within." The corner of my lip curled. "We're all damaged goods, unfit for human consumption."

Jon snorted. "That's why you are who you are, isn't it? Robinson fucking Huntingdon, Earl of this shitful patch of ground away from everything and everyone we love, and rescuer of assholes like yourself." He swept muscle-bound arms in a wide circle to encompass the living room, which was the largest part of my cabin home and in dire need of expansion.

I stared at the semiconscious men littering my floor, each of whom would wake with a hangover worse than the next. My heart clenched at the sight of the broken boys—*men*—I collected, rescued before they suffered a fate worse than mine. Before they hit the realm of unredeemable.

Each thought they'd already met wrecking-ball status. I knew better.

I grunted over my coffee, letting the dark ambrosia unpack what I kept hidden from the most prying mind: my own. Sleep itched the corners of my consciousness as I processed Jon's words, though I rose a full hour earlier.

My response came out more than a little salty. "Yeah, but it's my shitful patch of ground."

The cabin walls closed around me, a too-tight fit for a woodsman and a displaced trust-fund-kid-cum-officer-cum-CEO who had learned to rough it alongside the rest of my outcast crew.

Never created with the girth of five large men in mind, we inhabited out of necessity the space I had originally built by hand for a contingent of only two. Recurve Ridge nestled among a brutal section of the Adirondack mountain range in

Upstate NY. Full of unforgiving granite outcrops and pitfalls, not to mention my own improvements to every defensible aspect of the land, it suited each of our flawed personalities to perfection.

I'd always intended to build a larger bunkhouse behind my cabin sometime after my other tenants arrived, but seeing as we were now all shoved into the cramped space, that time had come. I flicked my toe at a beer bottle that drifted near my foot. It rolled across the bare floorboards and bumped into a half-empty glass of cheap whiskey.

If I expanded, the space needed to be usable. More than just room to sleep. I drew out plans in my mind's eye for an additional kitchenette, their own bathrooms—the latter because I was a pedantic asshole and refused to share. A man cave for toys and... more toys.

Change required topping up supplies, and that meant a trip out of Recurve Ridge and back into the dark lure of civilization for someone. Heading off the ridge to a place where only one of us was welcome incurred danger for us all. The rest may as well wear a *shoot on sight* tag knotted around his neck and have a bull's-eye tattooed on his ass.

My stomach protested the thought of losing one of the boys I had collected before they healed enough to seek their own futures. I covered my disquiet beneath a long draw from my mug. Scalding, bitter liquid seared my throat that instantly craved a second hit of the dark ambrosia. I relished the sharp pain that numbed a different sort, no matter how brief.

What didn't kill me created a new evil, or some bullshit affirmation regular people invented to protect their cloistered lives. Pain offered a tainted strength that propelled me forward, each of us craving his preferred brand of poison.

The youngest man in the cabin stirred on the floor.

Cracking a swollen eyelid that looked like it bore the brunt of fisticuffs from the night before, Will offered me a sloppy salute that might have been a thumbs-up and returned to his sloth-like state. The man beside him, who sported a home-job military-grade haircut, lay face down in a puddle of his own drool.

I might have worried for Miller's existence if his barrel chest didn't lift every so often in the deep sleep of an inebriated man. That, and he snored like a local drunk.

What else did we have to celebrate but surviving one more day against our personal battles?

I served with both Will and Miller in the Middle East, working shoulder to shoulder as their commanding officer for too many years. The latter retained a desire to address me as *sir*, though I no longer held any right to the title. Jon, I had found in the midst of his blackest moment, while my newest recruit, Alan, fell into our ramshackle life through a design of fate I didn't stop to study too hard, lest it replace their heartache with a loneliness once they left.

My lost, broken boys.

A piece of my splintered self featured in each man, giving us a common, if neutral, ground. Their healing provided me with a selfish version of pride as I strove to give them what I couldn't fathom for myself: redemption.

A life outside this pitiful existence.

These loyal men looked to me for protection and had decided to stick around to make a hash of my self-imposed serenity. Some part of me liked that a few salvageable qualities remained from my previous life, because the mission I set us on didn't allow for error, only a skewed sense of morality.

One of the assholes broke wind in his alcohol-imbued stupor, filling my living room with a vile stench. I slugged the remnants of my coffee and thrust the cup at Jon. One bushy eyebrow rose, and his beard twitched.

"Make sure they clean up after themselves. I'm out."

Jon said nothing as I stormed from the house into the welcoming arms of the forest blanketed in snow. A stubborn Eastern white pine stood above everything else, its many stoic faces battered by winter's kiss.

I needed to shoot something.

THE WEIGHT OF THE AXE SOOTHED MY CALLOUSED palms as it sliced a parabolic arc through Recurve Ridge's crisp winter air. Sharp pine and warm, earthy mulch wrapped around me in a cocoon only the forest could offer as comfort as I disturbed the thin layer of snow that fast turned to slush beneath my boots. The numbing cold edged beneath my jacket, but I was more at ease here than I'd ever been in the city among everything I hated.

A city that hated me in return.

One day I would return to the lights and face my nemesis, but for now... I took a sense of peace in the ache of muscles tight from a lack of work that craved action. Sweat soaked my shirt with each swing, log after log. But as good as the repetitive action felt, it wasn't enough.

Shooting was my preferred method to redirect the coiling violence that writhed beneath my skin. The twang of the bow and a breath of mountain air at my cheek settled a sense of peace into my heart. Despite firing off several dozen quivers earlier, the tension remained, the sort no bow or amount of spent arrows could fix.

I returned to my axe, a therapy Jon taught me when we first scouted land for the cabin together. My next exhale clouded around me, condensation obscuring my vision before air and breath melded in an invisible seam. A neat pile of split logs lay by my feet, dusted by a skiff of fresh snow. My therapy billets of chopped wood far outweighed our actual usage in the cabin. I kicked the halves over to the heap and hefted the next round onto the stump.

Snow crunched underfoot in the wrong direction. The mountain stilled in a pensive air.

The only warning the forest provided that all was not well.

Hair rose on the back of my neck. I pivoted, reaching toward a change my brain reacted to but hadn't processed yet.

Fleeting sounds traveled between the trees, shattering and rebounding to displace its origin, but the predator in me refused to be distracted by splintered echoes. I closed my eyes, my breaths softening as I listened to the forest. The irregular stumble of prey that had already forfeited its life filtered into the clearing.

A dual need—*to hunt, to protect*—rose in my chest as I swiveled on my heel, tracking my prey's path across land I knew too well to allow its escape.

I marked the thrashing gait against an invisible map in my mind as I scanned the spaces between scant evergreen foliage. There—a flicker in the shadows between the trunks. The light shifted, then again. This section of the forest around my cabin was thickened by nature rather than design. I never bothered to clean out the underbrush and smaller saplings that vied with the natural giants, seclusion being the aim of the game.

My game.

My blood heated as my boots carried me one step forward, then another, each lunge faster than the last as the panicked flurries neared. I wanted to pause and study the rhythm of the creature's flight, but my heart put together what my mind still fought—the frantic, fleeing form was *human*.

Another person in my patch of the forest where no one else should be. Only those with a preconceived death wish sought access through my trees, not one whose survival instinct kicked in to extend a life. My land didn't come under the category of *safe* by any definition, occupied as it was by some of the deadliest creatures in Upstate New York, including the local human contingent.

Which begged the question: What could be so big and bad that it drove desperation in my direction in our coldest season?

Nothing else came close to the ruckus a person created in their struggle to survive. A black bear lumbering through the Adirondacks in search of its dinner had more grace than a stumbling amateur hiker on a trail rated beyond their ability. Pure panic sat under its own category for the average, untrained person.

Good thing that neither Jon, me, nor any of my boys back in the cabin counted as the *average human*. Years of training kicked in as adrenaline dumped into my system at will.

My prey appeared to be a solitary chaos. I paced the clearing's boundary on silent feet, seeking what tore through my section of the woods. The flighty sounds stumbled on alone long after its predator had been outrun. Snapped twigs brushed the pads of my fingers as I passed, their sharp edges digging into hardened calluses.

I stepped around small depressions that disturbed pine needle mulch and bared the earth in tiny sections. No heel prints indented the exposed soil. I knelt at the side of the damage path, letting my fingers sink into the exposed dirt beneath the cypresses' overhang where less snow gathered. The shallow imprint had no defined edges. Less than what a full-grown man would make, which meant my prey was either a small-framed person or a child.

Or a barefoot woman running alone.

That thought spurred me into the depths of the forest that had become my home over the past five years. I learned the ridge's secrets though never divulged my own in turn, relieved by its silent support. The perfect companion for a man who took society's eviction notice and hung it over his threshold in place of a welcome mat.

A flash lit a path beyond the trees. I frowned. Skin had a way of throwing light in the darkest places, an easy giveaway for any unassuming target. I spotted that earlier when she first darted away.

When had I become so sure the runner was female?

That should provide her more endurance than a child. I filed the extra information away as a wild guess at best. Regardless, those rare flashes gave me something to aim toward.

The dodging pattern transformed into a primal path, the brain existing in pure survival mode after more than a few minutes after her critical incident. Soon the spike would deplete, and she'd crash.

I intended to be there when she fell.

But for now, she ran.

I timed my breaths with her movements, catching the second the pattern changed—a falter in step, a dodge around a fallen log.... I weaved between scarred trunks and snagged a flailing limb as she shot past.

The body attached to the slim extremity followed as I swung the cold arm in a broad arc. She grazed the next tree, knocking small heaps of snow to the forest floor, tangled in the undergrowth, and crashed face-first into my chest, slamming the breath from us both.

No startled cry ripped from her as I cupped a hand behind her head, worried I broke the poor creature's nose. A handful of twigs and pine needles trickled from her damp, mussed hair and streamed over the back of my hand in a steady cascade. She didn't make a single sound or move at all.

The woods settled as I wove my fingers through her dark chocolate curls, a natural silkiness detectable among the snares. What should have been long, luscious waves resembled a hawk's nest that tumbled over my knuckles, massing about her head like a dark halo to a fallen creature.

A tearstained alabaster face turned up. Eyes older than her maybe nineteen, early twenty years perhaps stared at me. Her gaze slid out of focus, glazed with unadulterated terror. I doubted she saw me or anything else in front of her. Despite her pale skin, ice cold beneath my roughened palms, her body warmth soaked into my torso too fast. I registered the lack of clothing barrier at a sensory level before my eyes took in the additional information. Barefoot and naked.

She was naked.

In my arms.

Bruises bloomed on every surface in a wide array of blacks and blues, all recent. I scanned her arms and legs, but there were no telltale yellowish tinges, no evidence of older abuse. She was blessed with deep blue irises ringed with violet, a hue somewhere between midnight and dark ocean. I wanted to fall into her eyes and never escape. Fear, along with exhaustion, dulled their luminous quality, but her stunning beauty still sucked breath from my lungs. My chest closed tight on expired air that refused to escape.

Whoever hurt you just topped my shit list.

A ripple of renewed energy slid through my heated veins. I didn't quell the urge to find who had ruined her and revisit the pain she suffered on the asshole tenfold.

Biting back a growl, I scanned her body for more immediate injuries. Puffy pink lips were split in more than one place and torn in others. I leaned forward, tracing the rounded depressions with my gaze alone. Were those *teeth marks*?

Someone ripped her from whatever coddled world she had existed in before her assault and threw her into my dark territory where civilization and soft people had no place.

That made both her person and her vengeance mine to safeguard.

Fury seared my insides as I stared at her bare form, my gaze utterly uncontested. The woods fell into an eerie purgatory. No call echoed through the close-knit branches often filled with the soft chatter of my furry and feathered neighbors.

The girl took a shuddering breath that should have jerked her back to the present but didn't. Her pulse fluttered beneath my fingers in an erratic rhythm that began to slow as her body accepted her current predicament over the ongoing struggle to escape.

One breath became many. She gulped at the frigid air in shallow gasps that barely made it into her lungs before she expelled short pants in racking, tearless sobs. My heart wrenched as I held her tight, weathering the remnants of her fear and wondering what the fuck to do with her.

I was used to triaging broken bones and burns or worse on a battlefield, not recuperating a shattered mind in a fragile body.

I stared over her head, my jacket heavy across the taut line of my shoulders. No threat appeared from the gloom that might obscure an enemy. The only other heartbeat came from the prey in my arms, and even that thumped at half the rate I expected.

My gaze swept back to the girl, and a different muscle turned over.

I traced a light fingertip over plump dusky pink lips, noting every tear in her swollen skin. Keeping my touch gentle, I cataloged each mark, lodging the damage in a running list entitled *due rewards* for when I identified whoever had hurt her. The bruises mapped her torment in a stunning array of torture that cost hours of her life not so long ago.

Four close-together spots looked like finger marks. I sought out the thumbprint, finding it where I expected over the other side of her shoulder. The handprint dwarfed her dainty frame. I picked out more of the same prints in varying sizes. Each mark on her differed enough to suggest a line of attackers. A similar puzzle covered her torso.

I didn't need to check her legs to know they would show the same.

Christ.

"How many?" I grated, grazing my thumb along her arm.

My other arm wrapped tight around her back, holding her to me. *Unprotected, my ass.* Anything that came at her had to deal with a whole lot more than a tiny, unarmed, and untrained woman.

The girl stood statue still during my inspection. A cool breath brushed my cheek through the untamed growth there. What did I look like to her eyes? A great brute of a wild mountain man, perhaps. A far cry from the silk-blend suits I had worn after my uniforms were stripped away. *Three lives in a single lifetime.* We all wore many hats in different seasons. My scars were covered with checked shirts and a beard, while she stood bare before me.

Exposed. Raw.

"Where did you come from?" I didn't expect an answer as

I fell into her galaxy-dark gaze, processing the too-still woman in my arms.

My mind kicked into gear, and it took me too long to realize that she stood still and quiet, not a shiver in sight. Cursing myself as a goddamn fool, I shucked my jacket free and covered her battered body. My lungs closed tight when she didn't flinch, though the damage to her fine-boned frame bordered on horrendous. That she was still standing at all was a miracle. Shock did that to a person.

I'd seen soldiers trained for combat situations struggle with the reality of the traumatic aftermath when enemies returned to plain old human forms. This slip of a girl had no defense mechanism to rely on other than what her mind provided, and now me. I shoved back the violence that pulsed beneath my skin, aching to erupt and tear the woods apart for her.

"What's your name, sweetheart?"

Darkened eyes shifted to my face, the lone sign she heard me.

I caught her chin between firm fingers, careful not to incur further damage. Either someone was overzealous with their impact play or abused this girl well past a horrific level. It didn't take much nous to select the latter option as her fate.

"Your name," I repeated, cradling her face between my hands, and prayed she'd emerge from her head for me. "You're safe. I promise. What's your name?"

She stared at me through hollow eyes, and I swore she wouldn't answer. Then those pale lips parted, and she offered me a part of herself I'd covet for eternity.

"M-Mari."

The inflection of her British accent whispered around me. I struggled to hear her, though she pressed against me. I squelched the need to hunt the fucker down and show him what being the recipient of those bruises felt like firsthand.

Sliding an arm across her body, I wrapped my jacket tighter around granite skin covered in a cold flush. How long had she run, how far? I cupped her bruises with as much gentleness as I could offer.

"Where did you come from, Mari?"

Her luminous gaze dimmed as she retreated. Whether triggered by my words or my presence, I'd likely never know. The girl possessed an ethereal beauty. Cleaned up, she'd be stunning, and I had a damn good idea what had made her a target for such an attack.

I kept murmuring, offering her what warmth I could, though she didn't seem to make sense of my words. A flicker of attention entered her sapphire gaze as her brain appeared to process her adjusted situation.

Carrying her wouldn't be hard, but we had a distance to reach the house, where I could offer a hot shower and food, plus medical supplies. She would need a whole lot more to heal her mind. I could provide the basics, at least.

As I prepared to hoist her over my shoulder and run her back, a part of me worried that placing an abused woman in a small space with five filthy men used to surviving in an all-male environment might not be my best idea, but it was the only option I had to offer her.

Mari blinked once and twisted in my arms. I held my breath as one hand rose. Soft, slim fingers grazed the rough edges of my beard, pressing close enough for her natural heat to brush my jawline. I held her gaze, keeping myself still and unmoving beneath her discovery tour, waiting for her to open to me. My heart slammed in my chest hard enough that she must have heard it firsthand.

Awareness slipped behind her eyes a second before her

palm cracked across my face. Fine fingers tangled in my untamed beard. I caught her wrist, confining her as she writhed in my arms, scratching and clawing in a delayed reaction. Holding her at bay without hurting her took little effort. The size difference between us bordered on ridiculous. I dwarfed her as a mountain overshadowed a pond nestled at its foothills.

Her knotted fists pounded my shirt in weakening thumps. I weathered her beating until she panted, her frantic energy spent against my chest. Mari rested her forehead over my heart, her arms limp over my shirt. Ragged breath huffed against my lips as she turned up her midnight gaze clouded with fear and desperation.

Need.

For the base conditions a body required: food, water, warmth.

Security. Love.

A thin, strained keening tore from her throat in a pathetic whimper that shrouded my thoughts in a tempting promise of violence.

What the hell happened to this woman, and who do I have to kill to make it right?

Mari

2

MARI

I THRASHED AGAINST THE TWIN LOGS OF PURE MUSCLE hefting me over the forest floor while for the second time in my life, a giant of a man kidnapped me. This time, my giant had kind forest-green eyes and spoke in riddles my mind couldn't untangle, though it did protest that I needed to run and run and run.

Dregs of adrenaline coursed through my body, though my hands shook against his back. The hit diluted my fear until I exhausted my supply, leaving me useless and filthy, unable to protect myself from whatever came at me next.

Not that I'd been able to protect myself in the first place, reduced to a fleeing mess the moment *he* dumped me onto the forest floor. My brain still screamed at me to run, but my body crashed against its fresh imprisonment.

Wanting to believe that warmth equated with safety, though I knew better.

My new mountain man walked for long minutes through a snow-laden forest I barely saw, his stride blurring into an unmeasurable time, my body torn between memory and reality. Pins and needles assaulted my toes as he rubbed feeling back into my limbs that twitched about on their own with renewed circulation.

I supposed I should be thankful, but instead I added the pain to my current catalog of bodily hurts that overwhelmed every sense while I tried to match my reality with my past and came up with a whole lot of confusion I couldn't unravel.

And so I hung across his shoulder, my body giving pitiful jerks in the arms of the giant who carried me, too-late reactions to a trauma no longer fresh.

The behemoth ignored my feeble efforts to wriggle free as though I were no more than a flea on a mangy dog's back. A horrendously strong and wild dog. I noted the beauty of both my captor and our surroundings in a disconnect. Beneath his jacket, my skin numbed, but instead of running cold, I blazed as with an injection of anesthetic, sweltering against his rough shirt.

All dark hair and soul-deep eyes that seared through me when he'd halted my flight through the forest. Now I hung over his shoulder, filthy and damaged, though cleanliness landed last on my list of concerns. *He* had stripped my identity away, baring me to the world as less than nothing.

Then, when I was at my barest, the man who carried me took my name. One of the few secrets I managed to keep to myself throughout my assault.

I gave that away too. Freely to the man who stood like one of the trees in his forest and refused to shift when I crashed into his solid form. Because surely this place belonged to him.

Rage broke through the fear steeping within me. I scratched at a hard lump on my arm and came away with bloodied fingers. Perhaps a splinter from my dash through the forest. I hadn't cared about what happened to my skin during the deep-seated need to *run*.

Something broke inside me as my mouth ran free in a

delayed reaction to everything. I cussed my new captor endlessly, uncaring of the outcome. What could hurt worse than when those hands had ripped me out from inside myself? But it was more than that. No matter what I told myself, this nameless, wild man felt *safe*. And so I unwound my fears, my horror in a place where I instinctively knew that he wouldn't hurt me more.

Before, my mind and body froze when the multitude of hands touched me, leaving their marks on my skin while I screamed in the silent confines of my mind. Now, those same words exploded from me in a delayed burst. The dual effort drained me faster than the manic energy that came on, leaving my breath ragged.

"You fucking monster, you *stole me*. Ripped me away. Let me *go*—" Breath lodged in my throat while a quiet voice in the back of my mind whispered, *It's not him*. But my mouth didn't care, the words tumbling forth without censure, seeking freedom. "Get your filthy hands off me! Don't touch me, you bastards," I sobbed as my rage dissipated, only to flare a moment later.

If he helped me after this, it would be into an early grave, albeit a well-deserved one.

Survival and freedom wisped by my outstretched fingers. I craved both like a starved woman, filling my lungs with an alien air, and wished I never left England in the first place.

It'll be an adventure. A learning curve.

My parents' disapproving scowls floated past the blurred forest that scrolled by my periphery with every heavy, though not ungraceful, footfall.

A learning curve. What a joke.

Joke's on me.

What had to have been hours of running for my life gave me plenty of fresh injuries. At surface level, the forest had scraped me bloody. On the inside, unwanted hands had flayed me raw. My single source of warmth and security came from the mountain of a man who carried but hadn't hurt me.

Yet.

"It's okay to scream, Mari. It's fine. You'll be okay. Promise." His voice came out rough, as though he wasn't used to speaking so much, though his words didn't strain with anger or fury.

I expected a mountain man not to have anyone to talk to, but apparently this one did. The trees, perhaps.

Words abandoned me after that, and I waited for the blows to come. Relief shot through me when he patted the soles of my feet in a comforting gesture as I slumped over his shoulder. A few soft murmurs, a simple touch, and he removed me from the panicked headspace.

Too easy.

My frazzled brain turned that one over and came up with a disturbing conclusion I craved and hated all at once. The reason I felt safe in verbally abusing him was because I wasn't afraid of him abusing *me*.

The odd things my brain noticed that I hid from myself in a bout of self-sabotage, ranting in broken rasps that I myself struggled to understand, let alone should expect him to figure out.

Attraction. Safety.

Trust.

My world tipped from one extreme to another, and I wondered if Gideon had pumped my bloodstream full of some exotic hallucinogen while I found myself... distracted.

The fear flowed again.

Hands reaching, sliding, grabbing.

Pinching and plucking and pulling.

Spread apart, wrists pulling and raw, fingers touching—

The scream built inside my throat, but it wasn't an incomprehensible sound that burst free.

"I don't want to be touched, you fucking prick," I seethed. My heart thrashed inside my chest, willing my newfound voice to die a quick and silent death.

"Foul-mouthed little thing, aren't you?" my mountain commented, patting my jacket-covered rump in a familiar gesture. "Is this the usual you, or is it traumatized you?"

When I couldn't answer, my words run through again, he sighed, shifting my weight to sling me across his chest instead of over his broad shoulder like so many potatoes in a half-empty sack. I stared into the underside of his mahogany beard, able to see little except the tips of thick eyelashes utterly wasted in the wilds.

I shook my head at his unanswerable question, barely able to recognize who I'd been, let alone who I was now. My frozen toes curled beneath me, under his forearm tucked beneath my thighs, to contact his torso, eliciting a soft puff of air. A masochistic smile curled my lips. If I hurt, my brain claimed that it stood to reason that he should too. How broken I'd become in the short space of scant hours. Had it been a day since my world imploded on itself? I closed my eyes, waiting for bile to rise as my stomach attempted to empty itself over his forearm.

But it didn't.

Thank God, because everything hurt.

Fingers groping, tongues—

My stomach *did* rise this time, bringing with it the bitter edge of acid that teased the back of my throat. I clenched the urge away with effort, removing my ability to speak.

The internal argument rioting inside my mind insisted I never wanted *anyone* to touch me ever again. So why did this mountainous lump of muscle with his hands around me seem safe? After the abuse I'd suffered at my boss's—and his *friends'*—hands, I shouldn't be comfortable with anyone, let alone this mountain god, manhandling me. Yet I allowed Mr. Everest to hoist me into his arms when my legs refused to support the weight of my shame.

Maybe *allowed* stretched the point a touch too far.

I sank against Everest's hard chest, my cheek grazing rough cotton scented with man-sweat and the sharp tang of pine. I breathed in the scents of home and safety and laughed at myself inside my head. I'd clearly lost it, but I went on cataloging all the comforting features that made him real to my mind. His steady heartbeat became my rhythm. I counted each thump, matching my breath to his footsteps until they dropped into sync with every graceful movement.

Hands pressed to my sides, tearing at clothing, then skin. When they had reduced every part of me to shreds, they tainted my soul.

A raspy shriek battered against compressed lips I refused to open. Fear became my fuel, and I possessed an abundant store.

Sleep was no longer an option.

Despite no new adversary announcing themselves, I huddled within the protection of my mountain man's jacket as he halted. I craned around him, my body rubbing against the obscene amount of muscle he possessed. I swore he could be the twin of the giant pines that guarded the forest.

A soft huff that might have been a laugh brushed my cheeks. He turned so I could see the circle of ancient trees that surrounded us. In the center of the clearing sat a rustic log hut that looked like it had risen out of a Wild West story from the 1800s.

"Did you—" *build it yourself,* I started to say, but the rest refused to come out, my tongue exhausted after my tirade.

He seemed to catch my meaning and nodded.

The cabin had an air of strict neatness, as though the occupant couldn't abide any change to its exterior surface. A narrow wraparound veranda was its sole decoration, the boards bare and clean, lacking in personality or furniture. The windows were empty. No spiderwebs clung to its corners; no leaves tumbled across its clean-swept exterior.

The structure appeared as welcoming as an abandoned hospital wing.

Through it all, Everest stared down at me. A small, possessive smile lifted his beard at one side. Or maybe I imagined his kindness and he would become my new tormentor after all.

My insides frosted at the concept, though my heart took up a faster rhythm than when he'd been walking. When I tried to speak, my brain played ball, and real words fell out.

A tortured whisper worked its way past my lips. "Where are we?" I peered past his beard, ignoring the aches that vexed every abused muscle.

A strong jawline and high cheekbones were emphasized by a full head of tousled hair shot through with dark chocolate strands that highlighted their reddish neighbors. Trimmed neatly at the edges, it was longer on top and swept into a messy knot.

Something darker—harder—lay beneath his expression, as if this man had seen horrors and stored them within himself when others would run screaming. Deep laugh lines were etched around a wide mouth visible through his beard, though I couldn't imagine his smile. Moss green eyes surveyed me with a tinge of impatience masked by concern— and something else. Determination.

Or possessiveness.

That flicker of obsession rippled over me again, the expression one I recognized from my boss's face.

They're not the same. They're not the same—

I'd spent a few minutes at most in this man's arms. A kind temperament didn't redefine a lifetime of delusion. He might be the sweetest man I had ever met, or the flip side of the monster I'd fled. Perhaps he was the proud owner of one of the pairs of unknown, disembodied hands.

Though my mind denied the thought, a shiver worked its way along my spine.

His eyes flared, filled with awareness. "My home." My giant shifted but didn't release me.

The world rotated in a slow fashion that did nothing whatsoever for my nauseated stomach. Sensing my discomfort, Everest hauled me flat against his chest. I leaned into him, burrowing deeper as the urge to puke on him passed, then squeaked as my legs dangled well above the ground. My bare, scraped feet struggled for purchase against his pants' tough material.

I lifted both knees to wrap around his waist, but the immediate intimacy overrode my need for freedom. Fighting a closing sensation in my chest, I let him press my body to his as he lowered me to the forest floor in a controlled drop.

Cold pockets of damp pine mulch compressed between my toes as his jacket drew up, leaving my bruised rear hanging out for all and sundry to see. Lucky for me, there didn't seem to be anyone else around. I yanked at the heavy material, preserving any scrap of dignity I still possessed.

Like I deserve dignity.

Perhaps my ego perceived that thought as a joke. A brutal one at best, and I'd missed the punchline. Or maybe the punchline was me.

A soft sound drew my attention upward. My giant stared

down at me, too close, though he didn't shrink my world. Maybe the world shrank for him instead. His breath brushed my cheeks as he busied himself with wrapping my arms around my body to hold the makeshift barrier in place.

Calloused fingertips paused over my cheek and slid through my hair, avoiding snares by some miracle. A gentle touch for such a giant of a man. Everest caught a rogue strand that tickled my nose, tugged it lightly, and tucked it behind my ear. His unexpected, tender touch left me shivering.

The flash of possession that returned to those forest-green eyes said that this man would kill anyone who touched me without my permission.

And my stupid, broken mind *liked* it.

My stolen moment of peace lasted until the door to his hut swung open. Three strapping young men bursting with bulk stepped out onto the veranda dressed in an assortment of checked shirts and jeans, their outfits consistent as a uniform. A second giant, who dwarfed the man clutching my frozen form, followed the newcomers. Blond hair tumbled over bare shoulders. He reached obscenely thick arms above his head to grip raw-cut exposed beams that doubled his bulk. He looked capable of pulling the entire thing down on his own.

I tugged at the hem of Everest's jacket, wriggling closer to hide, but there was nowhere to go. The soft rumble that vibrated against my ear offered a second shock. He was capable of laughter? A smile crept up my face in reply, the expression both alien and forgiving in one. Then I remembered why I stood before him naked and bruised, and the muscles that strained to hold up my good humor died as I cowered into myself.

To my horror, fresh tears welled, prepared to join the filthy tracks already coating my face with God knew what.

"So, British, huh? Work visa?" Everest nudged the top of my head with his chin.

I shook my head, willing him to let me hide between his bulk and his jacket. "That was one of the threats," I mumbled, debris and sweat tumbling into my mouth. His body stiffened, perhaps imperceptible outwardly, but given our proximity, I experienced every one of his reactions as they were presented. "Stripping me of my documents. Taking away my identity if I didn't... comply."

"I'd send you home, but who would want you?"

Certainly not the overly religious parents already on the verge of disowning me for leaving my small hometown to visit the land of sin. I laughed off their backward notions at the time, but now....

"No one will take you back."

"You're so much more beautiful when you're ruined."

Bile coated the inside of my throat as my boss's voice echoed around my mind, trapped in the confines where his torturous words played on repeat.

My legs trembled. Pressing my weight forward, I stole a little more of the support Everest offered, sucking his warmth into my tainted bones. He nudged me with such a tender grace that I gave in and raised glistening eyes to meet his fathomless gaze. The soul of a mountain god disturbed by a mere mortal stared back. Understanding flooded his face, something akin to awe tinged with regret. He moved sinuously for a man his size, his body twisting, his bulk threatening to consume me.

My reflexes long dulled, I became a voyeur unable to fight off the pending attack as he engulfed me in a protective embrace. Salt streamed into my mouth, bringing with it all the accumulated grit and filth from my short burst through the forest. From *before*. I pressed my lips into a tight line, caught in his bottomless gaze that held knowledge of too many dark things.

Broken, ruined, I fell into his silent offer of safety and never wanted to leave.

I need to go home, but home won't want me anymore.

Which left me a begging orphan beyond her depth.

"Easy, Mari." Everest kept his hold light but firm, clearly expecting the deranged animal in his arms to bolt at the slightest hint of danger. Freeing one hand to tuck my head into his shoulder, he called out to the men behind us.

I ignored his muted words, matching my breaths to the steady rhythm of his heartbeat. The regular motion calmed me, the panic that nibbled at the frayed edges of my sanity ebbing.

Enclosing my hand in his, Everest pressed his lips to my temple. His touch offered a simple comfort, a brush of skin that barely equated to a kiss, but the sweet caress gave me a moment's extra warmth, a contrast to the grabbing—

NO.

Unaware of my roiling internal conflict, my mountain man marched forward, towing me alongside him. A roar consumed my overstimulated mind. The edges of my vision filled with dark spikes curving inward. Hands jostled me, shifting me from person to person. I tried for logic and failed. My mind took me back to that place, pulled and tugged in every direction.

Everest's face entered my narrowing vision, my anchor to a world I feared. Concern edged into his verdelite eyes. I made out my name on his arched lips before the world dropped out from beneath me.

This time when the darkness fell, the nightmarish creatures stayed away.

Robe

3

ROBE

"WHAT THE HELL IS SHE DOING HERE? WHAT THE HELL are *you* doing, bringing her here?" Miller ran a hand over his recently shorn head, bushy brows lowering as he offered me his customary scowl. He flicked a glance at the door to my bedroom, where Mari slept as she had for the past two days whenever I tried to look in on her.

She took to only opening said door to accept the thin soup Alan provided in a stream of endless bowls and freshly baked, buttered bread. When I tried to speak to her, the door shut in my face, though not before I caught a daily glimpse of the haunted eyes that seared soul deep in me. She was hurting, and I wanted to help, but I couldn't until she let me.

Not that I would allow the same response from her for much longer.

"How is it that we can't tell anyone about this little piece of hell you've corralled us into under strict instructions of secrecy, on pain of death and the like. Fuckhead," Miller added under his breath. I knew he wasn't finished. "But you get to have the girl? As per fucking always." He didn't bother to disguise the sarcasm in his voice, and for that, I loved him all the more.

The nugget of a man who'd followed me through so many campaigns, took bullets on my behalf, and walked away with the tinge of disgrace to his pedigree instead of a pretty set of medals folded his arms over his barrel chest and glared at me.

Jon shifted at my side, but I held up a hand. "Miller's correct. He has a right to know what I think at this point. You all do."

The blond woodsman's unspoken words hovered between us, though neither of us aired them.

"I need to know."

And he would. Keeping secrets from the men who gave up everything to stay by my side while my world imploded had never been my intent. Certainly not blacklisting the soldier who backed me every step of my downfall like a stocky, battle-scarred shield.

I didn't doubt his judgment or his loyalty. That he mistrusted mine in turn motherfucking hurt. They'd searched for her path, tracked her back to a spot that made no sense on the edge of my land. Done everything I asked with no answers. Now it was my turn to reciprocate and earn that trust back, unless I wanted the man with the yellow gaze who glared at her door with his arms folded to storm inside and shred her to pieces both mentally and physically to do what I couldn't.

Protect us all.

Miller took his duties seriously. A stark reminder of where my loyalties lay.

"She's a runaway. I found her panicking and flailing in the woods, Miller. And she's clearly been abused. Are you going to ignore that, pat her on the rump, and send her off to the next house on the ridge? Have a heart, asswipe."

Alan Dale, stripper and my best source of information about the city that abandoned me, sent the sturdy ex-soldier on the other side of the bar a scathing look.

I pressed my lips into a firm line as Alan beat me to saying the words already formed in my head. For a man whose IQ outweighed that of the entire cohort jammed into my living area, his tact lacked his standard brand of finesse. An unusual slip for him; Alan's ability to blend was the trump card I kept stowed in my pocket for a rainy day.

I narrowed my gaze, taking in the faintest downturn of his lips that belied his smile. True worry etched his brow. In all the scant tells the younger man let show, he exposed only what he wanted me to see—and act upon.

I bared my teeth beneath my beard. *Manipulation like that is an open door, my friend.*

The curl of Alan's lip when he looked at Miller told its own story. His gaze flicked between me and the closed door where Mari now slept in my bed. It might seem arrogant of me to place her there, but hell, she ran into my arms and home. I watched Alan, looking for what I might have missed in my first pass. Annoyance didn't match what rang in my barman and friend's gaze.

Concern.

"She escaped some sort of hell," I hedged, unwilling to admit that, though she ranted at me the entire walk home, I hadn't gotten a single piece of useful information out of her apart from her name. "And she's been abused. That much is clear, but where—*fuck*." I glanced at Alan.

The youngest kid in the room raised an eyebrow as if to say, *Caught on yet?*

The brat put together what everyone else hadn't without my saying so, and I was a solid forty-eight hours too late with that intel. Of course he picked up on what I'd missed. His display of emotion didn't bother me; on a deeper level, I knew what had happened to her. One simple fact remained obvious to us all—there was no *next house* on the ridge.

Gideon Blackthorne's neighboring property matched the thousand acres of my land. His compound sat on the eastern boundary away from the cabin, on the other side of what the boys had fondly named Recurve Ridge. The forest Mari dove headlong through divided the distance between us, miles of scrappy woodland and sentinel pines that explained the surface scratches covering her body but not the rest of the damage she incurred.

Our remote location, paired with invisible fence lines we both made an effort to maintain without laying eyes on each other, provided both me and my sole residential neighbor a reminder of my failure in NYC. My presence gave his purpose—banishment for failing to keep me in check.

His boss had no concept of forgiveness, something I needed to teach both parties one day soon.

We kept our distance from each other by means of a keen dose of mutual hatred. The old adage about keeping enemies close ran through my mind, but all I wanted was his head in the center of my arrow range and a clean shot on a windless day.

The soldier turned businessman crossed the law at least as many times as I had, but if a moral line existed, he fell in at the furthest edge of the black.

On our other side, a tall ridgeline of the next mountain rose, harboring a few small vacation homes owned by NYC politicians and CEOs along with the odd athlete and a reclusive artist who avoided politics and people at all costs. Those were rarely used until the holiday season, though some hunting went on throughout the year, whether legal or not.

At the base of the mountain, a few small homes contained the rest of the local population.

As we harbored our own issues with that side of the law, we stayed the fuck away from everyone else, unless those activities crossed over our boundaries.

Like they had today.

I held Alan's startling azure gaze as each thought turned over in my head. I'd wanted a shot at Gideon for a long damn time. Now that the opportunity had landed in my lap, I couldn't grasp a clear course of action.

Pursue the need to destroy Gideon and wipe him from the face of the earth, or the desire to wrap up the girl he took a hand in abusing, protect her until she could manage on her own again, and then return to clause one.

Choices, choices.

My bartender's knowing smile irritated me, but not as bad as it did Miller, who strode toward the exotic dancer with his clenched fists raised.

Alan raised his own hands, palms stretched outward, his explanation falling on deaf ears. "We can keep her safe. No one should have to go through whatever happened to her—"

Miller swung at the kid as soon as he ventured within range.

"Like a fucking schoolyard," Jon spat. "You gonna break it up?"

"Alan needs to stand up for himself." I kept an eye on my young spy and knocked my shoulder none too gently against Jon's.

The moonlighting exotic dancer backed up at speed, his grace and balance enviable. For a man with fists thrown at him every half second, his backpedaled crabwalk looked nothing like a man scrambling to save himself from an ass kicking.

In fact....

I narrowed my eyes. "Shit, he's good."

Alan bobbed low on his heels twice and then rose in a smooth movement.

Timed to perfection between punches, the slighter man straightened into the empty, undefended space between a blur of fists and jabbed Miller square in the nose.

A muted chorus of sympathetic hisses filled the room.

"There it is." I canted my head as Miller, clutching his nose, delivered a sharp side kick to Alan's ribs. I winced for them both. "Damn. Schedule hand-to-hand training for tomorrow. It's meant to be a clear day."

Jon nodded his agreement, his brow creased as he tracked the two men's progress across the room. "Could do. Might also want to teach your new girlfriend how to fend for herself."

"She's not my girl," I growled, low enough to strain my throat at the effort.

But the plain fact that Jon had called her *mine* sat all too well in the cavity that once housed my heart.

A hand banged against the wall of the room *she* slept in, and Jon shook his head. "Enough." He thumped a fist on the kitchen bench, but neither man halted their mini battle despite pants and blood splattering my walls. "I said—*ah*, fuck it."

He leaned into the foray and grabbed both boys by the scruffs of their necks to separate them at shoulder height. *His* shoulder height, which meant two pairs of feet dangled well above the floor.

Alan raised a hand and waved in my direction.

I rolled my eyes, noting Miller's opposite reaction. He folded his arms across his barrel chest while still dangling in midair and glared first at his opponent, then me.

I sighed. "Put them down." The big man hesitated. I clenched my teeth, my patience fraying. "Now, Jon."

"Don't you two start up again, or you'll be cleaning outhouses for the next month. Got it?" Jon glared between the pair of younger men, both his junior by at least half a dozen years. The thirty-four-year-old giant took a step back, bracing his tree-trunk arms overhead against the thick, exposed beams that supported the ceiling, matching their girth.

Alan's nose twitched. He made it all too easy to read his thoughts as his mouth opened to object that we didn't *have* outhouses. The intent seemed to dawn on both men at the same time.

"Yes, sir," two voices mumbled.

I caught a fleeting smile that disappeared from Alan's face at speed. The brat would end up killed or come limping back with his ass handed to him if I didn't do something about their attitudes soon, but right now we had other concerns.

"Miller. Spit it out." I leveled him with a stare that said he'd crossed a line, but the soldier who had saved my life too many times to count sent that stare right back.

The balls and testosterone clashing in my house were better suited to a barracks. I needed neither when I had an injured girl in my bed with God only knew what damage haunting her mind as well as her fragile body.

"Fine. You bring home a girl who happens to turn up in our woods. Your woods, Robe." Miller looked between us and threw up his hands. It might have been comical if his eyes didn't bore their intent into mine. "You want to save her, but what if she's a plant, Alan? Jon? Did you think about that?" He rotated on the spot, catching each man's attention before his singular focus returned to me. "Did you?"

I nodded. "I have. And I'll risk everything to secure the

safety and well-being of a woman who's been treated so... harshly."

Miller's lip curled, and not in a nice way. "You haven't changed."

"I hope not." I smiled, offering an olive branch.

Miller glared at me for a moment longer. Clumps of hair from his home buzz-cut job stuck up too tall from the top of his head. His mouth turned down when he failed to find what he sought in my face. A moment of stillness strained the oxygen in the room while we conducted a silent conversation about events the others weren't privy to.

"Remember what happened last time?"

I remember saving lives, getting them to safety.

"I remember us getting shot at while you had a little romance."

I let the old sadness grip my heart. It hurt, knowing the woman I almost gave both our lives for wouldn't come back with me. At that point I still had a career, and afterward, a business.

Perhaps that choice had saved her a worse future here, where Mari lay.

"I remember acting human, even if I'd lost my sense of humanity by then," I murmured.

Miller's grimace transformed into a snarl. I wasn't the only one affected by what we'd seen and done during those peacekeeping missions, every one of them bullshit. He pivoted on his heel and stormed from the house.

Alan sidestepped, waving him out the door in his typical flamboyant fashion. I half expected the younger man to say something, but the cabin filled with a strained silence.

"Miller—" Jon started forward, four steps too late.

I held out a hand, pressing my fist to his chest when he pushed against my arm. "Leave him. He'll cool off."

"Will he?" Jon rubbed the back of his neck. "He reminds me of...."

"Me, twenty years ago. Full of righteous indignation and a misguided sense of loyalty." I gave my best friend a lopsided grin he didn't return.

"Your moral compass might be screwy, Robe, but your loyalties are fine." Alan pushed away from the door that swung shut after Miller's exodus. "Are we going to have dinner or what?"

I waved him away, grateful for the distraction despite holding the same reservations as Miller. I kept those to myself, given that my moral compass never pointed true north. Maybe I hadn't found my north yet. Miller was right; I broke both trust and procedure by bringing her to the house, but where else did one take a distraught and abused woman?

You should have taken her to her car, or the highway, or called an ambulance and sent her off without a whiff of fanfare.

I couldn't hand her off to a law enforcement lackey who might or might not be in someone else's pocket. She turned up on my front lawn, convenient as that may be, which gave me the right to seek vengeance on her behalf. My body burned for it.

A bored soldier is a dangerous soldier.

A cute adage, but true, nonetheless.

A reckless soldier is a dead soldier.

My mind slipped to her asleep in my bed as I acknowledged the truth that burned in my veins. As soon as she gave me what I needed, I'd take action, but not before.

"Wait until she wakes again. I want to know what the boys discovered this time out."

Not that I expected their recon mission to come up with anything new. Whatever was there to be found, they had already seen it when they went looking two days ago when she first arrived. We were chasing a ghost long fled while the real thing lay in my bed, silent as though she had lost her soul somewhere in the woods.

My damn woods.

It had been a good hour since Mari last slammed the door in my face. That gave us more than enough time for Alan to work his magic, though Will had just as magically disappeared.

"Are you going to starve us out?" Jon glanced sideways at me. His gaze dropped, focusing lower.

A familiar thrum set every nerve ending alive. "Probably."

"Asshole."

"You know it." I nudged him. "We need to talk about the company."

"Isn't Yana coping?"

My business partner had a limited range of use, and her expiration date encroached. A brilliant personal assistant, Yana had neither the drive nor the inclination to run a multi-million-dollar organization. If I didn't find a replacement soon, Knight & Watchman would fold.

I pressed my lips into a hard line. "Yana wants to retire, Jon. And she's earned it, running everything for the better part of five years while I...." I couldn't finish that sentence.

Jon acknowledged my hesitation. "Your grace period is up."

"Looks like it." I rubbed my hand over my head. "Fuck it. If I go back, I lose everything anyway."

"You can do most of it remote, you know," Jon consoled me. "None of us can go home, Robe. Not back to work in any traditional fashion, except maybe for Alan. Hire someone else to do the job. Let her pick another office manager for you."

It would take an entire boardroom to manage what Yana

covered in a week. Glorified personal assistant perhaps, but as a stand-in CEO, she managed to keep a Fortune 50 company in check while I hid from the world.

"And turn my company over to a stranger? At least for now I have some facade of control."

Jon held my gaze. "Life changed, Robe. Maybe you've been in hiding long enough."

I ground my teeth.

Alan winced.

"Keep it down, yeah?" he called from the bar.

I nodded and fixed my gaze on my bedroom door. Maybe a pretty little distraction would quell the fear roiling through me. Hot on its tail, a strong dose of protectiveness arrived, followed by the lightest brush of lust. My cock stirred, and I shoved the thought away.

Inappropriate, asshole. Someone else fucked with her, and she doesn't need an outlaw brute humping logs in her path to get a taste of the girl in our midst.

Focusing on turning my anger to revenge, I let the protector in me take root. I should have been used to betrayal by now, but I surprised myself every time I brought home a stray to add to my collection.

When I had laid her down in my bed and taken stock of the damage on that first day, it required every ounce of my control not to tear the house apart for the rage flooding my system on her behalf. Marks covered her body. Some originated from hands, while others came from blunt trauma. We were damn lucky hypothermia failed to make the list from her mad dash to escape her demons. I had cleaned the passed-out girl as best I could, my gaze impassive as I removed the gunk and grit from her fragile form, distancing myself from the gorgeous woman who deserved better.

I hadn't checked deeper than skin level, but I bet I'd see

worse if I looked between her thighs instead of merely washing her with gentle hands and keeping my eyes averted. A rape kit was laughable; Gideon and his boss had the local sheriff and cohorts paid up a decade in advance. She'd be lucky if she didn't end up with an extra cache of bruises and trauma if I sent her down the mountain. And so, I cleaned her.

No woman who had suffered what she did deserved to wake wearing the filth of her abuse. Shame shone from those eyes the moment the dull light in them faded. Telling her she couldn't go back to whatever life she was living previously sat high on my priority list, but that didn't mean I looked forward to breaking the news.

Letting her fall back into overwhelming despair would be the grossest neglect. I had existed in the shame-filled realm long enough to know intimately how that ruined a soul. I'd do anything to save hers. I needed to know who hurt her, and I wanted to make her safe by removing her aggressors from the face of the earth. My little rescue project unknowingly created the perfect distraction to put a pause on my inability to return to the world.

A world that hated me enough that I had removed myself from it in the first place.

Perhaps my chance at redemption had arrived after all.

Mari

4

MARI

I WOKE SEVERAL DAYS AFTER I LANDED IN MY mountain man's cabin in a stiff bed with a hard pillow beneath my head, and it felt like heaven. A long sigh grazed swollen flesh on its way out of my throat. Everest and his men left me alone because I silently demanded it, but I knew the end of my grace period was almost up. I could *feel* it in the pensive air that filled the cabin like the hush in the hour before dawn. Still, the warm air within the structure allowed me to breathe free and easy, and for that, I was grateful. My gaze flitted about the unknown room, seeking out the shapes obscured by the dim light, but nothing nefarious moved there.

My body's apparent recovery *somewhat* suggested an extended rest period. My nerves should be jumping and my heart pounding, or so my head informed me as I languished in someone else's bed when my feet itched to tear through the forest and escape. To escape...

And go where?

I didn't have any answers my mind liked.

Silence surrounded me, though not the strained sort. For

the first time in unknown hours—*days*—I reveled in a sense of quiet as the panicked, primal instinct to run retreated, the sense of peace that followed distinct from the blood still rushing in my ears.

Pushing all thought aside, I sank into the mattress. Warmth pervaded every limb, weighing me down in a cloud of safety and protection. A heavy quilt covered me, scented like the woodland area that surrounded the cabin. That smelled like *him*.

And so did I.

My eyes popped open.

Assault. Cabin.

Wild man.

Everest.

The room rocked, my senses swimming as I fought back the urge to puke as a memory slammed into me. At the speed of a sloth, my body caught up with my brain's message. I gripped my arms in curled fingers, my torn fingernails scraping at hands that no longer touched me, and found my skin smooth.

Skin I hadn't dared to touch in the last days, skin that didn't feel like my own. Too many times I dug my nails into my legs, wanting to tear the flesh from my body, but didn't have the strength. And so I took the bowl of watery soup I barely tasted when the knock came at my door, ate as I was commanded, and then cried until salt crusted my eyes and I slept again.

This time when I ran my hands over my body, the urge to rend my flesh from my bones and inhabit someone else's carcass like a shell was absent. This time, I felt like...

Me.

Silky and clean, like someone had spread lotion all over my body.

I blinked at the wooden ceiling, womaned up, and peeked beneath the covers.

The grime and filth that had covered my body from my horrendous streak through the mountains was gone. Someone had washed me, cleaned me, and put me in a hard bed that gave me no doubt about who owned it. I still didn't know his name apart from the one I'd labeled him with, even though he knew mine. My own fault. I couldn't face anyone right now. Myself most of all, but that also included dealing with anyone who would start asking questions I didn't want to—*couldn't*—answer.

Everest my mystery man would remain until I had a chance to thank him and find a way off this mountain. The place might have been Mordor for the distance it put between this hidden world and civilization. Because sure as a Sunday roast, I was *not* in civilization.

Just give me a blue check dress, some small dancers, and a scraggly dog.

Pity I seemed to have misplaced those glittery red heels.

The rustic room offered more space than I'd given the cabin credit for from the outside. An *It's bigger on the inside* comment rolled around my mind, but I rejected the humor as inappropriate when I should be planning my escape.

Rough-hewn walls suggested a hand-built structure, confirming my first assessment. It didn't take too much brain-power to know that the owner used his personal well of formidable strength to construct the place himself. Paired with his obvious stubborn streak, the man and his house had become endearing in an odd sort of way.

Woven mats in tans and whites lifted an otherwise dark room that provided relief from the glare of the overcast sky outside viewed through a slim window above the bed. Basic wood furniture filled a few available spots—a single bedside table sat beside the king-sized bed I slept in, and a simple chair in the corner. I wondered if Everest had made those too.

The icicle-framed windowsill housed a collection of hand-carved items. None were perfect, though each had been created with the same painstaking attention to detail. A darkened doorway led off to one side, either a wardrobe or bathroom. Given the climate and location, I guessed the latter.

No one who lived out here required more than a few changes of clothing.

The austere existence suited the giant of a man, a polar opposite to my life experience, though I never considered myself a princess. The image of a fluffy frou-frou dress flew to the forefront of my mind and transformed into a high-end red-carpet-worthy ensemble in my vision. No, princess I had never been—*would never be*—which was the way I liked it.

Besides, a princess had a factor of innocence, and after the last forty-eight hours plus—I had lost count of the days in this bleak house—I could no longer claim that in any capacity.

Bile rose in my throat. I clutched the coverlet in whitened knuckles and prepared to launch myself out of the bed, praying I'd make it to the bathroom in time. If it turned out I got it wrong and the darkened room was, in fact, a closet, I'd have some explaining to do.

A laugh, alien to my headspace, bubbled in my chest. Rather than war with the reeling sensation in my stomach, the burst of impromptu emotion settled. As the urge to be sick faded, I rolled beneath the heavy quilt, which emitted a cloud of all-male scent.

I inhaled a deep breath filled with the scent of pine and leather and black coffee. A sense of peace washed over me. My heavy eyelids drew shut, leaving me in a weighted void I didn't try to fight, surrounded by Everest's personal brand of pure, wild mountain maleness.

———

DUST MOTES SWIRLED AROUND THE ROOM IN A delicate dance when my eyes cracked open an unfathomable amount of time later. Sleep had become a timeless void where I fell endlessly. Thin slivers of windows sat above the bed, letting in little light and leaving me guessing at the time.

Grit itched the corners of my eyes. I swept the remnants of slumber away while faux fairies pirouetted between the narrow, slanted sunbeams that filtered through the unadorned windows a little longer. Their presence softened the unforgiving and unapologetic male lines of Everest's room.

My dreamless, uninterrupted sleep gave my brain time to process the last few days. I'd lost track of time during my headlong dash, with only the few hideous flashes of grabbing hands that refused to leave me alone to backfill the absent hours. Though still sickened from my ordeal, sleep appeared to have removed the immediate edge from my shock. My stomach rumbled, leaving me in hope that, despite my brokenness, some remnant of myself might be salvageable as I smiled at my body's ability to KBO.

I ran my hands over my stomach and limbs in an instinctive check-in, cataloging bruises and swelling in various places. *Still naked.* That hadn't changed while I slept. To my relief, the aches seemed to be mostly flesh based, though some delved deeper than others. I didn't suspect a single break in any bone.

The soles of my feet throbbed from a thousand pinpricks from my scramble over the forest floor, and my wrists and ankles stung where I'd been tethered to my boss's table for *entertainment purposes.*

Hesitantly, I reached between my legs. My breath seized on a panic attack in the making at the concept of checking. The sensitive flesh there was still swollen, and as I probed a little deeper, I discovered that, although sore and tender, nothing had been torn or ripped the way I'd expected. Everything seemed revoltingly normal. My head couldn't grasp that. The only casualties were my innocence and honor with a side serving of impending fear that wouldn't quit.

Minor complaints.

A dose of lingering horror permeated my mind at the discovery. I leaned back into the hard pillow with a long sigh that verged on a sob, grateful for its staunch support.

"Inch worm, inch worm, measuring the... something something," I muttered, out of tune and out of memory for the right lyrics of the childhood ditty that evaded me.

"A woman in my bed is a new occurrence for me," Everest remarked, breaking into my solitary assessment. "The boys don't mind sharing when I choose to rest. Or not." His ambiguous comment charged the meager air in the room between us.

My gaze snapped to where he leaned against the doorway. I winced at the involuntary reaction, my heart pounding at the huge shadow he presented, then slowing as I registered his voice. While my body had begun to heal, my bruised brain swirled like a dirty martini after a hard night at a dingy bar.

I pressed my hands to my temples, my skin flaring at the sensation of cool mountain air after the warmth of the weighted blanket, and I squeezed my eyes shut to prevent the room from swimming around me. "Oww, Everest."

He huffed a sound that could have been a laugh. "I didn't mean to make you move. I'm sorry," he murmured.

That he could speak in such a soft voice despite his giant barrel of a chest surprised me. Steady footfalls announced his entry as Everest crossed the room. I shifted beneath the blanket, burrowing deeper on instinct. Shivers not unlike the sort that afflicted me in the forest rippled across my skin despite the weighted quilt's warmth as I sucked in shallow breath after breath.

He's not going to hurt you. He's safe. He brought you here—

And undressed me, if removing his pine-and-mountain-scented jacket counted. Washed me, looked at me, and touched my body without permission.

Not that I'd been conscious back then to give consent.

This never would have happened if I stayed in Britain.

Where my parents would have dressed me in their neck-to-ankle cultish clothes and married me off to the highest bidder by Christmas in their small village outside Bristol. I mean, the next most interested suitor. Part of me found that funny still.

The other part couldn't laugh anymore.

Cowering beneath the pathetic shield of blankets that trapped more than protected me, I peered over the stifling edge as he maintained his slow but steady progress toward me.

A red-and-white checkered shirt hung open to expose the expansive chest that its buttons had strained to confine when I first met him. The light that fell in sharp relief hinted at deep, carved muscles I'd become acquainted with during my sojourn over his shoulder for half the journey to his forest home. Beneath the brushed cotton, tails of ink peeked between the loose panels of his shirt. Dark hair and a freshly trimmed beard complemented his forest-green eyes that simmered with an intensity focused on one thing—me.

I'm not the only one he cleaned up.

Each measured step provided me with plenty of time to scream bloody murder or scramble away. Neither urge presented itself, a relief after the never-ending running and running and running. Craving security, I exhausted my supply of both energy and fight.

If I'm going to die, let it be here in a hard bed, near a harder man.

But it would be by my choice.

In what might have been the single stupidest decision of my life, I put my trust in him.

All of it.

A silent prayer left me that if he broke my tenuous faith, it would end fast. I clung to the facade of safety that let me pretend my life would continue on as per normal. But I couldn't.

Nothing will ever be normal again.

His gaze never left mine as he approached, reaching out to pat the quilt around me like a mother hen. Careful to avoid all contact, he perched on the edge of the mattress, which dipped under his mass. I tumbled sideways into the dip, a slow-moving target pinned beneath a bear of a beast.

His features tightened under the shortened beard, almost horrified that the barrier between us might be broken—albeit through a swath of thick fabric—and retreated a fraction.

The visual brought on a fit of giggles while I fought to maintain a straight face. *Inappropriate.* Pushing my smile back with no small degree of horror, a stunted squawk passed my lips. The strangled sound would have terrified a bear on the hunt.

My savior sat back, his weight slipping to the edge of the hard mattress, eyes flaring with alarm.

The giggles returned for round two. Everest froze with every bout of hysteria that left my lips in snorts and suppressed grunts, panic written across his features. I laughed all the harder. My vision blurred as tears leaked free, and I raised my hands to scrape them off my face but couldn't.

My hilarity died a short death as I realized my arms were trapped beneath the quilt and his weight, though he gave no indication that he noticed. I braced for the panic I expected to swamp me, but nothing arrived. Although I'd been tied down what felt like only hours before, though both my mind and my body promised me the trauma happened much longer ago, this seemed... safe. Like his restricted space gave my anxiety no place to develop.

No frantic flailing, no thrashing, no cursing.

Shit. I swore at him.

Hurled abuse right in his face, if I opted for honesty over ego. I could write my behavior off as part of my survival instinct, but screaming whatever came out had been a stress-relief mechanism, pure and simple. Taking my reclaimed freedom and doing whatever the fuck I wanted with it, I cussed out my wild mountain knight in the process.

The last of my unhinged mirth subsided in an inhale beneath his watchful gaze. Eyes wary, Everest leaned forward, his hand half raised. He paused, as though considering the action. When I didn't shy away, he closed the distance and brushed hair from my face.

"It's okay. I'm okay," I lied. My voice came out soft and raspy, refusing to cover my falsehood, though nothing could be further from the truth. "I don't know your name. To say thank you for stopping me. My escape from...."

Where, exactly? The pits of purgatory? An icy hell? I'd take either option to escape the violation my body had been subjected to while my mind tried to flitter free but failed.

A small smile curved his lips. I wriggled harder, trying to

free my hands to trace over his features, but his weight compressed the heavy quilt over me, rendering me immobile. The draw to him doubled as my breath shortened. Even in my admittedly hysterical state, I knew I shouldn't want to touch a man I didn't know who resided in the middle of the woods with others who, like himself, screamed *dangerous*, but I couldn't help myself.

He leaned into my space, those forest eyes of a woodland god lighting with a promise of more I wanted to delve into. My body heated beneath the blankets, suffocating, my skin on fire but still craving the warmth of him. The only air I wanted was whatever he would give me.

One look, and I'd let him claim me.

What is wrong *with me?*

I'd gone from running for my life like the typical victim in a horror movie to embodying the farce of the debunked Stockholm Syndrome myth. That was *not* reasonable. But after what I'd endured, what did my new baseline consist of, my new normal? I had no benchmark to align myself against.

"Robe Huntingdon." He pronounced his last name in a stilted way, as though he hadn't said it in some time.

"Mari Merripen."

He raised an eyebrow, the arched sort that featured in a double-page magazine spread.

And now I knew his name.

A sense of power flushed me from head to toe, as though he'd divulged his deepest secret. Maybe I banged my head in my mad dash through the woods, or perhaps he'd given me a sedative that scrambled my thoughts. I clung to the threads of false evidence that I hadn't yet broken and tried to convince myself life would return to normal. Not a single word of my mantra rang true.

I dropped my gaze to his chest, imagining the hard ridges

of muscle that had pressed against me with every step through the forest. The hard ridges my palms had been molded against, and now I wanted to see if I imagined it right, the phantom caress of his bare skin against mine.

So freaking broken.

The thought of him naked sent a shiver rampaging violently over my skin. I clutched at my elbows to hold it in, but there was no chance that he didn't notice me gawking at him like a lovelorn teen deprived of contact with another living person.

What the hell was wrong with me? I'd been assaulted, I lay naked in a strange—albeit beautiful—man's bed, and now I wanted to screw everything in sight?

Broken, broken, fucking broken.

His lips formed my name, though no sound came with it. "Did your parents hate you? I've heard the English can be like that." Rolling off his tongue in a smooth glaze of honey and whiskey, his musing brought me back.

I spluttered at him, my mouth hanging half open. "No! I mean, well...." A smile tilted the corners of my lips, then, to my horror, formed into a grin. "Maybe a little."

"Mmm-hmm." He coughed, the corners of his mouth twitching around his raised fist. "I thought you might prefer to wake up clean, feeling fresh. If I've made a mistake, then I am sorry." His dark gaze held me captive as he trailed one calloused finger down my cheek.

One part of my screwy brain wanted to know what else that finger could do.

The other part declared outright that this man never made a mistake. An exact dose of confidence coated every aspect of his being, just like another man I knew but refused to give brain-space to, now or ever again. Refocusing on Robe, I studied the hard angle of his jawline exposed through the edges of his beard, the way he tilted his head down, watching me with a mixture of concern and amusement. His attitude spoke of a man kind enough to remain shy of the line that would transform him into a royal asshole. I hoped.

God complex much?

While I obsessed over a man I didn't know, maybe I could add *delusional* to my growing list of pathologies to declare before a cute doctor handed me a nice white jacket and led me into a cozy padded cell.

I wiggled again, and he leaned closer. Air evacuated from the small space between us. Even beneath the blankets that pinned me, my skin rippled with the anticipation of his touch, craved it.

That didn't help at all.

"No, you made no mistake in cleaning me. I feel...." I inhaled a breath of him that went straight to my head. *Leather, coffee, pine, and forest spice.* He might have washed me, but he clearly hadn't taken the same liberty for himself in any recent capacity, or maybe the woodsy essence just clung to him. A flush ran through me at the thought of him beneath the covers with me—or with no covers at all. "I feel smooth and clean. Thank you. Did you use lotion? Did you shave me?" My brow dipped at the suggestion, and I knew I should be horrified.

I added another line to my mental *broken* list.

"Arnica. For the bruises. My sister sends baskets of feminine goodies in the hope I'll convince someone to share my reclusive existence. It hasn't worked yet." Robe shrugged. "My en suite is yours alone, whenever you need it. I'll share with the boys. Use the products. Be comfortable." He hesitated, then stroked one fingertip over my cheek as I watched him with widened eyes but didn't shy away. "I'm sorry if I overstepped. I'll get you some clothes."

Overstepped what? I didn't have boundaries anymore. The ones that once existed had become twisted, maimed things that were better off bulldozed than trying to repair the gaping holes left behind.

"Thank you," I whispered.

My voice thickened with emotion that he... that *anyone* could care after what happened. The thought overwhelmed me, choking the tender skin of my swollen throat. Another emotion flushed through my body, and this time it had no connection to his proximity.

Shame.

His gaze shifted from the fathomless void I'd become accustomed to seeing to resemble a normal man's gaze rather than that of a mountain god. Staring at Robe Huntingdon was like looking into the sun after contemplating a black hole—both terrifying and enlightening.

"Well, Mari Merripen, stay and have coffee with me. The bar is that way. You have nothing to fear here, from me or from anyone in my house. Rest. Recover." He offered me a lopsided grin. "And when you're ready, come out and meet the rest of my household."

A refined accent clung to his words, as though he belonged to another time. Robe's cultured speech threw me. For a man who lived in the literal sticks, his education clearly far outweighed my Catholic school days. It would be as easy to imagine him as an NYC suit as to think he came from old money and had been afforded a full education, despite the contrary evidence of his choice of living situation staring me in the face.

Paired with his neat beard, relaxed but confident demeanor, and the fact that he appeared to *care* about the woman he rescued despite the way she had been ripping up his trees, I watched the rabbit hole open beneath my feet and prepared to dive in headfirst.

I am in so much trouble.

He tapped the quilt at my side, his knuckles scarred and calloused. In a swift movement full of a dancer's grace, he stood and headed for the door.

"Wait!" I called.

"Yes?" Robe turned back, raising one of those manicured eyebrows.

"Am I...? Do I have to stay here?"

Can I go home?

After all that I'd been forced to endure, I didn't know if I had a place to call home anymore.

Robe stared at me for a long moment. His gaze swept over the lump I made in his bed, huddled beneath his quilt. "If you want, although I advise waiting to return to your life until you're healed and we've... talked."

Without another word or offering any explanation, he strode from the room, leaving me alone.

It took every fiber of my self-restraint not to call him back again.

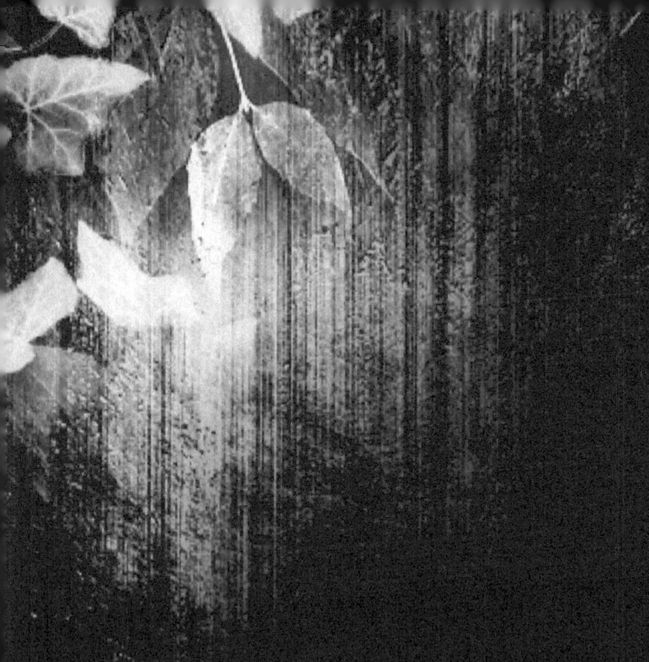

Robe

5

ROBE

THE TRUNCATED STORY OF MARI MERRIPEN IRRITATED me. Not her presence in my house, but the fact that I didn't have enough information to keep everyone who relied on me safe because I didn't understand the scope of the dangers surrounding her yet. Both Jon and Miller had raised their concerns, doubling down on my own, though there was little I could do to alleviate them. Alan initiated his mysterious information network, and I knew he would dig up more for me on command.

Maintaining Recurve Ridge as the best not-kept secret this side of the city had been our mantra as my little herd of wounded men was built up into the ramshackle family we'd become. Over the past few years, Blackthorne and Petersen knew we were hiding in plain sight, but so long as I didn't venture back toward the city, I could keep my little patch of mountain air and rustic life.

Petersen hadn't made a move on my business yet, though a coup wasn't outside the realm of his vengeance.

Snow crunched beneath my boots as I tracked through the woods, trying to follow her path back to where it originated for the fourth time, though I lost the trail a few hundred yards from the house, the elements washing away her presence more and more with each passing day. Still, I knew her trail now. We all did.

And the connotations of her arrival on our doorstep, at least proverbially speaking. Mari was the puzzle we knotted ourselves around, attempted to solve, driving ourselves mad with the singular question we mulled over. *Friend or foe? Can I trust the woman in my bed?* The measurements of her flight, what remained, were hard to gauge due to the twisting nature of her panicked trajectory, and today's fresh falling snow was determined to outwit me in my own territory.

Mari had wended her way between trees until she'd run a mile instead of the short distance she covered. We were damn lucky she still had all her toes given the time she must have spent pounding snow to slush in her birthday suit, for fuck's sake.

"Over here." Miller raised a hand above his head, waiting for me to catch up. "There, and there. To...." He tracked her invisible path with a quick eye trained in conditions much harder to navigate than my mountainside. "There. And then... nothing. Like she fell out of the sky."

"I don't think she parachuted in, Miller."

He grunted as I caught up with him. "Never know. Kid could have skills."

"You're a crabby old man." I folded my arms over my chest and stared down at him. We'd been over this. Her route, the impossibility of her arrival.

"Feels like it. Where the fuck did she come from?"

I stilled, our banter dying in the wake of the same question I'd asked myself over and over, only to come back to the same singularity. My gaze pierced the trees' tall shadows that led in the direction of Gideon Blackthorne's ridge-side residence.

"We both know the answer to that."

"Then let's go. We've got what we need to finish the job."

"What job?" I glared at him. "Don't end up dead on his doorstep. We have no evidence, no strategy. Barging in is a stupid fucking choice. We don't know numbers inside the house right now, or if he's there at all—"

"A better reason to break in."

"—*and* the reason George Petersen keeps his distance is that he has his hound to babysit us while he wallows in the city."

"Such a poet." Miller bared his teeth.

"Fuck off."

"Grow a pair."

"Pathetic. I could hear you whiny bitches going at it like a married couple a mile off." Alan appeared in a crouch by my feet, his honed hunting knife drawn across his knees.

He was perfectly placed to rise and gut either of us—or both of us—before we knew he was there.

Miller jerked back. "Creepy little fucker."

"You love it." Alan rose in a smooth movement, sheathing his blade. "What do we do?"

"Who did you leave guarding Mari?" I searched the darkness between the trees for any trace of the evil dwelling too close to my doorstep for comfort. One misstep over that boundary line, and I'd take pleasure in ending my neighbor's life.

Until today, I'd have called myself a melodramatic asshole, but now....

"Don't get your knickerbockers in a twist. Jon's watching her."

Not really. Or not in my bedroom, at least. I hoped. The

chances of Mari accepting the presence of unknown men as soon as she woke clenched something inside my chest.

"What the fuck are knickerbockers?"

"I love you, too, darling." Alan batted his eyelashes at Miller. "I thought that since we have an expat in the house, I should perhaps brush up on my British lingo."

"Stupid ass." Miller snorted and turned away, his hands flexing at his sides.

I should try to ease his concern, but I harbored the same gut feelings even if I didn't believe Mari was a threat.

"We should go back."

"Yes, sir." Miller pivoted on his heel and stomped through the woods with all the grace of an addict on the way to his next hit. Though his type of fix couldn't be found in the direction he was headed.

Exhaling hard through my teeth, I motioned for Alan to follow my ex-troop. My aim had been to get a little closer to Gideon's compound, maybe sneak a peek behind his walls, but my desires didn't make my words to Miller any less pertinent. If one of us had to head back to NYC and risk raising the attention of my nemesis there, it would mean facing simultaneous battles on dual fronts.

"Come on."

Alan stood on the spot, ignoring Miller's temper tantrum. "I'll find out who's home, if you need." He offered the solo mission up like an easy traipse through the woods, not a solitary suicide run if he were caught.

I held his stare long enough for him to drop his head. "Not tonight. I need you in the house to settle the others when she... talks." *Or I make her talk.*

Not that I took pleasure in the idea of forcing a traumatized woman to do anything. Still, Miller's ongoing silence and orchestra of huffs reminded me of the potential threat she posed, pretty package she looked or not.

"Maybe tomorrow?" He perked back up like a kid desperate for a treat.

I narrowed my gaze. "Housebound, huh?"

"A little." He offered a wink and an ass wiggle as he followed Miller's path with all the fanfare and stomping steps but in utter silence. "Let me out?"

Message received.

"To run amok?" I smiled, though he couldn't see it. "We'll see."

SEVERAL ADDITIONAL HOURS AFTER DEALING WITH Miller's personal brand of torture in the art of charged silence and *not* whining, I sent him and Will out on a barest-minimum reconnaissance mission. I checked the windows every few minutes, but the cleared area around the house remained exactly that.

"Is she okay in there?" Alan asked in a casual voice, mixing me a cocktail I hadn't ordered. "Want me to check on her?"

A sound that might be a growl but that came out as a reluctant laugh surprised us both. Alan twirled away, making extra drinks for the hell of it, or so it appeared.

I kept the bar well stocked, a feature that ran the full length of the open-plan combined living-and-kitchen area, created post-build for one purpose. Not because we needed the distraction of alcohol or kept it as an emotional crutch, but because it gave Alan something to do with his hands. Dancing and fixing drinks were his way to deal with the shitty hand life dealt him.

A steaming mug of tea sat on the bar top where he worked.

Though some of us were further along the road to recovery than others, we all had our own Band-Aid fixes to help us deal with the world we'd fallen out of favor with. I reached for the tea, but Alan batted my hand away with a quick shake of his head.

"Not for you."

"Fine." I pressed my lips together, then ran a hand over my hair and attempted to answer his earlier question. "I have no idea. She seems chipper enough for a woman who's been abused to the edge of her sanity. Is that something to worry about or a sign of healing? I'm not the right person to assess her for this. Maybe she'll crash, or maybe she won't be able to leave the room. She needs medical attention at the absolute least and psychological support we can't provide from here. But she seems like she'll survive, at least at a surface level. I didn't scare her as much this time. I don't think."

I shot a look sideways to where Jon leaned out the cabin door, his back to me as he stared into the silent depths of the winter-blanketed forest beyond.

"The boys should be back soon." Jon gripped the lintel harder beneath thick fingers that suited his oversized frame, still staring after Miller. "When's our little ray of sunshine waking up?" He stepped back into the cabin, dwarfing me as we stood side by side.

Alan twisted away from us and whistled an obscenely jaunty tune as he pottered about between the bar and kitchen.

I elbowed Jon in the ribs as my easiest target. "Tell me you're not sweet on her too."

"Oh, hell no," Alan answered for him. He ran a hand through his hair, a grimace twisting his features.

I was used to hearing the end result of his ideas; by the time a thought fell out of his mouth, he'd already either approved or discarded it.

"She needs therapy, but not here. Which...." His grimace became more pronounced, baring teeth and gums at his hatred of the idea he voiced.

"Means either bring someone in or send her away. Yeah," I groused, the same thought whirling about my head. "I'm not a fan either."

Jon growled behind me, and Alan turned his attention in my woodsman's direction. All at once, my bartender's easy facade dropped away to be replaced with cold eyes and a tight white slash of a mouth.

What did Miller call him—a creepy little fucker? He sure as hell wasn't wrong. A groan left my lips as my gaze swung between them, waiting for the next crazy to fall from someone's thoughtless mouth.

Alan's eyes turned predatory when the big man didn't back down. Some of the color returned to my bartender's face. "Oh, yes. He's got eyes for the little darling. And speaking of, here she is. For you, sweetcheeks." Alan passed the waiting mug of steaming liquid out of my line of sight.

I spun on my heel, almost knocking Jon on his ass. No small feat in itself, that. But then I turned and took in Mari.

She'd dressed in the compression running tights Will had handed over upon request with no small dose of reluctance and a black long-sleeved thermal top Miller had donated, his slight build being the closest to her smaller form, though he topped her by a good half a foot.

But Miller wasn't who I thought of when I looked back toward my bedroom.

The slinky black material covered Mari from head to toe and clung to every curve of her breasts. The thermal draped over her ass in a gentle swell that invited a perfect one-hand grip. Clean and damp, her hair was knotted in a messy bun on top of her head. She wore a wary smile that appeared to be her default setting, and as predicted, she weighed in well above stunning.

"Mari—" I started, but Alan cut me off.

"Mari! What a pretty name," he all but cooed, bracing his forearms on the bench and leaning forward, not quite invading her space. "I'm Alan Dale, pole dancer extraordinaire, and you've already met our most gracious host. The big blond one is Jon Littleman. Will and Miller are about somewhere." He tweaked her nose in slow motion, and she giggled.

Giggled.

"How come he can make her laugh while I get a crazy woman who seesaws between hysterical and mute?" I asked the room, unable to pry my eyes off her.

"Because you're the size of a mountain, and he chats people up for a living," Jon replied out of the corner of his mouth.

Alan was the closest thing we had to an intelligence officer, though he hadn't started out that way.

"Fair call."

We both folded our arms and stared forward.

Two heads whipped our way at the movement.

Alan rolled his eyes. "Subtlety is not your strength, Robe. Jon, samesies. Waffles, sweetcakes?"

Mari smiled behind the tea mug she clutched to her chest, though I noted her fingers weren't quite as white as they had been when she accepted the gift from Alan. "I thought I was sweetcheeks."

"You, tiny girl, can be both." He dropped a kiss on the tip of her nose in a cute, brotherly fashion and danced away.

She blushed.

My groin tightened. The obvious heat that rose in her at Alan's words spiked painful pleasure straight to my cock. My chest expanded, and I eyed Alan with dislike for the first time. In my periphery, Mari shifted on her feet, swiveling her head my way. I adjusted myself discreetly, though Jon caught my eye with a knowing smirk.

Bring a girl into a house full of military men, and we all started behaving like a ragtag group of randy motherfucking pups on a hormone-fueled trajectory through puberty.

"Thank you," she murmured.

Her gaze rose to catch mine, which froze her where she stood. Jon stepped up beside me, and her thick-lashed eyes widened.

"Don't mind the great lump over there. Or Jon." Alan waved a dismissive hand our way. "I'll make sure you're safe here, sweetcheeks." He shot the pair of us a warning glare. "Now, finish up your tea, and we'll get something a little stronger into you. It's medicinal. Promise."

Keeping his light tone, Alan pranced about the kitchen, dancing to a beat no one else could hear. As he swirled, he jerked his head once in her direction. Somewhat belatedly, I took the hint.

I stepped forward, though I had no idea what to say. I went with "If you need more rest, feel free to keep using my bed. It's there as long as you need it."

"And you'll sleep on the floor? I can't imagine you two sharing a bed." Mari gestured between Jon and me with a small laugh. Her look turned speculative, a hint of sass breaking through the barriers she'd erected for obvious reasons. It made her that little bit more endearing. "Maybe *he'd* fit, though." She nodded to Alan, who swept out in a great circle and exchanged her tea mug for two generous fingers of whiskey. She hid behind her cup, closing us out behind a spectacular display of English manners. "Thank you," she said again, reverting to her not-so-foul-mouthed default of prim and proper British.

Cute as fuck, and she wasn't even trying.

Jon coughed, his fist pressed over his mouth.

"Oh, I'm too much man for these great brutes," Alan said, redirecting the conversation, though his eyes sparkled as he caught my eye. "I wouldn't object to a lumbersnack like that, of course, though Jon and Robe have shared plenty of times." He leaned across the bar. "Miller and I got drunk one night too. Experimented with more than a kiss. I wanted to try that out with Will, but he's a little... well, virginal isn't the right word, but you get the idea." He winked at her.

I bit back a groan that bordered on something inappropriate. Add one female to the mix and an excess of testosterone became the order of the day. Was every asshole in the room going to smile at her? I couldn't risk opening my mouth in case something ridiculous fell out. I glanced over at Jon to check how he fared under this assault of sweetness.

His shoulders lost their habitual hard line. The hint of a smile I hadn't seen since we built the cabin played on his face.

We were screwed. Every single one of us.

"Alan wouldn't know," I reassured Mari as she stared at me with wide eyes. "He's... ah, I'm not sure how to explain him." I gestured toward the bar, offering her a rueful smile. "But he's a good boy."

"Oh, thank you, master," Alan roleplayed, lifting his gaze to the ceiling, hands raised in a silent—albeit sarcastic—hallelujah.

I snorted back a laugh at the kid's antics. Alan was damn good value and a benefit in the house. He sent me a wicked grin and wiggled his ass in a suggestive motion. My palm itched. I took half a step forward, prepared to deliver.

Mari chose that moment to take a large sip from the whiskey Alan had served her. She swallowed with her eyes closed, pleasure and peace warring on her face. Every line creased in panic I'd become familiar with now smoothed over, and I began to recognize the girl who withstood the horror her body and mind were forced to experience. The girl who *survived*.

When she opened her eyes, the three of us stared at her, unable to tear our eyes away.

"Oh, I...." She blinked, then peered up at me through her thick, dark lashes. "Isn't it odd how a little extra pain can dull the edge of everything else?"

Jon started at my side like she'd slapped him. He spun on his heel and took the short flight of stairs to the forest floor two at a time, the thump of his heavy footsteps likely to clear wildlife for half a mile around.

"Damn," I muttered under my breath.

The girl in front of me wasn't the only one who bore scars, though hers were fresher than everyone else's. Some of us, Jon the perfect example, didn't wear ours on the outside.

"What just happened?" Mari took a hesitant step in my direction, her head tilted back as she tracked the empty doorway.

Jon didn't reappear, and I knew he'd be gone for hours. The flare of her eyes betrayed her alarm, as did the way her whitened knuckles clenched on her glass. For the second time, she didn't run away.

I might not be able to make her smile like Alan could, but that she moved in my direction floored me. I stuffed my hands into my pockets to prevent myself from winding my arms around her or doing something else that was just as inappropriate. Whenever she managed to self-heal, she would still be in no way ready for what my heart wanted. For once, my brain didn't object to bringing her closer either.

"Ignore him," I murmured. Sucking in a long, slow breath in an attempt to calm the blood that roared through my veins at her proximity, I gave in to my baser desires and slid my hand around her waist. Instinct forced me to gentle my touch as I drew her into me. "Jon has his own devils."

She didn't pull away from the contact, didn't rant or scream. My world narrowed to her. I let out a long breath, keeping it under the same ethos of control, and looked across to Alan for support.

His forearms, a mixture of lithe dancer muscle and harder-earned bulk from working at the cabin, rested on the bar top. Long, inked fingers danced invisible patterns across the beer mats. His tea sat forgotten beside him as he watched us with a speculative glint.

Mari leaned into my side. That thin line I straddled between letting her heal and giving in to the selfish need to protect her at a much closer, more intimate proximity turned gray and fuzzy as hell. I'd stepped right into the middle of a taboo space with no exit strategy. The contradictory minx did everything backward. When I expected her to be cowed and silent, she thrashed out. When I expected her to run, she stayed.

Warmth seeped from her bones into mine as she nestled into me like she belonged there. I held her, my arm a light barrier between her and the rest of the world, though I tried not to make my touch restrictive. From the raw skin on her wrists and ankles I'd first observed when I washed her, I doubted she would appreciate having the little control she had over her own body stripped away a second time.

I met Alan's knowing gaze over her head, a small smile

playing on my face. My heart plodded along at its regular, steady rhythm, the possessive beast within me calmed by her proximity. I wanted to wrap her in my arms and defend her from every demon who came for her.

Alan paused, his gaze sliding between us. Something akin to yearning lit his brilliant blue eyes, but before I could delve into a wild speculation of what that expression might mean, he busied himself in the kitchen, his usual graceful movements jerky, his pale skin pasty.

Settling Mari into a perfect fit against my side, I couldn't work out what he saw in my face that terrified him to the point of distraction.

Or if the fear I read in his gaze came from somewhere within him instead.

Mari

6

MARI

M<small>Y HANDS TREMBLED AS</small> I <small>CLUTCHED THE GLASS OF</small> golden ambrosia, all too aware of Robe's possessive hold on my hip. His fingers sketched tiny circles over my borrowed clothing as he held me against him in an embrace both sweet and protective. It surprised me how well I fit against his bulk without the fear of disappearing altogether.

His enormous presence matched his personality, and neither overwhelmed me.

I should have been intimidated or terrified by the men who surrounded me in Robe's cabin. There was nothing *normal* about how my brain should have reacted while my world turned upside down and I clung on like a passenger on a weird sidecar ride. Perhaps I'd become more like Alice than I thought—or Dorothy. A mashup. *Bring on the blue caterpillar.* An inopportune giggle escaped me that I managed to muffle in his thick cotton shirt.

Robe traced roughened knuckles along my cheek in a firm, strong touch I didn't hate.

Better the demon you know, right?

My demons populated the outside of the house. From

what I'd gleaned, Robe's cabin offered a hell of a greater safety than my previous destination would have. I grasped the lifeline he offered with both hands, existing in survival mode, still burning energy at high speed. Each blink created a disjointed freeze-frame of snapshots rather than a scrolling memory.

What should have been running about in my mind was my future: the need to return to my apartment, call my friends back in the UK even though they seemed to have forgotten me the moment I left after graduation. Even message Mum and Dad. Had they tried to call? Did anyone know I was missing? How long would it be—

A sob caught in my throat, the answer already forming in my head. I hadn't spoken to my parents in the initial three months I'd been in the US post-graduation when I garnered my first career job, and since I came to New York, the trend hadn't changed much. Their opinion of my travels was made clear when, the moment I set foot outside the house, the door was slammed and locked behind me.

Caught in Robe's embrace and knowing the public face of the demons outside the barrier he and his woods formed around me, I declined the intrusive concept with my most polite British *Piss off, you bastards.*

Robe's arm flexed behind me as he drew me deeper into him in an almost imperceptible movement. I didn't fight his touch and had no desire to escape the haven he offered, different from the hands that—

Touched, plucked, pulled—

No.

I refused to let those psychotic assholes steal my peace now that I had discovered something else I craved. Something healing. Something more.

I am not broken.

I refused to be broken.

I will enjoy physical contact with another human again.

My new mantra. Especially huge protectors like Everest. But a reasonable, whole person wouldn't crave contact or find safety in the home of a wild man after what I endured.

Why am I so broken?

Tears pricked my eyelids. I dipped my head, squeezing my lashes tight to ward off the pity party raging inside my mind.

You won't win. I won't let you.

I made the promise to my foe—my boss, the person I trusted when I first came to this country—over and over. A baker's dozen of panicked breaths later, I found myself pressed flush to Robe's side. Chatter rose around me. I ignored it all, his presence providing the peace to block out white noise.

Familiar eyes met mine and held. Something wild, almost manic, flitted there. Robe didn't hide his demons like I suspected Alan did beneath a facade of smiles and misdirection. No, Robe chose to wear his trauma raw on the outside, like so much armor against a world he had retreated from. The ridge suited him in this way, both barren, bare rock the elements blasted against, but still they held firm. The shadows within his eyes spoke of scars I was sure lingered beneath his beard and shirt. He'd built his body up, either to physically battle what he had to face or out of necessity to survive in his own way.

I wondered what my own crutch would be when my brain freed up enough to allow my numbness to fade.

Robe held his silence as he wound his arms tighter around me, offering a physical barrier from the overcrowded room, and rested his chin on the top of my head. Roughened fingers tangled in my hair as he crushed me against his chest.

Warmth pervaded me, wrapping me in Robe's fresh forest-

and-woodfire scent. *My Everest.* I marveled at the steady beat in my chest that matched his heart's solid pounding against my cheek as I leaned into his embrace, taking the security his arms offered.

Leave. Run from the wolf.

Was he a wolf, though? I felt far less *Little Red Riding Hood* and more a Grimms' fairy tale where the heroine fell in with a group of uncouth men rife with faults who always ruined the day.

I snorted a little into his shirt, torn between aiming for a second bout of hysterics or settling on a keening whuffle noise.

Spoiler alert: the whuffle won out.

All broken here.

No one ever returned from those sorts of tall tales, or if they did, they weren't the same. Not the sort of story that suited me. I loved my urban life in New York City, so different from the one I fled my home country to avoid. The cult-escapee girl turned the CEO's PA, or something like that.

An all-male scent surrounded me, another grounding point of difference. No expensive perfumes worth a month's pay filled the cabin's living area with a posy of allergens. If Robe owned a single bottle of cologne, I'd eat my knickers. Not that I had any; they were left behind in my rushed exodus, along with all my other things.

I lost my phone, and I left my *car* parked out front of my boss's house. I might as well have called it my independence. Right now, I owned nothing at all: not pride in my body, the ability to call for help or to drive away to a home. All I could claim was a cabin full of men I barely knew and a half-empty cup of whiskey.

Somehow, for now... that was enough.

I chanced a peek around Robe's massive chest, peering

through the open doorway that the blond Viking—*Jon*—exited through earlier.

Their personal battles scared me. Robe offered me a slice of peace, and I'd take it in a heartbeat, needy creature that I'd become after the horrors I ran from. But the risk of ruining what they had, the community that had continued its existence in his cabin even in my scant days here, listening to their muted conversations, the occasional raised voices through Robe's heavy, closed door.... Well, half of me wanted to stay wrapped in his arms no matter the cost.

The other half of me, the part that had fueled my headlong sprint through the mountainside, screamed a different message.

—*run and run and run*—

Knickers were the least of my worries.

Run, run, fast as you can. Can you catch me, Mr. Mountain Man?

The niggle itched at my brain again. My old English professor bitched about alliteration overuse inside my head. But no matter how many times I said the words to myself, my feet refused to let me leave Robe's side.

I swallowed an onset of panic, locked in my own private hell. Serene on the outside, clawing and shrieking on the inside.

Like when he stopped me in the forest.

Help me.

More than broken, definitely. My jaw locked. I couldn't get the words out that would provide relief from my invisible cage. He stood right there, holding me, and I couldn't communicate what I needed.

Useless as a newborn, I forced my senses to revolve around him. The rhythmic beat of his heart fast became my benchmark, what I returned to when panic delved deep and took root. The hard ridges of muscle surrounded me in a warm, safe embrace. I didn't want to leave his arms or escape his cabin.

I wanted out of *me*.

Crisp mountain air and smoke that had nothing to do with a woodfire slipped through my firewall. I tapped my fingers on the tree-trunk biceps that surrounded me, lightly at first, then more insistently as I tried to bring myself back to the present.

Robe sent a single glance my way, and his features shifted from the facade of civilization he kept up for the men opposite us to something far more primal. He read the panic I couldn't communicate in any other way as I hit max capacity, my deafening silence my last line of defense as I shuddered with the aftereffects of delayed terror.

Everest released me, cursing beneath his breath as Alan set something on fire in the kitchen. He scooped an arm around my waist and leaned me against the bar like I weighed no more than a Mari-sized doll.

Long steps ate the floorboards beneath him, and then he swept one arm beneath the counter, collecting an overstuffed white paper bag. In a fraction of a second, he upended a pyramid of salt over the small inferno Alan had managed to ignite in a frypan.

Robe stood beside the lithe dancer, his arms folded over his chest. When I expected him to glower at Alan or dress him down, he surprised me by ruffling the younger man's hair. Footsteps and chatter filled the silence as men clattered up the veranda stairs to the cabin. Three faces peered in at me, two in open curiosity and one in poorly shielded hostility.

My safety net flung wide on the other side of the bar, I stared back, panic reigniting.

—*fight flight fight*—

But no enemy appeared for me to fight, and I had no way to escape. The bodies jammed in the doorway who were barring my lone escape route with their combined physical mass saw to that.

All of the men were the same level of dirty, each of them bound in muscle. *Henry Cavill, eat your heart out.* Their physiques were clearly sculpted by hard labor, not the sort built for show so common in the city. Even beneath weather-worn jackets, their combined bulk was impossible to hide.

Did Robe have a secret fighting ring buried beneath the house? A little private damage club of his own? I half expected Tyler Durden to stride inside the cabin and start mouthing off at the absurd tableau.

Cue the White Rabbit in three, two....

The men fit tight within the confines of the handmade walls, as it turned out. On any regular day, I might have been amused at their size. A low-level angst simmered to boiling point between the men as they all crowded the room, each additional body stealing precious space and air. Robe and Alan seemed to be okay with the constricted oxygen, while I backed up against the bar's edge.

Jon offered an apologetic smile and grabbed a beer from the fridge. A stocky young man sporting a buzz cut and a permanent scowl stormed through the house. His footsteps cracked whip sharp as he headed into another part of the house I hadn't discovered yet.

Will, the other young man Alan pointed out earlier, whose sandy fringe flopped over his eyes, watched me with enthusiasm, his cheeks reddening as he checked me out with no hint of apology. His easy, coasting gaze should have been creepy or unnerving, but his open face took the edge away from his assessment. Nor did he approach me with hands outstretched and grabbing—

I pressed back harder into the bar. The unforgiving border prodded between my shoulder blades as air evacuated from my lungs.

Robe used up the rest of the available oxygen to address Will, jerking his chin at the younger man with the soul-filled eyes. "Grab some firewood? We're going to need it when night closes in."

It struck me that the men should have been bantering with each other the way Alan and Robe did in their odd way. My presence silenced every single man inside the cabin's tight walls, changing their dynamic until they all teetered on edge, pretending a normality none of us felt.

Their combined judgment weighed heavily over my poor attempt at camouflage. I grasped at nothingness, my mouth open to say—something—but then I didn't need to. Warmth replaced the cold at my back.

I shivered at the abrupt temperature change as Robe shifted. Broad hands clasped my waist in a firm grip. His touch steadied me, let me breathe. I sucked in a fortifying breath as he slid into place at my back. His heart beat a faster tempo than before but then faded to its regular rhythm, taking my breath with it.

"You're super speedy," I murmured, sliding my fingers around the tumbler of whiskey Alan pushed back into my hand. I sent him a grateful, if weak, smile.

Dexterous and fast—Everest encompassed all the qualities a mountain man was supposed to possess. In any other place, he might be an oversized curiosity, but Robe Huntingdon's presence prevented me from screaming myself hoarse every breathing minute. Even in my panicked state, I knew that tearing back down the mountain with an icy night coming on was a bloody stupid idea.

"I try," Robe murmured, sliding his hand around my stomach and pressing me back to his huge frame.

Even more than his physical form, his sheer presence threatened to engulf me. At the same time, a protective bubble formed around us. Blocking out the rest of the room, Robe dulled the renewed conversation to a blur between my ears.

If I let him whisk me deeper into the mountains, would Mari Merripen cease to exist altogether? A fanciful notion at worst, but my body chose a different reaction to his touch. A jolt of desire shot through me, hot and electric. Submerged in my daydream, I choked on my whiskey. Arousal in my state shouldn't be possible.

Heat pooled between my thighs as he spread his fingers over my waist, pinning me to him in a gentle but unbreakable hold. Tiny shocks writhed through my system as I reveled in the ability to *feel.*

Gideon broke more than my body when he let his friends abuse me. A frigid shiver replaced Robe's warmth in the cold oblivion of denial. Yet I was attempting to play house with a group of men I didn't know, struggling to understand my motivations.

There was no way around that not-to-insignificant fact. I didn't know them at all, and I needed to go home. I had work —well, I used to have a job—friends... a family I spoke to solely on special occasions. Should a missing person's alert go on my wish list? I snorted into my glass. That was akin to an innocent teen who knew nothing about the world asking, *Will you cry at my funeral?*

What a morbid creature. My transformation was complete in the wilderness with no one but mountain men to witness my metamorphosis. But I couldn't go back—not to my apartment in NYC or work. Even the coffee shop between the two where I used to get my morning brew. Gideon knew all those places. And I'd seen faces—knew *his* face. Surely that meant home wasn't safe—nor was my workplace. All the familiar haunts were now off-limits, which left me nowhere to hide except to stay in place, right in Robe's path.

I knew this man could break me without a single word, just as he could heal me. But I couldn't bring myself to ask.

"What is it?" Robe asked, turning me in his arms as if by instinct.

My glass thudded onto the bar behind me, the dregs of golden liquor sloshing around the cut crystal base. Heat hit me on both sides. I twisted my head back to look up at Jon. The giant's hand hovered over my shoulder, concern transforming his dark eyes to liquid amber.

His warmth seared my body. Once again, rather than the connection attacking my senses in an invasive touch, I accepted it, leaned into him. I nodded once, and his fingers grazed my skin. A broad palm cupped my shoulder in a gentle squeeze.

"Mari." Despite his proximity, Robe's voice hit me from a distance too far away for clarity for my drifting mind.

"Robe?"

I turned my attention back to find him on one knee. He reached out to cup my face between broad, work-roughened palms as he looked at me. A nonthreatening position. My mind still functioned on some level.

"Come back to me," he murmured.

Behind me, Jon whispered his agreement, both hands sliding to my waist. Steadying, offering enough pressure to ground me.

Mad and unexpected, the dual contact worked.

I am safe here. These aren't the same men who took from me.

Not even close. Gideon's *friends* exuded their own brand of evil, and nothing in this world could make me face that again. Fool him once, maybe. My escape at his hands was the single reason my heart beat on. Fool him twice? Not possible.

Gideon took pleasure in watching others suffer, grandstanding for his moment of leniency when they begged for his mercy. I never gave him that moment, and I knew he hated me for it.

Robe's breath brushed my lips, warm and welcome. *Safe.* My eyes drifted shut, and I wondered if he would kiss me. Would I welcome the pressure of another's lips on mine again, or would I fear my soul could be stolen in a quick breath, leaving me an empty husk?

I will not be broken.

Too late.

"I'm here," I whispered.

His breath huffed against my cheeks. "Then open your eyes, sweetheart. We're not the monsters of those nightmares you face. Not in here, anyway."

Smiling at the image of this incredible group of men as monsters, I opened my eyes.

Robe assessed me with his fathomless gaze, and my stomach dropped at the uncloaked need written there. He reined in whatever was reflected on my face, reduced to something wary, protective.

The loss of his emotion hit me keenly. Part of me wanted to see his desire reinstated, but then I shook my head. "You're right. The monsters are out there."

The shivers returned despite the fact that I was sandwiched between two large bodies that brought my safety back in a mere breath. I glanced over my shoulder at Jon, releasing the bars of my new cage that had nothing to do with iron braces and frayed ropes.

Or shadows and glittering eyes and roaming hands.

The expression in Jon's eyes reflected Robe's concern, though a smothered, unvoiced need was displayed there too. My stomach flip-flopped. The tethers that wound themselves around me were scented with pine needles and soap and, most importantly, were of my own choosing.

Who knew soap would be something I'd crave.

Robe's eyes darkened with the sort of fixated obsession I understood could be so dangerous. "Do you want to stay, Mari Merripen? Because if you do, I cannot allow you to leave."

His words rolled around my head as I stared at him, my heart divided both ways. *Yes* was the only answer I wanted to give him, but I wasn't sure which part I agreed to just yet.

Maybe both.

Robe bared his teeth in a brutal smile as his next words contradicted everything I wanted. "Leave whenever you want, Miss Merripen. But I suggest you wait until we've organized a safe mode of transport. Running around at night through the forest is... dangerous."

It was the sort of practiced million-watt smile that made billionaire CEOs a hot-minute trend. All white teeth, dark eyes, not-quite-trimmed beard... swoonworthy.

My stomach flipped as he rose to his full height. "Thank you," I repeated.

I couldn't object to Robe's logic. The forest held its own plethora of threats, and I got the impression that I had taken up residence inside a cabin with five prime specimens the woods had on offer.

"Eat, sweetcheeks. Robe and Jon will let you catch your breath." Alan walked between the two behemoths and gripped my elbow.

He towed me across the room through the crowded space to a small, round table pushed against one corner. A window overlooked the pine forest beneath the house. I stared out, not realizing how high we'd ascended.

Flashing Alan a grateful smile, I tried to deny the anxiety that threatened to bloom into a full-blown panic attack despite the space I'd craved moments before. The air thinned, my vision graying around the edges. Conversation reached around me but couldn't touch me. I clenched my fists, and my ragged nails bit into my palms.

A calculated risk that blessedly worked. The sting of bruised skin brought me back. I swallowed gulps of crisp forest air that seemed to follow Robe around until it jammed somewhere between my heart and my head.

Alan pulled out the chair with a flourish, settled me into the leather-covered cushion, and placed a plate of golden-brown waffles on the table. The scent of vanilla and maple indulged my senses. Each sweet treat curled, crispy at the edges. My mouth watered.

"*Buon appetito*," Alan sang. The epitome of a cruise ship waiter, he sashayed across the room to take up residence in the bar.

Robe caught my eye in an assessing gaze. One eyebrow rose, the manicured one I already loved to hate. He folded his arms and stilled.

I raised my chin and pushed out a thin breath between pursed lips. Anger rose unbidden. That judgy, closed autocratic expression was back. Okay, so it wasn't just the eyebrow.

I stabbed my waffle, telling myself my appetite had rekindled because Alan put a plate of amazing food in front of me. *Not* because I swooned for a sexy mountain god who now seemed to think he could stake a claim on my eating habits. Never mind that I sat in his house, wore the clothes he provided, and was washed and clean because of him.

While I did nothing for myself.

The protective way Robe stared at me left me in no doubt that he wouldn't let anyone else see me in that state. Warmth bloomed in my stomach. *Still broken.* Holding his gaze, I cut a piece off my waffles and defiantly popped it into my mouth, chewing though my stomach revolted at the thought of swallowing anything. Robe tracked the movement as sweetness and carbs zinged through my overcaffeinated, tortured body that was already riding a whiskey high. I moaned in appreciation, forgetting Robe's attention, how he fixated on me, the room.

His eyes darkened, black flames wreathed in their depths that promised me I wouldn't walk away unscathed. I should hide and let the monsters play far away from me, but I wanted to push him, make him reveal every secret, every promise. Part of me needed his brand of darkness to forget my own.

And that was a terrible, dangerous idea.

Jon

7

JON

I POUNDED THE FOREST'S DAMP GROUND, MY BOOT falls far harder than necessary. The ridgeline opened out in front of me as I beat a new pass into the soft packed earth, winding my way between thick trunks. My breath remained light as I jogged away from the cabin, unwilling to let them see me wrecked, though I loved every man in the small home Robe had built for us.

Will and Miller appeared between trees. The stocky soldier smiled, an all-too-knowing look in his eyes. "Gave you the shits already?"

It took every inch of my control not to snarl back at Miller. Mari had been in the house with us for less than a month, and I couldn't bear sharing the space any longer. Too many memories surfaced every time she spoke.

I growled at Miller. "Maybe you should offer something proactive instead of having a temper tantrum in the middle of the house."

"Like you just did?" He raised an eyebrow in perfect mimicry of Robe.

I wanted to bitch-slap it from his face.

Normally, I got along well with Miller, all things considered, since my incursion into their world at his master's invitation. He followed Robe like a friendly stray, but the man was valuable. The rich boy turned soldier became Robe's friend over the course of a dozen skirmishes continents away from their homeland, saved his life during half of their missions, and for that I forgave him most of our combined grievances.

This was not one of those times.

"Find your manners before you step foot in that house." I pushed as much emphasis into the words as I could, shoving past the smaller man.

Miller might look intimidating to someone of Mari's build and height, but to me he was another short log in my path. His expression remained indifferent as I plowed past him. Will shifted at his side, the easygoing kid clearly torn between playing advocate and backing the fuck away.

Smart boy.

The latter option fell in the young man's favor, though Will's gaze weighed across my shoulders as I picked a deer trail to torture. I slammed my feet into the delicate tracks, obliterating all trace of their passing, all too conscious that Will saw me as a sort of mentor or a woodsman superhero to emulate.

I wasn't fit to be called either and tried to ignore the growing responsibility Robe thrust upon me unasked.

Unwelcomed.

Each of us played our role in his tattered family unit. Meeting the woods' silence with my own secrets while keeping Robe's was mine.

The boys' chatter receded as I pushed deeper into the forest. Shifting greens blurred into a gray haze that distinguished nothing and hid everything. Pine needles bit into my skin as I found my stride.

It didn't take long for the burn to start. I knew I'd have to stretch the lactic acid out later unless I wanted to walk like a cripple tomorrow. A quick glance over my shoulder assured me the cabin sat well out of sight.

The forest fell into a pensive snow-blanketed slumber around me as the echoes of my pounding boots reverberated beneath my feet. A half smile fell from my lips as I stared at the spaces between trees with a determined laser focus. Increasing the length of my steps, I sprinted like a madman through the forest, reckless and all too aware of the dangers nearby. I might be the size of a bear, but I didn't have the claws of one. At least, not the physical sort.

Branches scratched at my arms. I shattered twigs and crumpled garnet-edged leaves as I pushed my bulk between the behemoths that refused to bend for me. Was this what Mari had felt, tear-assing through the forest while pursued by a horde of invisible predators to land in Robe's lap? My heart pumped in my chest to the point of burning within moments at the thought of her endless terror.

At the exposed cliffside amid freezing battering winds, I turned a hard right. Appearing in clear view during the full light of day was stupid and out of character. Direct line of sight opened between us and our nearest neighbor at this range, situated a decent distance for sanity's sake.

We avoided the boundary, but Mari's abrupt arrival changed everything. Robe's priorities were rewired by instinct. *My* priorities. I no longer cared about invisible fence lines dividing us from the evil in plain view, intent on pushing myself harder as the memories began to flood in.

Ragged, fire-filled breaths tore at my insides, anchoring

me in a beautiful dance of heartrending memory that swept over the trees, obliterating the landscape.

Crisp lake air, so distant from the mountains I now called home, froze in the still fog that hovered over the mirage of a familiar lake in the brisk morning. Near the shoreline sat a pretty blue-and-white cottage I'd built for my new wife.

The image overlaid the weak sun pushing its final rays past the ridgeline, trying to announce its presence through my phantom memories.

The air around me drifted to silence as the heavy shroud extinguished reality. My pounding steps became the single slice of Recurve Ridge I allowed to break through my trance. A quarter mile into my self-imposed torture and my breath already wheezed out of constricted lungs.

My pain offered distraction enough to leave the hellish haven I'd created, assuming life would be grand, well away from city lights. I pushed my past away and concentrated on throwing each screaming thigh muscle before the other, setting a frantic pace along the scarred stone that understood my need.

Big men were never designed to sprint. I pushed through, determined on my self-flagellation. Watching Robe carry Mari into the house unconscious was one thing. Seeing her dressed in spare clothes, speaking her mind, and healing was another. In my head, Mari settled next to another woman I'd known who spoke out like that, both girls thoughtless and so damn sharp at the same time.

I preferred my women well-rounded, their figures robust with all the lush curves as the perfect foil for my work-hardened hands. Everything about Mari was wrong. Too skinny. Too pale.

Yet she called to me.

I shared that burden with every man in the cabin. I'd seen

it in Robe's face, and Alan's. The younger men would follow suit, and what did that make us but a group of fools panting after a woman we couldn't touch?

Couldn't tarnish.

Mari's fine frame reminded me of how breakable a woman could be despite her determination to survive. Live. The traditional fairer-sex stereotype never suited me, even as a younger man. Robe had staked his claim on the woman he rescued, and despite the fact that we'd shared girls in the past, I wouldn't cross that line.

More than a fool's errand, the fucker would offer to share. And having her—just her touch—would break me. Hell, I'd break *her* in all the ways he wouldn't. The rest of us needed to back off until he got his head—and hers too—into the right space.

Mari's emotional qualities shone through the plethora of bruises she collected in her flight, the sort of hook that lanced through a man's heart and reeled him in, both as unaware of the invisible process as the other.

Her fine bone structure gave her an ethereal beauty. Not quite pixie-like or otherworldly, she displayed a rare inner tenacity all of us respected on sight. Despite the state she'd arrived in—filthy, frantic, and giving Robe hell—I had to admit she made a sexy addition to cabin life.

I knew what Robe was doing, and even his *why*, but having her in the house with a band of not-so-honest brothers made for a terrible fucking idea. We all knew it. Alan put on his little flirty-as-fuck face that drove me up the wall, and I half expected to find Robe with a dopey-ass grin decorating his scarred mug.

My fist curled at the thought of throwing down a beating, though I never needed to use violence to coerce the men into line. The threat, it seemed, was enough. That, and Robe's weird brand of leadership that brought damaged men into his path, me included.

And cold little killers like Alan. Cute as the stripper could be, I'd seen the lithe man dance. If he considered this good behavior while wearing his best manners, I would hate to see him at his worst. Scratch that—I *had* seen him at his worst. I watched him garotte a man, cold and emotionless, then rifle through his belongings to make it look like a robbery and walk away whistling a soft, upbeat tune that stung my blood with ice.

Not that I could blame him for his vengeance.

The man he unalived had raped two underage male strippers who wouldn't be considered legal in any state the world round. The boys were close to Alan at the time. Despite my repulsion over the matter, our exotic dancer's bare-faced efficiency did things to my cock that only Robe had managed before him.

I'd seen that face on one man prior, and I'd never questioned him on his methods when he was in that mood either. Each of us was collected by Robe because we filled a role, outcast from our family, society, and the law.

Mari changed that status quo the moment Robe brought her into the house.

Unable to deal with the resurgence in memories, I speared deeper into the forest. Robe wouldn't fuss. He knew a man would take his grievance out on the well-trodden paths by his own choice of tool and return clearheaded.

For a moment I'd been grateful for the woman who'd immediately consumed me. Until she spoke and that same thoughtful tone brought me back to a past I'd long assumed I would escape.

Mari's head of dark hair with its gentle waves and deep navy eyes reminded me of another face—one taken from me too many years prior to count. A face I last saw when ropes tethered me to my own fence posts, the sort drilled nine feet into the ground and set in cement to prevent the damn things from moving.

When I first started working on the lake house, I never thought that the home I'd built for Jenny would turn my love of the place into something beyond loathing.

I slammed my soles into the ground, counting each step while in my mind's eye, I watched my wife spread out on the ground beneath hooded figures, no farther than twelve feet from my boots. I screamed myself hoarse, then and now, the sound echoing off sheer rock face that speared my pain high across the valley, but it made no difference.

The remote location became a blessing that then transformed into a nightmare I relived alone in my too-large bed.

Jenny had no chance to get away from them, all soft curves and stunning eyes. A woman I wouldn't break by accident. A simple laborer, my nature made me too rough for a woman with no substance.

The scratches of fine twigs became deep rents in my shirt as I burst out of the trees, slamming my boots into the rocky ground.

Thump thump thump

Beneath the icy air wafting off the lake, I strained against the ropes shackling me too tightly to the fence posts I laid myself, unable to tear my hands from their bonds. My black-edged gaze seared small details into my mind. Flashes of flesh, metal wrist watches and signet rings, colored angles of tattoos that curled around their hands in a matching set as bloodied fists rained down on her broken body.

Suddenly those curves were fragile things that shattered with each steel-capped kick.

Pound pound pound

Thump thump thump

A dark, still mound, indiscernible from a matted heap of kelp, lay before me along the shoreline when they walked away. No word, no glance. No jeers or cries of satisfaction. A job complete, punishment extracted for a crime I didn't understand.

She'd spoken out against a then-small local politician before we left the city, a passionate woman protecting others' rights. We moved away without another thought, a proud new husband with a glowing wife who consumed my every waking moment. Cooking with her, finding new scenes for her to paint, watching her as I worked among the trees.

Jenny never looked back, never searched for me, but she knew they were holding me there the entire time.

I couldn't reach her, but she didn't face her end alone.

Alone was where Robe found me less than an hour later, hanging from my ropes. Tears long shed crusted my cheeks, my throat raw. He untied me, bore my weight when I retched and reached for her. I lifted the first stone and the one after until we formed a cairn over her body. Robe worked alongside me in silence, and though he didn't pray with me, he stood sentinel until I was done.

He waited while I'd vomited into the sink and grabbed the few things I needed to leave the life I cherished behind me forever in favor of the vengeance he promised. He said nothing, remained unmoving when I found the positive pregnancy test in the bathroom she hadn't announced yet.

I cried anew, and still he waited.

Then, when my heart had released every iota of emotion within its confines, we walked in silence to the place my feet pound now. Laid a foundation for a new life in a place that bears as many scars upon its bare rocks as I do upon my soul. The cabin might feel rustic now, but it was far less stark than when we started. A few rough logs nailed together. Care factor came well after, once we established the status quo.

After I met Miller. Found Alan and Will.

When, day after day, he trained me.

Honed my body, sharpened my mind from the blunt instrument I'd been, unable to protect those I loved.

Mountain air now sucked into my wheezing lungs in shallow waves. I forced myself to return to Recurve Ridge, away from the ghost of my dead wife and the lake house. My own harsh steps reverberated through my bones, shaking my body to my core, but I refused to stop, ignoring the burning acid in muscles pushed too hard.

One more step, and another. I ignored the bleak, void presence of the compound opposite.

Until Mari said otherwise, we couldn't risk attacking Gideon or show our faces, singular or otherwise. Until she named him, everything we thought we knew got filed under *suspicious*, nothing more. Robe required proof before he went off half-cocked, while the rest of us seethed over unhealed scars, prepared to extract vengeance for hurts long past.

Besides, what was a small band of criminals capable of achieving against the expensive personal arsenal at his disposal courtesy of that once-small-time politician?

The moment Robe brought Mari into the cabin, he had unwittingly created a division between us. The broken man who hid behind a facade of manners and rules only some of us played by held himself to a high standard and was possessive as hell. If he claimed Mari, he wouldn't want anyone else touching her—and that broke all our house rules about sharing what was ours.

Still, I figured he'd come around at some point. But right now, and for the first time in a decade, I didn't have my feet in his back pocket. I made a mental note to get Alan to make me pom-poms so I could announce my siding with Team Mari.

Somehow, I didn't think Robe would mind.

It would be interesting to see how the other boys interpreted that change.

I drew to a halt on an exposed rocky outcrop, soaking up the weak sun's warmth. My shirt stuck to my skin that was coated in chilled sweat. Light glared out my vision, and I blinked away the kaleidoscope that splayed a brilliant array of color behind my eyes.

My sight cleared after a moment. I stared across the lush valley floor that arched upward in violent lines at either side. Recurve Ridge rose to the north, following the trail from which I'd burst out of the forest and leading deep into the dell where Robe had built the cabin. Opposite our hidden location as the crow flew, Gideon's concrete palace had been eked out of stone like an irregular geode that slit the landscape, an open scar unable to heal. Exposed and unapologetic, his compound created an eyesore we couldn't ignore. The gray behemoth marred the ridge's natural beauty across the broken abyss from where I stood, separated only by thin, crisp air and a scattering of tarnished leaves lifted by the mountain's breath.

A flicker drew my attention a second time. I knelt, letting damp mulch cool my hot palms as I scraped my fingers into the dirt beneath it. Never taking my eyes off the house, I raised my hand, rubbing the fine particles between my fingertips. The crumpled leaves filtered through the air, highlighting what hid in plain sight before they were whisked away on the brisk current of wind assaulting the barren rock face.

Twin lasers slashed the air in horizontal lines, drawing two identical dots on my chest.

I straightened, forcing my shoulders back, and stared in the direction of Gideon's snipers. I might not have fought on the battlefield Miller and Robe had experienced, but I trained with them, and I trained like them. In no way would I insult the hours Robe spent sweating beside me by backing down.

Come at me, you fucking assholes.

My hands loosened at my sides as the wind whipped my hair around. The distance required a decent shot, even with a sniper rifle, though I had no doubt Gideon's men would be able to account for the gale that assaulted the ridgeline more days than not.

When no shot pierced my chest, I nodded once and made my way back along the domed rock face. I didn't glance back at the compound with its twin lights that no doubt lit my path, but even when the trees closed over me, obscuring its view of my back, I knew we'd jostled the hornets' nest.

A manic grin split my lips, emitting the sort of restless energy I possessed when I first arrived at the cabin.

Robe needed to know I sided with Team Mari all the way.

Mari

8

MARI

CONVERSATION CARRIED ON AROUND ME AS I FINISHED my regular morning waffles. After six weeks of Alan serving me the things on a daily basis at my best count—though I hadn't been game to mark out a calendar on Robe's walls or risk asking for one or a phone—I thought I might start to *look* like a waffle. I ignored the snippets that offered a sweet reprieve from the dark thoughts tangling me up in their knotted strands, luring me back to the darkness.

Never again.

The waffles were my comfort food. I needed that, as my period hadn't turned up yet. And being six weeks late, whether the absence was stress related or not, terrified me of the repercussions. Alan knew; I hadn't brought it up with anyone else. He seemed my best and most likely advocate, the one least likely to hit the panic button.

The day after I mentioned my quandary, a pregnancy test found its way into my sweater collection. I didn't ask how, but the negative result left me relieved, though I still worried at a low level.

And so...waffles.

After losing myself in Robe's protective embrace and doing my best to sandbox my head in an excess of mountain-man energy time and again, my days blurred, each running into the next. I was determined not to let it happen again while I remained in his house, intent on preserving the slim pickings of my sanity. Vagueness became my constant retreat from the world, from everyone. Including myself.

Focus, Mari. Go home. Be safe.

But I didn't have a home I could go back to, which meant nowhere was safe for me. Except right here. The haven Robe offered with open arms and a guarded smile, though Will made that easier when he produced a pretty sundress with the tag still attached and a pink knitted cardigan so soft I swore I could sleep in it. Not a word passed his lips as he handed over the present, not reacting to my open-mouthed stare, and then left the cabin with long strides while Alan watched on from behind the bar, a broad grin covering his face.

"Go on. He wants to see it on," the bartender encouraged.

I gestured with my free hand toward the open door. "But he's not here."

Alan sent me a knowing smile. "He'll see you."

I took him at his word and changed. Will must have seen and liked what he saw, because the day after, a few more dresses and knits arrived in my bedroom. Now I wore them snow day or no snow day, and it also helped that the fireplace off to one side of the kitchen roared all day long regardless of the weather.

After finishing my daily quota of waffles, I scraped my chair back, got up, and edged through the throng of males that occupied the small living area that was not at all big enough to contain their combined mass and testosterone. The food and whiskey had done almost as much for me as the enforced rest of these past weeks. I understood the unspoken solo assignment. Sleep, heal, repeat.

But I wasn't a princess, and Robe's hard bed had no pea beneath the mattress.

I moved among the men, hesitating when fingertips or elbows brushed my skin, but the touches weren't intentional. No one grabbed at me or hindered my progress. They wanted me to eat waffles, so waffles, I would.

I knew I should reestablish a new normal even if my facade masked my pain because right now, I needed to function in the face of a household full of strange men.

Strange as in odd. Not all of them remained unknowns in my heart, which fell under a separate category of odd altogether—though they seemed the safer option as opposed to... out there, where the police couldn't help me because my boss's bosom buddy was the most powerful man in NYC. I did my best to face that reality, but denial offered such a pretty distraction.

I took another step forward and managed to draw the attention of everyone in the cabin. Alan's gaze lightened as he looked up from where he spoke with Will and Miller, the barrel-chested man who still glared at me.

I dropped my eyes too fast and cursed myself. Gripping the plate between whitened fingertips, which made the whole thing shake rather than prevent its tremor, I placed the crockery on the counter, then lined the cutlery up in a neat stack. I didn't just seek denial. Anything that could whisk away the dreamlike memory wraiths that taunted me from the edges of my vision with their nightmarish touch was welcome.

If I screamed, would anyone hear me? A philosophical question about downed trees and woodsmen crossed my mind, and the room shrank.

Robe and Jon stood off to one side, speaking in quiet tones. The latter's shirt stuck to his skin, transparent with sweat. Tiny tears decorated his cloth-covered arms. He took off earlier, as appeared to be his habit, and had come back sweating. I wasn't sure what Jon did out there, but he couldn't look at me when he returned. Whatever strange family unit Robe had put together, I screwed with it just by being here.

And yet a desperate, torn part of me wished Jon had taken me with him.

Where Robe presented himself as a hardworking, controlled specimen of strength, Jon's wilder nature won out in his tangled, untrimmed beard and hair, the unkempt button-down shirt in contrast to Robe's pressed wardrobe.

My fingers twitched at my sides, itching to pick the debris from Jon's beard, but the giant's presence consumed as much energy as he expelled. Together, he and Robe formed an impenetrable barrier, locking me out when, for whatever stupid reason my chaotic thoughts chose to fixate on, I wanted into their combined space.

I closed my eyes and listened, and the same voice that had been soothing me since my hell-mad dash through his woods worked again. When I opened them, Alan stood in front of me, dancing. His sinuous turns and undulations would have earned him a rabid fandom on socials, but from what I'd learned about Robe and his men, they hid the things that made them each so unique and formidable. A small smile broke through my chaotic headspace.

Alan never stopped dancing.

At the back of the cabin, someone thumped the floorboards in a deep, heartwarming beat, drawing the lithe man into a series of twisting turns that caught the eye. The interior space filled with harsh claps and a pounding tempo suited to the mountains around us, tribal and rhythmic, that stopped my mind from going back to—

Fingers prodding, pushing, pulling, twisting—

No.

Would I end up joining the ranks of Robe's hidden world? The thought flip-flopped my stomach, but as I watched Alan dance, devoured the flirtatious movements, the secret smile he offered as a quiet intimacy in an overcrowded room, the fear of an unknown future drifted away.

"Thank you," I murmured when he halted in front of me, conscious of the ball of energy Will created that thrummed on my other side, though the young man remained still. "That was amazing."

Something darker and far more formidable replaced his bouncing energy. I didn't have to turn around to know that Robe stood behind me.

"Good to know my efforts are appreciated." Alan grinned, though his sparkling eyes conveyed something else to Robe in a silent conversation they held without including me.

Robe's palm came down hard on the benchtop. I flinched, backing up by pure instinct—right into the wall of the man who'd caused the reaction. Alan's eyes narrowed, but he backed off, both hands raised, palms out in surrender, though he flicked a reassuring look my way.

A light touch grazed my hip as Robe locked his forearms against the bar on either side of me, leaning forward to prevent my turning to face him. He stared at me through the reflection in the mirror that sat behind the top-shelf bottles, the rare sort he preferred to stock.

"Tell me where you came from, Mari." Robe renewed his interrogation with a sweet voice, his demeanor so different from when he battered the counter with his open hand.

The switch in him was instantaneous, though I had

wondered how long it would be before his voice hardened, belying his kind tone. After all, these men didn't live out here in the middle of nowhere for no good reason. They hid from the world, or maybe the world hid from them. Either way, the words, his or mine, needed to come out for that to happen, and I already tried that while I dressed in the borrowed clothes he provided. My protector. My interrogator.

I saw him as a threat to my safety. He saw me as a threat to everything and everyone he held close.

He might be right.

I opened my mouth and replied with a gurgling mess I had no intention of repeating any time soon. "You could have tracked my trail back through the woods. From the damage I inflicted on those poor trees, I clearly didn't bother trying to hide it. I was just intent on getting out." That was enough to start the shivers again.

I shut my explanation down, biting my lip. He wanted an answer, a reaction, and he got one. I shrugged my apology, but how else did one run for their life? Concealment hadn't been my intent; distance and survival were my sole aim. I sucked on the metal tang that flooded my mouth from my split lip, giving myself permission to shut up.

"We did." Robe's voice brought me back. "Several times to be certain. Your tracks disappeared in the middle of nowhere. You managed to carve up my section of the woods. There was a disturbed patch, then nothing. Like you were meant to end up here. Miller is an expert tracker. If he can't figure out where you came from, there's something wrong."

"It was like you fell out of the sky and landed right near us. An angelic delivery." Miller's eyes accused me of some unknown crime, but his haughty tone prevented my disjointed explanation from flowing from between tight lips.

Something about the way he posed, displaying a degree of

entitlement the others lacked, though several had a military bearing.... I frowned, turning over what made his glare so out of place in this crew of muscle-bound misfits. It had been bugging me the whole time I'd existed in their living space, flying under the radar.

Miller jeered, his lip curling. There it was, in the tilt of his chin, the narrowed judgment in sharp eyes that missed little. Everyone else in the cabin reeked of genuine hard work, and though I didn't doubt for one second that he did his share, Miller's demeanor included something the rest lacked.

Privilege.

"Private school boy?" I asked, still studying him, and knew I'd called it right.

His mannerisms told the story for him: the way he threw his shoulders back, how he stormed about like he owned the place. All he lacked was the sports car and a doting mother on call.

Robe laughed, his chest rumbling behind my head, and reached out to clap Miller's shoulder in a blow that had to sting. Miller's whole body rocked forward.

He glared at me for a moment longer. "What, you're a shrink now? Is that what you're here to do?"

I blinked. "I beg your pardon?" My accent thickened when I got cranky, but it earned me a grin from Robe's reflection.

At least his interrogation had stopped, though Miller's had taken its place.

"I think he wants to know how you turned up in my woods, right on top of us, when there's no trail and no proof that you came from anywhere at all." Robe's tone remained conversational, though his gaze roamed over my body that bore the marks put there by too many assailants for even me to count.

And I tried—in my dreams every night.

Phantoms of invisible hands traced over my body beneath my borrowed clothes. I jerked, resisting the urge to rake my nails over my skin and peel the sensation free. Unable to bring out my crazy when my mind sent out a warning signal that this was not the sort of conversation I wanted to vague out on, I settled for wrapping my arms tight around my body.

"I don't know what you mean." I twisted away as if he stung me, but the veiled accusation ripped at the safety net of my new future.

An unknown future, which left me in a forbidden space. Tears prickled my eyes. I inhaled too fast and swallowed a mouthful of mountain man. Any other day, that would have been hilarious.

I'd spent hours talking myself into being able to trust Robe while I lay in his bed or stared at myself in the mirror in his bathroom before I emerged. My body still bore the marks of my abuse, though the bruises had yellowed and faded from their original dark splotches. Inside? That looked... different. Worse. Invisible parts of me I hadn't known I cherished were tainted with dark desires that weren't mine but had left their stain all the same.

Until this moment, it hadn't occurred to me that Robe and his men needed reassurance that they could trust me too.

We all had demons that followed us, though theirs were much older than mine.

I wanted to scream at the injustice of it, that I had been the one betrayed and abused. Hunted until nothing more remained of the prior girl who'd borne my face than a pathetic animal craving absolution for a crime it didn't know it had committed.

But as I stared around at the small circle of men, that

same sense of pain flitted through every pair of eyes, their demons not so different to my own.

"I had to drop off things at my b—at a place down the mountain," I started, cautious of releasing any details.

I had no idea why I kept trying to protect a life no longer mine to claim or refused to give more information. I needed to keep some trump card for a dire moment that might sink or save me. For all I knew, they were friends with Gideon, and I'd be tossed back into his home. Numbness started at my toes and worked upward at that thought. But another part of me told me I could trust Robe... and I was back where I started, ready to tear my hair out and face the cabin en masse as a bald woman.

What the hell. I can't be more broken than I already am.

No, just dead.

A heavy silence blanketed the cabin, blocking off the rest of the world from me, or maybe me from it. Which shook me deeper, until I struggled to continue.

"You know, the expensive-looking house that has the luxury European cars parked around it, the sort that never gets dirty on an unpaved road. I made my delivery. My b—Gi —he asked me to stay to help with some entertainment." I hiccupped a laugh. "I didn't know that meant me."

"Oh, sweetcheeks." Alan reached across the counter to clasp my hand. Understanding gleamed dully in place of the sparkle that I wanted, *needed* to fill his eyes, and already I missed its comforting presence.

I took the offering, squeezing his cold fingers. Alan's perception grounded me, gave me the clarity to plow on. "The man I trusted led me into a room full of people. Men. A table stood in the middle. Ropes and leather straps hung loose from it, and there was a dark stain in the center, though the thing looked like it had been scrubbed clean. Maybe. He'd created a... a torture room, with tools and other implements on the walls. Not some play dungeon with canes and whips you might expect in an online show. All razor edges, spears and needle-sharp knives. We never got to those." I choked up, shudders returning to shake me head to toe.

I drew in a deep breath, aiming for something fortifying, and managed a pathetic death rattle as Robe gripped my other hand.

"Why did they stop?" he asked.

Robe kept his voice soft, but it failed to disguise the undercurrent of violence he promised for reasons of his own, a history that predated my tumble into his life. The air stilled, but whatever he felt wasn't aimed at me.

"I don't know. Everyone left in a hurry. They bundled me into a ball of cloth and dumped me in the trunk of a car. New car smell will make me sick forever. Then they lifted me out. Two men carried me. More, maybe? Too many hands." I tried to look up at him but instead squeezed my eyes shut, blocking out the sensations that assailed my body as if I still lay tethered to the table.

Conversations erupted above and around me as though I were no more than an object to be discarded. A nuisance. A puzzle to be solved.

Robe stroked along my spine, removed the phantom hands touching me, but I couldn't quite quash the feelings, too high on the adrenaline that had flushed my system anew. His breath against my neck warmed me. I sent him a grateful glance, though my words stalled. I tried to make them come out but gagged instead.

"Think, Mari. What happened? Where did they take you?" Robe murmured.

My heart pounded, sweat breaking out on my arms, leaving me flushed and chilled at once. "Someone tossed me into the air, and I landed on the ground. I didn't look around. Then all my wrappings were pulled away. I lay there, bare… naked. They stripped me of everything. Then they moved away, and I ran. I didn't look back. I ran," I repeated, desperate, for some ridiculous reason, for the men surrounding me to believe my story.

Desperate for acceptance.

Alan squeezed my other hand to the point of numbness, but I didn't care. The tears that streamed down his face matched the ones that glazed my cheeks.

"You know him? The man who did this to you?" Robe extracted my hand from Alan, taking both of mine in his larger, work-roughened paws. He rubbed gentle circles over my skin, his fingers moving in a slow rhythm that matched my short breaths until they lengthened.

"Yes," I croaked, jerking my head in a half nod, unable to say more.

"Good girl," he murmured, drawing me closer. "Does he know where you work?"

All the questions that should have been asked and answered long ago but weren't because we orbited around each other, playing house and being too fucking nice.

I hiccupped a laugh that cracked and died a horrible death. "Yes."

"Where you live?"

"Yes."

Robe drew me into his arms, folding a wall of muscle and determination around me. "Shit."

"Yeah." I pressed my cheek to his chest, seeking the steady beat of his heart that had become the metronome I lived by.

We stood like that for an eternity. Some immeasurable time later, I clung to him when he lifted me in a gentle grip, cradling me to his chest as he walked me through the small house and into his bedroom.

My breaths timed to the regular, strong throb of his heart, I took comfort in the strength he offered. He'd been there when I crashed, and despite his questioning, I didn't fear him for that, for wanting to keep what he'd built safe. For wanting to protect me and those he loved.

Robe settled me on his bed, tucking the covers around me with care and a tender touch. He brushed a lingering kiss over my temple and started to rise.

I closed my fingers around his arm—the part of it I could grasp—panic rolling over me. "Stay. Please."

Robe's gaze shuttered in the semidarkness, and he squeezed my hand. "I'm here. Jon and I, we used to—" he started, then broke off, swearing.

"And you tell me I have a potty mouth," I murmured, unwilling to scare him away.

He laughed darkly. "You do have a potty mouth, Mari Merripen." He perched on the side of the bed, stroking my hair back, tracing light fingertips over my cheeks. With every action, he maintained the same slow rhythm, never rushed. He always asked permission with his hands, a dipped head before he pushed a boundary or tested my limits.

I can trust him. I can trust him. I can trust him.

Drawing in a long breath, I surrendered to his ministrations. "Tell me what you were going to say," I whispered. *Tell me a story with a happy ending.* "Please."

Robe hesitated for a breath before he resumed touching me, his strokes smooth and easy like I might have imagined the hitch. The need to commit my safety to someone else while I escaped from the fluttering hands drove my panic higher.

My tears started again at his gentle touch. He gathered me

against him, sliding his body beneath mine to pillow my head against his shoulder. His body surrounded me. Our legs tangled together as I found a comfortable spot curled against his ribs, supported by his strong arms and the tender touch of a roughened mountain man.

"I was going to tell you that once upon a time, two men knew a woman they both loved. More than once, actually. But it didn't work out, no matter how hard they tried. But they wanted to share everything they cared for."

"Did they ever find what they were looking for?" I asked sleepily, covering a yawn.

"Not yet." Robe curved his fingers behind me head and squeezed gently. "Sleep, Mari. I won't leave you."

"Maybe you could share me too," I mumbled, not really listening to what I said as I drifted away. I tried to cling to him, the room, but I was too tired. Slipping.

"Maybe," he whispered.

Or maybe I imagined that too.

Humming a folksy tune I didn't recognize, Robe lulled me to sleep in a heady mix of dulled terror and growing trust of a door that maybe opened both ways.

9

ROBE

THE MOMENT I THOUGHT I HAD AN ANSWER, IT turned to shit in my hands. Or in this case, into a black-souled asshole. Several of them, though only one would be left alive at the end of our encounter. But before I got to deal out an ass whooping, even a verbal one, I had the small problem of facing off with my household stripper.

"No. She's not even close to ready for intimacy." I glowered at him, my mind on Miller, who waited for me in the shadows beyond the house's doorway. "This'll have to wait for another time."

Alan glowered at me, a more Milleresque behavior than I expected from him. "Giddy up, Robe, or someone will do it for you. She's been here for *weeks* now, and we're still treating her like a fragile piece of fucking glass."

"I know she's not glass."

"Then treat her better," he countered, refusing to back down, the damn brat.

"She's been abused!" I roared. Clenching my teeth, I shot a glance at her door, where Will stood guard. He watched our interaction quietly, and knowing his history with his father, I didn't want to play his personal trauma out in front of him. "I'll... think of something. Give her a job. Maybe you could train her to make cocktails." I glanced at the doorway again.

"It's not enough. She needs intimacy. That girl needs to know she's loved." Alan stopped shy of grabbing at me.

That single word stopped me cold.

"She has no fucking family left and no one who can claim her," I snapped, stepping into his space, ready to shake sense into the kid. He knew that; he was the one who cyberstalked her on my damn orders.

"She has you."

My gut sank even as my head wanted to accept what he suggested. But a few random touches and support while I interrogated her nicely to get what I wanted shouldn't count as a claim. Still, no matter how I disparaged the idea, the possessive monster in my chest approved.

I stared at him. "You're out of your mind. She's hurt. She doesn't want me pushing into her life and making her feel invaded. Now—"

"Have you asked her?" Alan popped his hip out like a bratty teen and threw me a *fuck you, daddy* smile to match.

"Watch the attitude," I retorted, brushing him off. "I'll be back whenever this is done. Fucking behave." I shook my head and turned my back to him, ready to rant my way out the door.

"She needs you." The plea in his voice struck home, but we were out of time.

"Robe." Jon canted his head toward Miller, who was still waiting for me.

I blew out a breath. "We can talk later." I dismissed my bartender and pushed the whole encounter out of my mind the moment I set foot over the threshold.

The stocky man stood at the house's entrance, his expression dark—well, darker, considering his usual demeanor tended toward watchful and angry. He snarled, and I guessed he'd called my name more than once in the past few minutes. His shoulders sat in a hard line as he shifted his weight to one side, then disappeared around the doorway and into the forest below.

Jon raised his eyebrows as if to say, *What now?* I shook my head and followed Miller's silent exodus.

Crisp snow crunched beneath my heavy steps. A frigid wind left winter's late calling card. If Mari had traversed the forest a few weeks later than when she arrived in my arms, she would have died of exposure before I got her inside the house. Hell, thanks to unseasonal weather, that very nearly happened any damn way.

It annoyed the shit out of me that I still didn't know how long she ran for, or how far. Regardless of the fact that she still wouldn't tell me what I craved, I harbored my suspicions.

I found him in the shadows at the bottom of the cabin's stairs.

"What's up?"

"We have visitors." Miller snapped off that short sentence like it had offended him, omitting *sir* at the end along with his customary sharp salute, though his fingers stiffened at his side as if the habit refused to be repressed.

Even four years after leaving military service together, he struggled to complete the transformation into his new version of normality.

I opened my mouth, on the verge of saying, *"I'm not your commanding officer any longer,"* but it didn't matter. The words wouldn't have any effect, leaving us at a silent impasse. We'd had this conversation time and again. Miller wouldn't change his ways any more than I would. Perhaps that made us the perfect pair, coupled in a mountain-scenery version of purgatory, blocked away from everything we loved—and everyone.

Except for the three people back in the cabin.

Four, counting Mari, if I included her in the emotional sliding scale of our lives.

Miller insisted on holding to the tradition that had disowned us both, no matter what I said or how raucous the house became with every new member initiated into our patchwork family. It didn't matter that I no longer deserved his loyalty or his respect for letting so many down when I couldn't save them.

And yet he offered the balance of his life to my sad cause when he remained the one free man among a bunch of broken outlaws.

"Brandon? I know he's organizing a local community gathering." I shrugged when Miller glared at me. *Now I know how Mari feels.*

"Blackthorne's here."

I slipped my hands into my pockets and stared Miller down. "What does he want?"

He tilted his chin up. "He didn't come alone."

"That's not what I asked."

The corner of his lips twitched. "I'll bet my cut on our next job that it has something to do with our guest."

Of course it does.

I knew Miller didn't approve of Mari's presence in our home. He hated that she'd etched out a place there, stolen the hearts of men starved for something more than the meager existence we'd carved out of the mountain side. We could have been dwarves to her princess, but Mari wasn't quite that sweet.

Other chores came before pleasure, either of the homely or carnal variety. If I pushed her out, I'd have more than

Miller to deal with. Mari needed the respite from whatever reality had chased her in our direction, not a wheelbarrow load of randy men who were desperate for a sweet smile and soft lips.

And yet, she ran to me.

Into my arms.

I shook my head, shifting my focus to where it needed to be, not on the pretty head of curls inside my house.

Focus, Huntingdon.

"All right. Where is he?"

"Boundary line. Opposite that ugly fucking tower he calls home."

I nodded. "I know the place." Turning on my heel, I headed in my nemesis's direction, already rehearsing what I would say when he asked about her.

Who else would he inquire about? Not the picket line one of my regulars organized at the edge of my property. Gideon Blackthorne's Mari-shaped drawcard sat in his back pocket. I just needed to wait for him to incriminate himself during the next few minutes.

Other men, like our good friend Blackthorne, might play shadow games. But I ran cold, devoid of emotion at the reminder of the man who drove me from the city I once called home. One ruined veteran and a background of family politics made for a sensational news story on our return from the desert in the wake of too many scarred souls.

Knight & Watchman had flourished between us, right up until George Petersen stepped in. The current mayor of New York City ripped our lives to shreds. Then I realized Gideon had been working for the pompous little ass the entire time. Both our lives weren't ruined; just mine, and whoever followed me.

Miller scraped out of their little coup, a stroke of pure luck on our side. Maybe he came up as insignificant. Who knew why Petersen made the decisions he did. But that slice of luck favored us, leaving me with one man who could walk through the front doors of Knight & Watchman without being arrested.

The rest of us took more... covert entrances.

I might have gotten my business back when Blackthorne walked away, but the man who used to be my partner and fellow officer knew too many of my tricks. Good thing I had a team for that. Gideon Blackthorne had showed enough colors during the past eight years to leave me on the edge of extreme discomfort at having him too close.

After encountering Mari on my doorstep, I knew exactly where in the black Gideon stood.

On the other side of the fucking line.

Miller halted my progress. "Are you going alone?"

"I can find my way a half mile and back." My words came out short. "I'll be fine," I offered in a softer tone.

Miller's snort told me that though I might look like I made the journey alone, he would have my back from some distant point.

Before I could take another step forward, cold metal pressed into my palm.

I looked down at the matte black handgun he offered, but I didn't take it. "No."

"You go out there alone, he will kill you."

Blackthorne could; he even might, but I didn't think so. Not today. The man never made an appearance on my lands unless he deemed it necessary. Assuming I read the situation correctly, by taking Mari into my family, I had forced his hand.

Now I wanted to see how he played it out to the new threat I presented.

She contained all his scarred evidence, and I'd bet everything that he wanted her back. His previous experience was a kindness compared to the sort of torture Blackthorne would use as his personal trademark if I handed her over.

That wasn't happening on my watch.

Even if I'd read him wrong, whatever Blackthorne wanted, killing me wouldn't help him achieve his aims. My boys were well trained. If I died, they would disappear into the forest, and no amount of money or power would ever help him locate a single man—or Mari.

Until they were ready to take him down.

"I'm good."

"Suit yourself." Miller's tone suggested he may as well have said, *"Enjoy being slaughtered."*

I laughed under my breath and strode through the forest. The farther I walked from my house and the closer I came to Gideon, the thicker the trees became. We honored a tentative agreement not to cross each other's boundaries, but the distinct lack of wildlife in an otherwise populated section of the woods suggested Blackthorne broke his end of the bargain on a regular basis.

Keeping my focus forward, I pretended I didn't notice the sniper I walked below. As no bullet pierced my back—Blackthorne would never be so bold—I wondered how many men he would lose before our conversation ended. I counted six in the trees and three on the ground. If I missed any, Miller would find them.

The stocky little nugget from Georgia was a bloodthirsty bitch. Despite his compact frame, he could be as silent as Alan on his feet as he stalked his prey in his own playground. His favorite method of handling situations like this involved cutting throats in a literal sense. His broader skill sets included hiding bodies and removing all traces of their demise.

If Alan was a cold, psychotic little killer, Miller was our resident ninja.

We both saw bloody battles in the desert, fought back-to-back on more than one occasion, trusting the other man to hold his own. Thanks to Blackthorne, I also experienced a dagger in the back by my own people while he worked with the enemy enough times to learn a few extra tricks. Nor was I remiss in sharing that knowledge around.

Blackthorne waited at a point between two stones that, though they might look ancient, were put in place by Will during one of his initial scouting missions. Without being asked, he took on the responsibility of surveying and ensuring that the boundary lines between Blackthorne and Huntingdon lands were marked against any accidental incursion.

Anyone could call our "agreement" bullshit; we'd crossed that line on both sides more often than we'd met face-to-face in the past eight years. As an added bonus, Will had set up land mines on our side, just in case our nice neighbor changed his mind about our farce of a truce and crossed the boundary en masse.

I guessed he hadn't counted on anyone coming across the treetops.

Another little trick in our tool kit.

And something to talk about when I debriefed the men after I returned.

If I returned.

Gideon Blackthorne came into full view as I stepped out of the trees. Something hit the ground with a muted thump behind me as I eyed the man dressed all in black like some superhero villain. Dark hair was slicked back off his angular face. Thin black eyebrows and sculpted lips etched a permanent sneer on what should, by some metric, have been a handsome face.

A leather jacket that no doubt cost the same as the supplies to build the entire cabin hung over broad shoulders that could carry the weight of a full unit of men and not flinch. I knew that from experience. My nemesis completed his tailored outfit with black jeans and highly polished black loafers.

He didn't walk through the forest in those. Not with a shine like that on the tops.

I held his pale blue gaze. Something crackled in the underbrush at my back. *That's two.* I held back a grin; I could tease Miller for being slow after the fact, though I knew his current body count was double that.

Gideon's forces would be down by a handful of men before he turned tail and headed home.

"What do you want?" I worked against mounting tension in my spine to set my shoulders in a relaxed line. Letting my hands hang free of my clothing, I rested my weight over the balls of my feet, not looking like I wanted to launch myself at him but maintaining the option either way.

Unformed figures shifted in the woods behind my enemy. Three men equipped with semiautomatic pistols emerged from the forest and took up position at Blackthorne's back.

Not taking the pistol was a mistake.

It wouldn't help against those guns. I'd be dead before I raised my hand, riddled with a hundred bullet holes before I managed a double tap.

Gideon would be my land's proud new owner.

"Oh, I wanted to have a friendly chat. Neighbor to neighbor. You know, with a man I once worked beside." Resentment glimmered in his eyes as he gave me a derisive once-over.

I wasn't sure what bee had shot up his bonnet, but he had no reason to be unsettled about the way we parted company last time we spoke—him with ten proverbial guns pointed at my head and me retaining the business. Pretty sure the man hadn't changed a whit.

"Have you tried knocking?" I held his stare and smirked.

"We don't have that sort of—" Gideon stepped forward, placing a single foot over the invisible boundary line. "—relationship. Besides, you've taken something that belongs to me."

If that *something* didn't happen to be Mari, I'd put his lack of empathy down to a rich-boy temper tantrum. A sense of guilt—and a loss of control—stiffened his neck. I could almost smell his fear, and that gave me a reason to bite.

I opened my mouth to object, but we both knew it would be an outright lie. "I've taken nothing that didn't cross onto my land."

"Semantics." Gideon chuckled, an unpleasant and not-so-veiled threat. "I'm impressed, Huntingdon. You're more of a politician than you think."

My teeth clenched, pain shooting along my jaw. "I suggest you get off my land."

Blackthorne threw his head back, the forest echoing with his laugh. "I bet you've been waiting to say that for years." Soulless pale eyes the color of a wintery sky stared back at me.

It ached that I knew in my gut that he'd hurt Mari, that it was he who had touched her and enabled others to ruin her body and break her will.

She's more resilient than you think.

He was right to be scared of her. If she spoke out, she

would be a true threat to his comfortable, fucked-up lifestyle. But forcing her to say the words made me as bad as him. No, she needed to tell me in her own time. Coming out in public was the worst of ideas. Petersen would remove her from existence if she directly threatened his position as mayor, and his association with Blackthorne would do that if the truth of her assault was brought to light in the public arena. Hence the dual complication. Petersen would pull the trigger by proxy of one of his mercenary minions if Blackthorne didn't first.

Fire boiled in my chest as my fingers flicked at my sides. Watching the man opposite me, I forced my hand to relax.

Gideon's laugh died at whatever he read on my face. "The other day, I lost something important. I'd like it back."

Fuck, I gave him too much. "Why?"

My shitty deflection offered a poor barrier. *I should have prepared better.* Even though I'd known he would ask about her, I hadn't put thought into my defense of Mari, too distracted by the woman herself.

Gideon's gaze narrowed. "We both know why."

Yeah, but I want to hear you admit it.

"Return my property, Huntingdon." Gideon stepped back, and the games were over.

But I haven't been playing.

She was never yours.

The dual thoughts roused the constant rage that simmered low in my stomach as I glared at him. He could read into that look whatever the hell he wanted; it wouldn't change the outcome of his spoiled-child tantrum.

Look at the Brit terms I'm picking up from Mari.

If she gave snarky me ammunition in that vein, she could stay as long as she wanted.

And for a few other reasons.

I nodded back in an easy motion. "Nothing here is yours."

Nor would it ever be. I gave him a smile as empty as his previous promise that he'd hold to the boundary line.

Liar, liar, black soul on fire.

Mari would have an entertaining little ditty to lighten the mood. Something cheery and inappropriate that would clench my chest and make me want to wrap her in my arms and never let go. I would have to remember to ask her later.

Ignoring Blackthorne's demand, I turned my back and began to walk away in slow, measured paces, aware of the target I presented to any one of his paid protectors who harbored a trigger-happy finger.

"You can't hide out here forever, Huntingdon."

I swiveled where I stood, my teeth bared in a harsh grin that silenced him in swift order. Releasing my breath in measured exhales, I took a step forward into his space. Three muted pops halted me on the spot. I looked over his shoulder in time to see his three shadows fall.

Offering him a bland grin, I gave Blackthorne a little wave, turned, and disappeared back into the forest. The music of his cursing followed me as I wished him the best of luck keeping those shoes of his clean on his four-mile walk across the ridge back to his fancy cement compound.

I found Miller in the deepest part of the forest between Blackthorne and the house, leaning against a tree trunk as wide as his barrel chest and dismembering a pine needle piece by piece.

"Good job. Leave any out?" Not that he would. The man was as pedantic in his body count as a hooker working Cypress Avenue on a Friday night. Still, I made the attempt to lighten the tense atmosphere that surrounded him. After all, the man had killed for me.

"He made it too easy." Miller's brown gaze clashed with

mine, darkness roiling there. The pine needle fell to the forest floor as he glared at me.

I nodded, his silent message received: *"I don't trust him."*

Neither did I, but I doubted Blackthorne would offer men as bait just to test our capacity. Another thing we knew too much about each other. He'd seen Miller and me fight in close quarters before.

"Good job. I'm grateful. Clean up." I set my jaw and picked up my pace. "I'll meet you at the house."

He nodded and disappeared back into the woods. There wouldn't be a trace of Gideon's men left by the time he finished.

I mulled over Blackthorne's words as I retraced my steps, careful to use the same path and footfalls as before. The fewer tracks we made, the better—even on our side of the boundary. There would be no further incursions tonight.

Gideon's resources weren't endless, and he'd lost as many men as he'd brought out for intimidation and protection today. That had to be hard on the wallet at some point, though he would offer better wages to the next load of gung-ho recruits keen to earn their stripes in whatever way they could.

No, I wasn't worried about him crossing into our territory again for a while.

As always, Will emerged in the evening and erased all remaining traces of Miller's and my passing, leaving the woods looking like none of us existed at all.

Hell, the kid was so good, I wanted to clean his record and get him inside my business the way I'd corralled him by the edges of the property. That invisible line set a hard fixture for us all.

Our boundary line is bullshit.

I maintained my stride while I argued with myself, and

after a few moments, I realized I had company. A sideways glance without turning my head showed a lithe, fur-coated body of a gold-and-white wildcat keeping pace by my side. The lynx slinked along, neither crossing my path nor threatening it. Just beyond the boundaries of the house yard, I paused, turning to face my little stalker.

Yellow eyes blinked at me across the void. A glimpse of sharp teeth and bunched muscle left me tense, though not in the same way as with Blackthorne. No, he was a true threat. This cat wanted to let his presence be known. I held the creature's stare for a long moment, one forest dweller to another.

The wildcat watched me with a sense of serenity. After a time, he presented his back to me with a flick of a spotted tail and wandered off between the thick trunks that swallowed him into their deepening shadows.

Watching the darkness for a moment longer yielded nothing but the ruin of my night vision. When no other threats emerged, I headed back to the house and hoped to whichever god listened that my boys remained safe.

Mari too.

Mari

10

MARI

MY SKIN GLOWED WITH THE ADDITION OF QUALITY products, regular showers, enforced workouts with Miller thanks to Robe's continued influence, and the good food the boys—read Alan—provided afterward. The last of my bruises had faded entirely, though my scars, some still pink or whitened at the edges, others darker marks that shadowed beneath my skin, remained. Even so, I almost felt like a new woman, or at least some semblance of the one I had been before.

But thinking about *before* hurt, so I stopped. My eyes hadn't quite lost their haunted stare. If I closed them, I could retreat into the comfort of Robe's scent, his warmth, and the physical presence he exuded. He had become my everything, my new source of safety when the grasping hands obscured my vision, stealing a tentative peace away from my grasp.

Outside of him, the bathroom became my place of refuge. When the house's usual occupants got loud and I crumbled, I excused myself politely, rounded the corner to the hall, and dashed into the confines of the small, bright space.

Then I stood in front of the mirror without staring into it and tried not to hate the woman opposite me who looked more put together by the day while I shattered on the inside. If I got lucky, the room stayed still. Or I puked.

Dealer's choice.

A creak behind me and a brief whisper of air was all the warning I had before the bathroom plummeted into pitch blackness. The distinct lack of windows in Robe's room made his en suite a coffin of darkness without the addition of safe, secure artificial light.

Fake—like the sense of security I wrapped around myself here.

I froze, invisible tendrils curling around my skin in phantom eddies as the terror resurfaced. Memories brought a twisted brightness to my mind's eye. Scrolling images of being pinned down in Gideon's house swept over me, all-encompassing. I opened my mouth on a scream that twisted into a thin pant as my lungs sucked at the meager air my throat afforded them, clenching tight on itself to deny me what I needed.

The room swayed, or maybe I did. It didn't matter, because the rabbit hole of memories spread open beneath my feet, and I tumbled forward. Cold hands caught and righted me. The contact jerked me out of my fantasy of reaching hands only to throw me into a new terror, this one unknown, the touch indifferent, almost clinical.

My heart beat too fast in my chest, my body heating though my cheeks remained cold and numb. The floor shifted beneath me again, though for a different reason.

He promised me his home is my safe place...

And I believed him.

A sob tore from my throat. I bit my lips, the sharp metallic tang that trickled into my mouth adding a level of pain to my hyperawareness.

Why aren't I running?

Where the hell would I go?

"You are so pretty, Mari," an icy, unrecognizable voice whispered in my ear.

Almost unrecognizable.

Because that same voice belonged to Alan, though none of his usual sharp humor etched the edges of what I'd come to suspect covered a damaged man beneath the camaraderie, showmanship, and snark.

No, his voice sliced through the air as cold as the heat of him behind me seared my skin. A single knuckle brushed across the nape of my neck, raising shivers and goose bumps across my skin. He trailed the digit along my spine, leaving a harsh, searing path of pain and ice in its wake.

"Alan? What do you want?" I shivered at the contact, the whole situation so *wrong.* Twisting, the other half of my body anchored to the floor, I tried to face him, but that one finger on my nape turned me back to face myself in the full-length mirror I couldn't see. "Turn the light on."

"You know that's not going to happen, don't you?"

A dull rush of white noise filled my ears. For all my panic, jarred somewhere between a will for flight and the inability to access those primal bodily functions, Alan's movements—or lack thereof—were the opposite: laced in tight control, a cruel smirk concealed in his words.

As though he was enjoying this moment, *knew* his touch brought me back to that place, and that amused him.

All of that sat at odds with the man I thought I knew.

"I trusted you," I croaked.

He laughed, a low sound that rippled across my body in an intimate caress of its own. "I know. Shall we?" One unyielding, cold hand flexed on my shoulder, holding me in place so I had no choice but to face forward.

Like a Mari-sized statue, I let him.

I faced the blacked-out mirror I couldn't see, my senses reduced to a hollow void at my back that was anything but empty. Alan's touch centered in two places, arms cocked around my throat and upper body to pin me in place, though my rigid stance made his icy prison redundant. Fear locked me tight as a statue as his fingerprints seared pensive marks at my neck and shoulders, waiting.

My own contact offered nothing so kind. Ragged nails curled into my palms, the harsh edges biting into my skin. Something trickled between my fingers. In the pitch blackness that pervaded the small space, I couldn't tell the difference between salt and iron.

Alan's touch disappeared, leaving me alone.

Mustering every inch of my courage that rooted my feet to the floor—*I'd be dead if Alan were a bear or Gideon or something* worse—I tipped my chin up, though he likely couldn't see the small act of defiance.

"I'll scream, and Robe will come running. What would he do to a man who broke his trust?" I bluffed, fighting the urge to deny the event and to sink back into Alan's warm presence, into the man I knew.

Alan won't hurt me. He won't.

My heart thrummed in my chest, fear's cold touch embracing me anew, etched with an awareness of the man I called friend. Despite all evidence to the contrary, my brain clung to the new truth I'd created for myself. That I could trust Robe and his men; that they would protect me.

Or maybe they were just men, like the others who hurt me.

"If you were going to scream, you would have done it

already." A lilt in his voice added a strange musical element akin to laughter to his tone. The cool draft of his breath kissed the back of my neck, though he didn't touch me.

The absence of his usual endearments, no *sweetcheeks* or *sweetcakes*, removed the personal aspect I'd come to adore in Alan, who was my retreat when Robe and Jon became too overly everything to my senses. This new version of the personable man stripped away my shitty belief system, leaving me barer than ever.

I'd created a fantasy world, weaving myself a pretty, happy ending that would never happen for a broken creature like me. Now, he trapped me within that reality.

A torn sob jerked in my throat, the barest sound making it past my lips. "What do you want?"

I expected his phantom fingers to return to tracing across my body, but he gave me nothing. Only that void of cold air at my back where he still stood, though his chest never made contact. Then cool fingers encircled my throat, holding me in place by their disembodied touch.

"I want to see if little Mari Merripen is worth the trouble she's caused." His tongue flicked out, licking the shell of my ear in a delicate, tasting touch.

The sob lodged in my throat met with a scream that vied for cramped space while I forced two words past them. "What trouble?"

Alan's fingertips rested over my windpipe, his touch lighter, more familiar, like his usual brand of flirtation. "Oh, you know. The sort of trouble that can ruin a man, a brother-hood. A friendship. The sort that could fuck up this house, including Robe and every man in it. All because you've got a pretty little cunt they all want to fuck."

I reeled, swaying where I stood. The unchecked dark

desire in Robe's eyes, the way Jon watched me, even Will....
But Miller sure didn't count in that group.

"What about you?" I don't know why I said that. Of all the
things that could have come out of my mouth, those words
seemed the least reasonable.

Alan's cold lips brushed against hot skin. "Oh, Mari. I'm
first in line. Robe denied me, wanting to claim you for
himself, but that's not how we play here. We've always
shared... everything. You should be no exception." He trailed
his knuckles over my shoulder, crested the curve of my
breast, and paused at my hip. "I've learned to take what I
want to survive. What I need to enjoy my fucked-up life spent
far away from everything I love."

"He'll kill you." *And probably me too.* But death's shade
and I had become used to each other. I doubted adding Robe's
penance to my life-threat collection would be any more
daunting.

"Maybe it'll be worth it to taste you."

The morose thought of losing Robe's trust, so hard earned
yet freely given all at once, the complex man he was hidden
behind a wall of muscle and checked shirts, tore at my heart.

"You might have given up faith in him, but I haven't," I
snapped.

My body returned to itself. Sensation slithered along my
arms and wakened numbed legs. I thrashed away from the
fingers encircling my throat, kicking out at anything at all.
But my tiny personal-assistant ass couldn't compete with the
trained killer at my back.

Alan's arms imprisoned me against his lean frame that
seemed far too strong for his sleek body. I'd become compla-
cent, trusting in the bulky mass of wild mountain men like
Robe and Jon, not understanding the threat of a lesser-built

man who could still overpower me. So I fought, but my throat still wouldn't let me scream.

I scratched and hit and flailed until Alan laughed, catching my chin to force my head back. He propelled us forward until my cheek hit a cold, flat surface that halted our progress. Gripping my wrists in one hand, his other found my hip and delved beneath the slinky material of my top to touch bare skin.

"*No*—" I choked, my voice cut off as he tipped my chin back, arching my neck at an unnatural angle, and placed his mouth over mine, stifling my words, snuffing out my air. The contact curled around me with intimate fingers, but he didn't kiss me. Rather, his sharp mouth muffled the cry that finally came to my aid, torn out of me by shock.

Too many hands, so many touching—

But the phantom prickle didn't come. Alan's slinking hands replaced the many, only two to focus on as he pushed long, artistic fingers beneath the waistband of my borrowed sweats to slip lower.

My breath caught in my throat as he leaned forward, his body arcing over me so I could feel him *right there*. The evidence of his raw need pressed into me from behind. His mouth brushed mine in a sweet kiss so out of place with the threatening environment he'd created by blacking out the room and pinning my front to the wall.

Hot lips vied to contest against the mirror's cold surface pressed to the rest of me as he flicked his tongue into my mouth when I dared part my lips and suck in a shattered breath. His kiss was brief but potent, and my legs trembled with strain and a thin thread of need. No one touched me apart from Robe, and Jon that once. Contact was maintained at the barest minimum, like I'd explode or destroy Robe's fragile world if I allowed Alan to push me too far, except for the one night Robe had let me sleep with him.

Now I'd never get the chance to discover if I had that power alone or not.

Alan stroked a single finger along the center of my panties, grazing my clit to settle over my heat. Wetness pooled there, my nipples tightening beneath the flimsy material barrier between us, my body taking over while my mind screamed a withering protest. Arousal stoked low in my belly, and my hips jutted forward, needing the release he offered.

Broken, broken, broken.

I whimpered, heat flaring in my cheeks, drying the tears that touched them. "I'm so fucking ruined."

"No," he cooed, cold lips searing my mouth as he swallowed my shame. "You're like us."

My heart exploded as his fingers slipped lower, slicking along my heat. I cried out, a splintered sound. For the first time in so long, my body's reaction to touch from another human came from need over fear.

I want *this.*

Alan knew. Somehow he understood what I needed more than I did when it came to my own body. That made it so much worse and better all at once.

I wanted to cry at the revelation. A moan lodged in my throat from the simple touch of his clever fingertips. He dragged his knuckles along my slit, taking his time. No sense of urgency layered his caress as pressure and desire built within me, aching for release while he continued at an inordinately slow pace.

"My sweet little Mari. Such a beautiful slut." He licked the shell of my ear and bit down on the lobe, sucking and nibbling.

I sighed, leaning back into him. "It feels so bad." The

moment his hand stilled between my folds, I knew I said the wrong thing. "I shouldn't be able to get aroused after what happened." It made everything in me so *ruined*.

"You're like us."

But the comforting thought Alan had given me that I *fit* here, like every one of the broken men in the house, coated my residual fear in a sugary sweet temptation.

To be licked off and savored.

Alan's finger worked me again while the heel of his hand ground at my clit. My legs parted a little for him, easing his access.

"Such a good girl," he murmured.

One arm banded around my chest, crushing the tops of my breasts. Frissons of pleasure rippled over my body, hardening my nipples to impossible pain-filled points.

I wanted to beg him to touch me there, though fear froze my lips. Every part of me thrummed with heat and energy, so sensitive there that any caress would hurt, no matter how gentle or tender his touch. For some horrible reason, that thought got me off too.

"What's going on in that head of yours, Mari Merripen?" Alan asked idly, still swirling his fingers around my needy flesh.

His other hand drifted across my ribs, grazing the undersides of my breasts. Those same fingers wound around my throat in a light circle not meant to restrict my air or threaten me, but rather to hold me closer in an intimate sort of gesture I'd never experienced before him.

"That feels good," I murmured, leaning my head deeper against his shoulder, letting him hold me up.

Alan's breath hitched, and I knew he was enjoying this too. His hips rocked against me, his thickening erection resting against my ass. "Which bit?"

All of it.

Those clever fingers teased around my nipple, stroking in slow circles that left me swollen and aching. I pressed my thighs together, but the action did nothing to suppress the arousal that spiked through me. A moan escaped my lips despite my biting them.

Broken, broken, broken.

Alan laughed against my neck. His torture ceased for a moment as his fingers traveled lower again, rolling beneath the thin material of my pants to dip inside. Smooth pads drifted over my clit, circling just once, which was enough to tease my splintering mind. I swayed on my feet, parting my thighs to give him access as he slipped two fingers twisted together inside me straight to the second knuckle.

I cried out, a shocked, wanton sound that echoed around us in the incessant blackness. Alan stopped moving, letting me get used to the intrusion. My pussy ached and pulsed, desire washing over me in a wave that both shocked and elated me.

I'm broken... like them.

The new mantra was enough for now.

"You want this, Mari?" His fingers shifted a little inside me as he moved his thumb up to play with my clit, rolling over the slippery nub with ease. "Like this?"

He pinched my clit lightly. I clenched around his fingers in response, unable to voice my pleasure. My brain refused to process anything more than the soul-searing touch he offered, teasing me until my mind frayed. Sensation arced through my body as I met the gentle swirls he swept over my folds, my hips undulating to match. I could feel his smile near my ear, his lips pressed to my neck.

Arching a little, I raised both hands behind me to wrap around his neck, giving him all the access he could want to my body. Granting him permission where he would have taken it.

Both sounded good to my pleasure-warped mind.

Those long, cool fingers tightened, constricting the slightest amount around my throat. I should have been scared, but deep inside, I now knew I could trust him. Alan wouldn't hurt me. That had never been his intent. Despite my restricted airflow, I sucked in a larger breath than I'd been allowed before.

"All this." I whispered the words to the empty air. "I want all of this."

"Good girl." He squeezed my throat again, teasing pulses that halted my air and gave it back again as his fingers stayed still inside me.

I gasped with the strange beat he favored, flexing his fingers within me as I sank against his body. My legs trembled as he squeezed a little harder, my pussy clenching down outside my control. I came, bearing down on his fingers, and he hadn't even moved them inside me yet.

"Such a beautiful little slut for me." His cold voice grew rough as he held me against his hard body. My body shook in his grasp that loosened around my throat, offering a sweet caress over the faintest marks there that still hadn't healed.

But now, even the invisible scars were on their way to healing.

A sense of power and strength swept over me, a skewed version of control. *"A pretty cunt for us to fuck."* Wasn't that what he said before? The knowledge he offered was a weapon I armed myself with, his desire bolstering my ability to become more than the victim in his arms.

Alan's twisted fingers worked in and out of my hot pussy, crooking and stretching me as he hit a sensitive spot. Still coming down from my first release, he brought me back to the edge I'd escaped. He pulled me against his chest, his heart beating out of sync, too fast against mine though he kept up the pretense that his touch didn't excite him as much as it did me.

Shoving the thought aside and letting him play his game that I craved as much as he seemed to, I clutched the lean muscle of his forearm to my chest, letting him support me. I didn't pull away, clinging to him to stay upright.

Alan wouldn't let me fall.

Still pulsing one hand inside me, he turned the arm I clung on to. His knuckles brushed against my chin as he tilted my head back once more. I stared into the darkness, knowing I was looking at him but unable to see anything at all.

The void remained impenetrable around his hands as his body worked against mine. The invisible touch erased the phantom memories, replacing them with *now*. His hips pressed against the swell of my ass, his hard length against my back.

Who's in control here?

I didn't bother to bite back the smile he couldn't see anyway.

"I wasn't going to do anything more than tease you, Mari," he grated. "But you're too sweet, little temptation." Alan's breath brushed my lips—and then he moved.

Maybe the lack of vision belied his speed as his mouth crushed mine, but nothing prepared me for the searing intensity of his lust, his need to dominate.

I had the sense from my still sometimes scant interactions with them, despite my months in the cabin, that those boys—Robe, Jon, even Miller—knew how to play the domination game. They made no bones about that. Alan's style of seduction whispered where their natural characteristics blared, and

I wondered if that would carry over into the bedroom with each of them.

Then the chance to wonder about anything at all was stripped away as Alan coiled himself around me until I bowed backward in his arms while he played with my body, leaving me to weather his lust.

Arousal blossomed in jolts of need across my flesh. My skin prickled as I rocked onto his hand, arching up into his kiss. Those sharp lips moved over my mouth, and his tongue sliced inside when I whined my protest at the sensations roiling over my body.

I couldn't think, couldn't see. He corralled all my remaining senses and melded me into a palpating creature until, sweaty and moaning, I came all over his hand a second time. His tongue danced with mine in long, hard strokes, his own need undisguised.

Raw.

I cried out as he ground his palm against my clit, working my body for his pleasure, pinning me against his hips. His movements jerked as he brought me closer to the frenzied edge again. This time, when I moaned his name into his mouth, I didn't fall alone.

Alan hissed his release against my throat, licking and sucking there as he slapped wetly against my back. Through my own haze, I vaguely perceived the way his touch gentled, soothing rather than ripping pleasure from my body, easing the tender flesh that fluttered around roughened fingers. He flicked against my inner walls in a languid motion I never wanted to stop in time with the aftershocks pulsing through me.

He wound his arms around me in the close embrace of a lover, perhaps with a side serving of obsession. I suspected my destination ended there too. My mind wandered for the first time to Robe, and I froze.

"Don't do it. Don't overthink it. I've told you, little hell girl, *he's* into you. We share everything. He's fine."

"But am I?"

The searing light to Robe's en suite flicked on. I hadn't even heard the door open. My eyes watered as I stared at my reflection, all kiss-bitten lips, cheeks stained high with color. Alan's arms were wrapped around mine, his hand still in my pants, a wet stain coating his fingers where I'd drenched everything.

Unable to make eye contact with the wanton creature in the mirror who looked nothing like the broken woman I associated with myself, I tipped my head sideways to stare at Robe. The man in question filled the doorway, his presence looming over us even though he hadn't stepped a foot over the threshold.

Those deep green eyes conveyed a shadow of too many parts, letting me glimpse the fury that burned within, then whisking away that glimmer of truth. I didn't need to glance back at Alan to confirm my thoughts. I focused on the tall mountain man who stood mere paces away with the presence of a grizzly while he eyed the bartender with his hand down my pants.

I am in so much trouble.

Something flickering in the depths of Robe's gaze told me his might be the sort of trouble I'd enjoy.

My eyes watered under the glaring heat lamp of the variety Robe favored. I suddenly remembered that I stood in his private bathroom off the room he'd given me to sleep in while I recovered.

His. Room.

My body clenched around Alan's fingers. As though

reminded of the compromising position we were in, he began to move his hand inside me again. Echoes of the knee-trembling pleasure he had given me warmed my body until I again bore down on his intruding fingers, my attention still locked on Robe.

His expression never changed, though he stared at us with ravenous eyes.

"Oh, do you like that?" Alan's drawl slid down my body in a series of sweet, sensual shocks, leaving me more boneless than ever. "Robe likes to watch."

I wanted to deny it, but a strangled moan tumbled free. My hips rocked against Alan's touch, moving with him like a puppet. Dazed, I tilted my head back onto his shoulder and turned to face Robe, still reacting to the pleasure another man wrung from my body.

He stood there, Robe Huntingdon, broad, scarred hands open at his sides. A foreboding sentinel to protect or to block a path of escape, though I didn't need either right now. His gaze dropped to Alan's hand tenting my pants with his knuckles, his wrist exposed out the top of the material, working my body with his fingers to his own rhythm.

Robe's heat-filled eyes glowed with desire. He brought one hand over the front of his jeans. His slight smile turned to a feral grimace as he gripped his cock with white knuckles and rubbed himself roughly as he focused on the scene before him. Those forest-dark eyes fixed on me alone.

"Mari. Show him how beautiful you are when you come," Alan cooed seductively in my ear.

The temptation to do as he demanded slammed into me. Alan worked me faster, the base of his hand grinding against my clit. My eyes drifted shut as I floated between the two men, one of them touching me, one observing. Each sense was heightened the way they had been with the light off. Part of me wanted to go back into that darkness, to hide. The other part of me *liked* Robe's lust-riddled gaze.

Alan circled his hand around my throat, restricting my air for a second before letting go. "Open your eyes, Mari." His voice roughened again, his cock pressing hard against me, though he'd already found his first release.

A part of me reveled in commanding the pleasure of both these men who demanded authority in their own right. What should have seemed wrong felt so right. Tension left my body as I arched into Alan's movement. My shoulders dropped back, which pushed out my breasts as I ground down onto his hand.

Robe's audible pants grew faster, every breath matching mine as he rubbed himself through his pants. His lips parted, his desire mingling with ours. Despite not being a physical part of the act Alan performed, Robe's presence consumed every viable inch of air in the room.

"Mari," Robe rasped. His hand pulsed around his denim-encased cock as he fisted himself. A deep moan tore from his mouth as I watched him succumb to a bodily need as he witnessed our debauchery that held his attention.

The urge to curl around his body and touch and lick and suck on him the way Alan was doing to me consumed my mind. My knees buckled, but the man at my back didn't let me fall.

The bartender looked up from where he nibbled on my neck, then resumed his activity, biting down hard. The sharp pain combined with Robe's groan in a headrush of pleasure. I cried out as heat smashed over my body, aching as my orgasm hit with the power of both men, though only one of them was touching me.

Alan licked at my throat where I bared it to him as I sank

into his arms. "So beautiful." He brought my mouth to his in slow, deep kisses. "So perfect for us. Isn't she?"

Robe's chest heaved as he stared through me, possession exposed raw on his face.

My head swam as Alan withdrew his fingers, stroking the engorged nerve-filled bundle to soothe the oversensitized ache he'd left there. The scent of sex swirled around us as he brought his knuckles first to my lips, glossing them, and then his. I tasted myself while he sucked the orgasms he'd drawn out of my body from his fingers.

Alan split his tongue between them, making a meal of it and acting the memory out, like I suspected he would do onstage. He brought clean fingers out of his mouth and kissed the middle one, aiming the gesture at Robe, who looked like he was struggling to remain standing.

I understood the feeling.

"Maybe next time." Alan winked.

After making sure he propped me safely against the wall, he strutted away, crossing the room until he reached Robe. The giant woodsman didn't move, still squeezing his spent cock as he stared straight at me.

Alan rose on to his toes at the doorway. Pushing his mouth up, he kissed Robe, smearing the taste of my pleasure against the bigger man's lips. I watched as Robe opened his mouth to accept his tongue and kissed the cheeky stripper back deeply. He raised one hand to grip the dancer's nape possessively until Alan moaned, his dominance ripped away in a single kiss. Alan reached for Robe's crotch, but the mountain man batted him away with a deep growl. My body thrummed with heightened need before Robe broke away, his gaze still locked on mine.

Shifting aside, he made just enough room for Alan to slip

through the gap between man and wall. Alan shot me another wink over his shoulder and disappeared.

I opened my mouth to say something, but my courage depleted without my wingman at my back. Robe didn't help. My Everest crossed thick arms over his chest, impassive and unmoving despite the scent of debauchery still floating in the thick air between us.

His cock tented a dark spot on his pants. I had no idea if he wanted me to ask to finish him or cover up and leave his house altogether. Lost on everything, the confusion seemed so much worse than before Alan touched me. The tentative pleasure and healing he offered dissipated.

Alan helped me conquer my fear that I would never be able to take pleasure from a man's touch ever again. Now... I didn't know where we stood.

Alone. On the other side of a small bathroom from the man I trusted.

A man I *thought* I could trust. But from the way he looked at me, I wasn't sure if he wanted to devour me or kill me for what I just did with one of his friends. His men.

None of Alan's whispered platitudes meant anything in this moment as Robe watched me through hooded eyes, his face an indecipherable mask.

That break in trust hurt me as much as it did him.

"I'm sorry." Nothing else in my mind seemed valid.

In the event that my brain thought up something else fun to do, I closed my mouth and pressed my thighs together. My body ached to collapse onto his bed, preferably sandwiched between Robe and Alan, and sleep.

Just sleep.

Robe raised his fingers to his mouth, rubbing them across his lips. Desire still raged in those dark eyes, green flames wreathed in emotions as indecipherable as their master. He inhaled my scent, then licked his fingers, a simple gesture that copied Alan's earlier show and signaled his style as slower, savoring.

More intimate.

Then Robe dropped his hand and pushed away from the door to follow Alan's exit strategy, leaving me alone.

I stood in his en suite, reeling from the loss of both men and wondering at the pleasure they helped me rediscover. My legs trembled once more and then gave out. I slid to a gentle stop on the cold floor, gathered my limbs about me in a huddle, and closed my eyes.

Mountain men were going to kill me.

Robe

11

ROBE

BLACK COFFEE SCENTED THE CABIN'S INTERIOR. MARI sat alone at the small table while Alan leaned against the bar, reading on his tablet. In light of my banter with Blackthorne, and how my bartender had screwed our guest, waking beneath a beautiful woman yet again had been a serious slip of judgment the night before.

That Mari had turned up so conveniently still didn't sit well, but the pull to take action propelled me toward her. Her taste lingered on my lips despite me trying to forget the way she watched me get myself off to her moans. A growl filled my throat. I clamped my mouth shut to prevent its escape.

I allowed her to stay in my home, in the safe haven of the men who trusted me with both their lives and their freedom, and handed that trust over to a woman who threatened my entire household and the tentative peace I worked so hard to retain.

That peace had become a burden I didn't want to shoulder for the short time Mari Merripen existed in our lives. Needing to know one way or the other, I broke the perfect silence inside the cabin, striding past Alan, who looked up, his brow dipped in a frown. The kid was too smart.

Passing him without a greeting, I headed straight for Mari. Dark hair curled around her face as she stared off, lost in her head. That irritated me even more. I wanted into this girl's life, but she evaded me on too many fronts.

I rapped the tabletop with knuckles dry and splitting. Maybe Elena was right, and I needed to use some of those damned beauty products she kept sending me. At least with Mari in the house, someone benefited from my sister's bundled care packages chosen with a sort of desperate hope. I'd stored them for so long, half were probably out of date by now.

I returned to the reason I'd headed back to the cabin in the first place rather than work my woes out on a poor tree that didn't deserve my pent-up rage today. My moods were getting worse with every day she stayed, and my forest sessions grew longer without the payoff of the high from the energy expenditure woodcutting and shooting once provided.

Miller called it therapy. I called it apathetic bullshit.

"Finish up," I said, offering a cursory glance at the waffle that dangled from her fork. "You've got somewhere to be."

"I do?" Mari perked up and shrank back in the same moment as her unfocused gaze narrowed on my face. "Where?"

"Robe," Alan murmured, giving his warning to my back.

I shook my head once, a tiny gesture, but I knew he wouldn't miss it. "Come on. I want to show you something."

"What?" Mari didn't budge from her seat.

My lips twitched as she held firm in her resolve. Did I trust her for turning up when she did, where she did? Not on my life or anyone else's in the cabin. Miller's words echoed in my head. *Like she came out of nowhere.* If law enforcement turned up at my door, her presence inside my home would be incriminating to say the least. But did that same victim deserve to have to fight the ghost of her attacker, or attackers, when her fears could seek her in the depths of her mind every night? Also no.

The crisp mountain air had cleared my head long enough to let me see a path into one potential future, and I'd be remiss if I didn't give her the best chance of survival possible. If that came back to bite me in the ass, at least the betrayal would be a sexy one.

I leaned down, bracing an arm on either side of her. "Do you want to know how to kick the ass of every nightmare you face from here on out?"

Her gaze darted from my eyes to my mouth and back again, but she didn't say a word. She rose half an inch from the chair, giving me all the permission I needed.

"Be gentle," Alan chided, whipping a tea towel against my bicep as I prodded Mari to precede me from the cabin.

"Like hell," I muttered loud enough for her to hear, baring my teeth at both of them when she spun on her heel.

Mari mumbled something that sounded like "Asshat" as she trotted barefoot down the cabin steps and landed in a solid two-footed jump onto the forest floor.

My grin widened. I tossed the smallest spare boots we had in her direction—a scuffed pair of Will's from when he first arrived—from the collection by the front door. She jerked a little as they hit the ground beside her but otherwise stayed still as she raised a gaze full of curiosity to me.

Her fear of me seemed to diminish as she tugged the boots on, and she hadn't been stiff or trembling when she drifted off to sleep the night before, her body softening in my arms. Damn, but she felt good there. Like her place was at my side, sleeping with me every night. It just seemed natural. I shook my head, banishing the phantom of her soft curves pressed into my scarred body, refocusing on our task. Mari waited outside the house, nary a shiver in sight.

Step one complete.

I checked her again, but she'd already planted her fine ass on the leaf mulch and looked up at me expectantly. I winced. Perhaps I should have provided socks, too, but this ad hoc session came with no plan in mind.

The next would be more proactive, if I played this right.

"Where are we going?" Mari finished lacing up her borrowed shoes, tying the laces twice around slim ankles to make up for the excess length. She tucked the ends into the tops, her eyes too wide by the slightest fraction, lips parted.

I pressed the tip of my tongue to the roof of my dry mouth to prevent myself from telling her not to worry. She wouldn't want to hear it, and it didn't matter what I said. The oversized fit of the footwear looked more than slightly ridiculous, but as no one else out here would see her, I doubted it mattered.

Making a mental note to ask Alan to get her a few pairs of wearable shoes the next time he went into town, I caught her elbow and steered her to the bottom of the house yard.

A small track opened out from there, one I worked my way along, creating a defensive system around the house. The lower area led to a rapidly flowing albeit small spring that gurgled merrily despite the season. Its tenacious year-round refusal to freeze amused me, and it had fast become one of my favorite spots.

Mari followed me, her lighter step almost overshadowed by mine. "What are we doing, Robe?"

"Not Everest? I kinda liked that." More than I'd admit. "We're training, wildflower. Turning you into a deadly little killer."

"I don't think I—"

"Have a choice? No, you don't." I caught her eye as I led her out of the enclosed forest.

Bemusement lit her face. "Are you always like this?"

"Innovative, protective, and upbeat?"

Mischief shone in her eyes. "Grumpy, frustrating, and high-handed," she countered. Her lips curled, and my gaze dropped to the movement for the space of a heartbeat.

Long enough to make the distraction a fatal one if I'd read her wrong. But hell, maybe I was bored and living on the edge could solve my first-world problems. If it were that simple.

"Have you done any training? Self-defense classes, or maybe you took tae kwon do lessons as a kid?" I circled around her.

Mari pivoted on her heel. "I did kickboxing for a few months while I studied. Never competed, but I had fun because I needed to burn off excess energy." She shrugged.

I canted my head to one side. Interesting that she'd taken a harder form of classes rather than boxercise at the local gym. "What did you study?"

"Besides the occupants of the library while I avoided my work? Business, macroeconomics. PR and HR. MBA. All the funky business letters. Ended up a PA for a bossy-britches CEO in New York for all of it." She wound her shoulders back while I stored the information she offered up.

"Not London?" I waited for her response, but my tame little Brit said nothing. "All right. Kickboxing, huh? Show me what you know."

She smiled and rocked back on one leg, stretching. Her eyes never left me, though her degree of wariness reduced, the worry lines across her forehead smoothing with each moment she spent at my side.

Her lips quirked, and my heart tugged.

"I'm no match for you, Robe. And I don't want to have to

fight again so soon." Her light humor dropped, replaced by shadows I recognized.

I hated myself for making her go back there but promised my heart this would be worth it in the end. "Give me a little demonstration," I coaxed.

Let me see what you're capable of, Mari Merripen. Show me how you break.

"A heads-up, it's been an age. I'll end up on my ass." She popped a hip in apology.

"Or maybe you'll knock me on mine," I teased. "Bring it, Miss Kickboxer."

She gave a halfhearted laugh and folded over her knees until her body bent in half. "I doubt it, Everest." She spoke into her shins while I tried not to stare at her ass.

Massive fail.

Still, she rallied, sassing me with the nickname, and that had to be a good thing. I stepped around her in a semicircle, offering her space as she straightened.

Mari's wariness returned, but this time, her expression cleared with focus. She edged a little closer, and just as I thought she might have given up, she tapped my knee with the toe of her oversized boot.

"You know, I'm terrified I'll hurt you," she quipped, stepping in close enough to nudge my thigh with her knee in a piss-poor attempt to get me to move or let her off the hook.

Neither of those things was happening, and for the record, I worried more about her hurting herself than doing damage to me.

I bared my teeth in response and grabbed wildly for her waist. Not a real grab; I wanted to see how she'd react to the change in aggression.

Mari skittered backward with a yelp that could have raised the dead.

I stuck my finger in my ear to pop it and winced. "Damn, girl. That wasn't necessary."

"You asked me to start."

"I asked you to spar with me," I corrected. Her breathing was way too fast for my liking. "Are you okay? I'm sorry I scared the shit out of you. I—"

Her boot thunked against the top of my thigh and left me with an instant dead leg. I kept my expression blank despite wanting to drop to one knee and yowl like a wounded animal. My thigh muscles fucking stung at the contact, though the thought almost brought a smile to my lips. I hid that too.

Mari Merripen has bite when cornered. Noted.

Add that to the list of things I liked far too much about this girl.

"Ow," I said in a sedate voice that betrayed none of the excruciating pain that speared my leg.

Mari grinned. "Sorry. I can go hard."

"No need to apologize." I held up a hand, and her grin grew wider. "Let's try this for real now."

"Is that what we're calling it?" She let me circle around her at a short distance, pivoting on her heel to prevent me getting inside her blind spot.

Pine mulch crackled underfoot as she joined me in a dance of bobbing and jabbing, feints and quicksteps. It wasn't strenuous work by any means, but her chest rose and fell, her cheeks flushing after a few minutes.

And those motherfucking shadows I hated seeing behind her eyes stayed away.

"Am I pushing you too hard?" I murmured, reaching out to brush the backs of my knuckles over her cheek.

I never got to make contact.

Mari batted my hand aside and used the opening to punch me in the stomach. I doubled over at the waist, wheezing, making out that the light jab did more damage than intended. She didn't take the bait, laughing at my pantomime and dancing out of my reach when I lunged for her.

Her feet moved fast, but her darting steps faded as I gave chase around the clearing. She wove between trees, laughing... until her tone changed and became more ragged. Her step faltered, slowing her progress.

I wrapped an arm around her waist, drawing her back into me in a grip that was firm but not unbreakable.

"Mari, sweetheart. Are you okay?"

"I'm fine." She gulped in harsh lungfuls of mountain air.

Her hands wound around my forearm, sharp nails digging crescent moon impressions into my skin where she clutched at me, but she didn't fight to escape. She offered a small measure of trust—a grain, if that—but I felt like we'd jumped off a small ledge together and made it down a steep incline unscathed. Kind of.

"Liar," I murmured against her hair, arcing over her to lean my cheek on the top of her head. Mountain air mingled with *eau de Mari*, filling my head with images that shouldn't be there while I held her, protected her. Even from myself. "I shouldn't have chased you."

She shook her head, but the negative never fell from her lips.

"Yes, you should have. And you need to teach her more than to run like a fucking rabbit terrified of losing her hide. Because if that's what she does with any damn predator, then the end result is a forgone conclusion."

My shoulders tightened, though no enemy stood at my back.

"Thank you, Miller." My words came out clipped at the end. "I've got this."

"Bullshit. You know I'm right."

Every instinct fought against what he said, but I knew he spoke the truth I didn't want to face. Finding a way to teach Mari eluded me the moment I froze up.

"He's right." Mari tilted her head back, looking up into my eyes, close enough to kiss if I lifted her off her toes and pressed my mouth against hers.

What the fuck, Robe? Head. Out. Of. Her. Pussy.

She needed to be healed, not fucked by a rowdy group of men. I closed my eyes, my lips tight. Alan's little playtime session had proved his point. I got it; Mari needed the contact, the security we could offer her—what *I* could offer her, but I wasn't ready to go there just yet. I couldn't trust myself, and I still wasn't sure how long I'd hold on to the grudge my stripper didn't know I carried that he took pleasure from her before I did.

Even more so that I didn't listen to him in the first place.

Now is not the time. Asshole.

I added that last part for emphasis.

"Yeah." I cleared my throat of my raspy tone and could almost feel Miller's eye roll from where he stood across the clearing. "You're right. I'm not the best person to teach that. Too many memories," I added to Mari, who still hung her head upside down like a small, dark-haired bat in front of me.

"No," she protested, gripping my arm tighter. "I liked fighting with you."

"And that's the problem. Go with Miller. He'll help you better than I can."

"He scares me," she whispered, her cheeks coloring. Tilting her head back down, she broke eye contact, her hair swishing over her face in a thick curtain.

"Good," I whispered back. "Maybe you'll listen to him. Go, then come back and kick my ass later."

"Not going to happen," she huffed, staring forward at some focal point beyond me.

"Not if you talk like that. You've got the goods, girl. Go use them." I unhooked my arm from around her waist when she let me go and pressed my fingers between her shoulder blades. "Go. You're safe with him, I promise."

The shorter man had taken more than one bullet for me and saved my ass a half dozen times over the years. Maybe he had a guardian angel on his shoulder, but the kill shots never took him down. Luck, perhaps.

I headed off to a small clearing, not wanting to leave Mari wandering around the forest and getting more disoriented if she chose to seek me out after her session with Miller. If she could walk by then. Her hesitant step behind me, the subtle snap of fine twigs as she left a trail of twisted forest debris in her wake like so many breadcrumbs, told me everything I needed to know about her state of mind.

Maybe I could get Jon or Will to help her find her way around the forest, learn tracking and how to survive if she got trapped out on her own again. Not that I'd let that happen to her, but I also knew not to leave her exposed without a contingency plan.

I worked my way along a thin trail that led to the closer edges of my property nearest the house. A point well away from other seasonal residences and nowhere near my enemy. Having his perimeter bordering mine added enough stress to our lives; I didn't need him in my backyard to boot.

At strategic points around the cabin in a quarter-mile radius, Miller and I stored an extra line of defenses. We placed some farther out as well, camouflaged at the boundary line and a select few choice spots on Gideon's lands, but we didn't check on those enough to make sure they hadn't been found.

Pushing his boundaries had never been my plan until Mari dropped into my life.

Running my fingers around the harsh limbs of a dead tree, I sought the opening where the hollow exoskeleton folded back on itself. I peeled the trunk back, taking care not to crack the weathered bark, and removed a recurve bow and quiver full of hand-fletched arrows. A long bow I favored and maintained myself had been given a home on the other edge of the property.

Beyond the stump, a rocky outcrop with a perfect line of sight gave a direct shot into Gideon's study from the cover of the tall pines that marked time as sentinels along the ridge.

I'd lined the shot up many times, and Gideon had no idea how lucky he was to still be breathing. Despite the rumors of why I left the military, murder came last on my to-do list, and the man remained attached to his heartbeat. After what we suspected he'd done to Mari, however, he might not stay in that state for much longer.

Gideon would come for me one day. That was the hard truth I lived. My boys were prepared for the day he did.

I curled my fingers around the curved bow, its familiar lines seated in my hand like an extension of myself. Slipping into the mentality of *I need to shoot something*, the rippling anger that seethed deep within me as a constant companion eased back within the edges of serenity.

Turning at the southernmost point of the base of the tree, I worked my way twenty-one long paces to my right. Jon and I had measured them together using his longer gait once Miller picked out the positioning.

I stopped and turned in the opposite direction from where Mari and Miller were practicing. A dual line of trees lay before me, the distance between them less than an extended handspan. At the far end of the narrow lane, a row of three small targets hung from a broken, burned tree.

I inhaled a long, slow breath and withdrew an arrow from the quiver over my shoulder in one movement, then notched the fletched end to the bowstring. My breath whispered from between open lips, releasing tension to the forest. Another breath in, and I raised my elbow, sighted the target through the space between the trees, and breathed out.

Airless. Quiet. Floating.

No roaring, no rage.

Nothing.

I loosed the arrow, string twanging a breath from my ear.

Again.

And again.

And again.

Collect, fire, repeat until I emptied the quiver a fourth time. My breath remained hollow as sounds of the forest returned. The spaces between the line of trees darkened, though my focus pinpointed. I hadn't noticed time slipping away. I shook out warm arms and stiff legs as I worked my way back along the trail to the clearing. Soft voices and the occasional expelled breath or groan filtered through scant underbrush.

Stopping just inside the tree line, I propped my shoulders against a sturdy pine, a smile sliding into place. Mari battled with never-ending fervor, lashing out in controlled jabs and kicks. Her breath was labored, her face flushed the hue of a ripe tomato, but her gaze narrowed, focusing on Miller.

She spun, semi-off-balance, and caught herself as he swung at her in a wide haymaker that would have knocked her into next week if she hadn't ducked. Mari dropped, flicking out a leg as she twisted. Miller's ass hit the forest floor with a muted thump that startled the odd dozing bird from the trees surrounding the clearing.

Mari stood over him, a proud smile curving soft lips as her color returned to normal, and offered him a hand.

She didn't need me to tell her what a bad impulse she'd acted on.

He hooked a boot behind her ankle and pushed instead of pulled as he rose until they reversed positions.

Mari winced from her place on the forest floor and rubbed her rump.

"Either punch the fucker in the face or run like hell, little girl. Don't offer chivalry. Niceties don't count when his aim is to destroy that pretty soul you keep locked away in here." Miller jabbed her between the breasts, anger creasing the deep lines of his face.

"Noted." Mari hissed as she rose to her feet a little slower than I would have liked to see her move.

Before I could catch myself, I shoved away from the tree and strode forward, already reaching for her. Growling, I pulled my hand back and folded my arms to prevent myself from doing anything stupider.

"Have you worked her that hard the entire time I've been gone?" I spoke to Miller but kept my focus on Mari, taking in the quick rise of her chest, the deep red stain that refused to leave her cheeks. She returned my gaze, just as assessing, though with more... *something* in her eyes. Awareness, perhaps. "She needs to heal."

"*She* is just fine, thank you." Mari lifted her chin, and when I said nothing, she turned to Miller. "Thank you for the lesson. I appreciate the time you took."

"You're welcome," he returned, his eyes hooded, his manic fury and coiled body quiet for once.

Something unspoken passed between them in that look

that raised a green-eyed beast in my chest. I frowned. Respect between them had been my goal, but now that I'd achieved my aim, it tasted bittersweet.

I wanted Mari's quiet looks, the unsated yearning in her eyes for me alone.

Swallowing back the urge to push away the man who'd had my back for so long, I clenched my jaw and promised myself I'd play nice. "Hungry? It'll be dark soon." The words came out harsher than I wanted, but Mari didn't back away.

"Both of you get thanks. I don't think I've spent that much time away from you since I first got here," she murmured to the pine needles scattered around her oversized boots. Her cheeks flushed pinker, brightening the stain from her exertions.

"That keen to get rid of me?" I snarled back. *Fuck, get your shit together.* "I'm glad you learned something."

"Want to take me on?" she blazed at me, all sass and filled with a desire for social proof.

Needy little thing, aren't you?

The thought that she wanted—*needed*—my approval reduced my simmering rage, and the Kermit-colored beast retreated.

I shook my head. "No, Mari. You've worked hard enough. If Miller's happy, then so am I."

She tipped her head to one side. "You two have a lot of love for each other, don't you?"

A challenge resided in her words, a sideward attack on our combined masculinity, but I shrugged it off.

"Yes, we do," I said simply.

Mari blinked.

"Go get showered. Use the hot water before I do." Miller gestured her forward.

"Thank you," she whispered again as she passed by him, almost close enough to touch.

She hesitated, and his fingers flexed. The beast returned, roaring, almost obliterating Miller's next words, low and softly spoken.

"Good girl."

My words.

I focused on not ripping Miller's head off while Mari walked away in a cloud of quiet confidence, a small, private smile curling her lips when she looked back, her step lightening.

Careful what you wish for, Robe.

Mari

12

MARI

MILLER'S GOOD HUMOR LASTED HALF THE LIFESPAN OF the bruises I incurred from my first training session. By the time the week ended, tender spots covered my body like he'd used a meat hammer instead of his feet and fists. Alan spent his nights applying cream to and helping me work out stiff joints. I knew from the looks he exchanged with Robe in silent conversation above my head that he worried the training damaged me too much.

The simple truth they both ignored was that I enjoyed the physical activity.

Moreover, I enjoyed the power working on my body developed in me, the confidence that I wouldn't be a useless victim ever again.

Robe gave me the few cheap and somewhat pathetic kicks I aimed at his thigh with the intent of bruising his ego and only succeeded in deflating my own. Miller built my limits, adding to my repertoire of attack and defensive moves, and trained my mind and my body to react in a specific manner.

Anything was better than panic.

The aching muscles and tender spots remained my badges

of honor, and when I didn't complain or say anything, neither did the boys.

Miller watched me each day, the distrust in his demeanor reducing with each drop of sweat I left in the clearing, my essence mingling with theirs on the ancient mountain range they called home.

Scuffing my socked feet on the floor, I procrastinated against opening the cabin door to let the still-frigid air inside, my toes curling within their warm confines.

Behind me, Alan snickered. I could *feel* Robe rolling his eyes.

And I could have happily stayed there all morning, facing a closed door in a warm house heated by the bodies of five enormous mountain men.

Until a single whisper behind me took my choice away. "*Wuss.*"

Chin in the air, I gripped the handle of the door, preparing to face another morning practice with Miller in icy mountain air that left me cold until I curled into Robe's arms in his bed again each night, and tugged the door open.

Arctic air blasted in my face as I shoved my feet forward and yanked the door closed behind me, but a much larger frame obliterated Miller's expected form.

"Morning." Jon watched me with an open face. Unlike the rest of the members of Robe's household, Jon held nothing back. His expressions reflected exactly what he felt at heart level, and warmth, both the temperature sort and compassion based, rolled from him like a tangible thing. The huge man rocked from foot to foot, a fine blush rising above the edges of his shaggy beard. "I'm taking on your training today. Wanna go for a walk?" He gave me a shifty sort of smile and jerked his head toward a trail I never used that meandered into the trees north of the house.

"Uh, sure." I offered a wonky smile, resisting the urge to look back over my shoulder, but I'd already closed the door behind me, so I wouldn't be able to see Robe anyway.

Telling myself that I trusted him like I did the others, I took the hand Jon stretched out. His roughened fingers, thicker than the ones on Robe's massive mitt, closed around mine. He didn't dwarf my smaller form; he obliterated me.

But as with many giants of men, at least in the physical sense, Jon appeared to be a great big teddy bear, cuddly and protective. I didn't doubt that he could rock an apron and cook up barbeque to match Alan's flair at the bar. Because houses had bars.

I rolled my eyes. Only Robe, honestly. That man created the limit.

"I wanted to show you a bit of the mountain now that it's less vicious out," Jon called over his shoulder as he towed me into the tree line that closed off any visual of the house.

As happened each time I stepped into the forest, my breath shortened. I snapped twigs that grew at odd angles out of the giant trunks we passed, recalling the bite of every stick and ice-laden foliage I ruined in my headlong dash from hell.

Breath hovered at my lips, but my throat remained a vacuum, and every major function in my body stalled for a black-edged moment. I gripped Jon's hand too tight, pulling him back.

"Stop." I gaped like a fish out of water, desperate and in need of the cabin's close walls and population to block out the memories that swarmed me.

Why am I not like this with Robe?

Able to call for help, touch him when I needed him. But I couldn't. It was like a physical barrier stood between us, waiting for one of us to shatter it, when neither of us could.

Or would.

Not like with Jon, where everything started easy. Too easy, because I let my guard down for a single second when I begged for his help and the reaching hands from my memory of that day swarmed back, obliterating everything—

The forest. The peace I garnered. My safety net. Jon.

A moment where light faded around me, and I sank—

Hard, warm arms wrapped around me, catching me before I hit the ground that wavered beneath my feet. Hard, like Robe. Warm, like the cabin's interior. I leaned my cheek against Jon's enormous pec and listened to his heartbeat thump away, so close and reassuring.

"It's all right, honey. I've got you." Jon repeated the words over and over like a mantra that came paired with a bonus wall of impenetrability.

Warm, like mountain sun on a clear spring morning.

Hard, like a huntsman. No, a tin man. The man who couldn't share his heart because he'd forgotten he had one.

Pleased with the analogy, I labeled Jon for something to do while my feet found their bones and I supported myself again.

I emerged for air, sucking in the mix of cinnamon and morning sun that lanced off his body. "You're like a big stuffie," I muttered, turning my face into his chest and pressing my lips against his sternum.

My mind froze while I stood there, kissing his—rather massive and very impressive—chest.

Way to go, Mari. Kiss random chests because they smell and feel nice. That's the way to live in a cabin full of men.

"Uh...." I scrambled for something to say, trying to extract myself at speed while going slow enough to cover my faux pas.

"Take it easy, Mari," Jon commanded.

I reacted to his tone, easing my way backward as he

steadied me with a dipped brow over hazel eyes shot with sunlight and cypress. "A step at a time. I know it's been a while now, but that's one hell of a trauma. My fault for dragging you into a section of the woods you don't know. Yet," he added, like his choice of words contained a hidden meaning.

Was it that simple? I could waltz around with Robe and let him leave me alone with Miller. The stockier man and I had developed a fragile rapport over the last week based on the number of bruises I accrued every session without complaint. Each aching muscle appeased my relentless taskmaster in working off some debt or sin I'd garnered alongside my scars. Every time my ass hit the deck, my throbbing rump earned me a fraction of his trust.

I hadn't realized how much I craved that until he failed to mask his emotion for a scant second one session. Brief, but that longing for *more* was there. To be... needed. Wanted. No matter how hard he worked me after that, Miller couldn't steal that knowledge back from me.

Jon, on the other hand, gave trust far more freely, his hurts displayed in place of his heart like a banner across his broad chest.

"No, not—wait. Yet?" I pressed my lips into a line, but they twitched despite my determination. "What's up your sleeve, Jon?"

The big man laughed, catching my hand again and closing his fingers around mine in a fierce grip when I tugged at his hold, my feet skidding over last season's slushy mulch. "Nuh-uh. You stay put, girl, right next to me. No wandering off, no getting lost. No freaking out... again." He sent me a meaningful sideways look.

"Otherwise, Robe will hand you your ass. Yeah, I know what a grump he is," I muttered to my shoes, the embarrassment of almost passing out on his best friend sinking in. "I'm so sorry," I offered in a quiet, muted voice, unwilling to disturb the growing silence around us.

Where were the birds when I needed a cacophony or rent-a-crowd on cue? *Oh, that's right, freezing their feathers off, or warm in their nests.*

"Don't apologize, Mari. I've known too many women who say 'sorry' over and over again because they've been broken and beaten and it's all they know. I can't believe that of you. You're stronger than he is."

"Robe?" My brow furrowed as I halted, looking up at Jon.

"Him too. But I meant—" He cleared his throat. "I meant those who attacked you. This forest isn't your enemy. I'm determined that by the time we're done, you'll be able to survive out here for days if need be. Weeks, if you have the right kit and can find shelter, which, after today, you'll be able to do."

"I will?" I echoed. "Are we orienteering?"

"Damn right."

I grinned as Jon showed me the smallest foods to be found in the harshest of seasons. How to find north beneath an entwined canopy, what tracks and scat meant, where to locate water. The information swirled around my head, but this was survivalism at its best, and I would learn, damnit. And so I listened, and remembered, and watched.

"Here. Wild strawberry." Jon crouched to dig at the slush-laden ground. I had no idea why he chose to scrabble about there, but he clearly had a plan as he proudly exposed a dead-looking, leafless root thing. He held out a crunched-up leaf from last season, frostbitten on the edge, and at my confused look, he then produced a more recognizable fruit from his pocket with a sigh. "Here you go, city girl. I went shopping earlier. Just for you."

Strawberries weren't the only thing hidden in his Mary

Poppin-esque pockets. After ingesting blueberries and a stunted blackberry I suspected came from an actual, out-of-season, berry-bearing forest bush without being poisoned, I popped the fruit into my mouth and moaned out loud. "Oh, wow. That's so sweet. Have you thought of making a hydroponics shed? Something solar powered so you can grow these all year round?" We both knew Alan was the only one who left the cabin at any regular interval, and maybe Will, though I got the impression he had less freedom than he wanted.

"Not a bad idea, honey. Bring that up with our resident chemist." He smiled at my confused look. "Alan." *So I guessed right.* "And yes, they're some of the best you'll find. But the fruit isn't the only useful thing." He held out a handful of broad dark green leaves before he shoved them back into the coat pocket they came from. "You won't find many of these about yet, but a few more weeks and you'd be able to pick a decent amount."

"Are you going to ward off a tribe of zombie beavers with that?" I asked, still savoring the berry.

Jon's laugh kept me going for a few more steps, but my legs felt like they were going to fall off after the number of miles we'd traveled. He managed to reduce my fear of the dark spaces between trees with his passion about the mountainside.

That, and the fact that we hadn't been attacked or poisoned.

"You know, if I picked a berry on my own, I'd die," I pointed out. "I can poison myself with non-expired milk in my own kitchen." The thought of my apartment sent my stomach into a tumble. I gripped the tree next to me that turned out to be Jon's bicep.

"You okay there, Mari?" he asked, his attention on me though he kept his tone light. "Dried strawberry leaves create a solid base for a vitamin C shot in tea. Alan makes it back home," he murmured, stressing the last word.

His point drove my thoughts into a spiral I couldn't escape.

"Jon, am I...? Can I...?" I couldn't complete the thought.

I'd been asking Robe if I could leave, but his reply remained the same every time: *"Heal, and we'll talk."*

But healing took time, and talking didn't seem as scary as it had before. The Great Lump still wouldn't answer my questions, though, despite my poking. I pursed my lips, tossing up the chances of getting information out of Jon, but I got the impression he'd be even worse than Robe.

Jon's gentle eyes watched me, and I forced a smile I didn't feel, unable to escape the nausea in my stomach. I needed a distraction....

"Tell me about how you got here. You and Robe and everyone."

Jon arched an eyebrow. "He hasn't told you?"

No need to ask which *he* Jon meant.

"No."

"Stay long enough and you'll be able to pick these on your own." Jon piled a small pyramid of shop-bought strawberries into my palm and started to walk while I picked at my treasure trove. The explosion of flavors in my mouth floored me, and I moaned my answer with my typical inappropriate timing.

"A local... politician murdered my wife." Jon's hand found my free one and squeezed hard.

"Oh, God. I'm so sorry—"

"Robe saved my ass from offing myself and brought me back here. I've helped him ever since. Miller followed along as always, brought back from his sojourn in the military. Will arrived a bit after, and then we... found Alan."

"You make him sound lost."

"We were all lost, Mari. Robe gave us a home." He squeezed my fingers in a tender touch this time.

"How long have you all been here?" It must have been quite a while, as he talked about his wife with an ease I didn't understand. "I can't imagine the horror."

"Nor do I want to again."

"I'm so sorry for asking."

"It's fine." He paused long enough for the forest sounds to fill his silence. "Seven years. Me, at least. Miller and Robe have been here longer. Alan and Will less. But it's been seven years since I lost her." His voice grew ragged with suppressed emotion.

My tin man.

I closed my eyes, my tears coming for him, what he'd lost. Who. Warmth brushed beneath my lashes as his roughened thumbs swiped the salt away.

"Don't cry for me, Mari," Jon said in his gentle tone. "My life was forfeit long ago. Let us give you what we can now." His touch lingered and then dropped, leaving the ghost of my tears whispering in its wake.

My next breath sucked in as ragged as his, and I began to understand the value of the forest's silence as we walked, its weight no longer suppressing but a comfort, until my questions bubbled over, unable to be held in any longer.

"What about Robe? And Miller?" And Will? The kid with sunshine in his eyes. Hell, what had the world done to these men who just wanted to survive and protect?

And fight.

Because they all had some darker aspect etched into their souls. Damaged. Broken.

Like me.

"Authorities accused Robe of murdering a superior

officer and his aide, among other things. Miller backed his claim to innocence, the steadfast little shit. They both ended up out of the military, leaving quietly under their own steam when the required evidence didn't come to light despite the power backing it. Otherwise, they'd be incarcerated—or dead."

"He—" My voice caught on the first word. "Robe killed someone?"

Jon paused and looked back at me. "What did I just say, Mari?"

I thought back. "That he's innocent?" Breath sucked into the void of my lungs.

"That he's innocent." Jon nodded once.

"So he didn't do it." I let my breath out.

"He did it."

My breath stalled. "What?"

"He killed them both, Mari. They had a local girl on the floor of a tent, kept there for God knows how long. Half starved, naked, and filthy. His boss and his little groupie liked to traffic women. Robe lost his shit, as you do." Jon resumed walking, his shoulders a tight line.

"As you do." *Conversation closed, then.* I worked my screaming thighs hard to catch up to the mountain attached to my hand. "Jon... what happened to the girl?"

"I don't know. None of us do. They carted Robe away and locked him up until Miller rode to the rescue and brought him back to home soil."

"Which is why he has to hide. They both do." I swallowed, tears pricking the corners of my eyes. "He has a sister. Any other family? Has he ever been back to... where does he call home?"

Jon paused midstep. "No."

Robe's life had been ripped away, and despite the injustice

that would have crippled a weaker man, he made a home for those like him. Broken, unwanted.

A single tear cascaded down my cheek.

Jon twisted when my feet stayed planted where they were. My mouth opened a few times, but nothing came out.

"It's all right, Mari."

"It's not *all right*. How can he be as strong as he is?"

Jon's beard twitched. "Because he's a stubborn asshole."

"I thought the same earlier." I hiccupped, my heart breaking.

A calloused thumb grazed my cheek, sweeping my sorrow aside. "And because he's fierce, loyal to a fault, and wants to save the world like some comic-book-worthy superhero. He'll protect you, Mari. We all will."

"But you can't go home."

Jon stilled. "He is our home."

For a while, the sound of our boots crunching through the underbrush and my short breaths filled the forest as I cried in silence for the horrors they'd suffered. I hadn't even gotten to Will's story, but something told me trauma filled his past too.

Robe collected people like himself. Jon was stubborn but had a gentle side. Miller was gruff but loyal.

Jon walked me through identifying a few edible barks, picked out wintergreen and stored some of that, too, and then showed me habitual nesting sites to source eggs. I followed in his footsteps, letting his love of the forest settle over the grief overflowing my heart for them all. But I learned more about Jon too.

How much he loved the forest, what he knew about the area around the house. Why he ran through the trees early in the morning. Why he stayed with Robe.

Why he didn't leave.

"You loved her." I didn't bother phrasing it as a question.

He hadn't wanted to talk about it, but the ghost of his wife hovered in the back of his attentive gaze every time he looked at me.

"With all my heart. I thought it broke, you know. Shattered into a million worthless pieces." He looked straight at me, leaving my heart thundering in my chest. "Until you arrived."

"You're not worthless. And you don't know me." The words fell out as I processed his response. "Wait, you mean like a... a... ward, or a friend or a niece or something. Right?" I swallowed hard, desperate for that nod, because the dark intent in his eyes said otherwise.

I couldn't be the feature of a man's wet dreams when I sort of suspected—okay, that was me lying to myself head-on —when I *knew* I belonged with Robe. Alan... he was a different beast. Literally. But Jon was his own person. He was Robe's *best friend.* And I was meant to be with Robe. My head knew it. My heart knew it. Having his best friend want me, even when I felt so safe in his arms, presented a huge problem. No, I'd read the whole situation wrong.

What sort of an insensitive, narcissistic bitch thinks like that?

We share every important moment, Mari.

Robe's words from before dropped me into a spiral of my own making while Jon hauled me out, giving me a free pass.

"Yeah, sure. Like a niece." Jon huffed a cloud of condensation that hovered between us, obscuring my vision for a moment. "C'mon. I wanna show you how to build a shelter in winter."

"I'd freeze to death first. Not like I'll be here for the next one, you know. I have to go home sometime," I said reasonably.

Or maybe totally unreasonably, as his broad back stopped

halfway up an incline. I pulled up a breath shy of plowing straight into his hard-as-nails ass. I knew it was tight and hard because, like a prepubescent kid in a movie, my progress ended on a sudden halt. I tumbled toes over teakettle, but instead of grabbing handfuls of breasts, I got ass.

A whole lotta fine, hard ass.

Damn, he'd be good in bed.

If I'd learned anything about a man's physique, it meant that a solid, warm chest meant unconditional love. A neat, hard ass, on the other hand, made for an excellent, long-lasting lover.

I swallowed, prying my fingers free as Jon—*Robe's best friend*, I kept reminding myself—turned to face me.

"I'm so sorry," I stammered. "I—"

"Why don't you go first?" Jon offered, standing aside to clear the path. "I promise I won't go head over tails like you just did."

"Um, of course," I whispered weakly, trying not to imagine him without clothes in bed with Robe—and me.

I squeezed my eyes shut and edged past him.

A threesome, Mari? After the bathroom incident with Alan? Are you shitting me?

Where the hell was my head at? Left up a mountain man's tight behind, for one thing.

We made a wide circuit that took us first north and then farther along the ridgeline, but Jon assured me we'd still be in time for whatever was being cooked back at the cabin that would slip inside the frozen barrier of my senses and send my stomach rumbling.

At a rocky outcrop, a glimpse of an imposing fortresslike building sent my blood thrumming too fast through my veins, overheating me and freezing me all at once. I stumbled over my own feet, wondering if Jon had done it on purpose, but as

I'd kept my mouth shut about Gideon's identity for self-preservation, how would he know?

Because there's no one else out here, Mari.

Of course they knew. But I couldn't bring myself to talk about it.

Jon caught me as I wavered on the edge of the path, my gaze fixed firmly ahead, my attention on the monstrosity behind me and who resided within those granite walls. Hell, even the building looked lifeless and overcast, a vacant castle on the hill.

A hand between my shoulder blades steadied me and propelled me forward all at once.

"The tree line is safest," Jon explained conversationally while my emotions swirled in an uncontrolled maelstrom. "Winds can kick up fast, and they pummel the cliff face. Stay within the forest. It's warmer, and you're less... exposed there."

I nodded and said nothing.

The mantle of silence seemed more comfortable this time. Jon's presence at my back remained a sturdy shield between me and Gideon's shade that followed me into the trees. Jon gave a murmured direction where the path split, crouching to show me tracks, and directed me how to look between the trees rather than at them.

The knowledge eked out an extra degree of power, building my confidence with every mile. I smiled for the first time in hours, nibbling my last strawberry as each step became less torturous.

And all the while, I thought about the boys and how they behaved.

Robe, the consummate protector/provider.

Alan, the comic relief with way too much heart—and other skills that heated my body.

Jon, the mountain of a man who found passion in the oddest places and was all the more lovable for it.

Miller, whose snarky, grumpy methods earned the results Robe needed. Fixing what Robe couldn't while always having his back. Ah, the wingman.

Will—

I stopped.

"Robe's sending me around the group, isn't he?" I asked without any other brain function firing whatsoever. I might have thought the comment through a little harder. I persisted anyway. "Isn't he?"

"We all want to get to know you, Mari," Jon hedged, though his stance shouted *stubborn asshat* all the way.

It suited him.

"Why does he want me to get to know everyone? I'm going home soon." I pushed back the fear that started to fray the edges of my consciousness. "Jon, stop." I tugged at the hand he'd refused to release for the better part of the day.

"Because—" Jon gripped my hand tight and pulled me an inch closer to him. I shivered, gooseflesh rising beneath the long-sleeved thermal top I'd become accustomed to wearing. "We need to get back. Light's failing."

He pushed past me, releasing my hand, and strode forward. I hurried to catch up, unable to keep pace with his longer legs that ate up the miles. My breath came in short pants that left me unable to think about anything more than powering on behind him.

"Jon—" I gasped as the trees thinned.

The cabin sat in its usual place in the center of the small clearing. It was a relief that the forest hadn't swallowed our home in our absence.

Jon turned back, his brow furrowed as he took in my

state. "I went too fast. I'm sorry, Mari. I'm not used to company."

"It's okay. I wanted to say thank you before we went inside. Before...."

Before there are other people between us. A full day with Jon had increased my comfort level, and I knew I'd trust him if the world came crashing down around us.

He offered me a strained smile, his gaze sweeping over me, less checking me out than making sure I hadn't fallen apart in the last few hours.

Alan whistled from the balcony, wearing his fluffiest apron, and catcalled, but my attention remained on Jon's broad back as I followed him into the cabin. The inside of the house was steaming in comparison to the sharp mountain air.

"Have a shower, Mari. It'll regulate your core temp." Alan flicked my nose as I passed him. "Then it's dinner in your room tonight."

"In the bedroom?" The room that belonged to someone else. Not me.

"Yes."

"I can't join you?" I frowned.

Robe had sent me out with his friends each day, and now I couldn't eat with them, pushed away like a prisoner.

Friendzone status revoked.

I swallowed around a lump in my throat that refused to be dislodged while Alan observed me with pity in his gaze. I hated it and folded my arms. If they were stubborn, I'd match them.

"I'd like to eat with you." *All of you. Please.* I wanted to beg but kept my gaze fixed on Alan, too scared to look around the room or risk being denied by someone else.

Alan's mouth opened, but a different voice answered me.

"No."

I blinked, frozen to the spot in panic as tears welled. "Why not?" I whispered, already knowing the answer. Robe's select few didn't include me. What he gave to these men, he could strip away from me just as fast.

"Because we have work." The finality in his tone etched a strike through my heart.

"Fine," I snapped with the last of my energy and shoved past Jon, unable to deal with Robe's warmth at my back, the pity in Alan's eyes, and a fresh, shattered heart.

Someone might have called my name, or maybe I imagined it and they watched me go in silence. Worse, maybe they didn't watch me at all because my presence counted as temporary at best.

Why am I fighting for permanency when I'm supposed to leave soon?

It wasn't until I peeled sweat-laden material from my skin and stood under a scalding hot shower, going back over the moment we'd returned to the cabin, that I realized I'd called it home in my head when we arrived in the clearing.

And that made my enforced isolation so much worse.

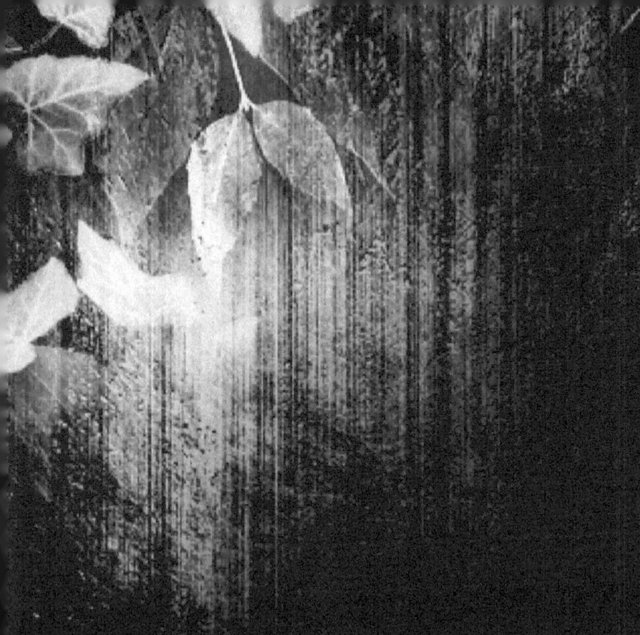

Robe

13

ROBE

THE FOREST SETTLED ONCE MARI LEFT THE LIVING area, and every man in the house breathed his relief. Except for Jon.

He glared at me, accepting the plate Alan thrust into his hands. I spent that night dozing in a recliner by the door, hyperaware of every single body in the house and subconsciously listening for any unusual sound outside. I hadn't been able to settle since the Blackthorne incident, blood thrumming in my veins as I worked through every inch of potential, both negative and positive.

There weren't as many of the latter, but we needed to do this.

I had always been sleepless the night before a mission, going over it in my head dozens of times to pick out the weaknesses in my plans.

"Not well done. Not after... the other afternoon."

I hadn't been backward in telling Jon exactly what our resident barkeep got up to in his spare time with our guest.

His tone bothered me, but we had work to do. "It went well?"

"It went well—until we walked inside." His teeth ground together. "It went fine."

"Fine? The fuck does that mean?"

"She asked questions."

"Which ones did you answer?" Alan asked over his shoulder as he grabbed another plate and headed for my bedroom.

"All of them," Jon groused, throwing a baleful look my way.

Alan hesitated midfootfall but then kept walking without another word.

"Don't get all pouty. You wanted to spend time with her," I reminded him, dragging my ass to the kitchen to serve up the rest of the plates.

Pulling a handful of greenery from his pocket that sure as shit didn't come from the forest, Jon deposited it onto the bar and started eating where he stood. "And it worked. Though I made her cry."

"Asshole."

"We were talking about you."

I smiled, though no part of that struck me as funny. "Of course you did. We need to plan. Alan?" I asked as he entered the room.

"Unhappy, almost in tears, and force-fed until she ate on her own. And locked in, on your orders. As usual, I've followed your command to the letter, oh Great One. This doesn't need to continue." He sent me a baleful glare full of blame and betrayal.

"At least we won't be interrupted."

"Fuck, you're an asshole," Alan cussed, swiping his plate from the bench and retreating behind the bar.

I ignored him, letting him continue his rant beneath his breath. "Miller found tracks on the northwest boundary after

I spoke to our... sweet neighbor. Three men, combat-style boots with medium depressions."

"Could be a hiker," Alan said through a mouthful of stew.

"Group of," Will corrected from the balcony. "I don't think so. They walked in a straight line, and some of the impressions crossed over, but not all. Like they were—"

"Hiding their numbers. So Gideon did a recce after you kicked his ass verbally. What's new?" Alan's mouth twisted. "Fuck. I'm usually better at reading Gideon's bullshit."

Jon glanced across at me and held my gaze. "We're getting distracted. She wants to go home."

I ground my teeth. "Will, Miller. Up for a nighttime incursion?"

Both boys nodded without speaking.

"Robe—" Jon cleared his throat.

"And I need a little intel from town, Alan."

"You got it," the bartender said.

I waited another minute for their objections, but Jon didn't interrupt me a second time, burrowing his attention into his food. "Good. Tomorrow, Will can take Mari into the forest. South side, well away from the house. It's important she's kept safe and out of this," I added in a gentler tone.

Will nodded, his hands flexing around his plate. "What do you want me to do with her?"

"Don't make her cry, for a start," I snapped, then closed my eyes. "I'm sorry."

"This is bullshit." Jon scraped his plate clean in record time and stalked out the door.

"Jon—" Alan began.

I held up a hand. "Let him go." Besides, that fuckup was mine to fix.

"I'll figure something out," Will mumbled.

"Good." I swallowed my pride. "He's moving, and I don't

want to miss an opportunity to make sure that move isn't aimed in our direction."

"It's not like there's anyone else up here much." Alan rested his forearms on the bar, his bright blue eyes fixed on me.

"Finish eating. You're heading out tonight. I need to know what's happening in New York." My chest ached at the thought of sending my boys out when I couldn't enter the city without earning myself prime real estate on death row.

"I'm out." Alan pushed the rest of his plate away. His apron floated to the bar top as he grabbed a prepacked back-pack from beneath the bench and shot out the door.

"See you in a few days."

"Check in whenever you can." I might not like how tonight turned out, but of all my boys, Alan was the one I most trusted to be able to make the choice between emotions and duty.

He winked and flipped me the bird.

He'd be gone as long as it took for the job to be done. That didn't put my mind at ease. It did mean I'd be in shit with the rest for sending him out alone when we all needed to focus on the enemy who'd stepped foot on the other side of our invisible barrier, even if by proxy. Not that I blamed him.

Miller had erased a handful of his men while we were engaged in neighborly chitchat, after all.

"Get your asses onto Gideon's land. Have a scout around and report back. Nothing else. Hear me? We'll decide what to do when you come home."

"You got it." Miller threw his plate in the sink and jerked his head at Will. "Let's go."

In a matter of seconds, the mass exodus left the cabin empty except for me—and Mari.

Her presence in my room burned me as I washed every

plate, stacking each into a neat pile and tidying the room. Once every surface gleamed spotlessly, I folded my arms and glared at the door. I'd given her enough time to eat and shower. She'd likely be asleep on the other side.

I clenched my teeth, calling myself a coward a hundred times over before I pushed through my frozen state and marched to the door.

I flicked the lock open as I knocked. "Mari?"

They were right—all of them. I'd been an utter asshole. To her and everyone under my roof, though group apologies weren't my thing. I could have explained the situation, but some part of me wanted to keep her from the darker side of our lives in the event that she ran and never came back.

Not that I blamed her, but I also didn't want to be the reason she threw herself headlong into danger when my safety net didn't include places where I couldn't see her.

Keep lying to yourself.

I got no response. No *Go fuck yourself, Robe*. No *Leave me alone*. No sobbing.

Just silence.

Her sassing me usually offered relief, but that didn't come either. If I'd broken her....

"Mari?" I pushed the door open and found her on the other side, the doorway an invisible barrier between us.

"Why make me stay if you won't let me in?" Her thin whisper broke at the end, scoring my heart.

"It's not safe. Anywhere. Here. You're not safe." My throat constricted, but I forced the words out anyway. "And I want to keep you."

Mari waited, her brow lowered as she peered at me through her lashes. "Is there another word to go with that sentence? Like an apology?"

Breath expelled from my lips in a laugh I covered as a cough. *What are you, thirteen?* "No."

"Mmm." She sighed. "I'm sick of crying, and I'm sick of being afraid. I thought...."

I waited, but she didn't finish her thoughts. "Will is your guide tomorrow. He's nice, so don't scare him." That earned me a sweet smile I memorized for later. "He'll protect you. As for the others... I've been trying to teach you ways to fight your fear."

"Is that what this is?" Lifting her head, she stared me full in the face, daring me to lie to her.

My throat dried on the truth I hid from myself. "Yeah."

"Okay. Good night, Robe." She reached across the threshold.

I grabbed her wrist, clinging to her. Knowing I shouldn't, unable to step forward or bring her to me. "I know I'm an asshole. Everything I do... I do it because I'm trying to keep you safe."

Mari stood stock-still for a long moment and then twisted her wrist in my grip. I opened my fingers, letting her pull away from me.

"I know," she replied, retreating into the darkness.

She crawled into my bed, and though my heart ached at the thought of not taking her into my arms for one more night, I stayed on my side of the doorway. When she settled, I drew the door shut but didn't flick the lock I had Will install despite his soft protests.

By the time the boys returned with their whispered reports, sans Alan, I had formed the plan I wanted us to follow the next day. Gideon's additional crossover bothered me at a deeper level than usual, and it had everything to do with the bundle of heartbreak burrowed in my bed.

While every man slept, I resumed my station by the door and waited for the sun to rise.

EVERY FOOTSTEP ECHOED LOUDER THAN THE LAST. I swore under my breath and tapped my throat mic out of habit. "Work in silence." I waited until the sounds of movement faded before stepping forward, my gun raised.

Gideon's compound was deserted.

My nose twitched every time the house settled or the mountain breathed, but after a full circuit of the place, checking room by room, I made it into his office undetected. I analyzed each vacant corner of the opulent room, though it became clear we were either very much in favor with luck herself or we'd missed one hellishly important boat.

"Call it in."

"Clear."

"Clear here." I opened each drawer of the desk, sweeping my hand over the glossy wood, and swore again over the channel. "Everything's been removed. He's closed up house." *For now.*

And gone... where?

The obvious answer settled in my mind. Back to NYC. Which meant I sent Alan into a potential minefield.

My brain whirred as Miller met me at the office door, his gaze sweeping our surroundings in a constant movement, his weapon raised to shoot out a dead camera.

I tapped his shoulder, and he jerked at the contact. "System's down. Jon checked it out."

"Fine," he muttered, still glaring at the mangled tech as though it offered him a personal offense. "What else do we need?"

"One more thing." I pushed past Miller and headed to a mezzanine level I spotted on my way through the compound.

I kicked a door open that stood ajar, then stepped into the arched space and stared. The open area without a railing looked out over a stage of sorts. An altar stood at the center, a white stain in an evil room.

A fucking altar.

But no sanctuary or revered altar had ever looked like this.

Manacles hung from blackened chains drilled into the stone at several points. My stomach clenched as I envisioned Mari's sweet form stretched out there while they tortured her into the shade of the woman I protected.

Whether he played at summoning demons or truly believed in it, the man's psychotic madness stunned even me. There was a slight dark patch in the upper center of the alabaster stone near where a smaller person's chest would be if they were laid out upon it. Every doubt in my mind fled that this was where he'd tortured her, whether by his own hand or by others. It didn't matter. I'd still kill him for it.

Miller swore colorfully behind me, throwing out a few choice terms we learned in the desert. "Fucking psycho. Are we done?"

"Yeah." My breath stalled. "We're done."

I stared around the area, wanting to burn the damn thing to the ground, but I knew I couldn't touch Gideon at that level. Not while Mari resided with us.

Nothing like a good bonfire to draw the prey to the flame.

"Not unless you want to take a souvenir home," Jon said into my ear.

"Don't touch a thing." I held Miller's eye until he relented with a grumpy-ass nod. *And clean up the damn camera.* I added that last as a mental note for myself and a text to Alan. "We've got no reason to be here. See you at the house."

"Watch your ass." Jon's line closed.

"What the hell is he doing?" I seethed, resisting the urge to throw myself into the icy stream to wash off the residue of Gideon's ruin as we made our way back through the woods.

"Pissy you missed your chance to shoot the twat?" Miller shot me an amused look over his shoulder, though his eyes glowed with dark promise.

If I lit the place, he'd help me burn it back to bedrock. There were other ways, more personal, where I could hit the asshole hard.

I glared back. "You're picking up Mari's terms."

His back straightened. "Yeah?"

"Show-off." I snorted. "Get tabs on Alan if you can. Let him know...." What? That Gideon escaped us *again*, moved everything off the mountain, and relocated elsewhere?

At least Mari is safe.

I sent Will out with her early in the morning after making sure the younger man knew to keep her away from the house. And now... I didn't have a clue where the line for *safe* resided.

I ripped the phone out of Miller's hand and shot a message off to Will.

"You're welcome." Miller twisted to face me. "You're never this rattled. She's in your fucking head. You know that, and it's costing your judgment."

"Solid assessment." I forged onward, away from Gideon's lair, intent on getting back to the house and washing off the sin-filled filth that coated me head to toe.

How she lived in her own body after having been stretched out there.... Bile rose in my throat. I pushed the bitter acid back by sheer will, unwilling to provide additional evidence of our incursion. My arms itched to wrap around her, crush her to me as I promised all the things that weren't mine to give.

"He'll wait for you to make a mistake, and given the headspace you're in, he's going to find one."

"He already has."

Miller snarked on. "It'll cost you a life or more. Are you willing to risk that?"

I bared my teeth in a feral grimace he couldn't see. "What do you want me to do? Send her away?" I waited, knowing we'd hit an impasse. Miller would have my back to eternity, but if I fell apart on him.... He was right about the cost, and the failure poked an already bruised heart.

"No. But you need to pull your head out of your ass where she's concerned." He stopped talking as the house came into view. "We all do."

A-fucking-men to that, brother.

My pack heavier than I'd swear it'd been when we left this morning, I pushed the door open to an empty cabin and then unpacked, unable to settle until Jon appeared in the clearing. Miller's phone bleeped. I grabbed it, looking for a message from Will, but Alan had replied in code to an earlier message.

If I barged in on Will and Mari, I could lose her, and my pride refused to let that happen. Neither would anyone else in the house. I settled in to wait.

Patience wasn't my strongest suit today.

Mari

14

MARI

FRESH MOUNTAIN AIR AND SUNLIGHT MINGLED ABOVE the picnic blanket I sat on while Will regaled me with stories of Robe's officer life in the military at the end of my third month in the cabin, or outside it. Not that I was counting. Much. Not all of them represented the grumpy man the way he would have liked to have been portrayed, digging at his pride, but some part of me enjoyed hearing tales of his fallibility, what made him human.

Not the machine that pushed forward into some unspoken vengeance for the ruined lives of the men who loved him, however their crazy household worked. And that love became obvious as Will spoke, animated as his hands told the story for him.

"He threw the snake as far as he could, still shrieking a little. It landed right at Miller's feet. The dude shot it, never taking his eyes off Robe, this look of utter disgust on his face. Robe bought him a lot of near beer—the base was a dry station—and got over it." Will's infectious grin brought on my own.

"Are you supposed to be telling me stories like that?" I

nudged his shoulder, enjoying the easy warmth he offered. "Something about breaking the bro code."

"Very American of you, Brit. But... you're right. I'm probably not." His smile dimmed as his gaze flicked to the tree line. He blew out a breath and turned his attention back to me. "It's good to share the memory with someone who appreciates that Robe's got faults."

"Oh, he's got plenty of those, all right." I twisted a pine needle into segmented pieces, adding to the pile near my crossed ankles, and decided to risk it all. "He looked... stressed this morning."

"He's got one hell of a grudge match with that man."

"Who?" I frowned, searching his face, so full of youth and innocence.

Sandy-brown hair flopped over his eyes. Will pushed it back, pursing his lips as he stared into the water cascading into a steady stream. The river meandered its way along the mountainside and tipped off the edge farther along in a never-ending tumble, though some edges were still covered in the occasional rare smatter of snow. Fine spray kissed his skin, his gentle brown eyes better suited to a poet than a soldier.

Will's gaze lowered to mine, dark and filled with suppressed rage. Any thought of innocence cowered beneath the intensity there. He blinked, and the tormented eddies disappeared, replaced by the boyish man I'd thought I understood.

"No one." He caught my wrist and placed a trio of small white flowers into my palm, their fragile petals curled at the tips from being crushed in his hand.

It took me a moment to pick out what they were, my head still full of his switch from a sweet younger-brother type I trusted to a mini wrath-filled demon full of dark passions.

"Strawberries. Jon showed me wild ones. Dead ones at the end of winter," I corrected myself.

"These flowered early this season. Like they were waiting for you." Will grinned. "Alan mentioned something about making a hydroponics shed. That came from your head, huh? They're my favorite." He added a few of the ripe berries that probably came from the same store as the ones Jon gave me to my palm and closed my fingers over them. "Enjoy." He leaned back, bracing his hands behind his head, and fully stretched out on the blanket.

"What are you doing?" I poked his side.

"Sleeping." He yawned.

"Didn't you get enough last night?" I popped a strawberry into my mouth and sighed. "Yum."

"I got thirty minutes of shut-eye after Robe—" He cleared his throat and shut his mouth.

"After Robe what?" I poked him again.

Will caught my wrist and levered up, stealing my space. I shuffled back, but his other hand clamped at my waist, holding me in place.

"Don't ask what I can't tell you, Mari." His voice strained, he leaned forward, rubbing his nose against mine.

Warmth sank into my skin where he held me, his body arced over mine, gaze darkening. The boy disappeared in a blink, replaced with the sort of unyielding man who prickled my skin, and my breaths shortened.

"What can't you tell me?" I forced myself to stay still despite the tingles that raced over my arms, his mouth so close that if he tipped his head, he'd kiss me.

A deep rumble filled his throat. "Christ, you smell like strawberries." Releasing me, he pushed back and resumed his position on the blanket, staring unblinkingly at the clear, pale sky.

"I thought you liked strawberries?" I frowned, trying to put the complex man I'd mistakenly assumed was a simple soul back together in my head.

"I do. That's the problem." His hand shot out to squeeze my wrist in a quick, intimate gesture that left my heart thudding in my chest.

"Oh." My pulse fluttered beneath his too-fast touch. I tucked my fingers together, making a basket for the berries he'd given me.

His phone buzzed. He wrenched it out of his pocket, exhaling a sharp breath. "They're back. Let me sleep for thirty minutes, and then I'll take you back to Robe."

I nodded, though his eyes closed too fast to see it, and stared at the waterfall.

But what if I want to stay here with you?

The cascading water gave me no answers.

Within seconds Will snored beside me. I ate my strawberries, wishing I could curl up at his side, and told my confused, traitorous heart to shut it.

THE NEXT SEVERAL DAYS CONTINUED IN THE SAME pattern. Each morning I pushed myself out of Robe's bed and dressed, ignoring the remaining scars and shadows of bruises beneath my skin I still saw no matter how much they faded and the shame I saw every time I glanced in the mirror by accident. My household of sexy captors forced me to eat amazing food, drink good coffee and better tea, and plied me with alcohol under Robe and Jon's strict supervision.

Alan's absence left a void in the house. His lighthearted jokes, flirting with everything in sight... I missed him. We all did, but at least they knew where he'd gone.

I spent days out with Jon learning the forest, or Miller took me to train while Robe shot nearby or chopped wood. Fresh-cut pine would forever hit the top of my favorite scents list. I'd never thought of woodsmen as attractive before, but muscles and fresh sweat and pine needles did it for me.

Also soap.

The longer Alan stayed away, the further Robe retreated into himself. Nevertheless, his brooding presence skyrocketed, filling the cabin until I found myself tongue-tied when he looked my way, communicating through a rare touch or conversations behind closed doors where my invitation didn't extend.

Every night I fell asleep in his arms, his bulk the foil to my nightmares, though they had nothing on the hole in my heart that remained from the night he stayed away. How much I relied on him terrified and healed me all at once. When I woke, a scream lodged in my throat and phantom hands trailing over my body, he secured my flailing limbs with a gentle but firm hold, lulling me back to a land where the phantoms reached out but couldn't touch me unless they were his.

My hours dwindled in a timeless fashion. I learned more about Robe, Jon, and the two younger men through listening to their conversations. Maybe professional eavesdropping could be my new thing when I got to... wherever life took me. *After*. With no place in mind, I headed toward a gray destination yet to take form.

When that boredom suddenly changed, I wished I'd never whined about it at all.

At breakfast on the fourth morning after the boys had returned from their mission or whatever the hell they'd been up to, heavy footsteps resonated outside the house that were so different from the footfalls of our sole absentee, they drew every eye.

"Do you get visitors?" I whispered as Robe and Jon took up position on either side of the doorframe.

Miller withdrew a matte black handgun from beneath the bar and sighted the entry. "No."

"Fuck me." Robe glanced out the side window and whipped the door open in time to catch the bundle that collapsed inside.

Alan lay on the floor, panting in short, staccato breaths, covered in dark fluid. Dirt or something else crusted his temple, and his hair stuck out at all angles. Deep circles hung beneath his eyes, and his skin had paled into an unhealthy, sallow hue.

"Alan!" I grabbed a cloth off the bar and shot beneath Robe's arms. His quick intake behind me said I'd crossed a line, but I didn't care. "Jesus, where are you—never mind. What happened?" I dabbed at his face, trying to locate the source of the injury.

"It's not mine. Mari, stop." Alan caught my wrist and pressed it to his chest over his heart. "I'm not hurt, sweet-cakes. Just exhausted."

"This"—I waved my dirty cloth to encompass his entire body dripping fluids, some of which looked like blood—"qualifies as hurt."

"If you say so." He dropped his head back to the floor and fell silent while I fussed, though he never let go of my wrist, rubbing his thumb over my pulse point.

Despite his words, his heart pounded inside his chest under the cover of his clothes. My pulse matched his beats until they slowed.

Finally, he turned dulled eyes to Robe. "You were right. He was in the bar."

"What?" Robe startled behind me, resting a hand along my spine as he leaned forward. "Fuck. Will, get him water and electrolytes. Shower, then debrief?"

His hand tightened on my back, reminding me that I didn't warrant an invite to that meeting.

Will scooted inside the door, and I wondered where he'd been.

Instead of arguing, I returned to my assessment of the friend I refused to leave. Even if they didn't tell me everything, this ragtag group of lost boys was mine to care for and protect. Dark red flakes, crusted at the edges, peeled away in my hand. I swapped my dry cloth for the fresh damp one Will passed over as he tipped water into Alan's mouth.

My clean cloth turned bloody fast. I gripped it tight. "If you're not hurt, who does all this belong to?"

Alan held my gaze for a long moment, then closed his eyes.

"How many?" Robe asked softly.

"Three." He paused. "Four—it doesn't matter."

"Fuck," Robe swore. He caught me beneath my arms and lifted me up, though Alan still held my wrist.

"Put me down. I want to help." I wriggled in protest, but Robe, in his typical fashion, ignored me.

"And I need time, Mari. Will you give us that?"

"She should know." Alan squeezed my hand, winding his fingers through mine as he pushed himself off the floor. "She deserves to know. He's hurt us all." He held Robe's gaze and didn't back down.

My heart thundered as the two men fought a silent battle over my head.

"This is how I usually feel," Will stage-whispered behind his hand.

I giggled, though his light words didn't hide the concern that tightened his easy features.

"Shut up or you can wash my ass," Alan muttered, then threw up his hands. "Fine. Run it your way, Robe. But shutting her in there"—he pointed to the room we shared—"doesn't solve other problems."

"I'll work it out in my own time."

"Stubborn ass."

"Agreed." I caught the elbow Alan offered with a stiff smile and let him walk me to my door. "You know where to find me when I'm to be let out of my prison."

Alan gripped my hand tight, pulling me a little closer, and my eyes widened. "You're the reason I came back," he mumbled into my ear.

I sucked in a long breath, shocked beyond my brain's ability to function. Alan's grip tightened. He paused for a long, intimate moment, brushing his mouth over my skin in the barest kiss. My heart thumped as my vision swam, obscuring his exhausted form. His grip lessened, dropping away.

Alan sighed and headed for the larger bathroom down the short hall that housed the bedrooms. His shoulders bowed as though he carried the heartache of every man in the house.

Of everyone he bore responsibility for.

I shut the door without looking back and leaned against it. My body trembled as I opened my hand and stared at the tiny pink cocktail umbrella Alan had pressed into my palm. Its features were marred with scribble, and as I tentatively opened the frail pleated paper, the scrawl transformed into a word.

Gideon.

I CLUTCHED MY SECRET TIGHT TO MY CHEST AS I WENT through my now-familiar day-to-day motions, knowing I'd never tell Robe what I understood about his covert missions or the risk they all took. Small things like where Alan went, his leaving me gifts, and the trail of bodies in his wake. I secreted every fragment of conversation away, each one a partial puzzle piece revealing who my old boss had been to me that vied against what Robe's crew knew.

I was under no illusions that the other men weren't as brutal in their own way. The whole situation should have made me run for the proverbial hills, but I hid within their walls instead. Robe and Jon went about their days oblivious to the dark glances both Miller and Will shot my way, though each had his different reasons. Tension grew every time Will stood close to me, but other changes tweaked the dynamic of our odd group.

After Alan's return, the fragile trust I'd brokered with Miller dissipated as though it had never existed. He refused to speak to me again, though his glares were gifted to me on a regular basis. All training stopped. Robe provided emotional distance between us despite remaining physically close, his usual sentinel self without the comfort, leaving me once again an island in a sea of wary mountain men. Alan caught my eye more than once, watchful and knowing. His smirk told me I hid nothing, even if the rest of the household remained oblivious to my plan to stay sane.

Those days fast transformed into one lost week and then another, each running into the next until I couldn't remember which month we were in. Spring set in, and I woke one morning to a bird call I didn't recognize and bright green foliage that took over Robe's corner of the world. Even the air smelled warmer from where I sat at the small table in the kitchen by the window. Robe still tried to get me to talk about who hurt me, but the more he probed with targeted questions on details he shouldn't have known, the more certain I became that someone had searched me on the internet or whatever they used for communications out here—a log TV, for all I knew.

On rare occasions, I wondered if anyone had looked for me. The UK girls I never socialized with, the family I never called, who disapproved and wouldn't want me back anyway. All I did *before* was work long hours six days a week for Gideon and then sleep through the next day. Rinse, repeat.

Over and over again.

Like in a toxic relationship, he stripped away my hours until family and friends faded, leaving only him in my future. And now, I didn't have that either.

My island shrank by the day, shared by an intense style of brotherhood that irritated me, drove me nuts with their over-protective streaks, and gave me anxiety attacks when they didn't turn up after dark. But they weren't the only things that went bump outside the cabin.

Determined not to be afraid of him, I confronted my old boss's shade as often as I could, walking in the forest beside Robe, knowing he provided a safety net if I crumbled. The more I reflected on my prior life, the more I recognized my situational blindness, both then and now.

No visible office leapt out at me within the house, though a single locked door I'd tried too many times to count denied me entry. Not that I had many chances to try, given Miller's renewed mistrust. I began to understand the men I coexisted beside, adding tiny fragments of each of their personalities to my new, somewhat tarnished, armor.

Things I liked started to turn up on the nightstand beside Robe's bed. An e-book reader arrived filled with my TBR from home, then a mug of chicken soup. A hairbrush and products to tame my curls that I suspected came from Robe's sister were neatly packed away in the bathroom. Pain medication, contraception, and tampons neatly packaged in a basket containing glitter indicative of Alan's flair were a welcome relief and right on time as my stress-delayed monthly finally made an appearance.

Finally, a potted orchid arrived.

I nearly cried, running my fingers over the leaves and watering it stupid until Will crept in and took my plastic cup away with promises to bring it back when the plant recovered from my overzealous affection.

Each night, Robe slipped into my borrowed bed, clothed in whatever he wore that day, his huge frame wrapped around me as I slept. When the nightmares became too much for him to handle alone, Jon joined us. The first time, it had seemed odd, but my sleepy head accepted the peace offering. The two huge men sandwiched me between them, providing me with a barrier from my demons in a restricted space that somehow appealed to the new broken me. Their combined presence beat my night demons away, allowing me a dreamless, restful sleep.

Alan spoiled me with music and dancing during the day, while Jon helped my body heal with lotions and taught me gentle stretches. The bruises, long faded, were etched soul deep. Just because I couldn't see them any more didn't mean they weren't still a part of me. Invisible scars ran the length of my body, and aches hit me at random intervals on nights when I slept in Robe's too-large bed alone.

Those were the nights I suspected he wasn't in the house at all, though when I asked, he would lie to me and say he slept with someone else. It wasn't his eyes that gave him away but rather Miller's, the hard man's yellow gaze sliding away, his jaw ticking until he left the room in his typical style.

I didn't push, too scared that Robe might finally say my tenure in the cabin was up. What I wanted and the reality of being shoved out on my own clashed in my head, and so I remained silent—and scared—until he returned to me and I slept again.

Bless Will for his good cheer and enthusiasm, the kid with his own demons who wanted to help everyone. After the months I'd spent in the cabin, I'd ingrained myself into their lives, and they were mine.

Most of them, anyway.

Then came the crux. I didn't want to leave. I didn't want to face what and who resided in the darkness outside the invisible barrier of Robe's home. I couldn't walk through the door on my own or return to work. I didn't want to find out who hadn't looked for me, or their reason for not making me the focal point of a search party.

What I *did* want was for my picture to feature on the back of a milk carton like a loved child, something I never could claim to have been. That would never happen for one simple reason, no matter how my head told me to at least *pretend* to want to be found.

Gideon would never allow it.

Mari

15

MARI

Hair clung to my cheek where I'd drooled on myself overnight. For a hard man and a harder bed, the damn thing eased tired muscles with the type of luxury reserved for royalty. On the nights and mornings I woke alone, I wondered where Robe slept while I occupied his bedroom. If he'd shared another's bed.

When that happened, a huge part of me wished he'd crashed with me.

Shoving my hair back off my face, I stumbled to the bathroom and threw cold water on my flushed skin. I didn't need the change in temperature from outside to wake me up; the icy tank water did its job just fine. Throwing an extra layer on filled my need for comfort. Those thin layers of thermals were pretty much what I lived in now.

The cold mountain air differed from the bite of a British winter even as the spring climate drifted into being. There, a permeating cold reigned. Bitter and icy on wet days, chilly winter sun offered a facade of heat in clear weather. Here, the breeze kissed my skin with a fresh chill still, absent the numbing bolt of my initial traipse through the woods. Here, I could breathe.

Thinking about home didn't have the same sense of loss as before, as though my perception had shifted. Still, the ache of knowing that Mom and D—my family would never take me back remained. I couldn't process that and buried the thought deep to avoid having to deal with it yet again.

Avoid, avoid, avoid.

I might as well wrap my previous life in police tape and lock it away. And I couldn't go back. Nope. No way was I doing this right now.

Forcing my thoughts forward, I padded across the hard floorboards to the bedroom door. A gurgle from my empty stomach offered the perfect distraction, and I *nearly* smiled. My head full of the expectation of coffee and toast, two things that differed from the UK that couldn't be simpler, the bitter bite of British coffee and crisp toast that tasted different there. Those were the things that I missed so much, I didn't pay attention to anything but a drive to get to that steaming mug.

Alan provided me with my preferred forms of nourishment every morning. Though I'd only been about for a short period, I knew that when I left Robe's odd band of men and his handcrafted mountain home, I would miss this place.

Even grumpy old Miller. Well, not so old, maybe. He seemed about Robe's and Jon's age, midthirties, perhaps a few years younger. And no part of him *looked* old; I'd seen him train, and on one memorable occasion, I passed the boys' bathroom in the hall when the door stood ajar. Stocky, barrel-chested, inked—call him what you would, but the beefed-up man possessed more muscle than any regular person should, including Robe and Jon.

Miller might hate me, but I knew he was right where he needed to be—at Robe's side.

Gripping the cold doorhandle, I shook my head at the romanticized notion. Coffee wafted beneath my nostrils, and I took a heady inhale that stopped me from pulling the door open any farther.

A good thing, as someone I didn't know stood in the middle of the room.

My eyes snapped open, and I froze. Peering through the tiny gap showed me nothing more, but it let me hear everything. A voice I didn't know filtered through to me, giving me pause. I listened for Robe's deeper tones, straining my ears and clutching the door tight.

"Are you sure it's all right to use your land, then? It's only a deforestation protest. I know you're not keen on losing your trees off the ridgeline, to keep your privacy and all. Hoped you'd support us. I can keep my group on the other side of the road if you need."

"It's fine. The land ends at the dirt road. You won't offend anybody. Plus, if you don't protest, who will?" That came from Jon.

"Those *neighbors* need to pull their heads out and take care of the world around them." That deep growl resonated beneath everyone else's voice.

I bit my lip, smiling anyway. *Good to know it's not just me he gets his grump on at.* I got the impression Robe would be angry at anything at this point, though not as much as Miller, perhaps.

"And there's the other matter of—"

"I don't think we need to work that over again," Robe threw out.

I rested against the cool wood of the door as he attempted his favorite form of distraction: misdirection.

Grumpy ass number two spoke up. "A mil bounty is nothing to be laughed at."

I searched the room and found Miller leaning against one corner, his arms folded over his chest as he glared at Robe or maybe the room in general.

Fail on that front, Robe.

Then the implications hit. *Bounty? As in bounty* hunters? *A mil... fuck, a million dollars?* My mind was jarred, unable to process anything else. I let my gaze wander around the sliver of the room I could see.

Robe shifted just enough to give me his side profile. One hand rose to stroke his beard in that unconscious way of his. A blue-and-black checked shirt covered his broad shoulders, and though I just pulled my sorry rear end out of bed, he looked like he'd been up for hours.

Or maybe he never went to sleep.

I still hadn't figured out where Robe slept each night that I occupied his bed alone—or with whom.

The man in question smiled—*smiled*—at the number Miller threw out there. "That's nowhere near enough to play with the big boys. He'll have to double it or more."

"You want them pawing at our door?" Miller snarled, rapping one fist on the wood at his back.

Robe turned away from me and stared at the stocky ex-soldier. Though his larger frame obscured my view, his straight spine suggested neither man had backed down. From the little I'd learned about them, I suspected this fight might end up being one they took to the literal death.

The other half of what Robe said registered. That small smile, the banter at a death sentence hanging over his head—he *enjoyed* this. Being the hunted, the outlaw. Like kids playing cops and robbers, but this time it read back to front. He was the good guy, and the others.... Well, whoever hunted him had to be the opposite.

Right?

Robe turned back to the other man in the room. A flash of bright royal blue obscured my vision for a brief moment before Robe came back into view again.

"Appreciate you coming all the way up to ask permission, Brandon. You're always welcome to do a little light protesting on my behalf and for others on the mountain. I understand the water has to flow through the properties and not be cut off or redirected from above. Keep your people inside my boundary lines and the violence to a minimum, please. I've got enough issues with—"

The rest of Robe's sentence cut off as the door shoved inward from the other side. I stumbled back, too absorbed in the conversation that wasn't mine to start with to react properly. The unexpected movement pulled me off-balance. A roughened hand shot through the opening and yanked me forward. I swore like Alan as I tripped over myself on my way into the short alcove that separated the living area and Robe's part of the house.

Heads turned in my direction, but I barely saw them, lost in the pair of narrowed eyes crowned with yellow spikes around the iris that were set in Miller's hard and unwelcoming face.

I opened my mouth—to protest, shriek, whatever—but he stepped inside Robe's room and shut the door behind him with a definitive click.

"How many doors have you listened at since you arrived?" he spat, clearly validating his suspicions.

A futile glance over his shoulder confirmed that the solid oak door stood between me and the relative freedom of Robe's and Jon's lesser interrogation at my surprise appearance. Being locked in a room with a man who'd appeared to hate me on sight would never top my to-do list.

"I got up to get coffee. You were all talking. I stayed back. That's all." I shrugged.

His lip rose in a cruel, knowing smile. "You think I don't know who you are or why you're here?" He took a menacing step toward me.

I couldn't focus on anything other than the slim gap between him and the door.

Instinct took over before I could think it through. I dashed around him, turning in circles on feet that knew his best moves as intimately as he knew mine. But that didn't stop me from escaping the dangerous man who stood between me and the relative freedom available. *Something* worked in my favor. I shoved at the door—which stuck in its frame right at the wrong time.

Miller shouted his displeasure at being outmaneuvered. He grabbed my wrist, twisting me into a Mari-shaped pretzel. I managed to use my momentum to pull us both against the frame. He managed a death grip on the door handle, yanking on it to imprison me against the solid wood. Paired with a dose of Miller-sized determination, our combined weight proved too much for the minor inconvenience of a jammed door.

We busted through together, presenting a knot of stumbling limbs and snarled words before the rest of the household that congregated in the living area beyond, along with the newcomer.

Miller let me go, and I stumbled on alone.

It didn't matter if he followed me now; every head not already aware of my intrusion turned in my direction. The unknown man faced me, his mouth dropping open. Behind him, Robe's usual scowl deepened. Forest-green eyes flared with deep-seated rage—directed at me.

"Get her out of here." His tone brooked no argument.

A calloused hand gripped my arm, yanking me backward. Ignoring Miller's insistent tugging, I held Robe's stare, begging silently for his permission to stay. Dipping my head, I tried to offer no resistance other than to the hand dragging me away from him.

I'm not a threat to your life.

A healthy dose of fear slipped in there as well. I didn't want to be left alone with Miller; the ex-soldier looked like he might attempt to beat some sort of truth out of me that I could never give him.

"It's fine. I'll go." The new man, Brandon, looked up at Robe, gratitude etched across his weathered face.

Robe nodded, answering the stranger though his attention remained fixed on me. "Never a problem." He escorted the blue-clad man out the door.

Miller towed me backward, away from the company of the men and the freedom I sought. I flashed my gaze about the room, projecting that silent plea Robe refused to honor. Will wouldn't look at me, and Jon's attention remained on the new man and Robe's back.

I glanced sideways at the bar, but Alan's usual spot stood empty.

Alan said he'd always be there when I needed a rescue. *Like right now.* No amount of fighting or screaming would change Robe's mind. I *needed* an intervention, and he could have helped me.

Robe's absence when I needed him hurt deeply because I put my trust in him. All of it.

My shoulders sagged, and I let Miller pull me away, offering no more resistance. He bared his teeth at me over his shoulder, triumph glittering in his yellow-shot predatory gaze.

"If I can't get the girl to come to the coffee, I'll bring the coffee to the girl." Alan appeared at my side, holding a full pot of coffee and three pristine China cups stacked on top of one another. He wiggled a cheeky eyebrow, then raised his gaze to look over my head. "Chop-chop, Miller. Off we go."

"You could pass for a British spy with those sorts of talents," I muttered under my breath, waving at the plate-and-teacup stack he carried with flawless grace along with his endless supply of sass, my relief leaking through the facade I threw on without understanding why.

Alan had seen me at my barest moment. I didn't need to fake it with him.

Miller dropped my arm. Glancing at the man behind me, he strode back toward Robe's bedroom. His back ramrod straight, he paused at the threshold as if straining against some invisible force and then pushed through.

I ignored his temper tantrum and stared up at Alan.

Concern laced his azure eyes that vied for brightness against Miller's odd yellow-struck ones as he looked me over, his lips thinned, then handed me a teacup. "I'd take that as a compliment, Mari Merripen, but right now I prefer to stay an American spy."

He winked and slid past me as I stared at him, my mouth hanging open. Not that I should be surprised; I'd sort of gotten the idea of what Robe and his odd little adopted unit did, an understanding gleaned from their continued interrogation since the moment I fell out of my reality and into his forest.

Alan admitting it outright, even if he only spied for Robe... I doubted he joked about that sort of thing.

And that made Robe's ridgeline home less of a safe place when a haven full of mountain men and friends was what topped my needs right now. Because harboring a spy sure as hell didn't seem to be the safest thing to do—at least not in the circles I suspected we all traveled in.

With a bunch of criminals. In the middle of the woods.

Running from the man who'd stripped me of my entire world in a country I didn't yet call home, though it was fast feeling that way. I *wanted* Robe's mountain to feel that way.

Tears prickled the corners of my eyes as I stared at Alan's back. Squeezing my emotions back into their tight compartments, I slipped inside Robe's bedroom. A dark hole burned somewhere around my nape when I turned my back to close the door with a final sort of click. Even though the conversation seemed to have dissipated outside, the amount of attention on me intensified the moment the door shut.

I pivoted on my heel to face the two men who seemed to be either dead set on removing me from the house or keeping me in it. I didn't know if I should expect to be stabbed in the ribs or some other creative way of removing me from the house—and life in general.

A few weeks ago, I would have curled into a ball and let them do it. Now....

Though it shouldn't have been a surprise after the time I'd spent in the house, the scene before me looked nothing like what I expected. Miller perched cross-legged on the bed, the tension slipped from his frame as he lounged in Robe's space while Alan played tea party below him.

I slid to the hardwood floor, my back to the bed with its solid, comforting presence, and clutched the steaming cup Alan had given me. The dark ambrosia that had been the cause of my morning drama glided down my throat in a searing stream. I sighed my thanks, smiling with my eyes closed. Fingers brushed over the top of my head, smoothing the bird's nest there until all the strands were to his liking, petting me in a familiar way that soothed away my spiraling fears and unsettled emotions back to their place. The massage continued soft and gentle, and I leaned into his touch, wishing we were alone so I could cry.

I finished my coffee, sipping with my eyes closed until I'd drained the cup. Somewhere behind me, Miller's phone buzzed. I opened my eyes, tilting my head up in time to see him scooting back on the bed.

He scanned the message and jerked his head toward the door. "Let's go."

I stared as he stalked from the room, leaving the door open. It wasn't until he disappeared that I realized Alan hadn't moved from his place across from me.

Which meant he couldn't have played with my hair. The lithe dancer wasn't *that* fast or silent. Right?

Alan's knowing smile lit a small fire in my belly. "Tricky little bastard, isn't he?"

Still lost in the memory of Miller's hand in my hair, I clutched my elbows tight around myself. "I didn't think you guys used terms like *bastard* or *muppet* or *bloody wanker*," I commented, nudging my empty coffee cup with my bare toe.

Alan snorted. "We don't. I'm trying to be more British on your behalf. Make you feel at home." He watched me with that same secret knowledge brightening his blue eyes. "Is it working?" His take on my accent bordered on abominable— and was apparently exactly what I needed.

I laughed, helping him clean up our tea—*coffee?*—party. "Yup. Sure is." I didn't try an American accent to mirror his British showcase, knowing I'd be worse than offensive. "Guess I'm free to leave."

The open door that I'd wanted to run through earlier now seemed a hell of a distance away. I sat without moving.

"I promise I'll protect you from all the bears out there," Alan whispered in my ear. He grinned roguishly and took my hand in a firm grip. "If they're going to bite, I'll make sure they target my rump first." He popped a hip and sashayed to the door.

Sucking my lip between my teeth, I let him lead me from the room. His eyes tracked over my face, lingering on my mouth. Invisible fingertips worked their way along my spine in a silent caress that broke when Alan fixed his attention on the living area the moment we stepped into it.

"I'll hold you to that," I whispered.

Alan grinned, dropping my hand and disappearing behind the tall bar for a moment. Robe and Jon stood talking to Miller in soft voices near the door, each of them glancing at me at intervals. No one said a word about Will's absence that mirrored Alan's before.

"Robe—" I started, only to be shushed by an extended hand.

Even Alan shot me a quick look, shaking his head. "Wait for him, Mari."

"I really think I—"

"For fuck's sake. Shut her up." Miller turned to glare at me one more time, and my patience broke.

"He's right, you know. Your friend. A bounty on your head is a danger to everyone you—" I pursed my lips. I almost said *love*, but that precluded me and cast a wider geographical net than I intended. "To everyone here."

"You think so, do you?"' Robe's face was wiped clean of emotion as he gave me his full attention. "What else do you know about my life?"

Then Miller of all people backed me up. "Don't be stupid. She's right."

"I am?" I stared, mouth agape.

That's an attractive look.

I ignored the little voice in the back of my mind. Since when had *Miller* started backing me?

About the same time as he'd played with my hair. I remembered his tender caress, his furious glares. Unable to understand his motives, I wrapped my arms around myself in the only barrier I could create.

"You are." Miller smirked, enjoying my discomfort.

"Are you going to add to this little calamity?" Robe asked in a deceptively calm voice, its edge sharp enough to slice through the cloud of bullshit floating around.

"I'm siding with our little stalker-spy." Alan emerged from behind the bar, way too cheerful for the time of morning. He grabbed my hand, shoved a fresh mug into it that was half filled with ice and black coffee, and filled it to the brim with Macallan whiskey.

"You're going to turn me into an alcoholic." I clutched the mug, considering downing the lot in one. Robe's intensive scrutiny was bad enough, let alone that of the entire household.

"Chug it back." Alan winked. "It's been a long fucking night." He tipped the top-shelf liquor directly to his generous lips, slugging its contents.

Robe made an exasperated noise. "Don't let him outshine you, Mari. Bottoms up."

"How is this responsible?" I stared between them, each wearing identical shit-eating grins. "There's way too much testosterone in this room."

"Uh-huh. Show us what you got, running girl." Alan planted lean-muscled forearms on the bar top. "We're waiting."

His pose came close to distracting me, but for some reason —maybe the culmination of damaged egos in such a small space—their recklessness drove my own.

Narrowing my eyes at Alan, I saluted first him, then Robe. "Cheers."

The caffeine in my stomach met a deluge of alcohol at the wrong end of the clock. Refusing to let my gag reflex take me down, I kept swallowing until the empty mug clanged against my teeth.

I smiled, holding my glory for a full second before I started hacking. Whatever had filled my lungs—a mouthful of alcohol fumes and impending doom, most likely—seared my insides as I gasped for breath.

"Nicely done, lass." Alan assumed that horrible accent again, thumping my back in an unhelpful fashion. "Couldn't have done better myself."

"Uh-huh," I choked out. My eyes watered. "That was fun."

Robe snorted, though something about the way he looked at me changed, softening a little. "Good girl."

My tummy flopped, and that had nothing to do with its contents.

"So, about that bounty." Jon pushed off the wall. Robe's distraction technique sucked if others resisted too. "Are you going to take this seriously, or are you going to self-implode?"

"And do we have to watch?" Miller snapped.

"You mean do we *get* to watch?" Alan shot back, wiggling his eyebrows. "There's good sport in that."

Miller shot an irritated glare in my direction, or maybe he'd aimed that one at Alan. He spat on the floor, and the only thing that broke through the echoes of his footfalls as he stormed outside was Alan's groan.

"You know I have to clean that up, you heathen." He glared at the glob of spittle on the floor as at a personal affront. "Muppet," he added under his breath.

"Your British is very convincing." I beamed at him and swayed on my feet.

"Whoa, sweetcheeks." Alan gripped my elbow.

I turned toward Robe. "I'm sorry for listening at the door."

His easy demeanor hardened. "Are you?"

"Damnit, Mari." Alan sighed and dropped my arm.

Robe's mouth thinned behind his beard, the motion somehow adding to the flint-hard stare he offered. "Listening at doors, downing grog like a pro, turning up where you shouldn't be. Is Miller right? Are you some sort of mini super-spy?" he mused.

"Hey. That was my idea," Alan protested from the floor, scrubbing as he stretched each leg out.

Robe kept walking into my space until I had two choices: let him run over me or retreat. Choosing life, I backed up in a stumbling quickstep, in no way aided by the amount of caffeine and alcohol mixed in my stomach.

"I'm not a spy. I'm not here to hurt you. I—what do you need from me?" I cried, flinging my arms wide and forgetting I was still clutching my mug. It shot from between numbed fingers and shattered into a thousand pieces beside the bar.

Alan groaned again, swearing beneath his breath.

Robe never stopped walking. He closed the distance between us until his chest brushed mine, leaving us at nose-to-nipple level on my side. The edge of the bar dug into my spine until I arched backward in an attempt not to suffocate against his heavy chest.

"I mean it. I am sorry for listening at the door." No lie there, after all. Not for the act of listening or what I heard. My apology meant that—

"Yet, you got caught." Robe's large hands rose, one slapping onto the bar top beside my ear, the other cupping the back of my head, cushioning it against the bite of wood behind me.

He lowered his head until his lips almost brushed mine.

Warmth draped around us in a heavy, soothing presence. His eyes said he found something humorous about the whole situation, but he didn't give any other glimpse of that part of him, reserving that peek just for me, a secret between us.

"You asked me what I want, but I don't know what *you* want, Mari Merripen." My name slid off his lips like a weapon, and he savored its edge. "Should I tell you all my secrets, give the lives of every man here into your shaking hands? You have no idea how dangerous you are. So fucking dangerous."

Someone grunted an objection. Miller, or maybe Jon.

I ignored them all. "I'm not a threat to you."

Robe's smile widened, his breath brushing my lips. "If I tell you everything, you can never leave. Whatever you choose, Mari, choose wisely. I can't let you go if you opt to know us all so... intimately." His eyes fell shut as though he was contemplating that thought, turning it over inside his active mind.

A mind that I knew never stopped churning.

Robe Huntingdon could call me whatever he liked, but he and the men of Recurve Ridge were lethal, each in their own way. Jon and his passion, Robe and his fire. Alan could be cold and machinelike, while Will's cheeky grin hid a damaged young man who craved the company of his ilk.

Miller....

I didn't know what to think about Miller, except perhaps that he had the most heart of all, ruined and broken though it was.

Alan's words chose that moment to ricochet around my mind in a series of dizzying echoes while I stared at Robe.

"You're just like us."

I licked my lips. "But you won't let me leave. I tried. The answer is always no. Not now. Something else to distract me. I *know* you're stopping me from leaving, Robe. A cage is still a cage, even when the bars are made of wood and whiskey."

As I spoke, his forest-green eyes flicked open. "Miller doesn't want you here. He believes that letting you go back to where you came from is best. Do you know why he believes that, Mari? Because he knows that without our—without *my* —protection, you'll be dead inside a week." He laughed, a soulless sound. "Hell, you wouldn't last three days. Your boss"—he spat the words, and I knew he understood every detail of what had happened to me—"would rip you apart. And he. Will. Enjoy. Ruining. You." His chest heaved as he punctuated each word with a squeeze to the back of my neck. "Is that what you want? A few days of freedom to prove your point, that you can?" His teeth slammed together as he dropped his hand and backed up a step.

"You're so much more beautiful when you're ruined."

A shudder threatened at the base of my spine, but I refused to give my fear the prime real estate it sought. "Thank you for that lovely threat, Robe. It makes a girl feel safe at night." My cool embraced me for a critical second, doing me proud.

"Mari—"

I shook my head, cutting off his protest. The whiskey buzzed through my system in a swell of numbness. I sent Alan a mental thank-you note for the effort. Planting my feet on the bare wooden planks so I didn't trip over my own toes or fall to the floor in my tipsy state thanks to the coffee-laced whiskey, I raised my chin in defiance.

"Keep your secrets, Robe."

No one stopped me as I walked back into the room I'd already managed to escape twice in one day and locked myself in.

Robe

16

ROBE

"He'll warm up to her sometime." Jon nudged my shoulder with his beefcake of an arm. Hell, the man made me look small.

"He blames her." I stared into the forest, but the green wall remained still.

From Alan's and Will's intel, I had nothing. Gideon's stronghold remained vacant.

"You know he will." Jon planted his feet.

"I don't think warming up to her is likely at this point," I murmured, "though there's a chance." A slim one.

"I fucking won't," Miller grumbled somewhere around the region of my ankles. He disappeared into the dim light and then reappeared, his chest heaving.

I leaned over the veranda railing to peer into the depths beyond. "What the fuck are you doing down there?"

"Burying bodies."

"Not under my fucking house." Not that I cared, but the smell of dead things got to me after a bit.

"You're in a right mood." Alan pressed a froufrou of a pink drink into my hand. "Taste test?" He fluttered his lashes.

Pastel pink glitter floated from his lashes onto the back of my hand. "Please?"

"Are you going to serve this to Mari?" I peered with no little dose of suspicion into the glittery depths, where tiny pearls danced in the bottom of the slanted glass.

"Thought it might sweeten Miller up."

I snorted. "Good fucking luck with that." Wrinkling my nose, I tossed the cotton-candy confection back. Sugar slapped the back of my throat. I prepared to gag on the rest when ginger and something green refreshed my palette. "That's... good?"

"Excellent. Thank you." Alan gave a swift bow, liberated my glass, and sashayed back to the bar.

My knees connected with the hardwood boards beneath my feet before I slumped. The ground came up at me fast. Both arms rose too slowly, and my nose crunched against the floorboards on impact.

"Six seconds. Might be your record. Good job," Jon congratulated the stripper.

"Mmm. Could have overdone it on the sweetness." Alan's voice came from far away as I tried not to hurl the drink up on my own boots.

"That better not be for Mari," I grated as I attempted to stand—and failed.

"Of course not." Alan had the grace to look offended. "I would never hurt my girl."

"She's mine." The words fell out of my mouth before I managed to raise my head all the way. Both knees solid beneath me, I tried to push up and couldn't. I blamed whatever Alan had drugged me with that I felt zero embarrassment at exposing my feelings for Mari in front of them. "Not yours."

"If you say so, sir." Alan winked. "Stand?"

Biting back a groan, I pushed upward a second time. My legs trembled like a dancer with hungry feet, but they held. "Satisfied?"

Alan grinned and slapped me.

My cheek burned. Not a soft blow, but the kid had a plan, and I wasn't privy to the intended outcome.

I stared. "Do you have a death wish?"

"Nope. Slap me back?"

"You do have a death wish." I raised a hand—or at least I tried to lift one. Nothing happened. My fingers twitched at my side, but for the time being, my limits included not lying face down on the deck. "This better wear off."

"I'm not wiping his ass," Miller yelled from beneath us.

"Noted." I took a swift catalog of body parts that appeared to be within my control. "What'd you use?"

"Vodka, triple sec, Cointreau, and ginger root. Oh, and mint. Quite yummy," Alan replied, ticking off his ingredient list on long fingers, then licked his lips. "That drink is for Mari."

"What else?" I ground my teeth together as feeling returned to my extremities. "Don't fuck me around or I'll slap you back, kid."

Alan grinned and raised his hand. A slim ring was wrapped around one finger, plain and dull. When he turned his hand, it revealed a small spike sporting a lethal-looking pinprick point on the back, covered with a tiny glob of resin. "Coastal taipan venom. Small amount. Useless if drunk, very effective when mixed with GHB that can be applied topically. Through the skin. Liquid X on speed during cocktail hour," he added at my blank look.

"Terrific. Who are we date-raping?" I asked.

"Oh, you know. A baddie here, a baddie there." Alan fluttered his hand, showing me his ringless fingers.

"Damn quick," Jon stage-whispered in my ear.

I nodded. I hadn't seen him remove the poison ring either. "No missions without a plan. My plan."

"Fine." Alan pursed his lips and drew an image out of his pocket of a tall man with dark hair sporting a face we all knew too well. "Here's a target I prepared earlier."

Beside me, Jon's breath picked up.

"No." I clenched my teeth to the grinding point, ignoring the ache blooming in my jaw.

"But—" Alan objected.

I raised my hand, glad to have full control of my body back. "I said no, Alan. We're not murdering, assaulting, or otherwise harming the mayor of New York City." I cast a sideways glance Jon's way. The big man stood rock still, his face pasty. I offered him a humorless smile. "No matter what sort of psychotic asshole George Petersen is."

"But, Robe—"

"I said *no*, Alan. It's too dangerous, and you jeopardize the lives we've built here, plus who knows how many others, by playing games when we can't be certain of the outcome." I tramped down the stairs, intent on hiding beneath the house to avoid the discussion under the cover of working out what the hell Miller had dug up that really did stink. "My answer is no."

"You're no fun," Alan called to my retreating back.

I didn't respond.

WORKING AGAIN FELT GOOD. MY SHOULDERS TOOK THE strain of moving earth beneath the house at a half crouch. I'd straightened early on and crowned myself on the damned underside of the cabin, and the faint throbbing in my head was enough to make sure I kept it ducked down.

"Dig there." Miller pointed out the low spots surrounding the footings. He followed me around like a nursemaid, hauling a sackcloth loaded with gravel to drop into the pits I dug to create a net of drainage aimed at preventing the entire place from rotting prematurely.

"Yes, sir."

"About damn time." Breath whooshed from him as he hurled what looked like half a ton of gravel into the purpose-built hole. "Offer respect more often, little apprentice."

I grimaced and attempted to straighten my back. "I thought respect was a thing you showed for your elder."

"Nah, you're turning into a cripple, old man." Miller returned to the heap of gravel that seemed to grow on its own beneath my house.

I straightened and banged my head on a length of timber I laid beneath the house to give it structure when I built the thing. A hiss slid between my teeth as I rubbed the offended patch beneath my hair, grateful for the distraction the bite of pain offered. Miller was right, even if he didn't recognize it. I'd hit grumpy old man before I'd even made it to forty.

While I didn't have the option of a future, he did. Miller knew he held all the cards—his main one being the option to throw me under the bus to get himself a short stint in military holdings and eventual freedom, though so far he'd refused to use it.

Same with Alan and Jon. I didn't want to be responsible for removing what little chance they had left for some semblance of a normal life they could garner outside my literal patch of the woods. Every time I tried to kick one of them out, the assholes kept on coming back.

Grumbling under my breath, I scooted out from beneath

the house, taking perverse joy in the simple action of straightening my spine. Something cracked and creaked, and I was pretty sure the sounds came from me.

"You're falling apart." Mari startled me out of my reverie.

"Starting to," I grunted, pounding at a muscle that chose that moment to knot my shoulder into the semblance of a pretzel I couldn't undo.

"Mmm."

I opened my eyes and stared down at her.

She stared right back. Something akin to defiance flickered in her gaze.

Lowering my hand from my shoulder, I took a step closer, then another until I crowded her space in the middle of the clearing, much like I had the first time I met her.

She didn't flinch or shove me back. Mari's conflict-avoidance strategy seemed out of character enough for me to give her a little push.

"Talk."

"About?"

My gaze narrowed. I dropped my hands to her waist and gave myself a single, opulent moment to sear the impression of her violent curves that hollowed between hip and rib in a slope I could fit my hands around before pulling her body hard against mine. The soft swells of her breasts contacted my chest. My heart raced in tandem with hers.

She sucked in rapid, shallow breaths, her thick lashes flared wide. Still, she didn't pull away. All those nights sleeping with her tucked to my chest must have twigged something inside that busy brain of hers.

"Don't you brat out on me, girl."

"Who said anything about bratting out?" She smiled, a coy little thing that curved her soft lips into a wanton smile.

A smile that went straight to my cock. Flipping her

around and fucking her against the nearest tree might be wrong, but it didn't make the fantasy any less appealing.

"Don't test me, Mari," I growled into her face, tightening my hands on her hips, waiting for her to freak out and back away from me.

She did neither.

The single reaction that's held true about you, pretty girl.

She never ran from me or flinched in true fear, and I loved that about her.

She pushed up on her toes, her slim arms curled around my neck, putting that luscious-as-fuck mouth inches from my own. "What's there to test?"

Visions of Alan ravaging her mouth, his hand sunk deep between the vee of her legs, colored my vision red. A feral growl broke in my chest. I held her gaze, then dropped mine to her lips. My own tingled in response as I dipped my head.

The hell are you doing? She's been abused, asshole.

She'd also been living in my house for the better part of four months, during which my entire household fell head over heels and giddy as fuck for her.

Though Alan had proved me wrong for all the right reasons, I still couldn't bring myself to tear through that barrier for fear of hurting her. Their dynamic was special, and Mari and I... we didn't share that connection. I suspected that every man in the house had similarly taken the opportunity to test their strength of will during the hours I gave her to them for training.

I sucked in a short, fortifying breath and moved her backward, untangling her arms from my neck with a methodical efficiency designed to retain my sanity and preserve her honor at the same time.

"Go inside, Mari. Stay safe."

"From whom?" Her liquid eyes shimmered. She wound

her arms around herself, highlighting how thin she'd become despite Jon gently pushing her to eat like a mother hen. Her bones still protruded at sharp angles from beneath the pale pink knitted thing Alan had acquired for her.

From the monsters who roam the woods. From me.

I raked a hand through my hair, spinning on my heel. The lure she dangled was a hell of a lot easier to ignore if I couldn't see her, though the fresh scent of lilies lingered where she'd wrapped her body around mine.

Long after she left me to torture myself with a fantasy I should have made a reality, I realized she hadn't asked which monsters I wanted to protect her from.

She asked *who.*

Mari

17

MARI

Once again, I found myself listening at doors.

Robe's voice cracked through a tense room, his mood penetrating beyond the thick oak door I hid behind. Last time, Miller had caught me doing exactly the same thing. Perhaps I should have learned from that mistake. The quote about the insanity of doing the same thing over again and expecting different results came to mind.

Yet here I stood, hunched over, hands pressed to the cool wooden panel, eyes glued to the thin gap that let me see into the room's interior while five men stood in an irregular crescent, talking about things they thought I shouldn't know.

Their lives. My future.

Not knowing what they did bloody well pissed me off more than anything else. Yes, I brought my natural Brit right to the forefront of this steep hill I would inevitably die on.

No, I'd learned nothing from last time.

After I'd been caught eavesdropping before, I made it as far as Robe's bed, where I'd lain on my back for a precise ten seconds before I dashed to the en suite and puked up the horrendous mix of alcohol and coffee Alan had stuffed into my all-too-willing body. I doubted the oak door had prevented any sound from traveling through, though my whiskey-soaked pride couldn't be bothered to be offended at the time. I couldn't hold my drink like in my early twenties anymore.

A situation I needed to remedy in order to keep up with these boys and their testosterone battles.

Keeping the longevity of my kidneys in mind, or maybe not so much, I pressed closer to the door, the heavy barrier muffling their conversation and obstructing my view while I attempted to not-so-subtly eavesdrop. Robe had caught me listening at doors once already and threatened my safety with him. I couldn't imagine how he would react to a second offense.

I peered through the slit illuminated by the windows on either side of the open doorway. The *always* open doorway. I swore that door never closed. Why leave it open when Robe and Miller seemed so concerned about insurgents, or what-ever nasties that went hump and bump in the night that scared this family of giant, tough guys?

And I knew they were scared. Their straight backs and tense jaws said as much when they looked outside that door and were all the more so when one of them was traveling.

When they thought I forgot to look for the person missing from our midst.

So why not get locks and close the damn things? And this one too. Which would put an abrupt end to my current habit.

I fixed my attention on each man in the room who I could see or sense. Jon with his deep voice and tempered passion appeared to be hiding near the window outside my range of view. Alan stood at the bar as per usual, fidgeting with every-thing and nothing in an attempt to keep his hands busy instead of fluttering over everything.

Will munched on toast at the small table. He alone

appeared calm, though his eyes darted side to side in a continual dance between bodies, as if gauging their intentions. As far as I knew, Will was the least threatening of all Robe's odd little patched-together family unit.

Opposite the entrance door, Miller folded his arms, mashing giant muscles against his barrel chest, and Robe surveyed the group, turning in circles and exuding authority while seeming like nothing more than a charismatic entertainer pitching his wares.

I stopped listening.

A few scant months ago, I'd stood in a similar position, watching the boys before me work and debate over life and deadly matters with little obstruction except for me, from whom they maintained a safe distance. Safe being a relative term relating to both physical and emotional fronts.

The difference was that now *I* could read *them*.

How far we have come.

Alan talked over Robe for a moment, but in the cacophony of voices, I missed what they were arguing over. The dissent in Robe's volume and the way Alan leaned across the bar top, one hand extended, made their positions clear. Dark eyes were raised to meet clear ocean blue, a show of disobedience and a challenge to authority.

Their clash, laced with passion on both sides, flushed me with heat. I didn't need to hear what they were saying to deduce what they *weren't*.

Ever since that day in Robe's bathroom with Alan, things had... changed. Robe's sense of security remained, but he reined in any physical response whenever I pushed him or bratted out, especially when he called me out on it.

And apart from a few occasions in desperate need, Alan barely touched me. Even his flirting took a back seat. The status quo hadn't been reset; it *reversed*.

I shook my head, pushing the thoughts aside as too complicated to untangle.

"Do you want to stay, Mari Merripen? Because if you do, I cannot allow you to leave."

Robe's seductive words rolled around inside my head, bouncing off emotions I'd thought were long dead. But the temptation—the *tease*—remained. Since I'd lived in his household for my short version of eternity, then surely I'd earned the right to know what sort of man—what sort of *men* —I shared a living space with.

That's how I chose to justify my actions, in any case. The Brit inside me roared her approval. *For king and country*—but of course, I had no homeland. Just me and Robe and his men —all of them.

His words whispered against my ears again. I swiped the fantasy away. He wasn't even *here*, for heaven's sake.

Forcing my focus forward instead of inward, I concen-trated on what the boys talked about, glancing around to ensure they were all still in the same positions I'd noted before.

Jon's easier tone interrupted my little stalker session.

"... packing, but nothing in any of the accounts has changed."

"Which means he has a different channel I can't fucking well see." Frustration laced Alan's voice, the deep sort that rarely entered our interactions when he spoke to me.

"He's gotten wise to us, then." Jon echoed Alan's irritation.

"We counted on that." Robe's smooth voice coiled through me like good Italian coffee. He rubbed a hand over his beard, his thinking gesture. I'd previously suspected the action hid his expression; now I wondered if the damn thing just itched. "So we find another way into the accounts."

Accounts? Who the hell were they stealing from? They weren't talking about themselves. Robe didn't look like he had more than two ancient coins to rub together, though his demeanor said otherwise. He talked of a business in New York City, but without any form of contact, how did he run it? Robe didn't seem the sort to willingly hand over a large business, and I doubted he owned a failing one. My brain whizzed into action in the way Gideon had trained it to when he hired me as his PA two years ago.

"Maybe everything is in a safe somewhere. At the compound in New York."

"Could be worth a look. Are you up to it?"

"I'll handle it." That gruff voice belonged to Miller, though I could no longer see him or Will. It couldn't be anyone else. None of the others apart from Alan were supposed to leave the house. "I'll drive into the city if need be."

"No," Robe snapped. "No one is going to Petersen's filthy little playpen."

"I might be able to—" Alan started.

"I said *no*," Robe roared.

Even if I hadn't been eavesdropping, I would have heard that one.

A gasp flew from my lips as my disjointed mind tried to place all of them within the room by their voices. Robe to one side opposite Alan, in their usual clash of bartender wisdom and traumatized millionaire, or billionaire, or whatever the hell Robe was. He might have the bearing of a soldier, but his deportment, even in his chosen rustic setting, spoke of excessive wealth.

I froze, though no one seemed to pick up on my audible mistake at Robe's outburst. Conversation resumed at a lower, placating level while Robe seethed. I took a step back, still waiting for Will's dulcet tones to soothe Robe's mini tantrum.

As soon as the thought occurred to me, I knew Will wasn't in the room anymore.

A warm hand rested on the back of my neck, halting my unconscious retreat. A soft gust of breath brushed my cheek as I stood frozen for a different reason than before.

Run, run, run—

Or don't run.

The sly little whisper slipped across my mind like a lover's caress. Everest's bollocks, did I *want* him to catch me?

My heartbeat increased, reassuring me that yes, in fact, I did want Robe to catch me.

The other, less confident part fainted away at the thought of facing him for the same thing a second time.

What if he evicts me from the house for good?

I could go home. Or... I'd lose my place in *his* home.

That same breath brushed the curve of my shoulder, drawing me back to the quandary I'd put myself in. *Again.* The silent man behind me stood still, his body heat emanating against my back. Other than his firm grip, he made no contact, didn't shove me through the doorway and into Robe's warpath or announce my presence where I had no right.

He should have ousted me on the spot, proving Miller right yet again.

"Easy, Mari," the youngest member of Robe's family breathed against my cheek. Tall he might be, but the others had height on Will. To a woman who stood at five feet and four inches with a ponytail, however, his six feet made him a mountain in his own right.

"Will," I whispered, biting back a whimper of relief. "I didn't mean to—" My shitty lie never made it any further.

"Keep listening, Mari," Will murmured in my ear loud enough for me to hear his request alone while denying it to any of the men in the other room, including Miller with his elephant ears.

"Why are you—" I started to turn toward him but halted when his lips brushed over my cheek, then rested against the corner of my mouth.

Those soft, arched lips moved in a light kiss as he spoke. "Don't move."

I couldn't if I wanted to, and... I didn't. Want to, that was. His stubbled cheek pressed to mine in a gentle caress, the contact lighting every nerve ending in my body with heat. The air shifted around us as his other hand settled over my stomach, holding me in place. He didn't pull me away from my tenuous position, instead settling his warmth against my back.

"We share everything, Mari."

Alan and Robe had said those words to me on more than one occasion. Though I'd listened at the time, I never took much notice of what they meant until this moment.

Alan's sweet touches. The way Jon looked at me, and now Will. My connection with Robe, a sense of belonging when he didn't seem averse to the other boys touching me—or him. Miller's glares, and that hand in my hair.... I recalled Alan's kiss on Robe's lips in the bathroom that day. The jealousy in his eyes, I suspected, came from the fact that someone else had touched me first.

Or maybe that fantasy sated my crooked, desperate need for comfort. For some semblance of love.

He was scared; Alan had said that. Robe thought me too traumatized for any sort of sexual activity. In true fashion to himself, Alan blew that fallacy out of the proverbial water and terrified everybody, including me.

His little experiment made the memories trapped inside

easier to deal with at night, locked in the dark with Robe's fading presence to combat my fears. I closed one hand across the top of Will's over my stomach, resting there in a sense of peace. *Comfort.*

Quiet without fear.

Will's tongue flickered out against the corner of my mouth, tasting. I released a breath that shattered the moment I freed it. Arousal spiked through me as I stood stock-still, held in place by a warm hand that spoke of the quiet confidence of a man who rarely touched me.

The room spun with our resident bartender's next words that removed the physical comfort of Will's touch altogether.

"He's more than doubled the bounty on you," Alan said casually, as though he were talking about a Sunday picnic. "Four mil," he added before anybody could ask.

Four? I thought they'd said it was one.

A few murmurs of appreciation filled my ears. Even Will laughed softly against my skin.

"Is that all?" Robe sounded insulted. "I could pay it off in triplicate from Knight & Watchman in half a week."

My ears pricked up. That little tidbit almost sounded like information.

Will stiffened, pulling me back into his body. The playful, seductive touch disappeared. His lips drifted away from my mouth, leaving the cold kiss of empty air in his wake. I mourned the loss of contact as I settled against his hard frame of lean muscle.

"Forget everything you hear in this conversation, Mari," he whispered, hauling me closer. "You don't need to be any part of this."

He tried to turn me away, but my feet were rooted to the floor. I refused to move. After a moment, he grazed his stubble over my cheek with a soft sigh and let me stay. A low rumble grew in his throat, voicing his opinion on the matter in his own way, but I ignored his protest and focused on what was happening in the other room.

"It's not about the amount of money on your head, Robe," Alan argued. "It's the fact that it means men are out hunting you. And if they're hunting you, they'll come here."

"We're going around in circles. Again," Jon groused.

"It's not like we're innocents," Robe said dryly.

Something banged on the bar. "Jesus fucking Christ," Alan shouted. "It's not about you or us. You've got someone else in this house. She's a little bit undefended, a little bit damaged, or don't you remember what he's already done to her?"

Air was ripped from my throat before either of us could move. Will's hand clapped over my mouth, holding me back against him as he swore under his breath.

I didn't have time to draw another lungful to replace the one I'd lost before the door was shoved inward from the other side. Miller stood in the patch of negative space between me and Will on one side and Robe on the other. Jon's furrowed brow turned my stomach. For some reason, his distrust *mattered*.

Miller growled in my face, and I drew my attention back to the threat in front of me. The stocky man's vicious gaze sang in victory. I couldn't back away from him, couldn't escape, trapped between the proverbial hard body and the rock of loyalty Miller provided.

Just not to me.

The way Robe inspired that sort of allegiance made me crave having someone in my corner, but I suspected I'd used up my goodwill with the stunt that got me caught a second time.

The stocky man's gaze dripped over my body, his lip curled in a snarl. Dark eyes blazed with fury as he focused on me.

I looked closer, so used to his anger aimed my way that I pushed past it to see what else his gaze harbored, and realized how close fury and lust were when they manifested. Heat lanced into every place he looked as though he offered a physical touch. My chest rose as I gasped behind Will's hand, fighting for air and security. The warmth of the man at my back who had teased me moments before turned cold and hard, offering no reprieve whatsoever.

No, I would face Miller's wrath alone.

His gaze coasted over the swell of my breasts, lingering there and then on my lips as Will dropped his hand, letting me suck in much-needed air. Miller's sharp mouth curled into a triumphant smile. His fingers grazed my wrist in an intimate connection before his touch roughened, slicing around my arm to yank me forward, out of Will's safe hold.

I stumbled through the doorway in his wake and collided with a solid chest I knew all too well.

Hands crossed over my waist at the small of my back, preventing me from going anywhere and keeping me pinned to his front. Robe's forest-dark eyes stared right through me, picking apart all my secrets until I stood bare before him, bereft of all that he'd stripped away from me in a single look.

Miller's heavy footsteps retreated, his path muffled as I lost myself in Robe yet again, though I heard him as he said, "She's making a habit of eavesdropping."

The simplicity of his words surprised me. I might have thought he would snark at my ineptitude at being caught or express glee at catching me yet again and proving his point, though I did feel his raw hatred directed at my back.

One large hand rose from my waist to cover my shoulder

blades, forcing my attention forward. "Well, you're here now. How much did you overhear?" Robe's dry humor didn't alleviate the hard look in his eyes. I had a lot of making up to do, if he allowed it. He tightened his arm around me, and that possessive look that lanced straight through me became my everything. "How many more times are you going to put yourself in danger, Mari Merripen?"

Tremors ripped through me, my shudders the opposite of his long, calm breaths. Robe squeezed my waist a little tighter, drawing me flush into his body. The material at my waist twisted in his grip, his roughened fingers scoring the skin beneath with heat and need. I grabbed his shirt the same way, like I did that day in the forest. The memory of his palms pressed to my bare flesh left me trembling in his arms. Bonus: at least I was wearing clothes now.

Robe's lips rose in a sinful smile, telling me he remembered the exact moment that sat heavy on my shoulders, a weight that wasn't mine to bear alone.

"I won't do it again. I'm sorry." The lie tore from my lips unbidden, and the moment the words were out of my mouth, I wished like hell I could retract them.

Because Robe saw right through my bullshit, and he wasn't the only one in the house who could strip away my fibs to expose my broken little self to the room. A dark laugh filled the space at my back, and I pressed tighter to Robe's chest, ignoring the amusement in his eyes as I tried to use him as my barrier, though he had more right than any to throw me from his home, leaving me to fend for myself.

"Hell, you wouldn't last three days."

The threat kicked my pulse up a few notches. All he needed to do to make that piece of prophecy come true was eject me from his protection.

"Girl needs a damn good spanking," Miller snarled as he strode away.

That seemed to be his usual attitude whenever I walked into the room. He'd tear into me, watching with those dangerous, cloaked eyes, throw down his barb like a tarnished gauntlet, and then get the hell away from me.

Coward.

Miller didn't approve of me being anywhere near the man he devoted his loyalty and love to, his fury clear in every purposeful stride. That wasn't what made him an asshole or a coward. It did leave me out of place. I fell under a temporary category in their lives.

Rather like a discarded toy, I twisted from the waist to face the aggressive soldier, though I was unwilling to dislodge Robe's grip despite what punishment he might have in mind for a second infraction.

"Nobody asked you."

But Miller's silent response to my words shattered under Robe's hard laugh.

"Damn, but you're trouble, Mari."

I turned back, letting my mouth curve in a hopeful smile. "Sorry?"

"No, you're not," Robe murmured, leaning down to rest his forehead against mine. "But Miller's right. You do need a good spanking."

I blinked, looking for the laughter in his face—or the threat, but for the first time, no danger presented itself there. A single bald, blatant truth I couldn't escape, however, did.

A promise.

I swallowed hard, trying to suppress the tidal wave of arousal that flushed me between the two points of contact where Robe held me.

Somewhere else in the room, Alan swore. Something clattered in the bar sink before he tore at the silence permeating the room. "Why don't you tell her everything? Like I've been saying all along." His voice strained at the end, a plea written there I didn't quite understand.

"Because it's a fucking stupid idea. We're trained for interrogation. She's not. Do you remember what's already happened to her? Fuck, just batter her up and lay her out on Gi—the table for whichever predator happens by." Jon detached himself from the doorway and stormed forward, as wild and bruised as I'd imagined from my hiding place behind the door.

If Robe encompassed a hard, passionate intelligence, Jon was everything... else. Savage. *Untamed.* This man would burn down forests and ransack houses for the people he loved.

Tilting my head back, I turned my defiance on him, letting out the anger and frustration at not understanding my position in this place, how Robe let me fluctuate day-to-day based around his moods, the lack of control over my own existence.

"I want to know what threats there are to me here," I murmured, glancing over my shoulder. "And what threat I pose to *you*."

All of you.

Jon stared back, his righteous anger cooling as he surveyed me with the same sense of appeal in his liquid brown eyes. I wanted to fall into him the way I did with Robe, but it wasn't either of the mountain men who dragged my gaze to the room's shadows.

Will leaned into the darkness just inside the doorway I'd been pulled through, looking for all the world as if standing at the edge of the light was the most comfortable place for him. Where his easy smile so often offered me reassurance, a deep frown now decorated his gentle face.

Among the excess of testosterone, he still claimed pride of place as one of the hottest men in the room, and holy mountain men, was the cloistered space filled with an abundance of hormones.

I trembled in Robe's grip, remembering the way Will's tongue laved the corner of my lips, tasting me. Teasing us both.

The hint of a sinful smile, so similar in its way to Robe's, tainted the tilt around his generous mouth. What would it be like for him to touch me at the same time as Robe or Jon did? Their rough-edged passion offset by the younger man, his touch seductive and caressing.

A raw sound ripped from my unwilling throat as I detached myself from Robe's too-close embrace. The moment I freed myself, the air cooled, leaving me exposed in a sea of men, raw hunger written on every one of their faces.

Wrapping my arms around myself, I sought out Jon again, knowing he held the linchpin to getting them on my side in this. "I don't think I can help in... whatever it is you do, and I don't want to be a threat to anyone here. But maybe I can be another set of eyes on something. Anything." I squeezed my own arms, indenting the soft material of the shirt I'd borrowed from Miller the first day I arrived and never returned, blaming its comfort when in reality I craved some of his strength. And he never asked for it back. "Accounts I can work on or... I don't know. Supplies, an inventory list. I'm good with numbers. Patterns. I can see what's missing."

I added that last bit in a pitch of desperation but spoke true; Gideon shunted me around departments to see where he could improve the flow of his businesses while never letting me view the whole of anything. More than once, I'd wondered what he was hiding.

I guessed after my experience in his home that I had been right, though I would never have chosen to find out that way. My brain itched to see his accounts in full, to work out what he concealed—and somehow, in some small attempt at revenge, call him out on it.

But I needed my mind to be *here* right now. I hadn't articulated my CV well. Jon's lips pursed; even I recognized that the point I'd tried to make was a piss-poor argument. He opened his mouth, but Robe beat him to whatever comment he'd lined up.

"All right."

I pivoted on my heel, eyeing Robe. He looked me over in that calm, studious way of his, one eyebrow cocked. A full smile enhanced the lines around his mouth that were hidden beneath his beard, showing white teeth. Even his eyes lit up at some humor he alone possessed.

This man is a sex bomb when he smiles.

It didn't happen very often, and that made each smile that much more precious. I was so used to reading serious, grumpy Robe that cheeky, cocky Robe offered a fresh shock to the system.

"All right?" I echoed, trying to enunciate my thoughts. My brain stalled, and nothing else came forward. Was I the brunt of a joke he kept locked away?

Still grinning, Robe's face lit with mischief. "You're right. A pair of fresh eyes won't hurt. Maybe she knows more about this than we give her credit for."

Silence filled the cabin as I stared at Robe. Jon pushed his way past Will, pausing to block the air flowing through the open doorway. He gave me a hard look that didn't quite veil his frustration, concern dipping his brow. Deep thumps radiated as he walked off the veranda, silence falling when he hit the forest floor and disappeared.

Despite the difference between Miller's and Jon's physical presences, in the absence of their two towering personalities, Alan's glee was almost palpable.

"Miller's going to fucking love this."

Mari

18

MARI

"Robe won't play with you, huh?" Alan stared at me beneath the soft glow of the bar. A twinkle lit his aquamarine gaze—his standard response to life, it seemed. His low-level sarcasm nicely underlined the pity party aimed my way.

Light failed outside beneath heavily pregnant cloud cover, leaving the woods in a dim, not-quite-dark haze.

"I have no idea what you mean." I pressed smooth, manicured hands to the clean beermat.

French nails were as fussy as I let Alan go, despite the array of colors he insisted I try. It didn't seem right, somehow, and the nude gloss suited my mood. Maybe tomorrow I'd try midnight blue.

"Uh-huh." Alan uncapped a top-shelf whiskey and emptied an eighth of it into my coffee mug.

Notes of peat and honey filled my head, giving imagery of an eighteenth-century Highland clan roused for battle. Or maybe the after-party.

"That's enough." I held out a hand to ward off any more alcohol. "Alan, it's nine o'clock in the morning."

A cheeky smile curved his sassy lips, showcasing his

popularity in his on-again, off-again job—both at the strip club and the one he did for Robe. "It's five o'clock somewhere, sweetcheeks." Alan tipped the bottle back, swallowing a healthy double slug, and managed to give me a sexy ass wiggle at the same time without spilling a drop.

"Talent." I giggled, then clapped my hands over my mouth. "Inappropriate much?" I said to the coffee that burned my tongue, the back of my throat, and my stomach but left me in a happy insta-glow that threatened premeditated trouble later. I wondered what he put in that whiskey and how long he'd been tippling my coffee without my knowledge.

"Gets you right there." Alan smiled knowingly.

I tossed back a healthy dose of my intoxicated coffee under his watchful gaze and then threw my hands in the air. "Fine! Robe is impossible. The silent, still sentinel one minute, all black mood and dark thoughts. You can *see* his thoughts swirling around. His head is like a fishbowl," I informed my bartender.

Alan leaned over his forearms where they were braced on the stainless steel bar. "If he only knew.... Oh, Mari, Mari. It's so obvious."

"Right? Then that mood changes. He goes from protective bear to... to..." I pressed my lips together and collected my thoughts. "To a sinuous fairy-tale beast in the next breath, royally capable of pissing me off. His emotions are a one-way door, and it's infuriating. If I approach him, the fire goes out and he shuts off." I sounded like a petulant child, but I didn't care.

Alan comprised my safe zone. Even knowing he collected information like other people collected flowers or toys, his charm worked as well on me as it did on anyone else. In a house full of borderline psychotics at best and full-on sociopaths at worst—including at least one murderer, per Jon —I needed to trust someone.

Anything for the cause, right? I needed a clarity check on what heeding my cause came under. Beneath the healing process Robe had set me on, I knew more than one thing had changed about me. Not that any of that was his fault, exactly, but I still struggled with those deep-level alterations.

I also still struggled on occasion with having the freedoms I used to take for granted whisked away, but not half as much anymore. My newfound need for constant physical comfort to prevent the nightmares, relying on others for basic survival and life beyond simple needs like food and shelter for the first time in my life. The men of Recurve Ridge protected me, and I didn't want to be without them. The cage I initially clawed against and whenever I fought against Robe's need for control had become my refuge.

A pale reflection of the figure that should resemble me stared back as I struggled to reconcile with the girl who shared my skin. But my reflection no longer suited my shape or shared my name. She died sometime during my race through the forest before I found myself entangled in Robe's arms. I adapted as best I could to circumstance, but I'd had enough of waiting and reacting.

Alan smiled. "Sweetcheeks, he's so enamored with you that when you approach him, he runs like a six-year-old boy."

I snorted, an unladylike sound, but the whiskey had sucked away my worry over decorum in this place. "Robe was never a six-year-old boy. He was born a full-grown man with six beards to choose from."

"Cheers to that." Alan clinked his glass against mine.

I pressed the alcoholic coffee against my lips, savoring the burn that sank down my throat. The sensation made my head swim and my eyes water at the same time. Spice and all things so, so nice, or something like that. "Alan, do I run from him? Do I try to hide? Or do I—"

Alan raised an eyebrow. "Robe is more than you can ever imagine. He's done things for all of us, helped us across that line we can't cross back over. Not one of us would—not even for him. Can you hide from a man like that, Mari Merripen?"

His first use of my full name since the day I walked into Robe's house hit me like a slap to the face. Despite the shock value he intended, I knew his words were truthful. Those same words also had an opposite, almost arousing effect. Robe had the resources to hunt me back to NYC and beyond. No matter where I went, I would always end up back on Recurve Ridge and back in his bed, even if I slept there alone.

The difference between him and Gideon lay in a moral choice. Robe wouldn't use me. Still, I wanted to wallow, and so wallow, I did.

"I'm a prisoner." I whispered the three words, wondering which truth Alan would throw at me next.

He paused. "If you choose to be."

I nodded, drinking the rest of my coffee in silence. Did I want to be Robe's prisoner or return to a different life? No matter which way we swung it, I had little choice in where I headed other than to go in the direction Robe pointed me.

Maybe I could make that happen on my own terms instead of on his.

An idea formed in my mind, aided by a cheeky bartender and the power of his wares. I pushed off the barstool and stood on unsteady legs. My feet pressed into ground that was spongy despite the fact that it looked as hard as it had been before, no matter which eye I closed. The floor wobbled, or maybe I did, and I grabbed at the bar for support.

Alan's warm hands closed over mine. "Are you all right there, sweetcheeks?"

I looked up at him and gave him a dazzling smile. "Alan?" I asked in my sweetest, most alluring voice. His eyes narrowed, but he nodded once. "Can you teach me how to lap dance, please?"

I wished I asked weeks earlier. The smile that split his face with mischief and mayhem filled the room with a glow. I'd put my trust in the right man.

MY LEGS ACHED BY THE TIME I PERFECTED THE MOVES Alan taught me. My *everything* ached. Muscles I didn't know I had hurt, and it felt almost too good after days cooped up in a house in the middle of nowhere with nothing to dispel the energy that coiled inside me without Miller's training.

My body awakened with the new activity, even if it was grinding away at an empty chair while the rest of the occupants were absent for... whatever they did. While I didn't often stand under the shower for long, I opted to embrace the luxury of the endless hot water system Robe had provided and let the steam clear my head while the heat unwound tension from my body.

Could I seduce Robe? Alan seemed to think I'd healed enough to take on the mountainous—pun intended—task. Even I had a degree of confidence over my scheme, once the effects of the alcohol wore off. And the head of the household did his damnedest to create moments he designed to drive me mad and then walk away, time and again. If what I was planning worked out, I'd have a definitive answer one way or another.

My skin still steaming from my volcano-level hot shower, I wandered into Robe's bedroom, patting myself down. His towels were massive—they had to be for someone his size.

They were also fluffier than any I'd used in the executive hotels we booked when I traveled with Gideon.

My hand froze over my heart at the thought of my old boss. *Ex*-boss. Tormentor.

Nightmare.

I'd managed to keep the chaos at bay for the few scant days since my last nightmare through pure distraction.

Never be alone.

Never stop talking.

Don't stop.

The ceaseless activity around and inside the cabin made that an easy task, and my usual short shower backed that up. Until I'd decided to do something out of my crafted routine and take a break.

Note to self: no more breaks for Mari.

I stared at myself in the mirror, taking in the no-longer hollow cheeks and the damp strands that clung to my shoulders and wound their way around my throat in a parody of a noose.

The pair of eyes behind me that burned with a black fire deep enough to seek out my soul.

His warmth radiated against my spine, tingles working their way toward my extremities until my fingers curled into fists at my sides. No man had the right to affect a woman the way my body reacted to his presence. I stared back, lost in Robe's gaze for a long moment. Then, in a delayed reaction that should have been rib-crackingly hilarious, I screamed the house down and scared the shit out of us both.

"What the—" Robe swore beneath the towel I threw over his head, peeling it back layer by layer, then patting his hair as though to make sure nothing had landed on him. "Fuck, Mari."

"Sorry," I mumbled in a small voice, wiggling my night-gown over my head. "I didn't mean to do that."

I tugged at the hem, but the thing refused to drop any farther. Lace crinkled in my hands. At the same time as Robe's head emerged from beneath the towel, I realized that I hadn't grabbed my nightie but the negligee I'd asked Alan to source for me earlier in a somewhat desperate plan to seduce my mountain man and never got around to deploying.

He stared at me in utter, breast-blushing silence that abetted my humiliation while his expression morphed from bemused to starving man in milliseconds. "I'd ask if you had that lying around, but... that's a moot point."

I giggled, then clapped a hand over my mouth. His eyes slitted, too focused on me, and the giggle became a full-blown laugh until even Robe cracked a rare smile.

"That's better." I poked his chest, aware that flirting with the beast might get me what I wanted—if not in the way I expected.

Maybe *expected* didn't apply to this situation. *Hoped*, or perhaps *wanted* might suit the outcome better. *Desired*....

His gaze darkened as it tracked over the sheer material, then lingered at the hem. "Isn't that supposed to cover more of you?" His tone was strained, reflecting what I read in his eyes—undiluted, raw lust.

That same gaze had a distinct effect on my own body. A warm flush started at my throat and sank lower, heat pooling between my thighs. I pressed them together and told myself that nervousness at my first sexual encounter since—

Alan.

The reset worked. I cleared my throat as the heat turned to cold stone in my belly. Forcing the nightmares back, I focused on the man in front of me, willing my arousal to return.

"Everest," I whispered, then shook my head, damp tendrils flicking side to side, showering us both in a spray of droplets.

No. I could do this on my own terms.

Time to woman up, Mari.

I threw on my best British attitude as his gaze narrowed further.

"It came with a pair of knickers, but, uh...." I offered a feeble wave in the direction of a set of drawers he'd allocated to me and wished he'd take the hint.

Or maybe I didn't.

Flee.

I took a step back, making room for breathable air between us.

Robe stepped forward.

His eyes glowed with intent as we promenaded across the room in a one-way defense—or offense, depending on which side of the equation I stood on.

Turned out my side ran defense, and I was shit at it.

Heat rolled off him as he shed his jacket to the floor, the need for its warmth expunged by this room that was already a thousand degrees too hot. Regardless, I kept backing up until a sharp edge jabbed my ass. I cursed the unidentified piece of furniture, but I refused to risk taking my eyes off Robe.

A predatory smile curved those sinful lips as he advanced, stealing my space. Both arms surrounded me in a thick cage, his large hands framing either side of my waist against whatever pointy object I'd backed into.

A big fucking mountain.

Also a very sexy one.

"What are you doing in here?" I gasped at thin air, unable to suck in a full breath when he stood so close. Nothing in this world came close to the feeling of curling up against his warmth, all comfort and sweetness and innocence. I'd broken my habit of sleeping with him to poke the literal bear, and look what happened. My eyes closed as I offered an undying pledge that I'd never deny my OCD needs ever again.

"I'm going to bed, Mari Merripen. Care to join me?" His breath brushed my cheeks, and the fire rekindled low in my belly.

Thank you, Everest.

My heartfelt gratitude resulted in a hooded gaze. His sexy-as-sin offer wavered between us, solid yet not.

Robe freed one arm to extend a hand. I stared at it, unable to lift my frozen one for too long a moment. Worried he'd withdraw his offer, my palm rose of its own accord. Long, roughened fingers curled around my softer ones.

I let him draw me the few paces to the hard mattress I now thought of as soft, crawling backward onto its surface and tucking my knees beneath me to stare up at him.

"This wasn't what I had planned," I whispered.

Unable to tear my gaze from his, I fidgeted with my lacy covering as he shucked his shirt into a puddle next to his jacket. His pants went next, and he advanced on me, closing the meager space between us. The wrist-thick erection that protruded from his groin drew my attention and held it.

Because who could take their eyes off a log like that?

I'm insane. I've been assaulted, and this *is what I think will heal me?*

He could rip me in two. Or three. Or four.

Chest heaving, I scooted back a few inches, as if that would protect me from the beast I'd incited, and reclined on his bed.

The lace negligee seemed a wonderful temptation on my behalf and a terrible accident all at once.

Robe loomed over me, his forearms braced on either side

of my head where I lay on the pillow. The space between us shrank, allowing a sliver of air to pass beneath him but in no way large enough to permit me a full breath to combat his overpowering presence. His knees fell to encase my hips. The warm, rock-hard mass of my Everest arced over me, though not a single square inch of our bodies touched.

My chest clenched, waiting for his rejection to cleave my heart. Would it sting or offer relief? A large part of me knew that as daunting as being loved by him seemed, it would break me if he pushed me away now.

We hadn't come this far together before. Every time we flirted, he disappeared or shoved me away before we made it to this point. My heart tried to hope, but I quashed the tiny seed before it could bloom, knowing the negative that hovered between us should he hold to his impossible—his *untouchable*—standard.

Refusing to let him go this time, I lifted my head, lips parted. An offering in the silence that permeated the sliver of light against dark that flitted between us.

A steely glare flattened me back to the pillow.

I wanted to growl at him or tug at his hair until I got a different reaction from him. The one *I* wanted. "Robe, I don't know what you want."

He surveyed me in the darkness. One corner of his lips moved, working upward as though he might smile. "Then that makes two of us, Mari Merripen." He dipped his head. His lips were millimeters from mine as his breath kissed my lips. "Something involving diving in without thought."

His words came out musingly, and I wondered if he'd spoken to himself or to me.

I didn't have to wonder anymore when his mouth covered mine in a gentle pressure that sent tingles rioting through my body. Nerve endings fired up all over me, pleasure lancing straight through my center until every surface was stripped raw and aching.

Robe pressed his forehead to mine, heat emanating over me from the single point of contact. Breath sighed from lips feathering and light. What started as a soft, sweet kiss changed within seconds. A groan ripped from his chest as his tongue swept over my bottom lip before he delved deeper.

Exploring became devouring, and devouring twisted into something deeper, darker, a whisper that etched itself on my soul, bearing his name. I arched into him, linked my arms around the back of his neck, and pulled his mouth down to mine. Our tongues danced and swirled as he let me press my body to his. A soft sigh left my lips, matching the thunder that rumbled in his chest, unvoiced.

Robe held to his frustrating position above me, unyielding. I shoved the nagging *what-ifs* aside and lost myself to him, letting the world and all my doubts fade beneath his onslaught. His skin heated from my touch along the back of his neck. I dug my fingers into his scalp, massaging the delicate flesh there, tracing over the heavy lines of muscle that extended into his hairline.

Robe groaned into my mouth and broke the kiss with wild eyes. His fist slammed into the pillow next to me, jostling me with its violence.

I squeaked, loosing the sound of something terrified of its impending fate.

He is more dangerous than the man I escaped.

The thought thrashed through my mind in a disjointed stream. I saw truth in it, but also something that existed between us—something I never had with Gideon but fought and ached for with Robe.

Trust.

The tiny sound I made hovered in the air between us, lost in a rush of breath and words.

"Mari, I'm... not suitable for someone like you." Breath hissed between his teeth as he twisted the pillow beneath my head. "I'll hurt you." Lust raged in dark, glittery eyes, leaving me a hot liquid mess below his enormous frame.

Still, his rejection stung like a motherfucker. My hand stilled behind his neck. I tried to draw him down to me, but he refused me—*again*.

Fine. Two of us can play this game.

I raised myself onto my elbows and grazed my lips against his before he could protest. "You're a different kind of dangerous, Robe Huntingdon. Your moral compass may not point north, and it might be a different shade of black, but you aren't anything like *them*."

The words scattered to ash in my mouth. I'd run out of innocence, that critical part of my soul ripped from me without choice. *My choice.* Not the virginal sort, but the part of me that believed horror movies were the stuff of the silver screen and nothing more. Now, I knew better.

The monsters lived among us.

Robe Huntingdon wasn't one of them.

"You have no idea who I am," he grated, his voice harsh and unforgiving.

Robe couldn't give my innocence back or take away the harm I'd suffered at the hands of another. No one could. He could give me love, new memories to replace the terror of those hours. He had given me the time and space to heal, and now I was ready to move forward with my choice of *who*. Maybe even somewhat ready to heal in my heart.

Tears filled my eyes, but I refused to let them flow—not anymore.

"Please, Robe." *Help me.*

His black gaze cleaved straight through me. "I can't be your therapy fuck, Mari."

Robe's stillness shattered as he pushed back till he was kneeling on his haunches at the end of the bed. A giant mountain god living in a house never built to fit such a demand. He dwarfed the building with his presence alone, even though it suited his physical form. But there was so much more to Robe than what the eye could see. I followed him, rising onto my knees, and crawled toward him.

His breath came faster. He watched me in silence, rock still, his hands resting on his knees. I'd called him a stone sentinel to Alan, so full of life, too full of energy, regardless of how he channeled it in dark ways.

When my hands brushed his thighs, I stopped. Looking up at him, I curled my feet beneath me. "I don't want your therapy. But I could use a teacher, a guide—someone to take me back to real life. A f-friend."

Someone to love and to be loved by.

I said all of that without extending an invitation for more, scared of what would happen if he threw me away, but I knew I could offer him something missing from his life. From all their lives. I wanted to be given the chance to try. I couldn't force those words past my lips, so I lay back and waited. Hoped.

Prayed.

Even if no god could want a twisted thing like me.

I knelt before him, begging.

His fingers rose from his knee to graze my cheek. "I'm not the man to take you back to reality, Mari." This time the corner of his lips did work, and he smiled.

The change in him was instant, ripping away the man who threatened torture and murder. He ran his household of broken misfits with an iron fist. That smile replaced him with someone he thought dead, ruined, but I saw him in a shot of clarity.

"I think you are." I leaned into his touch until he curved his hand around my cheek.

A dark gleam in his fathomless eyes was all the warning he offered.

The hint of a smile remained on his lips as that dormant growl rose in his throat. Robe's brand of fierce had become my standard, what I measured everything else against, but this kind of intimidation settled low in my stomach. A searing shot of arousal zinged through me, lips to tiptoes.

His fingers curved, brushing over my throat in a protective claim that promised violence to anyone who threatened me. Every caress staked a deeper mark on my soul, seeking possession. His touch verged on pure temptation, everything I wanted but knew I shouldn't take.

If we did this, our world would change.

Too late, I caught on to what Robe had been trying to say every time he pushed me away. His darkness clashed against whoever I'd become during my months in his house, and the heady mix threatened to consume us.

I shifted in front of him, lost in the dark glitter that surveyed me with humor and seduction. "Robe—"

"Too late, little lamb." He swept his arms around my body, locking me to his chest as he settled me onto his lap.

The energy coiled inside him thrummed against me, his movements fast enough to shock, silent enough to ripple the air as he moved. Everything I needed to know existed in the dark promise his eyes laid bare before he whisked that away too.

His sheer size and muscle mass stretched my thighs wider as I sank onto the hard ridges of him. Talented hands tangled in my hair, pulling my mouth down to his in a kiss hard enough to bruise, yet sweet enough to leave me sighing, pulsing on air, and needing *more*.

I rocked against the hard rise of his cock, my negligee a useless barrier between us. One of his hands dropped between us to squeeze the sensitive spot at the curve of my thighs as I writhed against his unyielding form. A moan dripped from my lips to sweep over his.

Robe caught the filmy material as I rose, drawing it over my head with care; then his hands were on my bare skin, dragging my tingling breasts over ridges of hard, inked muscle. My body became its own weapon. I used it the way Alan had taught me, grinding and undulating in a rhythm of my own.

Though Robe fisted my hair, drawing my head back, I never stopped dancing. His breath stuttered against my mouth as he held me in place, and the room disappeared into the fathomless depths of his gaze. Everything stilled between us. He slipped his tongue into my mouth, searching and tasting, finding my rhythm and matching it with his own as he released my hair and let me kiss him back, tasting him the way I needed to.

Firm hands curled around my hips, slamming me against him. The deep ache between my thighs intensified. Swollen, needy skin connected with his hardness as I moved over him and slicked his flesh with my arousal, soaking us both.

I wanted to say his name, something profound, but nothing came out other than an animalistic cry. The set of his jaw warned me not to break the moment, and my body obediently conveyed the conversation I couldn't voice. I squeezed my thighs tight against his hips, linking my ankles around his back, and let him show me what he wanted most.

The sheer size of him wasn't contained to his height or muscle mass. Robe's presence rippled with unleashed power as he ground me against his body, the extent of his arousal evident as he held my eyes. Lust overwhelmed his earlier hesitancy, and I drowned in the deluge of him.

A whimper whispered past my lips as he let me up for air, then claimed me again until I twisted into a writhing, hot mess on his lap.

And he hadn't even fucked me yet.

Robe broke the kiss, raising both hands to my cheeks as he drew away from me. "I'll tear you, Mari. I'll do more damage than any one of them did, even if you're ready for me. And I can't hurt you. Not you, precious girl." His lips grazed over my mouth once more, tender and lingering, and then again.

The insatiable urge that rose in me consumed any rational thought, leaving emotion and desire strung out in an impasse between our bodies. I shivered in the cradle of his hands, clinging to his shoulders as I wound my body over his. My limbs were fluid from hours of practice in front of the bar under a critical eye that had annoyed me then but made me thankful now.

Robe groaned, his touch turning rougher as he held me close, watching my movements with hungry eyes as I danced for him. His cock thickened between my legs, and I gasped when he pushed me down to grind my swollen flesh against him again. Sensation flooded my system. I arched into his brutal touch, craving him deeper.

"I. Will. Break. You."

"No." Insanity gripped me, the sort of madness that beckoned with pleasure and promised a different sort of pain. "I want you. Please, Robe—" My breath hitched as my brain caught up, but the words were already in the open.

Robe's hands swept my body, brushing my breasts, then moving over the globes of my ass cheeks, stroking and caressing. Every motion left me lust drunk on him. Eyes closed, head tilted back, I sought my own pleasure. His harsh moans reverberated inside the deep cavity of his chest with every undulation of my body against him. I danced until I edged onto a precipice, and I knew that once I tumbled over that limit, I would never be able to recover—not from him. And I still wanted everything he offered.

His movement halted, and I paused midgrind.

I opened my eyes to stare deep into Robe's. He panted at the same rate I did, as though he had been the one dancing. The air stilled around us, the moment suspended as my body throbbed, burning and needful.

His touch became firmer, and the moment broke as he grazed roughened knuckles along my spine. Those same hands caught me in an inescapable grip. He slammed my body against his, hitting all the right places where I teased myself into a frenzy, grinding against his rougher touch.

Once, then again.

Waves I reached for and then held at bay now splintered over me. I screamed, uncaring if I roused the house. The reaction of a woman who had discovered safety, trust, and acceptance, who craved his brand of fierce.

In the arms of a man she loved.

I snapped back as the thought penetrated my hazy mind. How could I fall in love? I had healed to a degree—on the outside, at least. Inside, my mind broke into a chaotic mess whenever silence fell. Whenever I wasn't with him, or with Jon.

Warmth filtered into my chest at the memory of his best friend's arms wrapped around me, my brief sense of peace absorbed by a sensible dose of guilt.

How could I think of one man while in the arms of another? And Alan, with his silver kisses and clever fingers.

Will leaning into me, talking of strawberries as he watched my lips. Miller's eyes on me while we trained, me wearing his shirt beneath the sweater Alan bought me, a secret I kept for myself.

Guilt provided a double-edged sword that razed me in both directions. My body tightened, fear tautening my muscles in painful twists as I gasped for breath. Perhaps I didn't need silence for the chaos to consume me after all.

This madness tormented me in different ways. I gripped Robe's shoulders tight, shock warring with recognition as my gaze mirrored his glittering one.

I love him.

And I want them all.

Every thought swept away as Robe rolled me onto my back, pressing his body over mine. His weight sank into me as a comfort rather than a threat. I wriggled beneath him, arching up for greater contact. His hips thrust against me, the coarse hairs on his thighs rasping against my curves as I wrapped my legs around his waist, tilting my hips up.

He pressed his cock to my opening and held himself there, pulsing. Animalistic and wild, he claimed my mouth in a savage kiss that left me with no doubt that we shared the suffering of our combined epiphany.

Robe tore away with force. A bellow rose from his throat, and a single word jolted me out of my haze.

"*Jon.*"

My hands tightened on his back. "Robe, please—"

The door swung open, Jon's mass filling it as he gripped the lintel above his head. Breath wheezed from his chest as he surveyed the room with a clinical, assessing glance.

Until that gaze rested on me.

"What? Is she hurting?" Jon asked, his tone terse as he strode into the room, kicking the door shut behind him.

The bed dipped with his weight as he settled behind me. Robe lifted me enough for Jon to scoot beneath my body. Denim scratched the backs of my thighs as arms the size of tree trunks wrapped tight around all of us, sandwiching me in the middle.

The pressure of being crushed between two giant chests might have been a pleasurable torture, except for the one thing I lacked.

I flapped at a shoulder, choosing the nearest one without bothering to check who owned it. "Air.

"Oh." Jon released our group, rocking back a few inches. Hands grazed my spine, stroking the healed scars there with a gentle reverence that shot heat through me as he took in my naked state. "Mari...." His voice turned husky and rough, so different to his sweet touch when he calmed my nightmares in this very bed.

I fixed my gaze on Robe, my brow dipping as I tried to process too many sensations and thoughts at the same time. Guilt still gnawed at me, but under his tense expression, I pushed that aside to focus on him.

He smiled, reaching around me to cover Jon's hand and press his palm to my body, though he kept his gaze locked on mine. "It's okay, Mari. This is who we are, who we want to be with you." He dipped his head to kiss me long and slow while Jon's hand curled around my ribs, his touch supportive. "We share what we love, and right now...."

Intensity was pinpointed on me as his mouth curled in a wicked, sinful smile.

Desire slammed into me at that look. I shivered in their arms, trying to work out why my body wanted the impossibility of what my brain had heard but struggled to process. The hints were there—the glances over my head, their dual touch... but it was more than that.

"You mean... all of you? Not just you two?" I squeaked.

Jon's chest rumbled at my back. "If that's what you want, too, Mari. We will never rush you. I didn't think we were going to—" He broke off the brittle words aimed at the other occupant in the room.

"Things got out of hand," Robe growled, his eyes full of violence as he flicked his gaze over my head.

I knew he remembered that day in his bathroom when he'd watched Alan play us both. His fingers dug into my skin, offering a deep, sensual massage to tender flesh in a touch designed to drive me mad with need for him.

Pressed between them as I was, my breath evaporated, basic body functions overrun with emotion and arousal. I let my mind turn that over for a long moment while they waited with patience for me to reach my own conclusions. I searched for a reason not to, but... the emotion I was lacking was fear.

I trusted the two behemoths as much as I did at any other time. Both men had developed our trust, crushing any doubt about what I wanted, what would be acceptable to them all, though I still trembled at the thought of what my body could take.

"I will break you."

I had no doubt that Robe's promise meant something to him, but I was ready for that challenge. Managing both him and Jon? Another impossibility to face for another time.

Not reassured by a long shot, I swallowed beneath Robe's watchful gaze and glanced over my shoulder at Jon. "I'm not hurting. Robe freaked out. I think."

"Robe did not freak out." The amused voice at my front belied the tension in his tone, though I knew he spoke the truth. Something else was there... but I couldn't pick it out. Robe broke the dark gaze he'd been using to lock me in place and tilted his head to one side. "Doubt. One very big doubt. I need to know I won't ruin her," he rasped.

Pinned between the two enormous men, the fact that they spoke over me about me without speaking *to* me was a nice reprieve. I settled between their twin masses, my thighs draped over Robe's hips, and leaned back into Jon.

He took the light pressure—I couldn't be more than that to him—without question, leaving me to think through the men's relationship once more. *"This is who we are."* I knew Robe shared everything with Jon; he rammed that point home enough times. I just hadn't listened.

It served to highlight my earlier doubts about my own loyalty to Robe, and my—at the time—ridiculous attraction to Jon. As I leaned back into him, letting the large blond man's roughened touch glide over my body, the thought no longer offered the same level of guilt.

My head cleared along with my heart. Did I want this? I turned my face to rub my cheek against Jon's semi-bare chest where his shirt hung to the sides of his body, testing my theory.

The big man's heart beat a little faster than I expected. I arched, pressing against hot skin. He removed his open shirt one-handed over his head, leaving his chest smooth with a smattering of fine golden hair over his heart. I hadn't noticed, caught up in my own thoughts and the way his hands caressed me in an intimate, loving touch.

Lost in them both.

Robe held a charismatic power over everyone, and I was no exception. The intimacy turned up another notch, though, when Robe's and Jon's fingers interlocked around my body. My breath shortened as I overheated in an instant. The thick ridge of Jon's denim-covered cock pressed into my lower back. I rubbed myself shamelessly against him, heady with their dual attention.

I discovered I had fallen in love with Robe, and now I was having a reaction to his best friend... the best friend welcome in Robe's bed—and mine.

Too many hands—but not the wrong sort. Not the sort from *before*, clinging and twisting. I'd asked Robe to provide me with new memories to banish the old, and he was rising to that challenge. An untempered stillness filled the room, bringing with it the potential for chaos, raising the tension being built between us all too fast.

Jon shifted behind me to provide stability. As he rocked me back onto him, his erection pressed against my ass through his jeans, and the mad thought of what it would be like to take them both at once flitted through my mind. If he let me go, I might have swooned.

Jon drew damp hair back from my neck and grazed his fingers over my shoulders. "Tell her, Robe."

"I'm scared of damaging you. That I'll tear you worse than they did." Robe's voice broke.

I froze. Not at his words, but at the brutal honesty he displayed as he exchanged a glance with Jon over my head. I was no more than an object pinned between two men whose closeness meant far more than a few impassioned moments between a man and the girl he wanted to fuck.

"You won't. We'll go slow. Together." Jon stroked my stomach in long, soothing caresses. His fingers passed my face to touch Robe's cheek in a tender, sweet gesture, leaving me suddenly certain of the nature of their relationship. Jon leaned forward, his lips brushing my hair. "Don't be scared of him, Mari. He'll give you the most wonderful loving you'll ever have."

Desire shot through my body as my gaze connected with

Robe's. His lit an insatiable craving within me. Though I understood his fear, I wanted to do the best I could to give him new memories too.

I let Jon tilt my head back to look into my eyes. The warmth and understanding I found there left me high on the sensation of being safe in the arms of two men I knew who, without a single seed of doubt, would protect me—would *kill* for me.

Two pairs of welcome hands roamed my body, removing the damage done there with each sweet, sensuous caress, begging off old memories, creating new ones to cherish. Together these men succeeded where everyone else had failed in breaking down the poor barriers I'd erected to protect myself, my heart, my mind.

And willingly, I gave all three.

Robe

19

ROBE

MARI'S HEAD DROPPED BACK ONTO JON'S SHOULDER in a stunning display of surrender. Heavy eyes dozy, swollen lips parted, she looked nothing more than delectable and nothing less than a treat to be devoured.

But, by a God who no longer spoke to me, she meant so much more than a moment's sweet satisfaction.

I love her.

Pressure built in my chest until I choked on it. Jon's gaze flicked once to mine. When I nodded, a single violent jerk of my head, he dipped his mouth to hers and kissed her.

Her reaction to him was instantaneous. Winding her arms backward around his neck, she arched to allow him to deepen the kiss. Mari gushed hot and wet, coating my cock in her arousal as I pressed against her entrance, teasing us both.

A bolt of pure lust sluiced through me as I watched them together. The cutest flush spread from the slender column of her throat over her chest, tracing pale pink flames to the tips of her lush breasts.

She moaned into his mouth, a languorous, blissed-out sound I craved. Her thighs relaxed around me, her needy scent permeating my skin. I could almost *taste* her desire, for fuck's sake. And when I could have drowned in jealousy, I took in her heady, sweet scent and let it flow over me, heightening my own arousal.

I slid my fingers between us, tracing over the soft curve of her toned abdomen from the hard work she'd put in dancing with Alan when she thought I hadn't noticed, from the hours letting Miller knock her on her ass until she could do the same to me. Strength emanated from within her. Pure determination when she fought—sweet surrender when she let go. I hadn't broken her, and she was ready. My fingertips were glossed with her slick need as I stroked the tender flesh I tortured in my desperation for her.

She bucked at my touch. Jon palmed her stomach, pinning her flat to his body as she rocked against my fingers spearing into her sweet flesh. A moan ripped between her and Jon, filling my ears with a roar that refused to die. I spread my fingers wide inside her, preparing her.

"Let me stretch you, sweetheart. I don't want to hurt you. Not like that."

She nodded once, her eyes wide as she pulsed her hands in a death grip on Jon's forearm. Her fingers didn't quite close all the way around the muscle there.

I grinned, sliding her pale thighs over my shoulders and bracing them there. Soft breaths came faster as I grazed the roughened patch of scarred skin that drew heady moans from her with every touch. My lips tingled, and I leaned forward to latch on to the tight bud of her nipple, teasing the peak with flicks of my tongue, working her with my other hand.

She exploded around me in seconds, a strangled cry breaking her next kiss with Jon. Glazed eyes, a touch wild at the edges, stared at me. I released her nipple with a soft *pop* and reared over them both to kiss her, leaving my fingers embedded within her sweet, hot flesh, teasing her with slow pulses so she writhed between us.

Her moans were our soundtrack, but I was a greedy asshole and swallowed everything she offered me. Mari tasted of coffee and strawberries and whiskey. Jon's fingers met my wrist at her gushing pink pussy and slid in alongside mine. Her cry shattered the pensive quiet of my room, and I knew the boys outside would rub one out—if they hadn't left the house altogether.

The feel of him working her body alongside me heightened my arousal. I offered her an apologetic look as I pulled my mouth from hers and slammed it over his instead, kissing him in a frenzy as we fucked her together with our fingers. Jon groaned into my mouth, one hand clamped behind my head, our tongues sliding together, and then he pulled away.

"For her," he reminded me roughly, shoving me back.

I nodded my thanks at the sacrifice he made of his own pleasure to serve us both and found Mari's face filled with wonder and awe. I leaned down to kiss her gently, though all the good intentions in my world didn't last half a minute with the taste of them both on my tongue.

She cried out against my mouth, her body already bearing down on our joined fingers, her muscles fluttering with the onset of her next orgasm. I brushed my thumb across her clit, extending her pleasure as much as I could before she crashed again.

"Stunning. Come for us again." I swept hair back from her face where it was plastered to her cheek. "I won't ruin the most beautiful thing in my life."

Jon caught my eye, and we sank our fingers deeper, easing into her secret places.

"Oh—" Her lilt shattered with her breath.

What started as a question ended as a drawn-out whimper. Her body trembled between us as a fresh gush of searing arousal coated our hands, and she slid boneless against Jon's chest. I licked at a droplet of sweat that had beaded on the top of her breast, concealing a groan. This night was meant for her, not for me, and she was still tender, inside and out.

"Good girl," I murmured, easing my fingers from her, along with Jon's. It took everything in me not to suck his fingers clean of her slick.

Jon leaned back, kicking his legs out on either side of me to let me draw her down his body until her head rested on his stomach. I slid my hand behind her nape, supporting her. My knuckles grazed the hard ridge of Jon's arousal. I pressed her back until his body tightened beneath us. His sharp intake fueled my own need, but I pushed the fantasy of having them both from my mind. This had to be about Mari, not either of us. A scene to play out another night, perhaps.

Her eyes fluttered, thick lashes sweeping down to close over her midnight gaze. "Robe, I can't...." She trailed off, stretching sinuously against Jon. She draped her arms over his thick thighs, her legs spread around my tapered hips where I lay between them.

I doubted I'd ever see a sexier sight in my life.

But she wouldn't thank me for ramming my need home into her tender body. My control already frayed to a tight thread, I looked to Jon for support. He nodded, offering a small smile as he traced the swells of her breasts, then along her throat in sweeping touches designed both to soothe and create a desperate, boiling ache deep within. Watching me have her when he held her body to his must be excruciating, but I couldn't do this without him.

I *needed* him.

To make sure I didn't go too far.

To make sure I didn't destroy her.

He retrieved a condom from my bedside table and tossed the foil packet at me. Humor glinted in his eyes, and I knew I'd owe him well after this.

Fisting my length to deny myself what I craved, I slid down her body and dipped my head to kiss the pretty little offering laid out before me, needing to taste her pussy before I sank balls deep inside her. Mari moaned, hooking her legs around my shoulders. I stroked my tongue along tender flesh, savoring her taste, then flicked it over her clit. Waiting until she trembled on the edge, I pushed my way back up her body and held her still, stroking her clit with my fingertips as I notched myself at her entrance.

Her sensual, hooded gaze latched on to mine as I pushed in a little. Hot and slick as she was, I found the edge of my determination, desperate not to disgrace myself within her sweet pussy before she came again. Mari's eyes widened as she opened her pretty mouth and gave me a sweet, splintered scream. Yet she let Jon hold her open for me, all spread out like a beautiful offering. Her pussy hugged my cock tight as I held myself back, aching to drive balls deep in her heat.

One more inch, then another. I paused to let her stretch around me, unmoving until her body softened with each shallow thrust until I reached halfway home.

Jon played with her breasts, rolling her nipples between his calloused fingers as he watched me impale her on my length. His pelvis tilted, and he eased his hips up so I felt like I was fucking them both—or maybe we were both fucking her—together. She arched and whimpered between us, all slick heat and searing liquid flutters as she let me in. Soft moans ripped at my heart and tightened my balls into heavy stones.

Not an inch of pain lit her face, her body accommodating me thanks to the combination of our stretching her earlier and her desperate need that matched my own. She took everything I gave her and reached out, drawing me closer even as she turned her head to kiss along Jon's arm where it was braced around her. He panted with her, his gaze shifting between us as he held her gently, straining against his own need—written baldly across his face—to flip her over and fuck her into the bed.

I gritted my teeth, the sight of her taking pleasure in us both too much. Maybe having Jon in the room for our first time hadn't been my best idea. I needed to last longer than a few minutes to give Mari what she deserved. After she got used to me, then we could arrange a playdate. Or five.

"Are you okay, Mari?" I rested my hands on her open thighs, straining not to slam into her for the pure pleasure of earning a raw scream from her throat as I filled her.

"Would you *please*—" She gasped for breath, rocking her hips against my hand where I stroked her clit. "—hurry up, Robe? I'm dying." The befuddled look she sent me teetered between lust and love, and I laughed.

I moved over her body, angling a little deeper, and leaned in for a kiss. "How about now?" I slid all the way home, not stopping until my thighs rested against hers and she took my full weight. "Better, sweetheart? Not hurting you?"

Her cry echoed inside my head, a fast road to pure, bliss-induced insanity.

"Much," she gasped. "No pain. It's... you. Perfect." Tears broke at the corners of her eyes as she wrapped her legs around my waist, urging me deeper.

I licked her tears one at a time, then returned to her mouth. Salt mingled with the scent of her pleasure from my tongue. A large hand cupped the back of my head, and a dainty heel arrived against my ass, both pressing me deeper.

"Fuck her, Robe." Jon's voice strained even as he encouraged me to sink into her, his body braced to take the brunt of my need that he understood well.

I acknowledged his plea with a short jerk of my head and began to move within her, taking care to note every twinge, every touch pushing me back to grant her reprieve, but none came.

She clung to me, lifting her lower body to meet every thrust. My control edged to its hard limit, I gave in to the need to rut her harder, unable to breathe as she took my full length time and again. Our moans mingled, tangling in an unreserved symphony that filled the cabin.

Her body rocked faster against mine, soft cries ripping from her lips as she clenched down hard a third time. Jon's fingers slid over her stomach to circle her clit, his breath heavy beneath her.

Mari's hot little pussy pulsed around my cock, taking me with her into oblivion as I roared her name, claiming her for whatever damned future we might eke out together.

Jon

20

JON

Robe's bedroom smelled of sated obsession. The two bodies slumped over mine were coated in sweat and sex that seeped onto my damp jeans. I rested against the headboard of my best friend's bed and tried not to disturb them. Rousing either Robe or Mari would be a mistake, but I had another reason for remaining frozen.

I swallowed back the heady arousal Mari's body offered, slung languid and boneless across mine, my best friend still embedded deep within her soft curves. Her peach-perfect ass split around me, soft and warm and so fucking tempting. The ceiling offered a focal point but such a boring one that it did next to nothing to distract me from the need raging in my jeans beneath a pretty, worn-out girl that more than one bodily organ of mine ached to claim.

Nor did the hard hand the same size as mine that gripped my fingers too tight offer a great enough distraction. I dropped my gaze to meet Robe's and let him attempt to break me. The pain finally gave me what I needed. When my cock no longer strained against the confines of my jeans, I managed to suck in enough oxygen to prevent my head from spinning.

"Thanks."

"I should be thanking you." Robe uncurled his fingers one at a time, shaking out the stiff joints as he flexed his hand. "Without you, I'd never—"

"Of course you would. Stop doubting her. And yourself," I muttered from beneath the girl in question dozing on my stomach.

Fresh arousal threatened at the sight of her spread over me, the scent of their joining leaking over my jeans. I bit the inside of my cheek, savoring the metallic tang. Their combined weight was the sort of torturous pleasure I'd take more of nightly.

Hell, I might even have a go at Robe if this kept up. A grin grew at the thought of the battle I'd face on *that* front.

A wary look creased his face. He eased back, drawing a blanket over Mari. Her legs tangled and draped around mine. "You all right with her?"

"You mean I don't have to put up with you snoring all night again?"

"Fuck off. I'm going to shower. Then I'll have her back."

"Hell no. You already shared. What if it's my turn?"

His wicked grin matched my own. "Maybe one day...."

"No." I expulsed the word in a cold rush. "No way in hell. One at a time. Nothing more." I held his gaze.

"Do I get a say in this?" Mari piped up from the region of my stomach.

"*No,*" we shouted her down together. I eased back to stare down at her. "No, Mari. We could damage you past the point of what we could fix. What *I* could fix. Neither of us wants that. Ever." I traced my thumb over her cheek as she offered me a lazy smile. I refused to risk more, no matter our desires.

Robe nodded as I drew her along my body to rest her curled form on my shoulder and tucked the blanket around her. I checked where my best friend stood.

His expression had turned inward, pensive. A wry smile cocked one corner of his mouth as he caught me watching. He rubbed a hand over his hair and turned for the shower without another word.

My attention returned to Mari. She rolled onto her stomach, pressing her body along the length of mine. I dropped a kiss on the top of her head, stretching my shoulders against the headboard.

"Thank you, Jon," she mumbled into my chest.

I clasped the back of her head, drawing her tight against me, reveling in the little sigh that slipped from her along with the last remnant of her wakefulness.

In all honesty, I hadn't minded Robe calling me in to share their first time together. Hell, better me than Alan, who didn't possess the physical strength to hold Robe back if his control snapped, or Miller, who was as likely to kill the girl as fuck her himself. Jury was out on Will, who harbored his personal cache of damage and secrets.

Robe gave me his blessing in letting me become an intimate part of their broken relationship, and I offered up a silent prayer of thanks that he trusted me to uphold it. Neither of us was a saint. We'd shared every woman over the past few years since my arrival at the cabin, but those were only brief flings. None stole my heart like Mari had. Most provided only a physical release at best, an uncomfortable one my body wanted that my brain resisted. Some of the women, often sourced by Alan from the fringes of society, took to our weird-as-fuck relationship guidelines. Some of them lasted one night, but most of them didn't even make it that far.

The thought of the two of us being with one woman who filled the gaps in our combined past, that dream we worked toward but were still unable to hope for, seemed unattainable at times. But as with Mari, both of us fucking the same girl would be... detrimental to her, physically speaking. Bodies weren't made to accommodate our combined girth, no matter how much she might like to try. Even some of the whores Alan provided had struggled, and after a while, we gave up on the endeavor.

Until Mari turned up on our doorstep, and the fantasy became that much more tangible.

I stroked her hair back from her face as tiny purrs rose from her. "Sleep, Mari." I nodded at Robe as he emerged from the shower, his body almost as large as mine, but by the grace of hard work, not God's design. "You too."

Robe paused, taking Mari in and how my arms are wrapped around her sleeping form. "Maybe later."

"You need rest," I snapped, gritting my teeth at the bitchy tone I hated.

"I know." The bedroom door closed behind him with a soft thud, his absence marked by a distinct cold air in the room.

My lips pursed, I soaked in the soft sensation of her skin on mine, memorizing the scent of her, and burned the images of her and Robe and the three of us tangled together into my mind for sleepless nights to come.

It was time for Mari to go home.

And soon.

Mari

21

MARI

I curled my legs beneath me, perched on Robe's lap in one of the kitchen chairs. His enormous body engulfed mine, his arms wrapped around me tight as I laced my hands behind his neck. Twists of gold flickered through the deep chocolate browns of his beard in the morning sunlight that filtered into the kitchen from the small windows either side of the door.

For once, we had the house to ourselves.

The quiet that rang through the space was so unusual that after we finished a meager meal of toast and coffee, we just sat entwined together, enjoying silence broken only by soft forest noises outside.

But in here... quiet reigned.

Robe's fingers tangled in my hair, stroking soothingly from my scalp around to the nape of my neck and back again. I tilted my head on the downstrokes, looking up into those deep eyes that had loved and ruined me so many times.

Yet, I was still here.

"What did he do to you? Gi—the man we both fear?"

Robe stilled, his strong fingers ceasing their massage. I

snuggled a little closer, pressing my lips to the cotton of his shirt where it covered his shoulder and peppering it with tiny kisses.

Somewhere between discovering a soul-deep need for each other and breaking away the physical barriers, we broke through some other walls too.

We might not say the name, but we'd come far enough to talk around it.

He sighed. "Why do you want to know?"

I slapped his chest. While I doubted the small dose of violence hurt him one iota, it stung my palm. "Are you kidding me? You've pestered me for five months to tell you about him. I ask once and you say no? That's a letdown."

"Fair enough." Robe closed his eyes for so long, I thought he wouldn't answer. His fingers resumed their trailing path up my spine and began a deep massage across my shoulders. I bit back the moans of pure bliss that pulsed at the edges of my lips when he started to speak.

"I worked shoulder to shoulder with him," Robe began, then halted, watching me. He sucked in a long breath and went on. "For three years, we went through officer training school. We served together twice overseas. There were periods during those years when we didn't see each other, but in the military, that's not unusual. Work long enough in the same circles and eventually you meet people for a second or third time, even if you haven't seen them for a decade or more. It's all too easy to fall back into old habits.

"When we met again, he'd transformed from being a reckless young officer on a small power trip with a chip on his shoulder to become something else altogether. I didn't realize how deep he'd buried himself in George Petersen's pocket until it was too late. A terrible assumption. I lost half my unit to an accident. It turned out to be a job he—my friend turned enemy—headed up, stealing weapons to flood the black market back home." His eyes were shot with remembered anger and pain, a distinct lack of forgiveness tightening his features.

I didn't blame him. "Why would he do that?"

"Petersen owned a paramilitary group he attempted to arm before he took office. I'm still not clear on the purpose— a coup or a political statement. Our old mayor friend switches his loyalty like a flag directed by the wind. Whatever his motivation was, it backfired on him. A lot of arrests were made. We were away, but the news made it to us all the same. Petersen still came out on top, ultimately preventing a gang war he'd sourced weapons for from taking over the city streets. It won him his seat in NYC. Fucked-up shit. But then... he's the politician." Robe's lips twisted. "He always manages to turn something crooked into a positive for himself."

I tilted my head. "I've seen pictures and I know the name, but I've only listened to a few of his speeches. I guess my boss kept that part separate from his business life, which was my focus. Actually, he was really good at compartmentalizing information to make sure people only got as much as they needed for a particular job. And... I'm not really a politics girl."

That comment might make me sound vapid, but I took little interest in a man who sailed under his own flag at the cost of others. Plus, I couldn't vote in the US, so it all seemed a moot point. Robe was right; George Petersen had earned himself a reputation for always turning a negative situation to his own interests.

My knowledge stopped there. Gideon kept me busy. Running between departments and maintaining his office made for a full-time position for more than one person. I managed that job on my own for the last year on my visa, never seeing what an evil man I worked for until....

I clenched my teeth tight, waiting for the inevitable sea of invisible hands, but they didn't come. Robe's touch warded my demons away.

"My friend, he...." Robe's arms stiffened around me, and he pulled me closer. "He made a good officer. Once. Not any longer." He tipped his head back, studying the ceiling.

I searched my memory, coming up with too many blanks. "You worked with him after?"

"When we returned from our last tour, we formed a partnership. He swore he hadn't been involved in the gun heist. I pretended to believe him, wanted to.... So many of my men faced disciplinary action based around what I now know were *his* consequences. The idea that he used the additional money to fund a joint start-up business hit me as wrong, but at the time, my family trust was locked away. I didn't receive that until my parents passed a year later in a break and entry."

"I'm sorry," I whispered, clinging to his shoulders.

"Don't be." He pressed his lips to my temple. "We opted to work in security logistics, a field we both knew well. As it turned out, we ended up with two teams, splitting the business in half less than a year after its inception. We... disagreed on the type of work. He wanted to focus on mercenary contracts that blurred the moral line. I took a stand." He offered me a humorless smile. "Funny how that line moves when it's convenient."

"You do what you have to in each circumstance," I replied, tracing the line of his mouth over his beard. "My boss is very rigid in his beliefs."

Peridot eyes gleamed an unusual shade of gold in the skewed light as he stared up at me. "There's always a choice,

Mari. Gi—he let me keep the business name. I paid him out, though he took plenty of equipment with him. Knight & Watchman began as a small security firm. Bodyguards and glorified mall cops." The corner of his lips tilted beneath my fingers. "After I let him screw me to the wall because I didn't want to play hardball back then, I realized who—and what— I'd become. I opened my eyes and worked out what the people around us needed, developing elite squads and security for hire, and founded a law firm to protect everything I'd built.

"I spent more hours counting dimes and protecting what I'd rescued than anything else. In the end, the expected attack didn't come from any of those avenues. He didn't need my money to bolster his efforts; he came with plenty of his own. His paramilitary squad turned into one of the most brutal teams of mercs I've seen activated outside the Middle East. While I let him distract me, he wormed his slimy way under the nose of officials who reopened the investigation. My men were disciplined. He targeted me as the weak link, turning over evidence only one person could have known, claiming he stole it from me while we did business together.

"I found myself dishonorably discharged, and when I tried to fight the charges he brought against me and Will, an offer of leaving under our own steam arrived. It was either that or remain loud, proud, and locked away for an extended period. *Treason* got tossed around enough that I knew we needed to walk. Miller didn't get charged, though I couldn't do anything more to help Will. Both men were so fucking loyal to a man who couldn't see around the shadow of the man next to him."

"Discharged dishonorably," I amended, then straightened, curving my fingers around his jaw to draw him back to me, looking straight into his eyes. "You're not the man they claim, Robe."

He laughed self-deprecatingly. "Aren't I?" He released me and shifted, pushing both hands through his thick hair.

No matter how rustic Robe Huntingdon's life had become, he didn't seem able to perceive the natural authority that exuded from his pores that every man reacted to. Kind of cute. If a mountain of a man could be called *cute*. But the haunted look in his eyes told me he hadn't forgiven himself for the hurt his actions had caused others.

"No." I prayed he saw the truth in my eyes. "You're not."

Robe let out a harsh breath, freeing his hair to slide his hands down my body, stopping at my hips. "You might be the only one who believes that."

I caught a lock of his short silver hair among the russet, running my fingers through its silky strands, thinking of the men who resided in the house with him, who trusted him and knew him to be so much more, but I knew he wouldn't listen to me right now. "I don't think that's true."

"Isn't it?"

He ran his fingers up my spine again, but when he reached my neck this time, he curved his palm against my nape, angling my head until my lips rested against his for a brief, fixed breath. His tongue sought entry, pushing inside with little resistance, his natural dominance rising.

Goose bumps rippled over my skin as I gave my silent permission, pressing my breasts to his chest and kissing him back. Our tongues danced, stroking and teasing until his grip found my waist.

He squeezed, then dropped his hands, reaching between us. "Ride me, Mari."

I drew back to look over my shoulder, but we were alone. "What if they come back?"

I sucked on my lower lip, trying to deny the urge to rub against him where I ached between my thighs. I never had Robe to myself; somebody else was always around. Call me selfish, but I didn't want our moment of solace interrupted.

"I don't care if the entire household watches me fuck you on the kitchen table, coating my cock with your fluids." Robe's filthy mouth sent ripples of desire shooting through my body.

One knee pushed me to standing. With a rough tug, my pants slid around my hips and tumbled to the floor, and then Robe pulled me back where I'd been a moment before, straddling him.

"It's going to be a quick, hard session, right?" My joke fell flat, the air between us fizzing and pensive.

Robe cursed as he reached around me, gripping my buttock and pressing his fingers against the sensitive nerve endings along the crack of my ass. He fingered my back hole, tracing around the edges as a distraction. I moaned, memorizing the new sensations as his other hand rose up my spine.

Without a single breath of effort, he took hold of the back of my shirt and ripped it open. The flimsy material stood no chance against his determination, splitting down the middle with his undeniable force like so much cotton candy to leave me bare on his lap.

In so many ways.

Robe rubbed the ruined shirt against my cheek. "No underwear, Mari?" He leaned forward and brushed his mouth over mine. Warmth bloomed against my lips, his beard grazing my cheek. Rough—like him.

"I kind of hoped...." My breath lagged, and I couldn't ask, even after all this time alone with him. Dipping my chin to escape his intense stare, I peeked through my lashes.

Robe growled, reaching between us to unzip his fly. His hard length filled one hand. A tiny clear pearl glistened at the tip of his cock. He ran his thumb across it, the weight of his gaze heavy as he smeared the precum over his mushroom head.

"Eyes up here, Mari," he rasped. "What is it Alan calls you —a beautiful little slut?"

Not *my slut*, but *a*.... I swallowed back a moan, knowing Robe needed to claim me, unwilling to share this moment with anyone else, whether they were in the room with us or not.

My beautiful little slut.

I remembered those words tumbling out of Alan's seductive mouth and giving me a thrill that day in the en suite, the day I began to heal. But those same words echoed by Robe? Pure sin ricocheted through me. Paired with his possessiveness, those words made my world spin faster. My body heated from the inside out, arousal coating my inner thighs. I balanced my hands on his shoulders and raised my ass to hover above him.

"Are you on the pills Alan got for you?" Robe forced my chin up with a knuckle so he could see my face. "Tell me you're on them, Mari. I want to fuck you raw."

Need ran down the inside of my thigh, coating us both with a craving only the other could satisfy.

"I'm on them."

No sooner had the words slipped from my mouth than his hands tightened on my hips, pushing me down to grind against his rigid length. My hips rolled forward of their own accord, seeking his tip, offering him entrance. I gasped at the contact, but nothing came out of my mouth.

His lips curving in a rough smile, he released his cock and

jammed me down. My lungs ceased functioning as I moved, easing back and forth to accommodate his girth.

"Robe—" I hated the plea in my voice, but I begged him—for sanity, a breath, *anything*—all the same.

"Uh-uh, sweetheart." His arms wrapped around me, pressing my liquid body flush to his chest. A few shallow thrusts and I gushed around the thick intrusion. My limits reached, he held me close until I molded to the shape of him inside me at this angle, easing the overwhelming stretch. "Better?"

I nodded, brushing my lips over his, needing the contact, his breath on me. "So good."

"That's my girl." Robe squeezed my ass with both hands, helping me rock over him.

He pushed up, hitting places inside me I didn't know were there, that had never been touched like this before. My thighs pressed tight to his, thick denim harsh against soft, marked skin.

Gulping air and breaking the kiss I started, I rose until his full length almost slipped outside, and then I dropped back down, aided by the copious slick of need that coated him tip to balls. His guttural growl broke something inside me. That urgent need he denied—I wanted that. I wanted him to rip through his control because of *me*. Something he couldn't deny any longer, just for us. I leaned forward and picked up my pace, using his body to steady myself as I rode him.

Pleasure rushed through me as he shook his head, urging me to slow, but I tipped my head away and pretended not to see. My hair tickled my back while he gripped my hips and massaged the same circles there that he had on the back of my head earlier. His touch spread bliss through every point of contact. I let my moans flow free, unchecked.

The way he looked at me—like I was his everything, his future, his *now*—jolted me out of my pleasure-induced stupor and brought my release rushing forward. My breath caught. He rocked with me, weathering the clenches and flutters where I bore down on him. He murmured my name and something else as the world shook and a shower of starlight obliterated everything—except him.

Robe cupped the back of my head, tugging at damp strands that clung to my sweat-beaded skin. I licked his collarbone, watching my hands tremble against his chest. Sweat traveled in rivulets between us, pooling in the apex of my thighs where I was joined to him.

"Fuck, Mari," he groaned. "Look at me, sweetheart. I want to see your face as I come inside you."

I lifted my head, the heaviest weight, and rested my lips on his, unable to hold myself up. The edges of my vision frayed into darkness as his next words left me lost between a hot and cold zone. My skin prickled, and I read his words twice, memorizing how his lips moved.

"I love you, Mari Merripen."

Robe pinned me in place and thrust up, taking away my ability to process anything beyond hot flesh pressed together. Rough hands dug into my hips, then my neck, holding my mouth to his. I played that moment over in my mind as he rocked me brutally against his cock.

When my body strained, he took over. Lips grazed mine in a kiss that rattled my soul. The deep rumble in his chest tightened my muscles once more as he worked us both to our limits, stealing my breath with every thrust.

A second, stronger orgasm rose, this one wielded more by my heart than my body, the brunt of its pleasure throwing me forward until I crashed into him, slamming us both into freefall. His mouth ripped from mine to release his roar as my pussy milked his thickening cock.

The cabin quieted in our aftermath. We breathed together in its silence, a tangle of hearts and souls and bodies, though I couldn't remember which parts belonged to me or to him.

Robe

22

ROBE

THE LONGER MARI STAYED, THE LONGER I NEEDED TO test out my theory. I stopped interrogating her in a bid to maintain the level of trust and intimacy that had developed with the woman I'd fallen for so damn hard. From the looks in the eyes of every man standing around the room where Mari had seated herself at our small table, I wasn't alone in my vulnerable state.

Perhaps I'd been in denial for too long... but I didn't want to shatter our fragile peace. Alan boycotted me from playing games with her, but even he saw the sense in trialing just how smart his little *sweetcheeks* could be. He detached himself from the bar and whipped a paper filled with figures and statistics out of... somewhere. He worked his way around to Mari's other side and dropped the sheet in front of her. I recognized it as one of the accounts pages from Gideon's business he'd already spent hours diagnosing, searching for weaknesses on transfers, anything that might give us an inkling on how and where his money went.

He'd pulled this set of transactions apart, leaving little chance that she could tell us anything new. We knew where the trail led—straight to George Petersen. The mayor of New York City was as filthy as the air his coveted city consumed.

"Pop quiz, sweetcheeks." Alan patted her head and gave me a look over his shoulder, though he still spoke to her. "Tell me what you see."

Frowning a little, Mari bent her head over the figures. She hummed beneath her breath, running her finger across lines, then down in a zigzag pattern. The room fell into heavy silence as she worked. I could see her mind churning, the critical part of her that had been missing all along.

My stomach dropped. How much damage had we—had *I* —done to her by keeping her here so I could play with her whenever I felt like it?

She reached out absently, flapping one hand.

Jon grabbed a pen from Alan's private cocktail writing collection behind the bar and tossed it to her. She grabbed it with a mumbled thanks and kept working, circling rows of numbers and underlining others. After everyone began to fidget, she made a line straight down one side of the page and added a little arrow off the side.

"The fuck is she doing?" Jon grunted in my ear.

Across from us, Miller folded his arms over his chest as he watched her, a stormy expression taking over his face. I curbed the defense that lurched to the forefront of my mind, but I didn't need it. Miller brooded in silence, stewing at the far corner of the room. We all knew what he was thinking, and more than a few exchanged glances confirmed my long-term fear.

"Mari's a setup, and you've allowed her into our inner circle."

"She's not loyal to you like we are."

"You risk everything we've built together."

But I'd risk everything to give her the chance to prove herself yet again to us. To me.

She *had* been set up, and no part of me wanted to believe that the girl I caught running for her existence playacted through the horrors she suffered in order to gain entrance to our world. But Miller's fears overtook that assessment. Even if her trauma was real, Gideon had inserted an oblivious Trojan horse into my home who he could take back at any time and extract crucial information from her pretty, dark head—even if he killed her in the process.

I love you.

Her reaction to those three words, nonverbal on her side though still present between us, told me everything I needed to know.

That she gave her loyalty to me, and she loved me back.

That she loved *all* of us—even Miller. The way she flirted with Jon, sharing confidences, looking after Alan when he crawled in the door damaged and hurting. Falling for Will's sweet sense of romance, an air of innocence surrounding them despite the inner turmoil I knew he suffered.

She loved us, and we all loved her back in our own ways, fucked up as our history made us. Words didn't need to be spoken to express what actions said on her behalf.

Another frustrated sound originated in her throat as she crinkled the edges of the paper. Mari's expressions trawled across her face no matter how hard she'd tried to conceal her fears in our early days together. I made a mental note to up my interrogation techniques, maybe plant a few false memories of my own in there as a confusion tactic, just in case.

I won't let her be taken from me.

And I refused to let my needs place these men and her in danger. Whatever I could do now still wouldn't save her life if he got hold of her again. Nothing would. I knew that. A heavy weight that seeded too deep in my stomach reeked of selfish guilt no matter how I justified it. The thought of losing anyone else broke me.

"He told her to tell us what she could see." I paraphrased Alan's words, knowing Jon was still processing everything I'd already come to terms with. He'd come so damn close to declaring himself to her—if he hadn't already in private. But I didn't think so.

"Shush." Alan sent another baleful look over his shoulder, wedging his ass against the chair beside Mari. "Ignore them, sweetcakes." He watched her fondly as she flipped the page over to check for information on the back.

She looked so damn innocent and sweet there, like she belonged between us. Beside us. My heart twitched. I had no defense against the pain that ripped through me. *We* were her place right now, though we couldn't be her forever home, and we weren't her forever people. Somewhere in the world, she had a home that wasn't us, and I had to return her to her place no matter how much that thought stung.

"Finished." She flicked the page at Alan, shoulders straight with a palpable energy I hadn't seen from her since I first paired her with Miller for sparring. "It would help if the pages were complete. Would you like an interpretation service as well?"

Alan made a show of turning the page around and held it out to her upside down. "Which way does it go?"

"Smart-ass." She huffed and snatched the paper back, then spread it out on the table. "Here, here, and... here. These are regular payments. Bills, maybe. Transactions that go to the same place, like a scheduled drop. It'll be something he— *they* set up as a timed transfer. Or whoever accesses the accounts." Her eyes narrowed as she corrected the ownership slip that didn't go unnoticed.

I wondered how much she'd guessed about who the accounts belonged to, considering no name was listed on the page.

"That's good. What else?" Alan folded his arms, mirroring Miller across the room, sans the simmering rage. His eyes were hooded, a sense of pride and possession lighting his face.

Jealousy smashed over me as she explained a few more basic things about the account and smiled back. I wanted her to look at me that way, damnit.

But hadn't I been the one who pushed for sharing her? My jealousy didn't spring from Alan's ability to love her, or earn her love for him back, or what I saw in their easy banter as they worked through the task together.

What hurt was that the trust she'd developed with him still felt tenuous with me in this fragile moment.

I shifted, taking an unconscious step forward before I checked myself. Jon's gaze darted toward me, and I cursed inside my head for giving myself away. Schooling my face to a blank canvas, I rocked back on my heels under the guise of rubbing my shoulder blades on the lip of the bar. Jon looked back at Mari, and I breathed again, unsure why I needed to hide my revelation over her love for my bartender, though the fucker still owed me. Their connection seemed to have been obvious to the rest of the household, but I wanted to keep that moment private for a while longer.

Maybe until I could have Mari alone again.

"It all looks normal, except that there are transactions that don't line up." Her gaze broke from Alan's to meet mine, an accusation blazing there.

"If you gave me full access, this would have been easier."

Her intelligence was a massive turn-on. I might have

grinned like a lovelorn teen if her words hadn't broken through my sensibilities first.

"What?" Alan and I said at the same time, and even Miller took a step forward.

Mari smirked, knowing she'd earned our attention. "Here. This transfer comes in and goes out several times. Kind of like a clownfish." She grinned. But when I offered her a small smile back, she shook her head as though she'd taken it as condescending. "He tried to send it somewhere, and it was rejected. Why? And here, it's come back again... but out of order. More than once," she clarified. "Like an electronic check bounced. The transaction changed, its progress halted. Listed as a scam, maybe. Why would you do that? Where did it go? This throws everything out, and the balances don't match up. See? Where's the rest of this?" She flapped her hand at the page, frustration and pride warring for prime real estate on her face.

I met Miller's eyes over her head. He offered a small shrug, conceding defeat for now. I had no doubt that he'd find another angle to attack her on until she wore him down like she had the rest of us.

I was the first sucker who fell for her, more than willing to man up and admit that her appearance in my section of the woods had been a turning point. Our twisted little band grew without effort, and I wanted to keep it that way forever.

Pity that can never happen, asshole.

Maybe karma from my previous life let me find the perfect girl—beautiful, clever, brave—but that same cosmic bitch slap also said I needed to set her free. I'd cloistered her away under a guise of health and recovery, but I couldn't claim those reasons any longer. Mari had stood up to us, pushed away Miller's bullying, his rage, and etched herself into each of our souls in her own way. Even if some of us—maybe just one—were in denial.

I knew she needed to be free to enjoy her own new life, even at a detrimental risk to us.

Away from us.

I swallowed a wave of grief in advance of that impending break for freedom without us to tether her to the ridgeline we ourselves couldn't escape.

Maybe she'll come back.

Yeah, and maybe Gideon would lay down arms and become part of the neighborhood watch.

"Show me that." Alan snatched the paper from her hand and ran his finger along her calculations, ignoring the chatter that broke out around him.

I stopped pretending disinterest and leaned over his shoulder, offering Mari a quick wink that drew a blush to her cheeks. She'd circled the suspect transactions. Alan stopped when he came to one reversal that had been heavily underlined. He whipped out a second piece of paper and lined it up seamlessly.

Mari craned to look over the pages that matched up line for line. "I knew you were holding something back. Asshats," she muttered with no small dose of amusement.

Alan glanced sideways, and I nodded my assent. If he wanted to test her, this was the best way. She'd spotted something we all overlooked the many times we'd trawled through these same accounts, some of the transactions Gideon's, others from an unknown source, though I had my suspicions.

Her eyes were fresh, and she provided a perspective I needed. My lips rose at one corner. Miller was going to be pissed that I didn't play this out logically but followed my heart instead.

I had a reason to keep her. Again.

"How about now?" Alan folded his arms and stepped back, his expression closed, cold.

Mari looked over her shoulder toward the darkening doorway as long shadows lingered in the yard outside. Her eyes darted around the room, settling on Jon, then me, and avoided Miller in his brooding depths altogether.

"I thought—"

"You thought right, Mari." I met her gaze. "Same job, different details. Show us what you see now." I closed my fist, letting my nails bite into my palm.

Come on, Mari Merripen. Give me a reason for you to stay.

Mari's head went down again as she connected each line to its transaction in a methodical sequence. There were faster ways to find the information, but seeing as we gave her half a job in the first place, it made sense that she took a longer path to get there, cross-checking her initial assessment.

And all the shit we missed.

"Who owns this account?" Mari ran her finger across an account number printed at the top of the paper.

Alan shrugged. "I have no idea. I can't find it, so it doesn't —*shouldn't*—exist."

"Fair enough." Mari nodded, taking his assumed skill set in her stride. She connected three transactions together and carried over a balance to one side. "These don't line up. Something's missing."

"They redirect to George Petersen's accounts." Alan leaned forward to wrap his arms around her upper body, brushing his thumbs beneath her breasts. "Can you do it with distraction?" He glanced at me as she shivered and then back at the page again.

"The mayor of New York City?" She frowned, turning the papers to look at the blank spaces on the back. Her lips pursed, and her tongue flickered out to wet the corner of her lips.

A collective sigh swept through the room, every one of us taking an appreciative moment over what that tongue could do, except for Miller, who stiffened as the ambience of the room changed.

"Yes, sweetcakes."

"A line has been removed here." She traced a fingertip across the back of the page, then flipped the page to point it out to Alan.

"Photographic...." He shook his head and then dropped a kiss on the top of hers before he whisked the papers away, leaving her playing with the pen. "You're so precious, Mari."

"Is that it? What happens now?"

Already engrossed in studying the figures and muttering to himself, Alan plucked the pen away and added notations to one corner of the paper.

Her head swiveled between me and Jon. "Robe?"

Mari wasn't stupid. We gave her specific information on some of our more clandestine activities she hadn't been aware of before. Whatever she suspected, we'd just confirmed it.

"Now you go home." Miller didn't budge, though his chin dipped as he glared at her, a muscle in his cheek twitching.

Mari's eyes widened, her curls already shaking side to side. "No." Desperation brought her to her feet. "I don't want to go home. I don't *have* a home. Except here."

I stepped forward, resting a hand on her shoulder. The contact sang with the same energy that lit her gaze aflame. "No, little runner. You don't get to go home. Now, I thought you might like to work." I stared at Miller in challenge, offering him a onetime silent warning.

He kicked the wall before disappearing out the door.

"Looks to me like he's the one always doing a runner," Mari muttered.

Jon laughed, breaking the tension. "She's not wrong."

"I know I'm not. That's why you're keeping me." A cute and snarky-as-hell smile tilted her soft pink lips.

I slid my hands along her arms, circling them around her waist. She let out a soft squeak of surprise but didn't pull away. "That's one of the reasons." *The other is that I can't let you go no matter how much of a threat you might or might not be to me or the men I'm responsible for.*

Not that I continued to believe Mari would willingly hurt us.

Crooking a knuckle beneath her chin, I tipped her head back and leaned down to claim a kiss. I meant it to be brief, but... that didn't happen. Once her lips parted, I was gone. My jeans constricted my blood flow as I leaned into her, trailing my mouth along her cheek to her ear.

She sighed, linking her hands behind my head and arching into my touch. "That's good."

"Good, huh?" I paused, holding her in a firm embrace, blocking out the rest of the room and lowering my voice so she alone could hear me. "I can think of other things that come under that heading."

Her soft giggle nourished a flame of arousal that burned deep and long for the girl I loved. I always longed to earn one of those pretty little sounds from her.

And now I had.

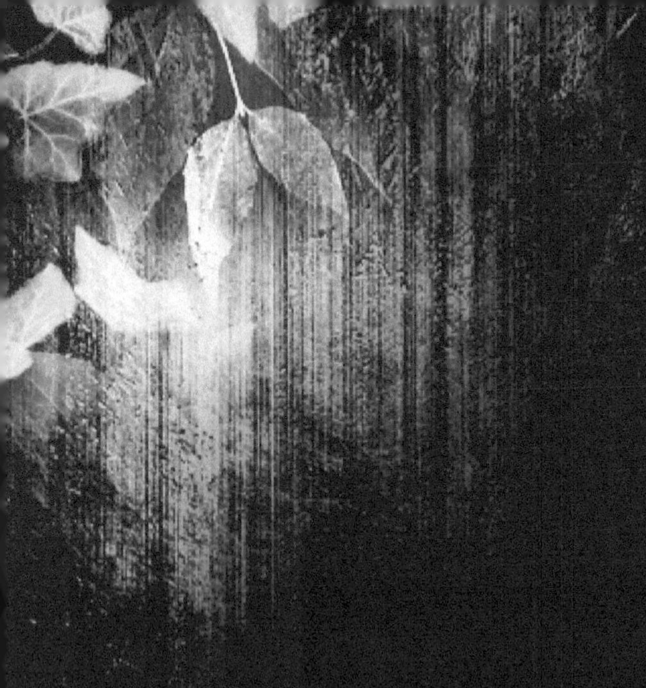

Robe

23

ROBE

Brandon: He moved us on. No police, men
in all black holding automatic weapons. A
few broken ribs, maybe a bone or two, and a
whole lotta bruising.

I REREAD BRANDON'S MESSAGE FOR THE THIRD TIME,
my phone creaking in my grip. The sun hadn't even risen yet,
and already the day turned to shit.

"I'm out." I tossed my phone onto the bar as I strode
through the kitchen and grabbed my jacket off a hook on the
wall. "I need a bike."

"Whoa, Robe. Slow down." Alan popped up from beneath
the bar, a half-empty box of beers clutched in his arms. He
leaned down to read the message before the screen blacked
out. "Shit. Hold up. I can be there in a second—" He looked
around for a place to unload his burden and ended up
dumping the box on the floor.

"No, stay with Mari," I snapped. "Will, Miller. You're
with me."

"Sir."

I didn't know who said it, nor did I care. Only that they did what I required.

"Maybe you should think about this." Jon gripped my shoulder. "He expects you to retaliate."

A deep growl rose in my chest as I faced Jon head-on. "I'm not retaliating. I'm looking after my damn people."

People I let on my land, promising them security.

A friend I'm responsible for.

Now Brandon's protesters who relied on him—and by proxy, me—for protection were hurting.

"These aren't your men, Robe. They knew the risks when they asked to form a picket line on your land." Though Jon kept his tone light, it belied the reproach in his eyes. "Be smarter. Isn't that what you taught me?"

"I gave my permission, which makes them my responsibility," I grated. "Get out of my way."

Jon held my glare for a breath. His broad form filled the space between me and the exit, a blockade I'd break, though having his permission would be easier. His frown deepened as he folded his arms over his chest in a show of discomfort.

My rage boiled over, and I wondered what it would take to make him move without doing permanent damage to the man who'd had my back since I walked out of New York City with nothing but the clothes I wore and twenty bucks in my pocket.

A sigh gusted from between my clenched teeth, frustration and understanding mingling in the pensive air between us. Jon dipped his shoulder to let me storm out of the cabin, Miller and Will trailing at my back.

As I hit the veranda, where I shoved my feet into my boots, a small commotion drew my attention back to the bar. A glance over my shoulder confirmed that Mari stood rubbing her eyes in the doorway to my bedroom, her sleep-mussed hair looking sexy as fuck.

"What's happening? Where is he going?" She spoke to Alan, but her gaze found mine and locked on.

My heart tugged at the mix of confusion and betrayal written on her face. I pushed a residual dose of guilt away and focused on the people who needed my attention right now. Broken bones meant a hospital, which entailed leaving our relative security on the ridge to head into the public eye. My personal vendetta had been revisited on innocents. Guilt gnawed at me from the inside.

Without a second glance, I walked away from Mari and the hurt straining her face.

THE BIKES WERE HOUSED IN A CAMOUFLAGED SHED AT the back of the house. Like our weapons hidden around the property, the bikes were checked and maintained under the cover of night when the rest of the ridgeline's scant residents slept or went about their own business. Not that a little night vision mightn't stop Gideon or his team of mercs from getting a glimpse into our own nocturnal activities. Perhaps the turnabout was fair play, after all.

The midnight blue finish glittered beneath the dappled light as I pulled the cover off and ran my hand along the machine's familiar curves. The leather seat felt like an old friend as I settled over the dirt bike—a road bike in our section of the woods would be worse than useless. Hitting the mountain tracks cleared my head like nothing else.

It didn't take long to work my way down the mountainside, followed by Will. Miller, as usual, took his own route, crossing that boundary line into Gideon's land we were supposed to honor.

An aggressive rubber profile churned over dirt and stone beneath me. I didn't bother to look for Miller, keeping my eyes on the faintest track in front of me. I'd made my way down the rock face enough times over the years, and Will covered our tracks so the path disappeared behind him, even when I knew where to look.

I paused at the edge of a short cliff face outside visual range of the house. Shouts echoed up the rock strata, the picket line closing out in the attack's aftermath. I cursed myself for not foreseeing the event that was right on brand for Blackthorne. At least I didn't hear the gunshots I expected, which left me cloaked in relief—for now. I tipped my wheel over the edge of a granite block and stopped, scanning the ground below.

No path appeared where it should have been. For the life of me, I couldn't see beyond a breakneck drop and a sudden stop with a mortal end written all over it.

"On your left." Will edged around me. Sandy-brown hair flopped over one eye as he shot me a cheeky grin and dove off the cliff of death. His bike bounced on a slab of granite and disappeared over the next low rise, the sharp report of his exhaust heading down the mountainside.

Jesus fucking Christ.

The kid was a daredevil, and I was a crotchety old man. Shit, if boredom filled his brains, then I needed to give him something better to do on his nights off.

Kidding. We never took nights off.

I revved the bike and followed his path, bouncing across the hard slabs. My tire sank into a concealed layer of peat moss as I followed him over the rise. Minutes later I parked my bike at the bottom of the hill on the well-maintained dirt road that bordered the northern edge where my land met Gideon's.

Well maintained because I made sure we kept it that way, for a multitude of reasons.

The picket line had devolved into a bedraggled cluster of campsites scattered around the foothills of the ridge filled with haggard, rugged-up civilians. I counted maybe thirty heads milling about. Recluse I might have become, but if this was what Brandon considered small, I'd hate to see what a big protest looked like.

I sought out the balding head above the blue puffer jacket Brandon favored. His height and glowing dome made him an all-too-easy target. Rheumy sky-blue eyes lit up. He dashed to my side, speed belying his age.

Mind, after that trick at the top of the hill, *sprightly* might never describe me again.

Will gave us a short wave from where he was kneeling beside a man with a makeshift bandage wrapped around his ribs. My leg cramped, but not as bad as my ass. I swept one boot over the bike seat and stretched.

"What happened?" I asked.

"Three were sent off to Mount View Hospital. A few more went home. Quitters," he muttered under his breath, but there was little animosity in his tone. "No police turned up, though."

"Funny that."

Fucking hilarious.

I swiped my hand across my mouth as I searched the clusters of people talking in muted voices, noting the absence of several figures in particular.

"Where are the men Gideon sent?"

Brandon gestured into the trees behind a huddle of people in the opposite direction from the one we came from. Most were twenty years the junior of those in Brandon's picket line and underdressed for the conditions. My lip quirked. I knew what his next words would be before he said them.

"Over there—well, they were over there." Brandon rubbed a hand over more than a day's growth on his chin. "Damnit. I wanted you to talk to them."

I nodded, keeping my thoughts to myself. These people weren't anything more than social activists working toward a goal that looked good on paper. Their cause hadn't riled Gideon enough to send a small army down the ridgeline. Whatever the men he sent did, Brandon stayed. How bad could it be?

But I knew better and glanced into the trees above for the telltale glint of a scope. One hand poked out of foliage in a thumbs-up to disappear just as fast. I disguised a laugh as a hasty cough behind my fist and turned back to Brandon.

"I know I gave you permission to protest here, old friend." I held his gaze as he nodded. "But that time has passed. It will be safer for all of you if you leave now. Send me all the information you have, along with your costs, and I'll try to secure resources and votes for your cause in other ways."

Brandon reached around me and squeezed me between long, lean arms. "We worry about you, Robe. And your boys up there. Take care of him."

This last was directed at Will, who joined us, offering a hug Brandon returned, gratitude clear in his wide smile and crinkled eyes.

Brandon hesitated, his mouth open, though he didn't say anything further. I set my teeth in a hard line. The old man had no idea how close his people had come to losing their lives today.

If his group were any smaller, the casualties would have been much worse, or Will and I might have found a campsite filled with bodies. Their number saved him; that, and his setup on my land, not on the other side of the road.

Swallowing down my fury at Gideon's assault, I returned the embrace with care. "You, too, old man."

Brandon gave me a mini salute and trotted off, rounding up his members. Within an hour, a few posters and a large patch of disturbed ground were all that remained of their protest.

If Gideon had a problem with that, or his missing men, he was welcome to chat with me any time.

Mari

24

MARI

Steam wisped from my skin as I stepped out of the bathroom, pulling the fluffy sweater Alan had provided down over my stomach. My muscles ached, but the extra training Robe insisted on honed both my body and my mind. The additional mental work I garnered in Robe's office helped keep that muscle toned too.

I knew without looking that Robe watched me, increasing the heat in the otherwise cool room. Ignoring him, I balled my filthy clothes into a bundle and tossed them toward the hamper in one corner of the room without breaking my stride to tumble face-first onto the bed.

"Oh, my fucking God. That feels good."

"My little Mari, swearing?"

I raised my head just enough to crack one eye open and stared at him blearily. "Not even close." I face-planted back into the pillow, letting out a small moan at the soft comfort against aching muscles. Even my *face* hurt.

"You shouldn't make sounds like that, Mari." Heavy foot-balls announced that his presence was now a whole lot closer than where he'd stood a moment before. "You never know which monsters might be listening."

"Donchuntas amunnsster," I mumbled into the blankets.

"Your definition of monsters is skewed." Robe interpreted Mari-speak with proficiency as he planted himself beside me. The hard mattress that felt like cloud heaven dipped to accommodate his bulk.

"Maybe?" I rolled into him under the weight of gravity. Broad hands rested on my shoulders and began to work the soreness from my strained muscles, tracing circles on my spine. "Don't stop. Keep going."

"What's the magic word? You do have those in Britain, right?"

Britain felt a world away right now, one I never wanted to go back to. Ever. *Much*. "Fuck you."

"More cussing. Such a dirty mouth."

A ripple of tension followed his fingers as he resumed his massage. "I think I said don't stop." His fingers halted their progress. "Please?" The words slipped out of my mouth. I winced and waited for some testosterone-fueled repartee to strike me down, too tired to go on the offense.

But he didn't insult me as he worked each muscle group, warming my skin and easing the soreness I'd acquired at his behest. I moaned into his blankets, dropping my face back into the welcoming darkness.

"Remember what I said about monsters, Mari?" His hands closed around my ribs, almost encircling my spine to my stomach. "Jesus, you're tiny."

"Nope, you're just so big."

A heavy silence fell between us. "We're doing this?" Robe shifted, plucking at my sweater. "Take this off."

That I couldn't ignore. "What?" I took his advice and

thought about the monster in the room, deciding I wanted him.

"Mari." His voice lowered impossibly, and anticipation swept along my spine. "Take this off so I can finish your massage."

"Oh. I thought you were suggesting...."

Breath rushed from him, and he pressed down a little harder, digging calloused hands into my skin. "Are you disappointed?"

I rubbed my lips together, burrowing back into the bedding, and didn't answer him, afraid of what might come out if I did.

"Get up. Pants and sweater off. Now." Robe left me where I lay.

Clutching the hem, I turned in time to see him dive into the en suite I'd recently vacated. I tugged the material over my head and shed the pants before sliding between crisp black sheets. Something about being naked in his bed left me in a wanton state of mind. Then I remembered how I woke like this in his room the first night I stayed in his house, then the night he first made love to me with Jon wrapped around us both. The memories didn't make me feel any less aroused.

"I really was suggesting something else." He knelt on the bed, holding a bottle in one gigantic hand. "Roll over."

I stuffed my face into his pillow, breathing in the scent of him and Jon combined. "Oh, yeah?" I teased, slapping on my best American tough-girl persona, though my voice came out so muffled by the hard pillow that felt so fluffy after hours of training with Miller and Jon that my tone lost most of its effect.

The bed depressed as he settled his weight, straddling me with an enormous thigh on either side of my hips. I dared to take a breath, but he didn't squash me like I expected. Something cool hit my back, and then his fingers slipped across my body. He resumed his massage aided by the oily slick that let him work me deeper.

I relaxed, lifting my head the barest minimum to speak. "Where did you get massage oils? Is there something you want to tell me about the sleeping arrangements here, Robe?" I yawned into the pillow and plopped my head back down.

Robe paused. "My sister," he said shortly.

Of course I knew about his sister—her creams and body lotions were the feminine products I used. One more link to the outside world, along with Alan and Miller.

"She sounds like a good sister," I murmured. "You must miss her."

"I do." Robe's voice cracked like sharp toffee. He sighed. "She's all the family I have left. None of us have much to keep us here, yet here we stay."

He worked his hands a little too hard over my shoulder, but I let it ride. The damage there healed long ago, and I sensed his need to release whatever was eating him inside.

"You have each other, you know. Ow." A whimper busted through my short-lived vow of silence.

"You're right. We do." He paused. "Sorry."

"For attacking my back, or for not valuing the wonderful collection of broken things you've mended here?"

"You do sound like the professional shrink." Robe kept working, rolling his knuckles against stubborn spots.

After a few minutes, the tension in my muscles began to ease, and I suspected the remaining aches could be attributed to other stresses during my time in the cabin that went beyond working out.

I closed my eyes and let out a soft sigh. "That feels so good." Releasing my death grip on the pillow, I arched my back.

He stuffed what felt like a stiff tower of pillows beneath me. My spine appreciated the support, and I mumbled my thanks to the pillows, floating on fluffy darkness. An oxymoron as well as a mixed metaphor, perhaps, but it suited him.

Suited *us*.

Robe squeezed my sides, and I knew we both valued the warmth and silence of the moment he'd created.

For nearly six months, every inch of me had been terrified of Robe—and wanted him pressed against me at the same time, while he worried I might freak out or sneak away. And I had my own hang-ups. But suddenly, none of them seemed as important as they had before. The trust we'd generated over our time together that had stretched out inch by coveted inch landed us... here.

And I didn't want to leave.

I strangled the pillow in tight arms that undid all the work he'd put into my back.

"You're not the only one who feels... good." Robe snorted and started to free up my muscles again. "The girl who has my boys in knots fantasizing about what they think they can't have."

"They don't think that." I paused, letting my mind wander. Alan had said plenty of things along those lines while flirting. "Maybe one," I conceded.

"You're too nice, sweetheart." He traced a word on my back, too fast for me to make out. "Do you enjoy working on the accounts?"

"You told me to do it. It's not like anything else is taking up my time."

"Isn't it?" He hesitated over my ribs. "We need to cover you up before you get too cold. Are you tired?"

"Which do you want me to answer first?" I yawned again.

By the time I managed to mumble some inaudible response, I'd forgotten half his questions. "I'm not bored with the work, exactly. I like to be active, and I like to feel useful. That somehow I can help. That was why—" My breath caught, but he didn't push. I swallowed. "Why I chose the job I did."

"You're helping."

"How so? The job feels fake, like it's something you could all do without me, something to, I don't know, keep me here. Occupied. I take up everyone's time, alcohol, food, and hot water. According to Alan, I am a pretty cu—um, pussy you all want to fuck." I closed my eyes and stopped—everything.

Stopped worrying, stopped fighting the edge of sleep and combating my fears.

Robe's presence left me safer than I could ever ask for. Nothing could hurt me here, and if he stayed, I would sleep heavy and dreamless.

Which sounded pretty dandy at that moment.

Robe stilled. "A pretty pink cunt to fuck," he amended, adding his own touch to another man's words.

Shit. My tongue got loose with this man. *Noted.* "Okay, so I paraphrased."

"Did you?"

I winced. "It's pretty close?"

He growled, all low and protective and sexy as all get-out. "That boy doesn't know when to leave well enough alone."

"He's doing what the rest of you feel you can't." Okay, so I could add grump to my tired repertoire.

"Sassy girl." He caught my hair, turning my head to the side, and traced his oiled fingertips across my bottom lip.

My eyes flew open, fixing on him as he arced over me. I shifted my hips, trying to alleviate some of the pressure on the body parts we'd been talking about that came to life all on their own.

"Don't do that." Robe's voice deepened.

"Huh?" I twisted, but my body wasn't having it. I flopped back down. His other hand rested in the middle of my back, stroking across the curve of my waist in an intimate caress. "Robe—"

"This is a bad fucking idea today, Mari. My mood.... Stop," he breathed, fingers fisted through my hair, holding me in place. "Distract me. Who do you like training with the best?"

"I don't know." I considered wiggling my hips again, but he'd asked me to stop. How many times had I said the same thing to him in the beginning?

So... training. Was *anyone* an answer? I didn't spend half as much time with Robe as I did the other boys, despite wishing I had him to myself more often. He might be intense as hell, but my connection with him overshadowed the ones I had with everyone else by far... even Alan.

All of them had their own brand of damage, each man broken like me.

Alan's flirtatious nature concealed an intelligent boy who couldn't trust anyone, and he kept his mind—and hands— busy behind the bar. Jon's steadfastness melded with a savageness within that he let out in violent sessions with his axe. Will appeared soft and easygoing until I looked a little deeper and found a darkness welling beneath his shy smile. Not that I trusted a pretty face any longer, knowing his lethality made him as dangerous as the rest of them.

In fact, the only one brutal enough to train me the way I knew Robe wanted—

"Miller." The angry man's name left my mouth and felt right.

"Miller?" He snorted. "You do have a death wish."

"Maybe." I didn't have a better answer.

Robe resumed his massage. "Why?"

"He doesn't go easier because I'm not one of you. I mean, you're all nice and cute and look after me and spoil me, but… I learn more from him. Sure, he's grumpy like you, and stubborn. Plus, he has skills. I respect that now that I know more of what and who is out here. I know he doesn't like me, and I know he doesn't trust me. Hell, in his place, I might not like me either. He's protecting you. And he loves you. That makes him important."

Robe didn't answer me for a long moment, silent in his concentration. He pressed a hand between my shoulder blades that didn't feel quite so slippery, like I'd absorbed most of the oil.

"You fit better than you know," he said softly. "Despite the way you arrived, I'm glad you're here."

I smiled as he leaned down and pressed a chaste kiss to my temple. Tension melted from me as he shifted his weight, sitting at my side instead of on top of me, like he had no intention of moving all night. One hand trailed my ribs in the lightest touch, my lower body falling into sync with the gentle pressure there.

A heaviness pressed over me in an invisible blanket of security, my eyes drifting shut before I dropped into the realm of sleep and dreams.

"Me too."

Robe

25

ROBE

I squinted into the darkness, balanced on one knee behind a small rocky outcrop not far from the house. "My night vision is shite. I don't see anything," I confessed, aware of the Mari-isms slipping into my speech.

Will crouched at my side, a wild grin spreading across his face. "Getting old," he muttered, digging an elbow into my side.

Grunting, I shook my head. "Watch it, kid." I nodded when he gestured to the pathway that led to the house, still struggling to see anything.

"Three, two... one." Will shifted his weight and sprang up, his lean-muscled body arcing through the air before it collided with something that yelped as he landed.

A yelp too low to be feminine, but familiar. I frowned, pushing myself up on cracking knees as Will dragged the person forward.

"What damage did you do?" My jovial reply dropped as I recognized the bright blue puffer jacket bundled in Will's arms. The body inside it seemed smaller than I remembered.

Dark streaks covered a balding dome and the jacket in matching stripes.

"Brandon? Fuck," I snapped, gesturing for Will to lay my neighbor out on the ground. I pressed my fingers to his throat, searching for a pulse, and finally found one, light but fast. "Wake up, old man." I tapped his cold cheek as I searched his body for wounds with my other hand. Something slicked my fingers with fluid, and when I withdrew, they came up glistening, even in the darkness. "Get him inside."

Will nodded, gathering Brandon's still form and rising without effort. Not a damn thing on him creaked.

Shit, he's right. I'm getting old.

I shoved the cabin door open with my boot, holding it aside for Will to enter. "Futon. Open it up," I barked to Miller.

The stocky soldier reacted to the order in a flurry of efficient movement like we had never left the desert. His attention remained on the doorway in a show of situational awareness I needed to remember to praise him for later as he pulled the bedding open and flipped back the covers.

I gave him a nod of thanks, which was all I had time for before Will carried his burden inside the walls that gave us the facade of freedom and security. I remained in the doorway, noting the trail of blood that thickened with every step my youngest tenant took.

Brandon groaned, shifting on the futon Miller had pulled out for him, shooting me a quick glance. Miller's brow furrowed as he ran his fingers over the man's pale skin, noting the blue tinge around his eyes. He dove down the hall in the next second and returned with a black plastic case. He held a roll of gauze in one hand as he ripped Brandon's shirt open and then stopped.

Blood oozed in a constant stream from a jagged slit in the

man's abdomen. How the hell he'd made it up the ridge was a miracle. I didn't need Miller's subtle headshake to understand that no amount of gauze could fix the problem. He shoved it in anyway, then threw another thick pad over the top and pressed down.

"Maybe if we—" he started.

I shook my head, but I didn't need to stop him.

"Too late, young man." Brandon coughed, spraying blood over Miller's cheek. The stoic ex-soldier didn't flinch.

I knelt beside Brandon, cupping my hand behind his head. Will stepped back, giving me space, and headed for my bedroom door as Mari emerged, shoving hair back from her face. She was dressed in a long white cotton nightgown that concealed little, given the amount of material involved.

Will wound his arms around her, and he spoke in a muted tone. She'd be safe with him. I switched my attention back to the old friend bleeding out in my living room.

"What happened?" I asked, noting the sickly pallor in his face.

Miller caught my eye and shrugged. The man had a few minutes to live, and despite wanting him to be as comfortable as possible, I also needed information.

Brandon smiled, a weary expression that chilled me to my bones. "You're not safe, Robe. He won't stop."

"Who?" I pushed, gripping his hand tight. "I need a name, Brandon. Then you can rest."

Miller extracted a syringe filled with a clear liquid, resting his elbow on the bandage-clogged hole in Brandon's body, the dressings stained with blood all the way through.

"Wait," I mouthed to him.

He rocked back on his heels, his expression tense.

"You know who." Brandon coughed. A weaker dribble of pinkish fluid left his mouth. "Blackthorne is an evil man.

He took girls—" He hacked, evicting red spray from his throat.

Miller shoved me aside and plunged the syringe into Brandon's neck as blood pumped from the wound where he put pressure, a pack of clotting powder exploding in his fist. He was too late; the old man's eyes closed and his body… stopped.

Silence filled the cabin, punctuated only by Mari's soft gasp. In my periphery, I saw her pull at Will's hold, but he refused to let her come any closer. I was grateful for his intervention. She'd already experienced enough trauma and didn't need anyone else's ghost haunting her damaged mind.

I couldn't help raising my eyes to meet hers, Brandon's hacked-out words rippling around us.

"He took girls."

I stepped back to let Miller slide into my vacated space. He closed the man's eyes and began to straighten him with the efficiency of a man who had a triple-figure body count to his name as a medic. We'd lost enough men together both at home and overseas, and I knew he would be respectful in my absence.

Her mouth framed my name, but I didn't hear her or stop at the tears that flooded her eyes. Not when Will stared at me, his face stricken, and then looked back at her.

I strode from the cabin, murder on my mind.

***

THE OPEN TRUNK OF A LONG-DECEASED OAK TREE, ITS reaching, twisted shape rare enough to be memorable in its position at the edge of my land, housed my preferred long-bow. I gripped the curved wood that melded to my hand, testing the tension on the string. It would do me no good if it broke when I required its strength most.

I slung a quiver of handmade arrows across my back as I ran in a low crouch to the edge of a rise opposite to where we found Brandon. It struck me that he hadn't come from anywhere near Blackthorne's drive or the compound. Almost as if someone wanted me to find him.

I would give a solid answer to that demerit.

I stared across the valley that divided the land into twin thousand-acre blocks. More than once I'd stood on this rise during daylight hours, notched an arrow, and measured the shot I aimed at Gideon's study.

It would only work if he was there, at the right time, in the right place. I prayed tonight would give me what I needed most.

The house beyond the walls was lit up, the too-bright glow bleeding into the night from every room. Standing out in the open should have screwed with my usual sense of self-preservation, but right now, I didn't care. The pain of losing a friend had etched itself in my soul, another mark for a man I failed.

I didn't have the convenience of guilt. Instead, I chose a straight arrow from the quiver and notched it, narrowing my gaze at the window. My rage sent dose after dose of adrenaline coursing through my body. My hands didn't shake as I took aim, noting the wraiths that moved from place to place, but none shifted around his study.

Movement flickered lower, out on the edge of the wall. I stared into the blaring light, unable to focus on the figure without significant distraction. The height and build matched.... Who else would be out on the edge of his protection zone tonight? He knew I'd come for him. I aimed the shot, letting breath leave my lungs, holding myself still, silent.

Excruciating light flared my night vision out as I loosed

the arrow. A spotlight worthy of the Super Bowl burned my retinas. I took a knee to the granite, pressing the heels of my hands into my eye sockets. I groaned at the intense pressure that bit into my brain in an instant migraine.

Shards of stone and shot ricocheted around me. I scuffled back under the course of aimed fire forcing me to retreat. The distraction worked. My night vision fucked up, I could barely focus on anything beyond stumbling away into the darkness and out of the sniper's range.

Gideon Blackthorne had destroyed another life and walked yet again.

I staggered back to the house, snuffing out the need to hold Mari and focusing on vengeance, letting it consume me.

Nothing else mattered.

Mari

26
MARI

THE MAN I LOVED HURT AFTER THE DEATH OF HIS friend, and he refused to let me help him. He'd barely spoken to anyone except for Miller since Brandon had bled all over the cabin floor that night. When he came back... we all saw a part of Robe I knew he'd never want exposed. The man had too much pride and ego invested in his infallible status. That didn't mean I'd back down. I simply had to find a way around his stubbornness.

I slipped my arms around Robe's waist. "Take me for a walk?" I knew he wouldn't let me go alone, and today I didn't want to be without him.

His spine stiffened. "Will can take you."

"No," I murmured firmly, squeezing around his stomach as I pressed my head to his back. "I need you. Please."

His head turned to one side as he scanned the inside of the cabin without speaking. Blood still stained the scrubbed futon, though Alan and I had managed to remove all other remnants of Gideon's violence from the house. I knew they had plans to burn the evidence. We just hadn't gotten around to it yet.

Miller and Jon were nowhere to be seen. Alan left for the city a day ago. Will sat at the small kitchen table, eating cereal for lunch while staring at the wall.

"All right," Robe conceded. He unwound my hands from his waist, turning to face me. The lines in his face had deepened in the wake of his tragedy. "Where do you want to go?"

My heart still burned with the vision of Brandon's body tucked between the two large men while they tried to save a life taken by another.

"Will showed me a waterfall," I said shyly, thinking back to our afternoon in the meadow, lying side by side. "I thought maybe we could see where the river goes, if that's... safe?"

Robe stilled, then nodded. "It's safe. We'll be back in a few hours."

Will raised his free hand in a thumbs-up, still eating from the spoon in the other.

"Thank you," I whispered, finding my hand enclosed in Robe's. "Can we go now?"

"May as well."

He drew me out the door after bundling me in boots, a scarf, and a thick jacket that looked like it might belong to Miller. A beanie plopped onto my head, and he fussed, tugging it over my ears until he smirked at me. I held up floppy arms in the borrowed jacket, and Robe folded the sleeves back to create bulky wristbands. It fit, kind of, if I slouched into the excess of puffy material. I followed him along the same trail Will and I had taken on our picnic, though instead of the high path where the trail split toward the waterfall, we took the lower fork.

The dappled light deepened as we walked. A late chill obliterated the warmth I'd misperceived from my sheltered spot inside the kitchen. It swept over me, seeping upward from the ground instead of the frigid wind's tendrils that made their way beneath my borrowed jacket and assaulted my cheeks.

The forest closed around us until the spaces merged between the trunks. Robe stopped where the evergreen foliage crisscrossing above us broke off, exposing a curve in the river's bend. The water twisted, flowing in a declined stage before it tumbled over the edge a second time. I bumped into him and then stepped around to stand by his side, watching the water rush along its busy path.

"How are you feeling?" I asked, tracking a stray leaf that tumbled along, refusing to float on the top like anything in a bid for survival. The leaf bobbed, disappearing for a moment before resurfacing farther down.

"You brought me out here to ask how I'm feeling?" Robe turned sideways toward me, his hands stuffed in his jacket pockets.

I shrugged. "I thought you might answer me if we were away from the house."

He snorted. "You don't know me very well."

I raised both eyebrows and faced him in full, ignoring the beauty of the river for a moment. "You brought the body of a man you loved all the way down the hill after looking after him as he died in your arms three nights ago, then disappeared into the night and sought vengeance for his passing. And you haven't said a single word about it since. No one has." I watched him, pleased when he didn't look away. "I could put money on the assumption that if I don't ask you how your mental health has been since you tried to commit murder, no one else will. Am I wrong?" I challenged him.

Robe considered me, drawing one hand from his pocket to skate his fingertips over my cheek, tucking my hair behind my ear. "No. You're not wrong." He paused for a second and stepped a little closer. "Are you going to ask if I killed him?"

I blinked. "You're avoiding my question." My heart hammered a wild staccato in my chest.

"So are you." He coiled my hair around his fingers, bringing me closer. "I didn't, though not for lack of trying. Blackthorne still breathes. For now."

"Thank you," I whispered. I heard the words Brandon had uttered before he died. We all did. "I'm glad you came back safe."

Something had happened to put him off his goal. Robe didn't strike me as a man who gave up on a task without resentment over his failure. Either Gideon was gone, or something had reduced his ability to carry out the vengeance he sought that still burned dark in his eyes when he returned.

Either way, relief swamped me.

He hadn't died or been the one the boys had dragged into the house, unconscious and bleeding. I'd seen enough of that since arriving in the cabin to last five lifetimes.

Robe hummed, dipping his head. "I like having you in my home, Mari Merripen, with your British accent riling up my boys. I like what you make me feel too. It makes... everything worthwhile."

I stared as he lifted his gaze, focusing on something I couldn't see. He was so damn complicated, all soft edges and hard muscle underneath, or maybe he reversed that and twisted those characteristics around. The forest shifted around us with renewed life, so different from the haunted stillness I tore through in muted desperation months ago. Bird noises filled the silence, reminding me we weren't alone.

"Did he kiss you?" Robe asked abruptly. "Will, when he brought you out here."

I paused, recalling the way he'd arced over me, his fingers on my pulse. *Strawberries*. He'd been so damn close.

"No."

Robe nodded. His gaze dropped to my mouth, and he pulled me into him until my world filled with his leather-and-smoked-whiskey scent. I sighed when he curved his hand around my jaw, tipped my head back, and covered my mouth with his.

His kisses were usually rough, but this time he gave me a chance to catch my breath and hold it rather than steal it away. My head still swam at his closeness, his mouth gentle against mine, offering gratitude. I kissed him back, letting my tongue seek him out, rather than the other way around. My sighs were lost in the whispering brook as he held me close, wrapped in his arms until the light changed and dusk fell.

Then he walked me back to the cabin with one arm wrapped around me the entire time, as though he would never let me go.

I WOKE BESIDE THE GHOSTS OF TWO OF THE MOST extraordinary men I'd ever met. The large bed grew too big, too empty without them in it, and I took no luxury in spreading my arms out to either side. Jon spent the night with me, though I recalled a brief kiss from Robe when I opened my eyes at dawn to find him gone.

My legs ached. Fluid soaked my thighs, reminding me of the mini orgy I participated in the night before. Rather than embarrassment, my cheeks flamed with the need to feel Robe inside me again, and soon. Jon's hands playing with my body, easing each fragment of anxiety as it arose, blew me away but felt so right at the same time.

When I emerged from Robe's room for breakfast the day after I'd decided not to count sunrises and sunsets anymore, five sets of eyes stared at me, and I knew something more than our nocturnal activities had changed overnight.

Alan placed a mug of tea in one of my hands and a piece of toast in the other. He bent to kiss my forehead, then the corner of my mouth, unshed tears glistening in his sapphire eyes.

Shock bounced off my tarnished armor as I stared around the room. Will wouldn't look at me, and even Miller's glare had decreased its usual degree of animosity.

"What's going on?" I inhaled the black chai that Alan seemed to favor, its aromatics a calming agent as a familiar dose of panic edged in to haunt me yet again, and managed a single sip.

Robe crossed the room to stand in my space, much as he had that first day. Instead of a shot of arousal that set endorphins roaming free in my body, trepidation curled there.

"I need you to tell me who hurt you, and who you are—were—to him."

But he already knows.

I blinked. My secret was the unspoken truth we'd lived with these last months. I could say the words, but caution at his harsh tone stalled me. Whatever had passed between us the night before made zero impact on the stone sentinel standing before me now.

I held to my prior conviction, my chest rising with shallow, rapid breaths. "I can't tell you."

I got past this. You bastard, you healed me. Don't throw me back into that void.

Robe plucked the tea and toast from my fingers. I gaped as he leaned over me, broad arms braced on either side of my body, caging me against the bar top. A frisson spiked through me at the return to day one, like he'd just stripped away every inch of the trust and love we developed.

What I gave to him and every man here.

I didn't know what to do with that.

Apparently he decided on his lonesome that the time for slow movements and gentle touches was done. An emotion that had nothing whatsoever to do with panic built in my throat, threatening to overwhelm me.

"Tell me, Mari," he growled.

"Why?" I whispered, inhaling the scent of him, tucking it away in my memory. After all this time, *why?*

We both knew who'd hurt me. I didn't need to say it, didn't want to fall back into that darkness they helped me escape. My breath hitched, and I *knew.*

They were sending me away.

Not home, because I didn't have one of those, not anymore. No, he couldn't send me home…

Because home was *here.* With him. With them all.

A hot flush prickled over my skin in a shiver that went straight to my heart when I could have sworn that it would never work again. My time here had meant so much more to me than the best sex of my life. When I arrived in the house, I thought I wouldn't be able to have *that* again either.

A sense of loss swept over me, but Robe's voice anchored me to the present.

"Because I want to know I'm going to kill the right man for you." His rasp slid over me in a sinful, beguiling caress. His gaze darkened, filled with the heavy promise of his words.

He meant it.

And I didn't know what that meant to me.

My mind flitted back to the hands pawing at me, fingers pinching and pulling, tearing unknown secrets from my body and then trashing them alongside the remnants of my dignity as the pinches became slaps and the pulls became beatings.

The shiver evolved into a rage of tremors that racked my body.

Somewhere above me, Robe swore. His arms wrapped around my shoulders, crushing me into the safety of his chest, but it only served to exchange one cage for another.

I squeezed my eyes shut, reliving each moment over and over, my nights with Robe and Jon colliding into my past. Breath pulsed from my lips in an uncontrollable rhythm. Nothing made it into my lungs as I pushed at him, desperate for control.

Alan dancing with me around the bar.

Will's peace in the forest, a palmful of sweet offerings and dark promises.

Miller teaching me to knock Robe on his ass for the first time.

But the memories that had become a mantra now failed me. Invisible hands plucked at my body, filling my head with their harsh words—

Jon's steady hands on my body.

Robe's mouth on mine as he slid inside me.

The fight to reclaim my treasured memories as my own and keep them separate from the mess of *before* bent my body double of its own accord. I retched my single mouthful of Alan's lovely black tea onto the cabin's floorboards.

Voices murmured above me. Familiar hands, kind ones, not the hooked claws of my nightmare memories, stroked damp hair back from my face. A warm cloth cleaned my cheeks. Cool water pressed to my lips as I straightened.

The glass trembled in my grip, water sloshing to either side in its effort to escape its enclosure. Enormous hands folded around mine in the gentlest touch, their firm grip dropping a blanket of calm over me. I stared up into Jon's golden gaze, all too aware of Robe's presence at my back.

Rage and calm.

Safety and sweetness.

The two enormous men crowded my space, but rather than eliciting new fears from my addled brain, their combined presence soothed me.

Fully letting go of my fears for the first time, I leaned back into Robe's arms and smiled at Jon. "Thank you." I sipped the water, then swirled it around my mouth to remove the sharp tang of a shattered life that remained.

Alan passed me a bowl of chocolate mints with one hand while cleaning up my mess with a rag held in the other.

"You don't have to do that," I protested, grabbing for the cloth.

"Mari, let me," Alan murmured.

His tone, devoid of his usual contagious excitement, stopped me. Something more than our friendship lingered in his eyes, a gentle warning not to push. I bit my lip and nodded.

Jon released my fingers to bring his to my cheek, making sure the motion remained within my view the entire time. He traced over my cheekbones, trailing where we both knew the faintest echoes of bruises once blossomed beneath my skin, even if they had healed months ago now. Long fingers stroked the length of my throat and back, concern filling his amber eyes.

I held his gaze and inched my way forward to press my cheek into his open palm. Fire lit in his face, and I reveled in his approval. Jon lifted my hair to tuck a flyaway strand behind my ear.

Robe's arms slid around my waist, pulling me back to him. "You know we share everything here, Mari," he murmured, his lips brushing my ear. "And we want you, need to protect you. Even if you don't want... all of us yet."

But you will.

The unspoken promise hovered between us, winding around everyone in the house in a bond deeper than any I had ever experienced.

Movement shuffled in my periphery as I became aware of three more sets of eyes feasting on the vision of us connected. Every one of them held desire in his face, all aimed at me. And Robe. And Jon.

Even Miller, though his ever-present anger raged beneath the surface of his forced blank expression, a facade that he thought hid his roiling turmoil but actually exposed his need at the same time, even when he hated himself all the more for the perceived weakness.

I should have run from him. Robe. From them all, once upon a time. Now. My past and present mashed together in a heady swirl that left me swaying on my feet. I should have torn from his arms, screaming bloody murder. I should have protected my abused, healed body with my fists and all the skills Miller had instilled in me, one bruise at a time.

I did none of those things.

The weight of their need spun the room in a dizzying maelstrom. Robe's shoulders curved around my smaller frame. I sank into him and smiled deliriously at Jon, the glass slipping from my grip to shatter at my feet. My body followed in a graceful collapse as my knees buckled.

Two pairs of arms encompassed me, and I let myself fall.

Robe

27

ROBE

I SCARED THE SHIT OUT OF HER.

It was all I could think of the whole time Mari had slept off the dizziness that slammed into her the moment I tried to offer more of who we were to her. That my grace period was up and that lost her. Like I lost others.

But with Mari it wasn't the same. I wanted her.

We all did.

Miller's affection confused her. I saw it in the way she peeked at him over her crispy waffles and when she was curled on my lap and tensed every time he spoke. Her gaze tracked him whenever he entered or left a room.

Something had happened between them. I knew that much, and Alan made his own hints about the time they spent in the bedroom when I sent them away. A mess of my own making, of course, and not knowing irritated the shit out of me. Strange enough for the stubborn man, he broke the tension in the short term between us all, if not in the way he intended.

"That's too cute." Mari flirted with Alan in her safe zone

as he showed her his new stripperesque crop top and matching black glitter boots.

I bit back a snarl; I'd be sweeping that shit out of my floorboards for the next decade.

"Right? I'll give you a private show, sweetcheeks." He winked and tucked the clothes behind the bar before waltzing around to her chair.

"You know he's just horny for you, *sweetcheeks*," Miller snapped, his fists white at his sides as he stared at them from his end of the room.

Mari looked across at him with a display of innocence that left my heart swelling. She'd healed faster than any of us had believed possible. Jon grinned at my side as Alan patted her head, drawing her attention back to him, then scooped her off her chair, sat in her warm spot, and balanced her on his lap.

"You scared me!" She slapped at his chest with zero hesitation.

He grinned down at her, his gaze tracking to her lips. "Did I?"

She stared, unmoving.

The air charged, filled with the underlying static desire always present in the room if Mari stayed with any of us in the long term. His hands slid around her waist, his touch changing from protective to predatory. Alan looked up at me, and something feral in his gaze shifted before he refocused on her.

"If I kiss you in front of them, who would you ask to join in?" he whispered in his silken voice, the one he utilized for seduction and intel.

When he aimed that honed weapon at Mari, she flushed head to toe and wriggled on his lap in a way that earned a grimace from him while every one of us reached to adjust our cocks.

"Is that—" She stumbled over her thoughts, swiveling to take in Miller's glower and Will's always-eager eyes. She bit her lip, shaking her head. "Robe wouldn't approve."

Part of me—a very hard, straining part—*did* approve, but I kept that to myself.

"Come on, Mari. The big man likes a good show. Haven't you learned that yet?" Alan smiled, all cunning and sweet promises.

I leaned back and watched, as keen as my spy to hear her answer.

Mari swallowed, her attention flicking between us. "I don't think he's an audience to be pandered to," she murmured loud enough for us all to hear.

I hid my grin. She had me pinned, all right. Alan had earned the surprise I had in store for him, but I suspected she'd like where he took this—and what would come after.

He, on the other hand, would not.

Even Jon tried to prevent our resident stripper from digging his own grave with a subtle shake of his head, a rare intervention on his end.

Alan smirked at me. "Robe likes a show as much as anyone, remember? Trust me."

Mari looked over his shoulder, seeking permission. My cock swelled at the thought of her submission. I let a wicked smile spread across my lips, showing teeth.

She glanced back at Alan, but he didn't give her a choice. He cupped her chin and tipped her head back, claiming her mouth in a rough kiss that devolved into the realm of pornographic as she moaned, arching to accept his touch before us all.

Her neck curved, her attention focusing on him. He'd

wish he hadn't pushed this in a few minutes when I released the grudge I'd been holding since that day in my bathroom when he made her come before I'd touched her.

For now, he could have his way. A few more minutes wouldn't matter. Then I'd claim my vengeance for the time he'd stolen from me.

I raised my eyes to meet his startling blue gaze head-on as he kissed her with his eyes open. We never took liberties from one another. We were a unit, and that's not how we played it. How we survived.

But Alan refused to play by our rules. I looked forward to his punishment.

He settled in the chair, pulling Mari deeper onto his lap. Lean, inked arms wound around her waist as he deepened the kiss, his long-fingered hands wandering without interruption. She whimpered into his mouth as he scraped his nails beneath the tender curve of her breast, reaching up to tease her peaked nipple. He tugged at the hard nib, visible through her T-shirt, then pulled the material down to expose the slightest hint of dusky pink where it contrasted against a creamy swell and ran his thumb along it.

She writhed on his lap, twisting away from his hands, though her moans and soft cries told every one of us how much she loved what he did to her.

My cock strained at every sweet sound that slipped from her lips, her eyes squeezed tight. His gaze lifted again to hold mine, triumph glittering there as he laughed into her mouth. I was hard as steel, lacing my hands at my back in a familiar pose to stop myself from rubbing one out, a voyeur in my own fucking house yet again.

There would be plenty of playtime in a few moments. Alan was right; I did like a show.

Just not the sort he put on.

The moment his hands ran down her perfect thighs, scars and all, and teased the hem of her dress upward, I knew he'd already made up his mind to take their encounter too far. She stiffened until he cooed something into her ear, his voice too low for anyone else to hear. Her limbs went liquid soft, and she sank into him without resistance. I ached to know what he'd promised her.

Her head drifted lower to rest on his shoulder after he broke the kiss, both of their chests heaving. A show of defiance vied against victory to decorate his angular face.

No one moved, and she didn't object.

"Sundress season," Will whispered reverently.

Positioning Mari on his lap the way he wanted, Alan applied pressure to her thighs, drawing the pale flesh apart. He stroked his fingertip up the inside of her legs over the scars marring her skin. The lines had faded, but the heavier marks would remain, a forever reminder of her trauma.

My rage stoked anew. I watched them through slitted eyes, forcing myself to remain still as he murmured more soft things we couldn't hear into her ear. She shivered, grabbing at his wrists, but let him open her legs until her knees dangled off his thighs in a reverse straddle.

Her dress hiked up, her thighs spread open, the growing wet spot on her panties visible to everyone in the room. She released a shaky breath, relaxing for a second before her eyes flew open, clearly remembering that we watched. A deep pink flush stained her exposed chest, traveling up to her cheeks, and her gaze locked with mine.

Watching Alan brushing light fingers over her nipples and along her throat as she arched back might have been one of the sexiest moments of my life. The damp spot on her pretty white panties glistened, her arousal leaking around the scalloped edges as she held my gaze.

Jon shifted at my side, his breaths coming heavier. The room grew pensive. I didn't break my concentration from the show Alan was putting on, though awareness of the other three sets of eyes locked on the girl laid open before us flickered at the edges of my attention.

Biding my time, I waited until Alan kissed her again, spearing his tongue into her mouth at the same time as he stroked her covered pussy. She writhed for him, spread open for a one-man feast.

I turned my head and spoke out of the corner of my mouth. "Let him play. We'll have our turn."

Jon grunted, crossing tense arms over his chest.

More than one of us sported a raging boner; every man in the room watching her wanted the same thing: to push those panties aside and drive himself balls deep into her searing heat. Hell, even Miller gripped the windowsill with whitened knuckles to prevent himself from acting on whatever dark fantasy crossed his tortured mind.

Mari whimpered again, wriggling on Alan's lap, though for a different reason than before. He worked his fingers along her covered mound until her panties soaked to the dripping point. She rubbed herself against him, her head thrown back as he kissed her senseless. I doubted she knew what she looked like, splayed over his body, reacting to every touch with a fresh surge of need that scented the air of a cabin full of predators homed in on fresh prey.

When she stiffened in his arms, her body tensing as she sucked shallow, irregular breaths from the overheated room, his time ran out.

"Stop." My voice rang through the room, enhanced by years of practice.

Alan broke the kiss with a smile, releasing her with one hand, and reached between them to free his cock.

I held his eyes when he looked at me and shook my head once.

His mouth dropped open, the hand hovering over her dripping slit freezing midstroke. "What?"

I ignored his plea. "Hold her legs open."

"Robe," she breathed, blinking lust-drunk eyes as she tried to focus on me.

Guilt flashed across her face, warring with desire as she opened her mouth. Nothing came out except that pretty pink little tongue wetting her lips.

I'd never seen a sight so damn alluring in my life as Mari stared up at me, breath leaving her kiss-bitten lips in sharp pants.

"A little while ago, you two had fun without me." I watched Mari and ignored Alan, despite the objections he formed that went nowhere. Jon growled at my side, and he froze in place. "Jealousy crippled me that day. It should have been me kissing you with my hand in your pants." Mari whimpered at my description, but I needed them to hear me out. "Alan. You've had your playtime. I hope it was worth risking my wrath. You can sit this one out."

Mari looked like she'd stopped breathing altogether. I stepped forward, ignoring the protests of the man beneath her. Neither spoke as I tapped Alan's open hands with a hard finger, canting my head to one side.

"*Open her legs.*"

Alan's eyes lit on me, filled with disquiet and twisted arousal at the situation I forced him into. "Sir."

I couldn't tell if his tone reflected regret, but it didn't matter. His hands planted on Mari's thighs, he spread his legs wide, tilting her ass up for access. With her legs flung over his, she had no choice but to follow his cues. Held open, exposed, she shuddered her arousal on his taut body, the heady scent of her need permeating the air.

Even at this angle, I could see his straining cock jammed against the crack of her ass. I didn't give a fuck if he got off or not, but he wouldn't go behind my back ever again.

"Is this okay, Mari?" I trailed my fingertips along her scars, kneeling to lick each faint white line.

Her muscles tensed, but she could wait for her pleasure. Alan had jumped the gun on pushing her and could have done more damage than good. That he'd been right irked me. Still, I refused to continue until she showed me I wasn't forcing her for my own purposes. My control frayed thin, I raised my head, resting my cheek on the inside of her thigh.

She caught her bottom lip between her teeth and let it pop free, red and swollen from Alan's rough kisses. Her tongue followed, tracing the tender flesh, and I nearly came in my pants.

"Yes. Please, Robe. I want you. I want *this*."

My heart swelled at the way she begged, gazing down at me, adoration and need melding in the soft play of her voice. She'd given me a green light, and despite every prior reservation and fear, she was ready for me. For all of us.

I turned my head and kissed along her inner thighs, tracing the elastic edge of her panties. Keeping my gaze locked on hers, I licked her covered slit taint to top, tasting her arousal.

She gasped, her head falling back. Tension abandoned her legs in lieu of her growing pleasure as she sagged against Alan's body. He groaned, burying his mouth against the curve of her throat. Licking and sucking there, he marked her pale skin as he begged me with hooded eyes to deny him that pleasure too.

I let it ride, tugging the damp cotton from her pussy with

an easy lift of her ass. Mari moved like liquid in my hands with Alan's help. I peeled her panties down her thighs and off her body, then hung the soaked fabric on Alan's finger. "Hold this."

"Asshole." He mumbled some other insult as well, but I didn't care. He'd earned the punishment he wore right now.

Sliding my thumbs along her folds, I spread her open and dipped my head. Explosions burst across my taste buds as I swallowed Mari's sweet arousal. She mewled above me, twisting and writhing.

Alan did his job holding her still and kept her legs wide for me. I stroked my thumb over the rosebud of her ass, drawing a slick of her arousal to lubricate her there as I sucked on her clit. Alan's cock strained against the graze of my hand, and I gave his balls a hard squeeze through the denim, rubbing my thumb over his sac.

His groan filled the room, echoed by someone else, though I kept my attention on the pair in front of me. I wanted them both panting and covered in her fluids by the end of this. I released him with a hard smack to his bulge and returned to teasing Mari's asshole. She trembled at the touch, pressing forward and then pulling away. I knew she'd be scared, but she wanted this too. I thrust my tongue harder into her slicked pussy, easing my thumb into her dark hole.

Her debauched scream encompassed everything I loved about her. She broke Alan's hold, wrapping her legs around the back of my head and pressing my greedy mouth to her smooth center.

The dual sensations sent her body into overdrive, and she bucked against my face. Working my thumb back and forth against the tight ring of muscle, I teased every nerve ending there until her body gave out, letting me in. I slipped my thumb fully into her ass, encountering little resistance as I sucked on her clit.

She trembled between us, clinging to Alan. Her legs held me to her body as she rode out her orgasm against my face. Sweet, hot need flooded my mouth as Alan groaned his frustration aloud, rubbing his imprisoned cock against her ass crack and my knuckles.

I slapped his thigh hard enough to break through his rutting haze. He stilled, panting at me over her shoulder. His teeth clenched with the denied orgasm, but he didn't dare disobey me a second time.

The three of us dripped with sweat by the time her knees loosened around my head. I swiped my thumb over his jeans and collected her cum from my face, pushing up on screaming knees to shove my pussy-slicked fingers into Alan's mouth.

"Clean."

Mari watched us through heavy-lidded eyes as he sucked on command. I squeezed his balls hard again as a second reminder, not letting go as I played with him brutally, and the suction of his lips increased. My dark smile couldn't have been more fucked up.

"What a good little slut you make." I twisted his words to Mari and threw them back at him.

Mari echoed Alan's raw moan as she reached for me, frenzied. Afraid my pulsing cock would unload before I sank into her gushing pussy, I fixed my gaze on her while Alan's tongue licked her pleasure from the palm of my hand.

"Are you ready?" I gave her a moment to breathe before I ruined her.

Mari nodded, and I pushed forward, splitting her soft folds around the rigid veins of my cock. She mewled, flinging her arms around my neck for support and tilting her head up to press her lips against mine. We tasted her, the three of us—Mari as she licked her own pleasure from my lips and Alan tonguing my fingers like a virgin offering.

My commands forgotten, not that I cared, Alan pressed his hands to her hips, grinding against her ass. The head of his tortured cock jutted from his jeans when she arched toward me before I pushed her back, pinning them together. The rest of him was trapped and fit to burst behind a wall of constricting denim and the weight of the girl he craved.

I thrust shallowly into her soaked depths, dropping my hands to cover his over her curves, holding them both in place. The heat of her branded my swelling cock until I doubted I'd last more than a few minutes.

Alan leaned forward, glazed eyes raised to meet mine as he whispered into her ear. "The way you feel me now, imagine my cock in your ass fucking you at the same time as Robe ruins your pretty pussy. Feeling us both push and pull inside you, rubbing together."

Mari's beautiful eyes widened. She stared right through me, blinded by her impending orgasm. Her head tilted back, her soft lips parting on a silent scream. I'd never seen anything so beautiful or free. Her body clenched, bearing down on me and into Alan. She unraveled a second time between us, hot and stunning and needy.

After the tease he'd set up before and holding back as she fluttered around me, my own control edged past its expiry date. I gripped Alan's hands hard as I slammed my hips forward, no longer caring about being gentle. Pistoning into her, I ground her ass back against Alan's denim-encased cock, getting all three of us off at once. Mari moaned, pinned between two hard bodies as I snaked one arm around Alan, holding him to her.

He shuddered at the contact, pushing up to try to match

my movements, but I refused to hold back any longer, fucking them both with every thrust. Her body rocked between us, clamping down on my cock again as she massaged Alan with her perfect round ass cheeks.

She lifted her fingers to wind them through my hair, pulling me down for a deep, languid kiss, and I knew she hovered on the edge of bliss again. She'd already come twice, but she bore down impossibly again. I broke the kiss, baring my teeth, but she insisted, laving my mouth until I gave in and slid my tongue along hers, matching her pace.

Alan gasped as I turned her, angling her head back to seek him out. His mouth latched on to hers as I pushed us all to the edge. Alan fell first with a tormented keening, his head thrown back as he lifted his hips in the chair, pushed up against her, and came in his pants.

Mari arched, seeking my mouth. Her soft whimpers broke against my tongue, her pussy squeezing and fluttering around my cock. I jerked twice more and slammed myself home, painting her walls with pearls and possession. Alan's wet jeans nestled against the curve of her ass as I spilled my seed inside her.

Her nails tore at the back of my neck. She'd leave marks, and I loved it. I wanted my girl never to be afraid to touch me —to mark or need any of us—that way. She'd suffered enough.

I hung over them both, my arms braced on the back of Alan's chair. Mari sighed, pinned between us, a soft smile curving her plumped lips. Her body fluttered around mine as I rained tender kisses on her mouth.

"I love you," she murmured, nuzzling my cheek.

Those three little words said so much more, three important words that every man in the room heard. Purple-ringed eyes locked on mine, her lust and need rising to the forefront tinged with a heavy dose of love.

"I love you, too, sweetheart. So fucking much. All of you," I added, shifting my gaze to find Alan.

He nodded, sweat dripping from his forehead, reaching between us to press a trembling hand to my cheek for a moment. I kissed his knuckles, providing him the forgiveness he sought. Alan fell back, blue eyes drifting closed as he fought for breath.

Murmurs filled the room, but my eyes were solely for the two people before me, our bodies still entwined. Tiny flutters started around my cock as I softened to half-mast. I knew I should be ready to go again in minutes with Mari, but this time she'd wrung me dry.

I lifted her to my chest as I slid free of her warmth, leaving Alan in a similar state as when we started. The front of his jeans was darkened, a glistening smear coating his belly where his shirt hitched up. He gave me a tired salute, unmoving from the chair as his eyes closed again.

I backed up, tucking myself away with one hand while balancing her in my arms. Her scent swirled around me, leaving me dizzy with freshly suppressed need. I'd never have enough of this woman.

I pressed my lips to her temple, repeating his words to her from earlier. "Imagine what it would be like if we had you together."

Alan groaned, reaching down to free himself, working his cock again. Someone behind him laughed, though I didn't check who.

I smiled against her heated skin. Alan's torture had been fun to prolong, but now....

I crossed the room to Jon. Surprise lit his face as his eyes met mine, and I shifted her into his arms. He gathered her close, holding her to his chest like a coveted treasure. I knew he hadn't touched himself the entire time, though it must have killed him to watch someone else fuck her in front of him—again.

"Hold her" was all I said, redirecting her body so her legs slid around his waist.

She latched on to him, pressing her forehead to his shoulder while he stared at me with eyes hard as flint over her mussed curls.

"Robe...."

"You need her. She needs you."

Mari raised her head, pressing her lips to his chest through his shirt. I reached between them and ripped the buttons open so she could access his skin. Arousal swarmed straight to my cock, but I ignored it, focusing on *them*. My own need should be long sated, but the sight of her with him rekindled everything.

Jon's lips parted on a heavy breath as she leaned in and flicked her tongue over his sweat-beaded skin. I slid my hand lower, but he caught my wrist, pushing me away.

"No." He fixed me with a biting glare that warned me I'd hit a hard limit. "You can't screw with me or placate me like Alan. If she wants me, she can say so, and I'll fuck her myself."

Jon

28

I HELD ROBE'S GLARE, WAITING UNTIL THE CORNER OF his mouth curled up in a sensual smirk I wanted to lick right off his face.

He shrugged. "Whatever suits you."

"This suits me." I grazed my chin against Mari's cheek to push her head back. If she kept kissing me like that, I'd come in my jeans like Alan. That would do neither of us any good. "Robe asked you before, Mari. Are you too sore? Do you want this?" He'd been rough with her. I gave her the chance to deny me. Whatever she said, I would do it, no matter how much I fucking ached.

Her eyes still glazed from the rough-and-tumble two men already gave her, she met my gaze and nodded. Her cheek brushed my lips, and she pressed sweet kisses to my beard. Despite already being covered in sweat and sex, her body rubbed against mine like a kitten in its first heat.

"I want you, Jon."

My chest loosened. I leaned forward, parting her lips with my tongue. This would be quick, rougher than I intended. But after the scene that Alan and Robe had played out, I had little control of my own remaining in addition to what I needed to get her off. And I wanted to give her pleasure on my own, away from the rest of the horny assholes overpopulating the room, even if my resolve shattered the first time around.

I kissed her harder, delving deep. I didn't want to hurt her, bang her into a wall, and screw her thoughtlessly when she'd already been through enough. Levering my thighs wider apart in preparation to hold us both as she purred against my mouth, I struggled not to throw her to the floor and fuck my need out into her flesh.

The soundtrack of her moans lanced straight to my cock, pushing me past the point of no return. I ripped at my jeans, fisting myself the moment I freed my cock and notching myself at her entrance.

"Look at me, honey. I can't go slow for you, not today. Are you sure this is what you need?" The offer of an out jarred my throat, though I forced the words forward. Every second of restraint cost me a wisp of my sanity.

She nodded with her eyes closed, her lips curved in a sleepy smile.

Fuck. I'll break her if I'm too rough.

That last coherent thought jumped around my mind before I pushed her down on my length. A strangled groan from Robe somewhere behind me brought me back. I stared into her face. Her eyes glowed as she pressed herself closer, her walls pulsing around my desperate cock. I drove into her, retreating only to slam myself home again. She cried out each time, her screams rending into my soul. Her body clenched down, tugging me in and then pushing me away.

I stilled, though it killed me. "Too deep?" My voice strained as I held her in place.

She opened her eyes, twin soul-deep wells I fell into, unwilling to leave. "More. Jon, give me *more.*"

I drove forward, filling her. Mari's head tipped back, and she gave me the most beautiful scream, fluttering around me the moment I sheathed myself to my balls inside her depths.

Inhaling precious air, I eased myself back and cupped her ass with both hands. Her tiny frame could split right there. My groan drew another flutter from her hot pussy. The world narrowed to just us, obliterating everything else. My greatest enemy could have launched an attack, and I wouldn't notice.

I pressed a hand to her nape, turning her mouth to meet mine. Our lips brushed, not quite kissing as I traced hers with the tip of my tongue. She opened for me, and my control dissipated.

A feral sound tore from my chest, and her eyes flared wide with fresh awareness and need. My body responded to her whim, craving everything as I worshipped her. Gripping her hips, I fucked her hard, tasting her mouth with soft kisses while I brutalized her lower body. She screamed again, carnal sounds of pleasure and sin that sank into my skin, branding me as hers.

I stumbled, bracing one knee to the bar as I held her up. A few more pumps, and that's all I had left before I soaked her insides with my cum. I buried my face in her hair, desperate to collapse and take her with me, but I couldn't—not yet. She clung to me, still moaning and writhing through her own aftershocks well after my orgasm had ended.

My legs shook, failing me as my energy dropped away in the aftermath of our fucking. I turned my back to the bar, leaning against it and holding her to me, unwilling to let her go. I'd held back for so damn long, and now that Robe had offered me a taste of what she felt like in my arms... I had no intention of letting her go. Not now, or ever.

"Get your hairy ass off my workspace," Alan muttered without cracking an eye. His hands were clamped around his cock, covered with his own release a second time. "Fuck me, that was good."

"You liked that, huh?" Robe's gruff voice laced with amusement reminded me that there were more people in the room. "Glutton."

"Probably."

God alone knew who else had jacked off to our display. I didn't really care. She didn't seem to mind the eyes that followed every movement she made. Her hands dropped away from my shoulders to twine in the material Robe had ripped before, resting her cheek to my chest. Pain and pleasure flicked through my system despite being still hard inside her—and far from willing to move.

I met Robe's silent question over her head. He jerked his head to one side, and I shifted my attention around the room. Will grinned broadly, tucking himself away and wiping his hand on the back of his jeans. He'd fallen for her hard, and we all knew it. The kid might be a fighter, but he covered the lover-boy base enough for the entire household.

Robe worried about the younger man who couldn't bring himself to admit to his emotions for Mari, and with damn good reason. Will had his own traumas to battle hidden beneath that perfect exterior, and I knew he was scared he'd revisit his own childhood on the ones he loved most, which made him unwilling to get closer to Mari in case he hurt her the way he had been.

Which left our problem child. Miller's fists clenched tight against the windowsill, twin indents left beneath where he'd slammed them down at some point during our fuckfest. Not that I blamed him. I'd been as needy as any of us to drive myself balls deep into her sweet body when Robe offered her to me.

Miller raised his head to look at me, his hard face strained with the sort of desperation that leads to bottomless obsession. He wanted her as much as all of us, but in refusing to admit it, I knew that deep-seated need would turn inward and consume the man whose determination and stubbornness rivaled Robe's on his weakest days.

Instead of running toward whatever fear she brought out in him, he dove away from it. His attention landed on me—no, Mari. Last week his opinion included tossing her out and forgetting her altogether. Today his familiar fury rose, twisted with something else I knew but didn't quite understand.

Pain.

Robe said he'd come around, but his fears could ruin him and her both.

Will made his way across the room, his walk cocky as any kid in his twenties after a boys' night out. He shot an arrogant grin at Robe. "What did I tell you, huh? Sundress season."

Alan laughed, a dark, rich sound that left Mari pressing herself tighter to my chest.

Robe rolled his eyes as I shook my head, gathering her into me. I couldn't complain when the beautiful girl I lusted over wrapped herself around me and refused to let go.

"Fucking kids." I couldn't help the smile that worked its way across my mouth.

Holding her sweetly while Robe fucked her was one of the hardest things I'd ever done. The feel of her body molding itself to me as he rocked inside her haunted me every night until I wrapped myself around her sleeping form, wondering when I'd be allowed to sink inside her tight body and have her mouth on mine as she screamed for me.

Now I knew.

Still unwilling to leave her heat, I cupped one hand beneath her ass. Mari melted against my chest, dark eyes flaring wide as her body reacted to my growing length. "Bath time, kitten." I kissed the tip of her nose and then slanted my mouth across hers, desperate to seek solace in her willing body.

She responded with an endless hunger, wrapping her legs tight around me and bearing down again.

"I said bath time. Mari, stop that."

"Why?" she asked thickly.

"She's as bad as fucking Alan," Robe growled.

She tilted her head to one side. "Maybe," she acknowledged. Her mouth pressed to mine again, her lips plump and open for me. "Thank you."

I carried her to the hall, aiming for Robe's room with its double shower and large bathtub. I didn't think he'd ever used it before now, and it seemed like the right time to christen the thing together.

"Bedroom's that way," Robe muttered, containing his laughter as he jabbed my shoulder in the right direction.

I nodded and made a beeline for the room before I fucked her in front of them all again. "Thanks for that."

Mari giggled. It might have been the best sound I'd ever heard outside of that scream when I first thrust into her. My cock ached at the memory, thickening until she moaned into my bare skin.

I kicked the door to Robe's bedroom shut once I found it and fell to my knees, Mari still clinging to my hips. Her body pulsed, trembling muscles easing to accommodate me as I stiffened. She'd broken me from my habit of grief, and now I couldn't get enough of her.

"I love you," she told me, smiling.

My heart shattered for a future I couldn't deny, terrified of repeating my past with her. I groaned, squeezing her in my arms too hard. Anything to keep her safe, though my physical bulk might not be enough. "That's the sex talking."

Mari smiled, molding her lips to mine in a long, slow kiss that promised no lies. "No. It's my heart."

Tears pricked my eyes as I eased her back onto the carpet and shifted my hips. The words were there. They were right fucking well *there* in my mouth, but I couldn't make them come out.

Mari smiled more gently, lighting up my world. "It's okay. I know. And it's enough."

I swallowed past the rock of my heart that rose to fill my throat, trying to convey to this stunning woman all the things I felt about her but couldn't say in a mere moment's glance. She returned my kiss, then pressed her lips over my heart.

Any last remnants of control dissolved. My body crashed into hers, alongside part of my soul.

Mari

29

MARI

I TRAIPSED BETWEEN TRUNKS, RUNNING MY FINGERS over the different types of bark and undergrowth that snared me in patches. Robe and Miller followed me at a decent distance to allow me a sense of freedom as I delved into my history with the woods at my own pace. Their muted conversation was often loud enough to be heard, though I couldn't make out the words, and their company offered comfort and the relative freedom to wander through the woods, retracing part of my journey that brought me onto Robe's land in the first place.

He suggested I take a hike, in the literal sense. Find my way back and do whatever I needed to feel safe on his land. I knew he'd readied me for my return to the world, but I clung to the illusion of living my best life with my boys at my back in a forever sense.

I'd moved on from broken to healing to lying to myself. I mean, why not? A girl needed life goals, and denial was currently my lane.

Inhaling a long breath of crisp air belonging more to winter than spring as it crested the ridgeline in a swift gust that rattled the forest around me, I knew I'd leave a slice of my heart here when Robe made me leave. Part of me wanted to go back, to pretend that I could have a normal life, but Alan had made it abundantly clear that *normal* had left the building long ago for Mari Merripen.

I didn't know how I would return to the world at large, just that it had to happen soon.

The cozy sanctuary my five lethal boys offered reduced my fear. I couldn't be better protected anywhere else.

My legs strained as I walked faster, nearing the tall cottonwood where I first crashed into Robe. It made a significant addition to the landscape and my destination. Robe asked me to stop there, as the ancient tree marked a point close to the eastern border of his lands.

Earthy scents and warm sunny kisses melded into a spring morning lanced with shards of sunlight from a high, cloudless sky. I stepped between trunks where a tall pine had uprooted, leaving a space in the canopy where sunlight struck the forest floor in an array of soft greens.

The cottonwood stood a few paces ahead. I stepped up to it and trailed my fingers around its thick girth, wondering at the age of the enormous sentinel. It reminded me of the two innate protectors who followed me. Their conversation behind me stopped for the moment, or maybe they spoke too low for me to hear.

Robe still kept most of their work secret—whether out of a sense of security or for me, I wasn't sure. But they'd let me into their small empire despite Miller remaining unwilling for the most part.

I completed my half lap of the cottonwood trunk and nose-butted a broad chest imbued with the faint scent of cloves. Scrunching up my eyes to prevent tears leaking from them, I took a step back and pinched the tip. "Ow. Why do you all have to be in the way," I grumbled, not really angry. Robe must have caught up with me when I let the forest's quiet beauty distract me. "Sneaky bastard."

"You always did have a potty mouth when others weren't looking," a smooth American voice that was neither Robe's nor Miller's drawled above me.

I know that voice.

I stumbled backward, my heel catching on a heavy tree root as I stared at the man who orchestrated my abuse at the seat of his personal power through watering eyes and landed on my ass. My mouth popped open on a scream, but the sound I needed refused to exit my throat, strangled by a resurgence of world-ending terror that shifted the ground sickeningly beneath me.

"Shhh." Gideon Blackthorne, ex-boss and personal pimp-slash-abuser, crouched before me, one manicured finger pressed to his pouty lips.

Dark eyes surveyed me with a touch of amusement at seeing me all sprawled out and panicked before him. In another life I might have found him attractive. Once. Now the only emotions I experienced upon staring into his aquiline face were terror and disgust.

"Get away from me," I whispered, my voice ragged, like I'd run for hours through the forest, sucking at air that wouldn't let me breathe.

Again.

"Mmmm. I think we need to have a little talk first, don't you?" Gideon's head tilted to one side. "You have let yourself go. Huntingdon isn't caring for you," he tsked.

I managed a hollow laugh. "You think it's okay for men to gang-rape a woman, and then she should be able to get up and walk away to live a normal fucking life?" I whisper-shrieked the words, unable to call on the volume I needed.

My heart thrummed heavy in my chest, rising to my throat. If I could have puked it out, I would have on the spot. *Anything* to prevent the rush of renewed memories coiled invisibly beneath my skin. So many hands, mouths, the *teeth*—

"You're not worthy of being called a human," I forced out between numbed lips.

"Perhaps not. It makes no difference. You can tell him, by the way. He already worked it out."

"I know." I scooted back a pace, scraping my heels through the mulch to expose dirt beneath. "He'll come for you."

Gideon waved a hand as though Robe's history meant nothing to him, though I didn't miss the dark flash in his eyes when his jibe elicited no damage.

I tipped my chin back, trying to suck in a big enough breath to scream. Where the hell were my boys?

"Make sure you don't incriminate yourself at the same time. Will he want you when he knows what you used to do for me?" He leaned closer, looming over me, obliterating all light above and around us. "What you're doing for me now? You're never alone."

Two fingers brushed the bump inside my arm where a small scar lay, healed at the same time as the rest of the damage from that day. His face blurred.

"No," I breathed, horror squeezing my heart. I swore it jumped a beat. "No, that's not true."

"Isn't it? Don't his men get hurt? His... friends?"

My throat closed, the forest wavering. *Brandon.* Was I solely responsible for the old man's horrific death? "You didn't—"

He shrugged. "Perhaps. Perhaps not. Will you take that risk?"

I shook my head, unable to answer him. "No."

Time stilled as my stomach flipped over on itself. I turned my head to one side, taking my eyes off the demon predator before me for a half second.

I can't stay.

My new truth, the one that ruined me. I was the danger Robe always believed me to be, and now my borrowed time had run out.

"Occasionally they ask about you. Your parents. Friends...." He smiled, a slow taunt that unwound like a mechanical beast with a target in its sights.

"My what?" I blinked at his drastic change in pace. But that was Gideon's best negotiation tactic—pulling the rug out from beneath his opponent. I didn't know if that meant me or Robe or if I was just an incidental pawn in a larger war. "You—"

"I watch what you do. I talk to your mother. Your old professor. The friends who think you've dropped off the map. Oh, and we're fucking. At least, according to the group chat." He pulled my old phone from his leather jacket, the device charged and filled with active messages that scrolled through in regular, recent conversations.

"I'm not missing." My hands were numb. And my tongue.

"Not in the least. Alive and kicking. You won an award at work last week." He flicked me a lazy smile, so similar to Robe's that my insides revolted.

"But my life—" I struggled with the concept, knowing my eyes bugged out of my head and that he was watching me suffer for his pleasure again.

Stop, I can't—

Miller—

His name was the cry that formed on my lips, knowing after our training how deadly and cold he would be against this worst of enemies when Robe's obsession over us both would blind him, but my throat closed at the critical moment.

Help me—

"You didn't beg. You know I can't forgive that, don't you?" he said conversationally as acid seared my veins. "You were supposed to beg, pretty little Mari. It was twelve." Gideon tucked my phone away as he rose and brushed at his leather jacket like I'd sullied him with my presence alone.

"Twelve what?" I croaked.

I have to warn Robe.

He'll throw me out.

Or Miller would end me on the spot, and he'd be right to do it, righteous fury burning in his strange yellow eyes.

"Twelve men." Gideon watched me, emotionless, un-anything. "Twelve men you entertained before we were interrupted."

"Stop—" I gasped on a desperate note I knew he wouldn't heed.

Gideon paused, running his fingers over the zip on his leather jacket. The scent of it made me want to puke.

"It could have been worse." His lips turned up in a soul-less smile. "It could have been me."

He walked away and left me lying on the forest floor, retching at the memory of a dozen ghosts I'd never escape.

Robe

30

ROBE

"FORGET THE BOUNTY. LET'S CONCENTRATE ON MORE important things."

Like removing Blackthorne from the face of the earth.

Miller grunted, keeping pace at my side, though I knew the Mari-sized steps killed him. Given the choice, he'd be over the treetops and back again by now. Sitting still had never been his forte.

"Ignoring the obvious will bite you one day."

"So will your temper." I nodded to the large tree that came into view. "Once we catch up, you're free to do whatever you need."

"I'm not." He bared his teeth in a grimace to the forest beyond. "You know I won't leave until you're both inside the house." He paused. "Preference on alive."

I grinned. "I don't need a babysitter."

"She does." He gestured to where Mari appeared between the trees, darting out from a different path than I expected her to take.

It took me all of a half second to realize something was wrong.

So fucking wrong.

Miller took a quarter of that time and wrapped her in his arms, cupping her whitened cheeks. He stared into eyes filled with the same emotion that had been written across her face the day she crashed into me months ago in this exact spot.

"What happened?" His voice trembled with underlying rage.

"Nothing." She threw a smile on her face that might as well have cracked straight down the middle for the lie.

"Tell me the truth." His tone might be kind, but Miller's words were an order.

"I saw—I thought I saw something. It all came rushing back. I remembered," she whispered.

Tears tracked along her cheeks as Miller folded her into his chest, one arm tight around her back, the other hand stroking her hair in long, slow motions. Every action soothed her, providing a safe haven where she could crash.

He might hate that she lived with us, but he didn't hate *her*, not any longer. Like me, Miller loathed what had happened to her in the first place, what haunted her now, though I doubted he recognized the difference.

Yellow eyes met mine over her head. She shuddered against him, clinging to his shirt as though he were the one thing in the world that could save her. I knew that feeling because I'd been there. Only once, and just briefly, but I understood. His lips pursed, and he cocked his head toward the tree.

I nodded, walking a wide circuit around the cottonwood's broad base. Mulch scattered in a circle that might have kicked up in a flurry or panic, recalling the events that brought her to me. No other disturbance flagged my attention.

I cursed beneath my breath, slamming my palm against the trunk. Neither of us shuddered at the impact. I was a fool to think bringing her out here would help. The concept seemed so simple back within the safe haven of the house. Here, her ghosts were almost visible, haunting her months later.

She needs to go home.

I could have prevented this in so many ways. Sent Miller ahead, as he'd requested when we left. Gone with her, held her rather than make her face her flight alone.

I might have lost her for good. If she left, would she come back to the ridge?

To me?

A deep growl reverberated in my chest. I punched the hardwood again and again until my blood decorated its impenetrable surface. Then I threw on my big boy pants and rounded the tree to take her from Miller. I hefted her feather-light body weightlessly in my arms, and I carried her back to my house.

The last time I took this path, it was a beginning.

Taking her back—that felt like an ending.

MARI'S BODY FIT AGAINST MINE AS SHE SLEPT between me and Jon that night. Heedless that she wasn't awake to feel it, I stroked her hair over and over, hoping the calming sensation would settle the beast roused within me, but it failed.

"You want her to stay." Jon stared at me over her head.

I smiled humorlessly. "In any other world, I'd be on one knee, begging her to move in, and then I'd buy her a puppy."

Jon laughed too loud for the quiet house. I shushed him, checking on Mari, but she slept through our disturbance. It could have been the cocktail Alan mixed for her as a nightcap. She was out before Jon or I could beg her for sweet kisses, but her warmth would do.

Holding her would do.

Anything except sending her away.

I waited for Jon's suppressed laughter to subside. "You know, that's not how most people propose."

I thought about it for a moment and shrugged. "Never got to that part before."

"I did." The pain that habitually rippled his gaze when he talked about his earlier life didn't manifest. His face remained clear as he stared down at her, his heart right out there.

"Yeah?" I contemplated that. "How'd you do it?"

"Her favorite café closest to the lake before I built the house. I took a third of my savings and invested it in a perfect black pearl. She adored those. Loved the lake, couldn't stand the ocean, and wanted a pearl. So I nearly sent myself broke buying her that and the lake house. Well, the land and the materials."

"She said yes?"

"What d'you think?"

I snorted. "Romantic."

"So, you'd do it with a ring."

"Is that what I'm supposed to do?" I turned the thought over and rejected it. Anything that marked Mari in the future had to be by her choice. "I think I prefer the puppy."

"Of course you do." Jon shook his head. "You're hopeless."

"I'm good with that." I pressed a kiss to the top of Mari's head. She nestled deeper between us, drawing a thin thread through each of our hearts that held taut.

"Love you."

We said it at the same time, but not to each other, though I did love him as a brother, a lover, and I knew he reciprocated. Jon huffed while I snorted.

"I love you too," her sweet, sleepy voice piped up between us as she linked her hands around each of our waists, drawing us closer.

Jon grinned while I went back to stroking her hair. I didn't know who she meant, but it didn't matter. We'd do anything to protect the girl who fell out of nothing into the woods and gave us back something none of us had claimed for far too long.

A heart to care for.

She loved us. All of us. And that was enough.

Robe

EPILOGUE

ROBE

Mari stirred on my lap as Jon pressed a cooled cloth to her cheeks, cleaning away the remnants of the delayed reaction to her horror from the day before. I should have looked for it and had failed her yet again. She worked out for more hours than I could count in the wake of her walk through the forest. And then she took that solid night's sleep and her fear, and she belted it out against her opponent the way we taught her.

But we'd forgotten to tell her how to stop. Her stomach emptied itself as she hunched over her arms, once outside the house and once back inside it, where she dry heaved as her limbs shook until her body gave out.

Miller grumbled while he held her the entire time, swearing lovingly in his own strange way, like he was proud of her for finding her limits and pushing through. Then she let each of us hold her, passing her around for cuddles until she returned to me. I fed her a few mouthfuls of water, and then she purred against my chest.

"Too much, too fast," I murmured, tangling my fingers in her hair.

Plus, I'd been a complete asshole, making her retrace her steps, dictating where she should find security after the months we'd spent wrapped around each other. The need to destroy everyone who hurt her burned within me, dolloping a decent helping of self-loathing onto my shoulders.

Cinnamon notes bloomed as I curled a glossy lock around my fingers. She used the shampoo and lotions I'd given her, and some deep-seated part of my inner beast roared its approval.

But as much as I wanted Mari to stay, I couldn't keep her forever. I imagined her in a white-picket-fenced yard, pregnant, a white-and-brown puppy lolling at her feet. But that couldn't happen, not with me. No world I lived in would ever allow it. Which meant I needed to give her a choice, the choice she should have been given earlier.

Then we got... distracted while I lied to each of us that we could keep her.

If she wanted to return to us, that needed to be her choice. In the half year she'd lived with us, Mari displayed a keen intelligence, a Miller-level-worthy loyalty to all of us, but especially the ability to deal with circumstances beyond her control whenever they were thrown her way, like with Alan and his skewed sense of morality. I had a place where she could use those skills and keep an eye on her.

Watch her—like a fucking creeper.

Letting her go broke my heart, but she needed to heal without me in her space. And there was that minor issue of professional help.

Jon sensed my hesitation. He paused in his ministrations. "She'll come around."

Mari shifted in my arms. "Robe?" she murmured, tilting

her head back. She stared up at me with a dozy gaze, her lips parted.

My cock hardened in an instant. I held back from dipping my head to kiss her, from laying her out on the floor and begging her to stay with my tongue between her thighs. She needed more time to heal. I knew that now.

I doubted that with five men who were already obsessed with her, she would get that time in this house.

The unspoken words that pressed against my lips threatened to break me.

"Sweetheart, sit up." I searched her gaze for any hint of internal damage. I couldn't fix every hurt she'd endured, but I knew someone who might.

"Thanks," she murmured, snuggling into my shoulder. She wrapped her arm around Jon's giant bicep, drawing him closer. "I feel a lot safer when you're both here."

Adoration lit Jon's eyes. I expected my face matched his, which made the next part so much harder to push out.

"Mari, it's time you got your wish." I forced the bitter seeds into a semblance of sweetness, coating them in a lure of honey. "Freedom."

She struggled in my arms, tangling herself into a knot between us in her panic. "What? No. I want... I want to stay," she whispered, the admission widening her eyes in shock.

I smiled, knowing how weak it had to look from the outside. "Get dressed. Take your time. Anything you need. Then come out. We'll be waiting."

Mari stiffened. I swallowed hard, extracting myself from her embrace, Jon mirroring my jerky movements.

"You said take your time. But you could have specified," Alan rasped forty minutes later, holding his face between his hands.

The shower had turned on and then off, and we hadn't heard a thing from her since. I was seconds from ripping the door off its hinges and getting on my knees for her when the damn thing opened and she crept out, her arms wrapped around herself. She was wearing one of those damn sundresses she loved, regardless if it was fucking snowing outside or not, and a knitted pink thing that hung to the hem so she appeared naked beneath.

Will looked on the verge of swooning or bending a knee himself, and I didn't blame him in the least.

"Ready to talk, Mari?" How many times had I said those words and in how many other versions?

She nodded, her gaze skating about the cabin, lighting on each man, even meeting Miller's rage-fueled gaze and holding her own without flinching.

My brave fucking girl.

Jon broke from his position near the door to slide in behind her, linking his arms around her waist. She sighed and closed her eyes, and I took that as my signal to start.

"You need to see a doctor, a real team who can help you heal. The right way. I've kept you from that long enough. I don't want to send you away," I reassured her. "You can come back after, if that's what you want."

Please let her come back to me. To us.

Mari nodded and said nothing.

"We need to know who you are from your own lips. I know we've been through this, and I know that we already know. But now I need the words." I needed it recorded, as evidence, and Alan was ready with all the right hardware.

"Tell us who he is to you. We can't send you back to your own world if we can't protect you." Jon's eyes held the same unspoken plea as mine, though she only looked at me.

"He's a CEO," Mari started, and I knew she'd already thought the words up, turned them into something that would betray no one but herself. Who knew how many times she'd rehearsed the part? "I am—*was*—his PA. Personal assistant," she added, sneaking a quick glance at Alan. "You know that. But my home... my life there, it isn't—"

Her brow dipped. We'd spent weeks, *months* telling her that she had to stay for her own safety, and here we were, throwing her into the lion's den. I knew what that looked like, and I had a solution. But first, I needed something from her.

Silence fell in the room.

"Stay here," Will piped up, his enthusiasm overflowing, as always.

"Ignore him." Jon curled a hand around the curve of her shoulder in an intimate gesture that belied his words.

None of us could bear to push her further. Mari's strength and resilience were a blessing in themselves. I doubted I could have been as courageous in her place. And for that, I would worship her in any way she wanted. I wiped my face clean of emotion as she cast a speculative glance my way.

"If you go back, you won't have a job, and you'll have to move. You can't be you, not anymore. If he's in a politician's pocket, then he can use those connections and pull to create problems. Will's right." My voice cracked, and the boys laughed. Mari managed a small, sweet smile. "You would be safer here." I paraphrased my ex-junior officer's words and ignored the startled glance the young soldier shot my way.

"I'll be fine." Mari waved a hand as though walking back into that viper's den would be a simple thing.

I clenched my teeth and didn't bother to fake a smile.

"You won't be fine, Mari." Jon tipped her head back and kissed the tip of her nose. "What they did to you is inexcusable. Unforgivable. It needs to be dealt with."

She looked up at the gentle giant of a man with such trust that had he been anyone else, I might have attacked him for stealing her attention.

"It does need to be dealt with," I agreed, catching her fingers to hold her hand in mine, memorizing the heat of her. "Why are you scared of going to the authorities, Mari?"

Her eyes flared wide as she started, and for a long moment, I expected her to deny it. Then she shook her head.

"I played a part in too many of Gi—his crimes. Some small things that I arranged for him. Hookers and parties. It took me a bit to realize how naive and stupid I was then, how it would look, but nothing like this." Her eyes welled with tears as she ran her hands down her arms that bore the marks of her horror. "I had no idea they were making slaves out of women." Her eyes took on a distant look I hated, and Brandon's words the night he passed echoed around the room.

I caught her chin in a firm but gentle grip to bring her back, tilting her head back so I could hold her gaze. "But there will be more if nothing is done about it."

"You want to, don't you?" she whispered. "You want to be the one who destroys him. But he's dangerous, Robe. More than you can imagine. I don't want you to get hurt because of my stupidity."

"That wasn't stupidity on your end, Mari. Corrupt men believe their power comes with no price. I know better. We all do."

"I can't tell you, Robe." She nibbled her bottom lip. Her head tilted farther back of her own accord, though it must have hurt her like hell to do it, in an invitation I couldn't deny.

I lowered my head, brushing my lips over hers. She sighed, leaning forward as Jon released her, melting in my arms, and I kissed her deeper, then sweeter until the taste of her seared into my tongue. My heart clenched on itself as I held her, willing her to do what I asked and deny me at the same time.

Go because you should.

Stay because I need you.

A moan worked its way from her mouth to mine. I wanted to be the air she fucking breathed.

When I drew back, her lashes framed heavy-lidded eyes crowning a curved body that begged to be fucked. I inhaled a slow breath before I broke my promise to myself not to touch her again, took her to my bed without anyone else in it, and let my control snap.

Then I'd be as bad as the assholes who tortured her, who made her run for her life.

I brushed my lips over hers, memorizing the shape of her mouth against mine.

"Stay," I murmured against her lips. "Tell me what I need."

Indecision warred in her midnight gaze, but then she relented. "Gideon Blackthorne was my boss. I... I...." Her bottom lip wobbled, but she held the impending tears at bay. "I didn't see other faces. If I think of anything, I promise I'll tell you." She hiccupped. "I can draw really good stick figures."

"Thank you, sweetheart. I know that hurts to say." I held her tight, my heart ripping into shreds. "You're the bravest damn creature I've ever met. God, girl. I love you."

"I know." She smiled through her sheen of tears, tracing her fingertips along my cheek. Her touch burned like she'd branded her claim there.

She'll come back.

I believed it. I had to.

I swallowed hard and pressed her back into Jon's waiting arms, my decision made. He nuzzled at her neck, inhaling her scent. Then he looked at me with a closed face and nodded.

I withdrew a pair of keys on a single key ring from my back pocket and let them dangle from my fingers. Alan pressed a small pile of plastic cards into her hands.

She picked them up, examining the freshly printed driver's license that featured her photo, albeit with a new name and address printed on it. "Marion Knight. Is that who I am now?" She traced a fingertip over the glossy card. "I can keep my first name?" *At least in part.*

The rest of the short stack included ID cards, enough to prove to the world that she was who we needed her to be. At the bottom of the pile sat a brand-new passport. A new identity to hide her from Blackthorne and thus Petersen, who kept his lapdog on a short, albeit invisible, leash. This identity gave her a new life and a chance to live it.

Alan tossed a phone into her hands. "Password's the same as your old one, and it's got all the same apps on it."

"How do you know my passwords?" Mari stared up at him with wide eyes.

"It's a talent, honey. I get to infiltrate everyone else's life. I just don't get to live mine." He tried to smile, but it didn't reach his eyes.

"Yet you struggle with who you are," Mari said, still staring at him.

Alan snorted. "Get out of here, sweetcakes, before I decide to keep you regardless of what the oaf tells you to do."

Jon laughed, squeezing Mari's waist between his giant paws.

She twisted to face him and pressed her hand over his heart. "My woodsman. My tin man," she whispered. Fresh tears tracked her cheeks.

Jon stared down at her, unbreathing. Yearning filled his face. My heart broke a dozen times for him over his wife, and a dozen more now on his second round. Every time he found someone to love, they were swept away from him, outside his control.

Tin Man suited Jon Littleman all too well.

"Mari," I called, bringing her attention back to me. "There's a car on the dirt road half a mile that way." I jerked my thumb behind me in the opposite direction from where she'd arrived. "It's yours. Everything's in your name. Illegal but untraceable. Alan hasn't let me be caught yet."

Mari lifted the keys, wonder widening her eyes. Her fingers brushed over mine. A shiver shot up my arm, and I pressed my hand to my thigh to prevent myself from touching her again.

"Are you sure?" She turned the pair of new keys over in her tiny hand.

"Am I sure? Hell no, sweetheart. But if you want that freedom, then you'd better run before I change my goddamn mind," I growled, echoing Alan's sentiment and meaning it no less. My lips pressed tight together as I bit the words out, only half playacting.

Mari giggled.

She fucking *giggled*.

Add that as one more reason why I'd fallen in love with her in a few short months.

Anyone with their sensibilities in the right place would have tripped off the veranda in their haste to escape, but not Mari.

A handful of chuckles echoed her sentiment around the room.

Mari squeezed the keys between her fingers as though testing they were real. "What's the second one for?"

Jon grinned, brushing his fingers along her throat. She shuddered at the contact, her lips parted in a response that went straight to my cock—and his.

"Robe's office in New York City." He spoke into her hair as he whispered the address into her ear. "There's a nice penthouse apartment on the top floor of the building. Key's in the bottom drawer of his desk, taped behind the back. It's yours." He nuzzled her neck, sucking hard enough to mark her.

A tiny moan escaped her lips, her eyes fluttering closed. When she opened them, Mari stared at me as she leaned back into Jon's embrace, the ghost of a knowing smile gracing her lips.

I clenched my fists, willing self-possession to take hold of me before I ripped her from his arms. A dual need tore through me. The urge to protect her roiled inside my chest, demanding to be released.

"Yana manages my company, but she's been begging to retire for the past year. I've struggled with handing over control of a multimillion-dollar business to someone I don't know. I'd like you to get to know her, see if she thinks you might make a good... replacement." I couldn't offer her any less for tearing away the life she had, for not pushing her through the proper channels when we had the chance to do the right thing.

Her eye for detail and her care factor in my house showed me everything I needed to make the decision.

Mari's pretty eyes narrowed. "Did you cyberstalk me, Mr. Huntingdon?"

"Through a screen, but never in person," I said in a rueful voice, as though that slim difference made it all right to inch my way into her private life to ensure who she claimed to be matched up with the woman I loved.

Lucky for us all, she did.

Her eyes darkened. "Your company? The one you ran with Gi—" She swallowed and stopped.

I didn't force her to say his name again. Once was more than enough. "Knight & Watchman. The same as the accounts you looked over. It's who we were. Who I was, once. It's a private security firm that deals with cases like yours. Perhaps you can make a difference there."

Maybe my purpose could become hers.

"Maybe you can come visit one day," she whispered, her eyes glistening.

I forced my lips up. "Is that a yes?"

Not to the question I want to ask you.

My heart ached.

"It sounds like you have a reason to leave the mountain, Robe."

"Bullshit," Alan yelled over a chorus of laughter. "He's afraid to go into town."

"If *town* is several hours away and situated in one of the biggest business centers in the world, then yes, I'll take that one." I gave her a rare smile, and she rewarded me with one of her own as laughter bubbled from her again. I tapped the phone Alan gave her. "The number of a doctor who can help you is programmed in there. Use it. But you can't contact anyone, not your family or your friends. That's the price of your freedom. One call and you blow your safety net to hell. And... don't Google yourself."

I let her see the fear in my eyes of what might happen while I wasn't there as a barrier between her and the rest of the world.

"I didn't think Robe Huntingdon was afraid of anything," she teased, stroking Jon's cheek as she disengaged from his embrace and sashayed toward me. Then she stopped, her eyes impossibly wide. "Mari Knight. On the license."

I nodded. "It's my family name. Huntingdon is the title I hold in Europe."

"Are you shitting me?" she whispered, one foot preceding the other as she crept forward.

My vision tunneled in on her. "I wouldn't admit it in front of anyone else," I murmured.

Mari moved into my space, stealing my air with every step until the hem of her dress touched me. She rose onto her tiptoes, brushing her lips over mine in the barest caress. "I love you," she breathed into my ear, so soft that not another soul could hear her confession.

I flexed my hands in my pockets. "Will you come back if I don't say it again?"

My heart thudded in my chest as her mouth moved, but she didn't kiss me.

"Half a mile up the path?" she asked, her breath hot on my mouth as she spoke.

"That's right." I still hadn't touched her, couldn't touch her. Otherwise, I'd never let her leave.

"Thanks." She sent me an impish grin, whirled, and flew out the door before anyone thought to stop her.

Five pairs of eyes tracked her escape across the clearing and into the trees. The forest's sentinels closed over her route until only the faintest trace of her scent remained among us.

Jon made a half-strangled sound deep in his throat and stepped forward.

I caught his shoulder. "Let her go."

He watched me, turning his teacup in his massive paws. "You're not keeping her?"

"Did you think she would say no? We gave her an offer she wanted, one she didn't need to refuse." I huffed a laugh. "She's not going to tell anyone about the men who fucked her over. Or us. I think we're safe." I followed the boys out of the cabin and watched them scan the forest for any trace of her.

Alan alone leaned back against the cabin, his hands stuffed in his pockets. He caught my eye with a small grin while the others pined over what they couldn't have.

I held his gaze, assessing him. "Want to check if she got to the car unmolested? Don't be seen."

Alan answered me with a fast grin and quicker feet. He hit the forest floor before the remaining boys could protest.

Leaning my forearms over the railing, I watched him disappear between the trees and head in the direction of the car I left on the road for Mari.

"Are you sure, Robe?" Jon braced his arms over his head at my side, gripping the struts that held up the veranda in a white-knuckled grip.

"I'm sure." I scanned the trees, a plan forming. I retraced her original path in my mind to where someone had dropped her onto my land in an effort to incriminate me. A short surveillance walk might be the thing to keep the boys from obsessing over a broken heart. "Besides, I don't think Mari Merripen-Knight is done with us yet."

And I'm not finished with her.

I gave her my name, and that was a two-way door.

Mari would return to us. I had no doubt of that, the same as I refused to doubt her ability to take on my company and run it like a well-oiled machine. Hell, maybe I'd venture back into my old life to see how she filled those shoes, give her a reason not to slip away and disappear on me altogether.

And when she came back, I'd know she chose us. Until then, I opted for a little vengeance to seek on her behalf.

I spread my lips in a dead smile as a familiar coldness blanketed my ruined soul.

"Who's up for a little recon mission?"

ABOUT THE AUTHOR

DOVE PRIEST is a dark romance author who writes surrounded by her collection of stuffies, including her fur babies. Her characters haunt her until their stories are told. She is a corset fanatic and has a closet collection of dark fairy-tale retellings.

Dove has other pen names but won't share them unless provided with black coffee.

Sign up to Dove's NEWSLETTER and get a FREE BOOK: HTTPS://BOOKHIP.COM/RKXBLFP

Join Dove's reader group: HTTPS://WWW.FACEBOOK.COM/GROUPS/512979953484214

instagram.com/dovepriest

ACKNOWLEDGMENTS

Robe and Mari have been in my head for so long now, it's hard to think of a time they weren't there. So many in my writers' groups and community have heard snippets of my *why* about writing this story, so thank you to all who have listened over the years while I figured out the mechanics.

The first and biggest thanks has to be to hubs. The man who asked the moment I arrived in the UK with three kids under five years old and my wrist in a cast what I wanted to do and listened when I announced, "I want to walk Sherwood Forest because I have a book idea and I'm obsessed," then simply agreed to add it to the itinerary despite the location not being on plans we'd discussed during our four-month absence. This same man has listened to abounding plot bunnies, supported every crazy whim, watched every version of Robin Hood on film, and laughed at my jokes when they weren't funny (let's face it, most aren't). I'm so grateful to be able to write these stories will all his support, and the kids' too.

Fae, you've been the other ear who has let me rattle on for the last five years consecutively on this project. Every change, woo, and woe, you've heard it all. Not once have you complained, and your epic support is more than I could ever ask for from my writing bestie.

Sarah, having a local writer (even when you moved!!) to talk to and hug it out with has been amazing. Thank you so much for listening and poking me in the right direction when my crazy overloads. I hope I can return the favor many times over.

McKinley, you are my fave editor. I'm never letting you go. Thank you for your tireless work on checking my Aussieisms (yes, it's a word, shh), my seasons, and all the botanical knowledge a girl can ever need. Also, commas. There is a plant named for you in my kitchen.

Kristin, you deserve more than cacti. No seriously, thank you for taking a chance on what is a whole new world (cue the music) for me. Becky too. Melbourne will be epic.

And readers. Thank you for risking your heart for Robe, Mari, and all my broken, scarred boys. I hope you love their strange little household on Recurve Ridge. This is not the end.

ABOUT THE PUBLISHER

Hot Tree Publishing loves love. Publishing adult romantic fiction, HTPubs are all about diverse reads featuring heroes and heroines to swoon over. Since opening in 2015, HTPubs have published more than 300 titles across the wide and diverse range of romantic genres. If you're chasing a happily ever after in your favourite subgenre, HTPubs have you covered.

Interested in discovering more amazing reads brought to you by Hot Tree Publishing? Head over to the website for information:

WWW.HOTTREEPUBLISHING.COM

facebook.com/hottreepublishing

instagram.com/hottreepublishing

tiktok.com/@hottreepublishing